· RETALIO ·

ALISON MORTON

PULCHERIA
PRESS

PRAISE FOR THE ROMA NOVA SERIES

INCEPTIO
"Brilliantly plotted original story, grippingly told and cleverly combining the historical with the futuristic. It's a real edge-of-the-seat read, genuinely hard to put down." – Sue Cook

CARINA
"This is a fabulous thriller that cracks along at a great pace and just doesn't let up from start to finish." – Discovering Diamonds Reviews

PERFIDITAS
"Alison Morton has built a fascinating, exotic world! Carina's a bright, sassy detective with a winning dry sense of humour. The plot is pretty snappy too!" – Simon Scarrow

SUCCESSIO
"I thoroughly enjoyed this classy thriller, the third in Morton's epic series set in Roma Nova." – Caroline Sanderson in The Bookseller

AURELIA
"AURELIA explores a 1960s that is at once familiar and utterly different – a brilliant page turner that will keep you gripped from first page to last. Highly recommended." – Russell Whitfield

INSURRECTIO
"INSURRECTIO – a taut, fast-paced thriller. I enjoyed it enormously. Rome, guns and rebellion. Darkly gripping stuff." – Conn Iggulden

RETALIO
"RETALIO is a terrific concept engendering passion, love and loyalty. I actually cheered aloud." – J J Marsh

ROMA NOVA EXTRA
"One of the reasons I am enthralled with the Roma Nova series is the concept of the whole thing." – Helen Hollick, Vine Voice

---

ABOUT THE AUTHOR

A 'Roman nut' since age 11, Alison Morton has clambered over much of Roman Europe; she continues to be fascinated by that complex, powerful and value driven civilisation.

Armed with an MA in history, six years' military service and a love of thrillers, she explores via her Roma Nova novels the 'what if' idea of a modern Roman society run by strong women.

Alison lives in France with her husband, cultivates a Roman herb garden and drinks wine.

Find out more at alison-morton.com, follow her on Twitter @alison_morton and Facebook (AlisonMortonAuthor)

DRAMATIS PERSONAE

Mitela family and household

Aurelia Mitela – Former Roma Nova government minister and imperial councillor
Marina Mitela – Aurelia's daughter
William Brown – Marina's husband, an Eastern United States defence electronics contractor
Miklós Farkas – Aurelia's long-time companion
Milo – Former steward of Domus Mitelarum
Gavinus – Former Castra Lucilla farm manager

Tella family

Caius Tellus – First consul of Roma Nova
Quintus Tellus – Caius's brother
Conradus Tellus – Caius and Quintus's young cousin/nephew

Military

Volusenia – Colonel, Praetorian Guard Special Forces (PGSF)
Numerus – Retired senior centurion, PGSF
Pia Calavia – Lieutenant, PGSF
Atrius – Guard, PGSF
Aquilia – Lieutenant, Roma Nova legions
Junia – Centurion, Roma Nova legions/PGSF
Styrax – Ex-legionary, Roma Nova legions

Former imperial government

Maia Quirinia – Budget minister and Aurelia's friend
Claudia Cornelia – Aurelia's former assistant at the foreign ministry
Silvia Apulia – The late Imperatrix Severina's daughter

In Vienna

David Soane – Viennese head of Soanes Bank, Aurelia's cousin
Edward Soane – David's son
Herr Goss – Assistant to New Austrian foreign minister
Commissar Joachim Huber

(aka Joachim von und zu der Havel), Vienna Gendarmerie – Aurelia's
cousin
Tante Sabine – Joachim's mother
Sándor – Miklós's friend, Aurelia's bodyguard

Other Roma Novan exiles in Vienna,
Burrus – Refugee
Turturus – Former military cadet
Lentilius – Soldier turned councillor
Regulus – Logistics manager

Roma Novan diplomats
Livilla Vara – *Nuncia* (ambassador), Vienna legation
Cornelia – *Nuncia*, Paris legation, cousin of Claudia Cornelia
Vibianus – Administrator, Paris legation
Grania – Administrator, Paris legation
Gracilis – *Nuncio*, London legation

Resistance members inside Roma Nova
Marcia
Sextus – Marcia's brother
Gaius – Marcia's cousin
Drusilla – Palace housekeeper
Lucia
Frontius
Anna – Miklós's business colleague
Janós – Anna's husband

Foreign governments
Sir Henry Carter – UK foreign secretary
Gerald Hill – UK external security services director
Charles Fitz-Glynn – Assistant to Sir Henry Carter
Mr White – EUS government advisor to Caius Tellus

PART I

EXILE

1

―――――

'Betrayal and collaboration used to lead automatically to a death sentence. You should be grateful this is the 1980s.' She refused to look at me and instead jabbed her spoon into the coffee cup, almost scraping the glaze off as she rattled it round the tiny amount of liquid at the bottom.

'Is that what you really think I've done, Maia Quirinia?'

'I'm an accountant, Aurelia, used to looking at facts and figures. And the evidence against you adds up, if you'll forgive the pun.'

This was my childhood friend, my fellow minister, one of the inner circle I had trusted with my secrets, my failures as well as my successes. The person who'd comforted me when I was nearly raped as a fifteen-year-old, whose common sense gave me balance and whose life I'd saved on the dreadful night of fires.

She looked tired; her hair was neat, but she obviously hadn't had it cut and shaped for weeks. She'd draped her coat – pressed wool from a chain store – over the back of the chair and kept the acrylic scarf round her neck. That and the knitted gloves she would once have been embarrassed to give to a charity shop told me how hard things were for her. And it was probably the same for the rest of them.

She glanced at the wall clock. Ten past eight on a freezing December morning in a Vienna backstreet. She wriggled on the hard wooden chair. The workman's café, warm from the fug of cigarette smoke, wasn't the most comfortable place to start the day. It was full of people arguing about the previous evening's football and how much everything cost, and the whirr and clatter of the coffee machines and the snappy retorts of the server trying to get to all twelve tables at once; crowded enough to drown our words.

'I have a job interview in twenty minutes.' She stood up. 'I'm sorry, more than you can imagine, but this is goodbye. If any of the others find out I've been meeting you, I'll be proscribed as well.'

She'd said it. That terrible word. Not that it meant much coming from a group of exiles stripped of authority and living on the edge of financial ruin, but it stung all the same.

Almost too shocked to absorb the full impact of what she'd said, I grasped her hand. 'I'll lend you some money. Don't waste yourself on some stupid office job.'

She looked down at my hand as if it carried the plague. I released hers.

'I don't have the luxury. I have to earn a living and bring money in for the others.' She gave a bitter little half-smile. 'I'm too old to do it on my back, so it's a return to counting beans as I did when I was an apprentice.'

She picked up her coat and handbag and glanced at me, then at the door. She snapped open her bag and took out an envelope. After a moment's hesitation she laid it on the table by my plate. It had a Roma Novan stamp and was addressed to me, care of the safe house.

'It came for you last week. I rescued it from the rubbish bin.'

She shrugged her coat on, nodded and made her way to the entrance. At the door she turned round once, then looked away, but not quickly enough for me to miss the tears on her cheek.

'If they don't want you, then more fool them.'

Miklós, my companion, and I sat in front of a roaring fire, cosy and warm after a good lunch and clutching glasses of seasonal *glühwein* in our hands. I pulled off the blanket he'd tucked round me as I was in danger of baking. I'd only been out of the convalescent hospital a week but after my morning trip he was fussing round me as if I was his grandmother instead of his lover.

'Quirinia looked so haunted,' I said. 'What in Hades has been happening there?'

'God knows, but you're safe. That's all I care about.' He gave me one of his lazy, warm smiles which was reflected in his brown eyes. I reached up to touch his curly hair and he gently took my hand and kissed the palm. After a few minutes he asked, 'What was in your letter?'

'Juno, I forgot to look.' I reached down for my handbag and brought out the crumpled envelope. I glanced at the return address. *Q. Tellus, Praetor Urbanus, Roma Nova.* On the front it was stamped *LICITA* – authorised. Was the post in Roma Nova now censored? I ripped it open along the edge.

My dear Aurelia,

I can only hope this letter reaches you; I suspect it won't but one must try. You may be surprised that I know you are still alive after Caius shot you. He told me when he summoned me to the palace yesterday and bellowed at me for a good half hour. I have never seen my brother in such a rage.

If you truly have survived, I congratulate you. But I must warn you. He intends to apply for your extradition or, failing that, a snatch squad. He'll try extradition first as Roma Nova has a treaty with New Austria. I strongly advise you to remove yourself immediately. Go to the EUS to your daughter and her husband, or to the United Kingdom in the north, anywhere that doesn't have a judicial treaty with Roma Nova.

You should warn the others like Quirinia and Calavia. Caius is intent on destroying the old order and particularly the heads of the Twelve Families. Please convey my condolences to Calavia. Her grandmother was executed by Caius's people three days ago, so even though in exile with you, Pia Calavia is now the legal head of her family. Since he seized power as first consul, Caius has become ever more brutal. There is some kind of ferocity which is driving him which hasn't been there before.

If you need to contact me send anything to the Swiss legation. They will inform me of any letters.

Take care of yourself, Aurelia.

My deepest respects and love,

Quintus

Miklós held me tight while I wept silently for my country, for my mother's dead friend, Senator Calavia, for her granddaughter, for my isolation and despair. He folded me in his arms, carried me up to bed and held me still close until I fell asleep.

I trudged downstairs the next morning like a seventy-year-old, instead of a woman in her mid forties. The gunshot wounds in my chest and leg had healed, and bruising from rough handling by Caius Tellus's political troops sent to capture me had faded. Even the deep graze from one of the Roman Nationalists' bullets on my face had healed although it left a white line across my cheek. I thought I was recovering my fitness but my little outing to meet Quirinia yesterday morning had floored me. Well, perhaps it was that damned letter. I clung to the oak newel post and caught my breath for a couple of seconds. The smells of coffee and fresh croissants and bacon drew me into the dining room.

'You're not fit enough to get out of bed,' Miklós said, 'let alone confront a crowd of stroppy Romans. They won't be grateful.' He sat down at the table opposite me.

'I must warn Calavia and Quirinia.'

'No, you must look after yourself.'

I read through the crumpled letter again. 'Quintus hasn't mentioned Silvia. I would have thought she'd have been Caius's first target for a snatch. Perhaps he still doesn't know where she is.'

'Unlikely. As you've said before, Caius Tellus isn't stupid. If he knows about you, he knows about Silvia.'

'Then it's even more important that I warn them. I cannot let that bastard Caius get his hands on the rightful imperatrix of Roma Nova.'

'Aurelia—'

'Order me a taxi, please.'

Miklós insisted on coming with me and made me take my walking stick. I didn't argue; the muscles in my leg were still weak from the gunshot wound and yesterday's jaunt had left me with an aching thigh.

When the taxi drew up at our front gate it looked like a private car – no light on top, no permit plate. I glanced at Miklós, but he was frowning at the vehicle. A thickset man, dressed in dark slacks, a polo neck jumper and black leather jacket, pulled himself out of the driving seat quickly, but not fast enough to conceal the bump under his jacket near his armpit.

'You took your time,' Miklós growled at him in Germanic, but then lapsed into his native Hungarian. The driver gave him back as good as he got, then shrugged and leant against the car.

Miklós answered him back, then turned to me. 'This is Sándor. He works for me. From now on he will accompany us everywhere we go.'

I went to protest, but Miklós's stern expression stopped me. Glancing at the heavy, then meeting the steady gaze from his deep-set eyes, I gave him a brief nod and eased myself into the back of the car.

We stopped at a secretarial bureau to have the envelope and letter photocopied, then made our way to the house the exiled Roma Novans were using as their headquarters. Sándor drew up in front of the two-storey eighteenth-century Biedermeier townhouse, its arms at ninety degrees to each other and occupying the whole of a block in a quiet suburb. One of the arms housed a small bar and bijou restaurant on the ground floor, but entirely separate from the rest of the building. Opposite were a delicatessen, a coffee shop and patisserie, bright lights shining and striped canopies overhead to shelter customers as they assessed the delicacies within. But the dirty upper windows and dull stone exterior of the exiles' house exuded an air of sullenness. Was I imagining things? Perhaps the tablets I was still taking were playing with my mind. But nothing took away the quiet air of menace of the two tall figures standing, legs braced, arms crossed, in front of the faded green double doors at the corner entrance.

Miklós helped me out, gave me my walking stick and took my other arm. The two guards, one woman, one man, tracked us as we crossed the road towards them. I recognised her immediately: Styrax, the ex-legionary from the XX Victis legion. She'd been part of the extraction group I'd led on our mission to find Silvia Apulia, the last surviving child of the murdered Imperatrix Severina.

'Private house – no admittance,' she said in heavily accented Germanic, looking straight through me.

'Styrax, you know who I am,' I replied in Latin. 'Now open the door. Please.'

She hesitated, then replied in a flat voice. 'I do not know you. I may not admit strangers.'

'Oh, for Pluto's sake, let me in,' I snapped back. 'I've only left hospital this week and my leg is aching from the hole Caius Tellus's bullet made in it.'

She looked down at the cobbled pavement in front of her. 'My orders are to ignore you. You are proscribed.'

I flinched inwardly at that word again.

'Well, it isn't as straightforward as that,' I said.

She jerked her head up. 'Truly?' She looked like a puppy who had been given a favourite treat.

'Fetch Numerus.'

Styrax flicked her hand at the younger male guard who disappeared into the house. She said nothing more, but kept glancing at me, then away, then once at Miklós. She shifted her weight from foot to foot as we waited in silence. Although it was sunny and bright that December morning, I shivered.

The door opened slowly, as if reluctant. A stocky figure, medium height, grey hair two centimetres in length, stepped out. Numerus, former Senior Centurion Numerus, my comrade-in-arms. But was he still my friend?

2

Numerus glanced at Miklós towering over him and then at me. He kept a good two paces back and neither smiled nor frowned. We'd shared hardship, danger, triumph and many a glass of beer in our younger days. Our bond had been tight despite the difference in our ranks. I'd been reassured after I'd first escaped from Roma Nova to find Numerus running this Vienna safe house. He was sound, steady as a rock. He was the only Roma Novan who'd visited me in hospital six weeks ago when I'd been recovering from death's edge after Caius shot me.

'We cannot receive you,' he said at last. 'You are proscribed, dead to Roma Nova. We cannot speak to you or associate with you,' he added.

'Well, at the moment, Numerus, you're doing just that, so you're tainted by association.'

He grunted. I thought I saw a tiny lift of his lips in the ghost of a smile. I stepped forward, intending to touch his forearm, but stumbled. Miklós caught me, but my stick clattered onto the cobbles.

Numerus bent and picked it up. As he handed me the stick, he searched my face. I looked back at him, willing him to believe in me.

He jerked his head towards the door and then stood back, allowing me and Miklós to enter.

The large hallway was lit by a single bulb poking through a dirt-coated chandelier that was new a hundred years ago. But there was enough light to see a utility table with two figures sitting at it, working on a pile of papers. Two others were arguing loudly at the other side of the hall. All four fell silent the instant they spotted me and stared. I'd been the late Imperatrix Severina's chief counsellor and Roma Nova's foreign minister; it was inevitable they'd recognise me.

Numerus gave them a stern look which set them back to work. He hurried us to the left and along a corridor with a parquet floor and doors at irregular intervals. He stopped at the second one and ushered us into a small room set up as a makeshift office. A battered grey filing cabinet stood in one corner, an upturned wooden crate and two cardboard boxes loitered by the wall. He retrieved two folded chairs leaning against the opposite wall under the sash window, handed one to Miklós and unfolded one for me. He retreated to the other side of his trestle table and flopped down in a steel frame office chair.

'Now tell me why you have come back here,' he said.

'To warn you all.'

'What about?'

'Caius Tellus's intentions.'

'Oh, really?'

'Is that so difficult to believe?' I said, almost despairing of the gap between us.

'Yes. Coming from—'

The door burst open and two figures in outdoor walking clothes marched in.

'What in Hades is *she* doing in this building?' the younger one shouted at Numerus. 'And with that damned foreigner?' She jabbed her index finger at Miklós.

'Hello, Calavia,' I said. 'I'm glad to see you alive and in full force.'

Two eyes burning with anger and hatred turned on me.

'If I still had a sidearm, I'd shoot you like the treacherous bitch you are,' she shrieked.

Miklós leapt to his feet, stood in front of her and shoved her back.

'Clean your mouth, woman. She's no more a traitor than you are. She nearly died trying to escape that bastard Tellus,' he said. 'And after saving *your* ungrateful skin.' He squared up to her, his features tight and his eyes raging. Calavia, still fuelled by anger, jerked her fist back to strike him, but her companion's hand shot out and grabbed Calavia's wrist.

'No.' The shorter but wiry figure of Colonel Volusenia, Praetorian Guard Special Forces commander, stepped forward into the light. Her fingers still gripped the younger woman's wrist. 'Stand down, Lieutenant.' Volusenia released Calavia but kept her gaze on her junior's face. Calavia took a pace back, her hands balled and face tight with anger and frustration.

'Right,' Volusenia said to me in a voice straight off the high Alps. 'You can tell me why you have the temerity to come here. You have two minutes before we throw you out.'

'To warn you.'

'Against what?'

'Read this.' I placed the original letter from Quintus on Numerus's desk. I knew she wouldn't take it from what she thought was a proscriptee's hand.

A full minute went by as Volusenia studied the letter. She grunted when she flipped the envelope over and saw the sender's address. She turned to Calavia, stretched out her hand and pressed Calavia's shoulder as if to comfort her, then handed the younger woman Quintus's letter and stepped back. Calavia's furious expression dispelled as her eyes followed the lines of the letter. Her mouth drooped. Even sitting a couple of metres away, I saw the tears roll down her face. She half -turned her back to us and lifted her hand to wipe her face. When she turned back, her cheeks still glistened. Volusenia looked at her, but Calavia shook her head.

'I would like to offer you my condolences, Pia Calavia,' I said. 'If you will accept them.'

She said nothing, but gave me a tiny nod.

'Very well,' I stood up. Miklós put his hand out to support me and I smiled at him, my only friend in this room. 'I have done my duty and warned you. You don't need me to tell you what a vicious and manipulative man Caius Tellus is. He has done everything in his power to ruin me, physically and emotionally, and through his lies has severed me from all my friends and colleagues.'

I looked at them one by one: Numerus, my old comrade who had helped me hunt Caius down for murder fourteen years ago; Calavia, with whom I'd shared mortal danger when we'd escaped from Roma Nova on the night of the rebellion, and whose life I'd saved from Caius's executioners; Volusenia who had at my urging brought the young Imperatrix Silvia to safety here in New Austria when the rebellion broke out.

'I will remove my unwelcome presence immediately,' I continued. 'I'm deeply saddened none of you believe I am innocent. I had more faith in you than you have in me.' My chest ached with the effort of trying to convince them, but I made a final effort. 'You must guard against seizure and at all costs keep Silvia Apulia safe. Try to persuade her to go to the north, to the United Kingdom or even America.'

'You don't need to tell the Praetorians their duty,' Volusenia snapped.

'Then make sure you do it,' I retorted.

'What did you expect?' Miklós said.

I'd kept my gaze on the back of Sándor's neck, too miserable to speak, as we'd ridden home in the car engulfed by driving sleet. As Sándor got out to close the black metal gates behind us, I slumped against the seat.

'I don't know. I thought they would at least talk to me when they saw me. We've shared so much.'

'You know how hard they all are,' he said. 'You *should* know – you're very much one of them.'

'Apparently not.'

Inside, he made us tea and heated up some *pogača*. 'Here, for energy,' he said, and pushed the oval pastry into my hand. It burst in my mouth at the first bite, releasing the full flavour of herbs and cheese. He'd made *pogača* for me after the first time we'd made love over fifteen years ago. We'd eaten them in bed, his strong brown finger searching every crumb that had dropped on my bare body…

'Tomorrow, we take the first step to protecting you,' he said. 'I'll book tickets on the Trans-European Express and you go to the United Kingdom then fly to America. Your daughter's husband is a strong man and he will make sure you are safe.'

'I'm not leaving Roma Nova.'

'It's left you, *drágám*.'

'No. The exiles are hurt and frightened. I must help them. We can't leave Caius to rampage and destroy everything.'

'But if what Quintus writes is true, he'll extradite or snatch you.'

'I have you, and now Sándor to protect me physically and once I'm fit again, I won't be such an easy target. I just need to put myself beyond Caius legally.' I shuddered at the prospect of being dragged back to Caius and handed over to his sadistic assistant for 'punishment'. And it would all be perfectly legal, from the New Austrian police arrest to deportation, handover like a package at the Roma Novan border and into the cells of the Transulium prison to await Caius's pleasure. My heart pounded at the terrifying thought of facing Caius's vengeance.

Miklós's eyes gleamed. 'I have an idea, but I don't know if you'll accept it.'

'What?'

He pulled me to him, his arm circling my waist, and kissed me lightly on my lips. The black curls brushed my cheek as he leaned forward to whisper in my ear. 'Marry me.'

I couldn't move. Not because his arm held me firmly, nor from reluctance to leave the comfort of his warm body, but from shock. I'd never considered marriage, not with my daughter Marina's father, nor anybody. Many Roma Novan women didn't. Unlike other Western societies, inheritance and names descended from mother to daughter; contracted or 'married' fathers were optional.

I gazed up at his face. He looked back steadily. Juno, he was serious. My heart thudded. I loved this man, his body, his mind, his laughter. It pained me when we were apart. But entering into a formal contract with him?

'Speak, Aurelia, or I really will think I've struck you dumb.' His wide smile reassured me I hadn't wandered into an alien universe.

'I – I don't know the words to say.'

He stroked my cheek with his finger. 'It's usual to reply with "Yes".' Now he was grinning. 'If you want a logical reason, it means you will take my nationality. If you're a Hungarian citizen, the Roma Novan authorities can't touch you.'

3

———

'*A feleségem.*' Miklós ignored the registrar and kissed me passionately. His wife, indeed.

Two weeks of form-filling, appointments and a nail-biting week's wait had followed Miklós's proposal before the *Oberlandesgericht* gave its approval to the dossier of pre-marriage paperwork we'd assembled. That and constant watchfulness for any attempt by Caius to extradite me had convinced me we would never be standing here before the registrar this morning before the office closed for the winter holidays. Perhaps entering the names of the New Austrian foreign minister and David Soane, my cousin and eminent Viennese banker, on the form as witnesses had hurried the process along.

Miklós released me and I thanked the two witnesses. The New Austrian minister kissed my cheek, glanced at his watch and hurried off with his security assistant.

David Soane pressed my hand. 'Come and see me soon, Aurelia,' he murmured. 'I have your document in my safe.'

Miklós fixed him with a steady look. That had been an awkward afternoon a week ago when David and his lawyer had drawn up a formal marriage contract that kept our property separate.

'You are marrying under New Austrian law, Aurelia,' David had said. 'You don't have all the automatic rights you do, or did, in Roma Nova. You must be practical about this. I'm sure Mr Farkas understands.'

Well, now I was Mrs Farkas – *Farkas asszony* – and I still wasn't sure that Miklós understood. I shivered. None of his beloved Magyar Plains horses would have dragged it out of me, but I didn't want to be formally married. Many Roma Novans didn't encumber themselves with such contracts. I loved Miklós with my heart and soul and he knew it. It was only because of Caius that I was going through this administrative fuss. Now I would be seen as an attachment to somebody else. But Miklós seemed happy so I smiled at him as he handed me my copy of the marriage certificate that the registrar had prepared for us.

After the chilly and short ceremony, we returned to the house and ate beef goulash and raised a glass of Bull's Blood wine to our future. Very traditional, Miklós said, in a cheerful voice, but I heard a wistful tone underneath it. Perhaps he was contrasting this expedient marriage with the exuberant weddings that were traditional among his people, but he didn't say anything.

We took a breath of fresh air, dogged as always by the charmless but armed Sándor a few paces behind us. The light-festooned Christmas tree squatting on the green in front of the cluster of local shops where people were drinking *glühwein* and talking and laughing together seemed so alien to me. This was the first year in my entire life I'd missed Saturnalia at home in Roma Nova.

Ceding my place at the head of the Mitela tribe for a day to the *princeps Saturnalicius* was traditional. For several hours, Domus Mitelarum would normally be overrun with noise, people, stupid but fun dares, overeating, games, theatricals and stand-up of dubious taste, arguments, falling in lust, laughter and progressive drunkenness. The under-steward would make sure the children were safe out of the way when the horseplay became too raunchy.

The atrium would blaze with light. Everywhere would be covered in ferns, spruce and pine. In the centre, there would be a large square table covered with linen, silverware, glasses, candles and the best china. Smells of roast pork, lemons and spices, everybody wearing over-colourful clothes, Miklós and I toasting each other and the assembled company with champagne from the Castra Lucilla estate, celebrating life.

Instead, I was stuck here in New Austria shivering, thrown out of my home and exiled.

. . .

Four days later, we stood in the queue in the cold, tile-floored public office of the Hungarian consulate, clutching our documents and translations, and registered our marriage.

'Don't look so depressed,' Miklós bent down and whispered in my ear.

'It seems such a lot of effort for a piece of paper,' I grumbled. Accepting it, I would lose a small part of my identity.

'But that piece of paper will save you from that man,' Miklós replied.

'I know,' I said and pressed his hand. 'I'm really very grateful.'

'I didn't do it for your gratitude, woman. I did it because I love you. Sometimes you need protecting from yourself.'

The clerk, unsmiling, probably from having to work the shift between Christmas and New Year, raised an eyebrow when Miklós thrust my passport application at him at the same time as the marriage registration. The only sticking point for the passport had been the *jus sanguinis*; I had no Hungarian ancestor that I could recall let alone prove. Luckily, the rules were relaxed for marriages based on long-term relationships; we could prove ours had existed for fifteen years.

As he picked through the sheaf of papers Miklós had given him, the clerk looked almost disappointed everything was in order. Perhaps he hadn't had enough coffee that morning.

'You'll only be granted an "overseas citizen" passport until you take up permanent residence,' the clerk frowned. 'However, you'll have all the same rights as any other citizen.' I smiled the most saccharine smile I could muster. I felt a ripple of guilt as I signed the application in front of him; I hadn't the heart to admit I didn't have the least wish to live anywhere but Roma Nova. He stamped and tossed it with the bundle of supporting documentation into his out tray, nodded dismissal and shouted 'Next'.

Three weeks later, Sándor pointed to a bulky envelope on the hall table. He collected the post every day from the outside box by the gate, but never usually informed either of us of its arrival. I was hot and sweaty, a towel draped round my neck, desperate for a shower after a murderous session on the exercise machines in the basement. Rehabilitation from my wounds was arduous.

'For you, from consulate,' Sándor grunted.

I tore open the envelope and stared at the blue pasteboard booklet with the gold lettering and state symbol. Thank Juno. Oh, thank Juno. I had my passport, my legal protection. I sank onto the telephone seat in the hallway and held the treasured document in my trembling hands as if it was the original Twelve Tables of Roma Nova. Moments later, the gate bell rang again. Had the postman forgotten something? Still clutching the precious passport, I went to open the door, but Sándor stepped in front of me and seized the handle. He jerked his head back at me. Of course. Security.

He opened the door enough for me to see over his shoulder without being visible. A uniformed New Austrian policeman with a white envelope in his hand. Sándor took the letter from the young man and thrust it into my hand as he kicked the house door shut.

The return address was from the *Neuösterreiches Ministerium für Justiz*. Oh gods, what now?

'Yes, on the surface it looks like a compelling case for extradition, but no, we're sure it can't succeed.'

David Soane's lawyer laid his pen down on his legal pad and removed his glasses. 'You've claimed and been granted political asylum by the New Austrian government and, provided you don't break any laws, you will continue to enjoy that status. You've also acquired Hungarian overseas citizenship by marriage, so if our government deported you for any reason, it would be to Hungary.'

I closed my eyes in relief for a second.

'However—'

'Yes?'

'I will ask a colleague specialising in extradition law to make a formal rebuttal of the application, if you wish. He will charge a fee, of course.'

Didn't all lawyers? David was being kind and paying for this one, though, but I didn't know if I had sufficient funds to hand, whatever I'd said to Quirinia all those weeks ago.

'Do it,' I said. 'I don't want any loose ends.'

I wrote again to Numerus, but didn't get a reply, nor to my letters to Silvia, Quirinia and Volusenia. The only letters I received apart from legal ones were from my daughter, Marina, and her husband, William, in the Eastern United States. She sounded happy and he content. They invited me again to go and live with them, but I couldn't detach myself mentally and emotionally from here. I kept giving my physical health as the reason but that would run out of steam soon.

Now I was better in myself and the hospital had discharged me formally, I wanted to stretch my legs, go for a run, but Miklós and Sándor had both vetoed it.

I filled my days writing a full account of what had happened to me from the night of fires when Caius Tellus had made his power grab last year, the abortive mission to rescue Silvia Apulia, my captivity and escape. So much had happened and I wanted it documented. No, I needed to get it out of my system. When I allowed my mind to go back to the night Caius raped me, shame and anger still flooded through me. Each day I would scribble out my anger, then type up a fair copy on the word processor Miklós had brought home for me. As I loaded each day's work onto the diskette I was comforted by the thought that at least posterity would know the true story.

'What were you doing up at four this morning, Aurelia? Again?'

Miklós stood in the doorway of the dining room, the towelling coat open at the neckline showing his smooth skin covered in fine black down. The belt was cinched tight around his waist and water glistened in the black curls. Warm desire rocketed through me. I wanted nothing but to surrender to and at the same time consume this man. I dropped my pen on the table and covered the two steps to him. I reached up, slid my hand down the side of his neck and kissed him long and hard.

'You didn't have any plans this morning, did you?' I whispered when I pulled away for a moment.

His eyes narrowed, then he shook his head and took my hand in his.

'Don't try to distract me.' He flicked my nose with his finger. 'You're like a horse straining to gallop across the plains. I do understand, really I do, but while we stay this close to the Roma Nova border, you must stay in the barn.' He pulled me to him, circled my waist with his arm and whispered, 'But we could burn a few calories together in the straw in the meantime.'

Miklós had gone into town early the next morning on some mysterious errand. Sándor sat in the kitchen with his black tea and magazine of dubious taste and I stared out of the window, bored out of my mind and intensely frustrated. Writing my account had made me realise I couldn't sit on my backside doing nothing while Caius was destroying everything in Roma Nova. But what could I do alone?

I dissected the *Acta Diurna* international edition, such as it was reduced to – mere propaganda. I scoured the international press, but most of them had moved on to other stories. My former colleagues in European foreign ministries only replied to my letters with sympathy and meandering about not interfering with other countries' internal problems. Probably written by one of their assistants and signed in a pile of letters.

Only Sir Henry Carter in the United Kingdom bothered to write his own letter; practical advice about enduring, building resources in conjunction with others and wishing me luck. His footnote, *'if the New Austrians chuck you out, we would be more than happy to give you immediate and permanent asylum,'* seemed like a tiny lamp in the general gloom.

I was curled up on the window seat an hour later, sipping my third cup of coffee, when I glimpsed a strange movement outside. A huge horse was the other side of the black railings of the gate. The rider bent down and stabbed at the keypad, but I knew from the way his body moved and curved it was Miklós. What in Hades was he doing with a horse?

'Get your tracksuit on,' he called from the open front door, and grinned like a kid up to mischief. He patted the horse who gave him back a soft breathy whinny. I tore up the stairs, scrambled into my running gear and was outside the front door in minutes. Miklós was bantering with Sándor who gave a short laugh back as I bounced through the door. Despite the chill, the day was glorious; blue sky and brilliant white winter sun. Sándor even smiled and waved as Miklós pulled me up behind him and we set off.

‘He's a bit of a slug,' Miklós said as the horse trotted sedately along the streets.

‘That's no way to describe Sándor,' I said. ‘I thought he was your friend.'

He reached back and gave me a playful slap on the thigh, but chuckled. I gave him a hearty jab in the ribs, then circled his waist tightly and laid my cheek against his back.

We reached the Prater and, on one of the bridleways, I slid off the slug with Miklós's warning not to run anywhere the horse couldn't go. We were 'on holiday', but couldn't afford to be stupid.

Juno, the sheer pleasure of running freely was almost overwhelming; the exhilaration of moving fast under your own power. The thud of your heart in the silence of cutting through air, over grass, weaving through trees, was one of the most satisfying feelings in life. Scientists explained it with talk of adrenaline and endorphins, but even with a frozen winter breeze hitting my face, it opened the senses and cleaned the mind.

I ran on, avoiding people, lamp posts, and rubbish bins by instinct. As my breath became jerkier, I slowed to a trot, realising I was becoming tired.

‘That smile on your face is well worth riding the slug.' Miklós's voice drifted into my consciousness as I came to a stop and gasped for a few moments.

‘Thank you.' I reached up and stretched out my hand to his. I laid the other on the horse's warm neck. ‘Thank you for this.' I made a moue. ‘I'll probably regret it in the morning, though.' He laughed and helped me back up behind him and we trotted back to the livery stable to collect the car, both content.

‘Don't stop. Drive on past the house.'

Miklós was slowing down ready to turn into the recess in front of the house gates when I grabbed his arm. He shot a glance at me. I jerked my hand forwards to urge him on. He put his foot on the accelerator and turned at the next junction, then stopped the car.

‘What is it?'

'Something's not right. The front door was open. And Sándor wasn't collecting the post.'

'Burglar?'

'With armed grumpy-guts there? Unlikely.' I looked around. Nobody on the street. 'Have you got your knife?'

He reached down into his riding boot.

'Back or front?' I asked.

'You jog along the front if you've got the breath – it'll look more natural,' he said. 'I'll climb over the back garden fence.'

He grasped my hand and tilted my chin up with the other to look me steadily in the eye. 'Aurelia, be careful. No heroics.'

I smiled briefly, then got out of the car and started a slow jog. I fished my bunch of three keys out of my pocket and, holding the fob in my palm, slotted each one between the fingers of my balled fist. At the gate, I crouched down as if to retie my running shoe. All I could hear was the murmur of somebody's lawnmower in the distance. But our house door was open at the same angle as it had been five minutes ago.

I straightened up, jabbed at the keypad and the gate opened. I took a deep breath and readied myself. This was my first test since I'd been shot. Suppose I couldn't cut it any longer?

Too late.

I crept up to the entrance out of direct sight line of the interior and flattened myself against the wall. I took a deep breath. I was trembling.

Pull yourself together, Mitela.

It would end one way or the other. Only one way to find out which.

I pushed the door open another few centimetres. No noise, no movement. Going for it, I slammed the door back and burst in. Dropping to a crouch, I panned round. The hallway was empty, nothing on the stairs, nothing I could see in the living room. Not the faintest sound from anywhere. But there was a sour, tinny smell, one I recognised instantly and it came from the direction of the kitchen.

When I got there, I threw up.

4

The first white police car screeched to a stop outside. Two grey-uniformed figures toting pistols, followed by a man in civilian clothes, hurtled into the house. Miklós stood slowly as one of the uniforms came into the living room. His reward was a service pistol pointing at his chest.

'I'm the householder who called you,' he said, holding his hands a few centimetres away from his legs. 'And this is my wife who found the body.'

The policeman nodded, said nothing, but holstered his pistol. '*Inspektor*,' he shouted.

Now, fifteen minutes later, the detective sat up straight in the armchair opposite us. He was tall, dark-haired and in his thirties. His beige gaberdine coat hung shapelessly, but didn't hide a brown cord jacket and slacks. Curiously, he wore orange and black striped socks.

He started asking the usual questions, simple to start with, designed to set a witness at ease. He scribbled everything furiously, but at length, in his notebook. We'd be here all day if we went at this pace.

'*Herr Inspektor*,' I interrupted him. 'Shall I just give you my statement in one go?'

He looked up at me. 'You seem remarkably composed, *Frau* Farkas.'

'I'm a former Roma Novan Praetorian trained in interrogation techniques and have conducted a good number of interviews myself.' I smiled to soften my words, but he blinked and sat back.

I told him in brief but comprehensive terms how I'd found Sándor spreadeagled on the kitchen floor with a *pugio* ceremonial dagger through his heart. He was lying in a large pool of blood which I estimated to be a litre to two litres. The note in Latin had been stuffed into his mouth, so that most of it protruded above his lips. I confirmed I'd entered the kitchen no more than two paces in, that we had moved nothing and had closed the door until the police arrived.

'I apologise for the vomit. It was a reaction to the smell. I didn't clear it up as I didn't want to disturb the crime scene.'

The young man waved his hand as in dismissal. 'Thank you for being so matter of fact.' He twirled the pen between his fingers and seemed at a loss for what to ask next. One of the uniforms interrupted him with the news that the forensic team had arrived. The inspector disappeared for a few moments, leaving a uniformed officer who fidgeted by the door and said nothing.

'Are you really okay?' Miklós whispered, holding my hand a little tightly.

'No, I'm bloody furious,' I replied. 'It's Caius, I know it is.'

'Sándor was as tough as iron,' Miklós said. 'I'm surprised anybody could kill him. He was a bodyguard for the head of one of the gangs in Budapest.'

'How did he get away?' Organised crime gangs usually had no formal retirement plans.

'His boss screwed his girl, so Sándor killed him. He turned up at the camp outside Budapest where I was living at the time and I got him away. He's lived in Vienna ever since. Until now.'

Juno. Sándor had radiated a grim strength, but I hadn't realised he'd killed.

'They'll want to search his room,' I murmured. 'Is there anything there that shouldn't be?'

'I hope not. I didn't impose border control on him when he moved in, you know.'

'Don't be peevish with me. I feel guilty enough.'

'It's *not* your fault.'

'If he hadn't been here, guarding me—'

I broke off as the detective came back in the room. His face had hardened.

'I have some further questions for you both, but I would like to continue this interview at the station. In any event, we will need to examine this house in detail. Please collect some essential personal items for a few days and be ready in fifteen minutes.' Miklós and I exchanged glances. Surely we weren't under suspicion? 'A uniformed officer will accompany you upstairs.'

Past the pristine stone and glass facade, the police station looked like any other; drab colours, a bored desk sergeant, faint smell of sweat and stale coffee. Miklós was silent as we proceeded down a chair-lined corridor and pushed through a pair of swing doors. He was almost reluctant to enter the interview room. It must have seemed such a foreign environment for him, threatening even.

I touched his hand and whispered, 'It's okay. Leave it to me.'

He said nothing so I pressed his hand a little harder.

The inspector came back with another, older, detective who sat down and clicked his fingers at the younger man prompting him to activate a recording device. After the usual preliminaries with our names and dates, the older detective, who hadn't given his name, pushed three photos across the table. The *pugio* that I'd seen sticking out of Sándor's chest had been shot from different angles.

'Would you like to comment on this weapon?' he asked Miklós.

'Never seen it before,' he replied.

'Really?'

Miklós tensed and he glared at the detective.

'I know exactly where it came from,' I interrupted. 'Until now, it's been in a locked display case in the Golden Palace in Roma Nova. It was in the personal collection of the late Imperatrix Justina, the previous imperatrix's mother.'

'And how do *you* know that, *Frau* Farkas?'

'I'm sure you've done your research, *Herr Inspektor*—'

'*Herr Leutnant*,' he snapped.

'You will know then, *Herr Leutnant*,' I emphasised those two words, 'that before the power grab in Roma Nova by Caius Tellus, I was the foreign minister there and imperial councillor. As a cousin of the imperial family I had the run of the palace since childhood. Moreover, in my service as a young officer, I commanded the Praetorian detail responsible for the imperatrix's security. I think you can take it that I know exactly which case that *pugio* was locked in.'

He glared at me, then turned to Miklós.

'Can you corroborate what your wife claims?'

'Don't you believe her? You're a fool then.'

I kicked Miklós's foot and shook my head at him. We couldn't afford to antagonise this policeman.

The lieutenant narrowed his eyes, then wrote something on a small piece of paper, passed it to the inspector, who glanced at it, sent a questioning look back to his superior, who nodded. The younger man hurried off.

'Who are you, really?' the older detective growled at me.

'I was born into the Mitela family and my given *praenomen* is Aurelia. As the head of one of the Twelve Families of Roma Nova, I hold the rank of countess, or *Gräfin* in Germanic, if you prefer. Currently, I am living quietly as an exile with my husband Miklós Farkas whom I married here a few weeks ago. The New Austrian foreign minister, a friend, was one of my witnesses.' I looked down my nose at him. 'I trust that will satisfy you.'

'We need to confirm your identity with the Roma Novan authorities.'

Oh, gods, no.

'I'm a political refugee, granted asylum with full rights,' I retorted. 'I also hold Hungarian citizenship. I showed your colleague my passport earlier.' I took a deep breath. 'My status is not in question. The main concern is the murder of my, no, my husband's driver. We are here to assist with that, not to be browbeaten on settled matters.'

'Very well. I have asked for guidance from my senior command as this goes well beyond a standard murder enquiry.' He stood up. 'I will send in coffee and sandwiches.' He flicked the tape recorder off and left.

I let a long breath out.

Miklós stood up, grasped the back of his chair for a few moments, then started pacing around like a wolf shut up in a zoo compound.

'How long do you think we'll be here?'

I tracked him as he circled the small room.

'I don't know.' I caught his hand as he passed by me. 'Stop. Come and sit down.' I dragged him back onto his chair and bent over to whisper in his ear. 'They're probably watching us and listening in, so sitting calmly as if unconcerned is best.'

'Well, it's all right for you – you're used to it. I've never been held in a police station.'

'Never?' I stared at him.

'No, never. Don't look so surprised.'

'Sorry.' I laughed, more in relief than humour.

He smiled back, and raised his eyebrows, making a comic expression. I pressed his hand.

'Try to endure,' I whispered. 'They can't hold us on anything. Playing the system and cooperating will get us further than not.'

Half an hour after a silent young policewoman had brought us sandwiches and coffee, the lieutenant returned with the inspector in tow and followed by an elegant suited man in his mid-forties who looked like a lawyer. He scanned our faces with an intense measuring look, then held out his hand and shook mine and then Miklós's. His grip was firm, but brief.

'Good afternoon, *Frau Gräfin* Mitela, *Herr* Farkas. My name is Goss, from the foreign minister's private office. He sends his warmest regards and apologies for any awkwardness to which you have been subjected.' He shot an almost venomous look at the two detectives. 'I understand that for technical reasons you cannot return to your house at present. The police service assures me they will have completed their forensic work within the next twenty-four hours. In the meantime, the minister asks if you will consent to be his guests at a government hospitality apartment. I have a car waiting outside to take you there.'

He hadn't paused for a single breath. I exchanged glances with Miklós. He shrugged.

'Thank you, *Herr* Goss. We accept. However, we would be more than pleased to cooperate with the police investigation. Sándor was my husband's friend as well as employee.'

'Of course.' Goss stretched his hand out in the lieutenant's direction without looking at him. 'The note,' he said curtly. The lieutenant thrust a transparent plastic bag containing an A5 sheet of paper at him. Goss smiled at me. 'Would you mind confirming what is written on this? I've made a rudimentary attempt at it, but I yield to your superior knowledge of Latin.'

Superior was a word he looked well acquainted with. I picked up the bag with the crumpled piece of paper, stained from saliva and spotted with blood. My mouth was dry as I read and translated it.

WE'LL HAVE YOU NEXT TIME. YOU'LL NEVER BE SAFE.

'At the expense of being obvious, this looks to be an overt political assassination attempt.' The immaculate *Herr* Goss sat across the dining table in the bland but comfortable apartment we'd been moved to.

The inspector wriggled in his seat. Goss had insisted any further police interview be held at our convenience at our temporary home.

'You don't agree?' Goss looked down his nose at the detective.

'Well, sir, it's a murder of a foreign national by persons unknown. We've sent the fingerprints to both the Hungarian police and the Roma Novan *vigiles* for their comments.'

I snorted at him. 'You'll get a negative answer from Roma Nova, no question of it. Do you think they'd dare assist with a murder committed by their own state political police?'

'We don't know that,' the inspector replied. 'We only deal in facts.'

'The note in Latin and the *pugio*, which could only have come from the palace collection, are strong indicators, I would say.' I failed to keep the sarcasm out of my voice. Miklós clasped my hand and pressed it. He gave me a tiny smile and shook his head. I took a long breath to calm myself. 'I apologise, *Herr Inspektor*, you are quite right, but I hope you can understand my frustration.'

He looked up, his face still grave. 'I can imagine why you would feel very frightened, *Frau Gräfin*.'

'It's not fright, it's anger. How dare that bloody man keep trying to kill me?' I stood up and went over to the window, staring down at the midday traffic but not seeing it.

I heard the door open behind me. Goss murmured something, then the door closed.

Miklós came to stand by me. 'Caius will keep trying until one of you is dead. And I think you know that in your heart.'

I almost shrugged his hand off my shoulder, but he was right.

A discreet cough broke the tension. I turned to face Goss, who was gathering his papers together.

'I will send a formal note to the Roma Nova legation for onward transmission to the Roma Nova authorities expressing our concern and so on,' he said. 'Have you been in contact with the *nuncia*?'

'No, I—' I swallowed. 'To be honest, *Herr* Goss, I haven't wanted to. When a regime changes, you have to assume the legations will change with it. Knowing Livilla Vara, I'd say she'll switch according to the prevailing wind.'

'You know her personally?'

'Yes, of course. I know all the heads of legation I appointed. She's also the heir of one of the Twelve Families, although Caius Tellus informed me they were being disbanded.' I grabbed the back of the nearest chair and bent over it. More than fifteen hundred years of mostly efficient government and history cut down by one brutal man. I straightened up after a moment. 'I don't know how secure her position will be, though, as Tellus had started dismissing all senior and middle-grade women state servants when I escaped.'

'So she wouldn't necessarily extend the legation's protection to you?' Goss continued.

'I can't count on it. If she's had instructions from Roma Nova, she might just as easily detain me and send me back there.'

'I see.' He touched his silk tie for an instant and looked away. 'Well, I'll consult the minister, of course, but I have to warn you that we can't provide this level of protection for very long.' He meant the policeman outside and this secure apartment, I was sure. 'Perhaps you would be safer if you were not so close to Roma Nova. Your daughter in the EUS, perhaps?'

'He just wants us out of his hair,' Miklós said after Goss left.

'I'd want the same if it was happening in Roma Nova, darling. No state can tolerate third country assassins operating on its territory. There's too much potential for political embarrassment, not to mention scandal if it gets out. I'm fairly sure that's why the foreign minister has sent his assistant and not come himself.'

'Maybe you *should* think of going to Marina and William. You'd have a comfortable life in the EUS and you have many business interests there.'

I caught my breath. 'Why are you saying "you"? You'd be coming with me. Wouldn't you?'

Oh, gods.

'I'm too European, Aurelia. If you think I sometimes feel uncomfortable in Roma Nova, I'd suffocate in those cities. And we couldn't live in the plains where we could breathe – the Indigenous Nations own most of that.' He took both my hands and kissed my forehead. 'I love you, my heart and soul, but I would give you up if it meant you would be safe.'

I had almost become used to his weeks-long absences when we lived in Roma Nova, but this – a permanent parting? My heart thudded with the horror of such a thought.

'Caius would put somebody on a plane,' I said in a voice hardly above a whisper. 'Or get his friend White in the EUS CIA to arrange an "accident" or have me deported back to Roma Nova despite my new passport. It could put Marina and William in danger.' His fingers gripped harder. I searched his face, but all I could see was sadness. 'No, I'm not going to be safe until Caius and I finish it between us.'

'There is one other possibility,' he said. 'You would be safer and have a way to make common cause against Caius Tellus. But it would mean submitting yourself to hostility and possibly abuse.' He stroked my cheek. 'I don't doubt your courage, Aurelia, but you are still fragile inside. And I don't mean your body. You need more time to recover, to rediscover your core. And even if you went through with it, I don't know if it would succeed.'

'I can't remain in this limbo, Miklós. It's like floating on the Styx unable to land. I know the exiles were hard when I went there last time, but they can't be worse than the judges deciding whether to let me into Elysium, can they?'

5
———

I dithered for days about contacting the exiles again. Miklós said it was driving him mad watching me unable to sit or lie still.

Given the reception I'd had on my previous visit would it look weak or pathetic if I approached them a second time? I hoped I wasn't too proud, but I couldn't bear to be half accepted, hovering outside the inner circle, tolerated at the edge. I knew I would be able to contribute. Why couldn't they see that?

I'd torn up several draft letters – formal, simple, comprehensive – but all essentially begging for a hearing. But in the end, I didn't need to send anything.

Miklós had gone with one of the police guards to collect post from our closed-up house. He didn't say anything when he came back, but just handed me an envelope. Local, from the postmark. I flipped it over to see the sender's address – the exiles' safe house. I tore it open.

From the Roma Nova Decuria of Exiles
  To Aurelia Mitela, sometime citizen of Roma Nova

'"Sometime"! How dare they!' I threw it on the table.

Miklós picked it up and held it out to me. 'Calm down and just read it.' I glared at him, but he was right. Having a tantrum was childish as well as undignified. Perhaps he'd been right about me still being fragile inside. My hand trembled as I picked it up.

The Decuria has seen the recent press coverage of the murder of a Hungarian citizen living in your household and noted the speculation about links to Roma Nova.

Exceptionally, as you are proscribed, you are invited to present yourself to us to discuss this matter next Tuesday at 10:00.

M. Quirinia

For the Decuria

Quirinia, as senior minister, flanked by Volusenia, the military commander, and Calavia, the next senior of the Twelve Families, looked up at me as I paused at the door of the faded ballroom in the safe house. My former friend was now my chief judge. I took a deep breath to settle the fluttering in my stomach. Juno, I'd given full-blown speeches in the Senate, debated in council, presented at international business conferences. I should be able to cope with this ramshackle gathering. In the dim light, the three women didn't look like Minos, Rhadamanthos and Aeacus, but their expressions could have belonged to those fearsome judges on the bank of the Styx. And their verdict would exonerate or condemn me as surely.

My sense of dread grew as I crossed the empty space to the back of the two blocks of chairs. Numerus escorted me down the aisle between the chairs filled with silent, staring people, about fifty of them. Quirinia, Volusenia and Calavia sat behind the trestle table at the front, facing into the room. I didn't look right or left. A short bench had been placed at the front, as if it were a defendant's bench in a courtroom. Numerus stretched out his hand and indicated I should sit there.

So, I was on trial.

I laid one hand within the other in my lap and waited. I'd made a bookful of notes and rehearsed a formal speech. But during an afternoon in the legal section of the Vienna business library, I'd almost leapt up and shouted '*Victis*' when I'd made an important discovery; more of a reminder of something I'd forgotten years ago. It was the key to unlock everything. But I didn't know if any of this preparation would help me. Nobody said anything after I sat; perhaps they didn't know how to start. But I was damned if I'd make the first move.

Eventually, Quirinia cleared her throat, picked up a sheet of paper.

'Aurelia Mitela, you have been summoned here to appear before the citizens to provide an explanation of your conduct. As a proscriptee, you have no right to be heard, but the *decuria* grants this as an exception.'

I held up my hand. Time for the bombshell.

'Before you go on, Quirinia, let's get one thing straight. No, two things. Firstly, you did not *summon* me. If I remember correctly, your letter *invited* me. Secondly, the proscription is *ultra vires*.' I paused, enjoying in a sad way the dismay on Quirinia's face, Volusenia's frown and Calavia's disbelief. 'Although she is the late Imperatrix Severina's direct blood heir, Silvia Apulia is not yet empowered. We may recognise her by consent and custom, but until she presents herself to the Senate and is accepted by them, she has no legal power to make any law or issue any legal instrument, including proscription.'

The silence was so thick, I could almost touch it.

'So you will delete any mention of this in connection with me from any records you are keeping,' I continued and glanced at the clerk scribbling furiously in a bound book. 'I will waive my right of redress for *inuria* and *infamia* for the moment, but the attack on my personal honour and my public shaming I will not easily forget.' I glared at all three. My anger had returned to boil inside me at the injustice of it all, but I gripped my fingers hard to stop it bursting out.

'Don't be ridiculous!' Calavia shouted. 'Of course Silvia Apulia can't present herself to the Senate at the moment.'

'Exactly so,' I retorted.

The three of them went into a huddle, whispering frantically together. Behind me, I heard murmuring from the other exiles. I glanced at Numerus. He didn't meet my eyes, but a smile hovered on his lips. A touch on my shoulder. I turned to see Styrax. She simply looked at me steadily then nodded. After a couple of minutes, Volusenia thumped on the table.

'Quiet.' She looked directly at me. 'The legal niceties may not stand, but there is little doubt of the reasons behind the proscription. You collaborated with the traitor Caius Tellus and betrayed Roma Nova by giving him countenance and support. There is no place in this community for you.' She looked away and I caught a look of regret in her expression. 'You will please leave.' She signalled to Numerus who sighed.

'So I'm not even granted a hearing? This is not a legally constituted court, agreed, but have you so departed from Roma Novan legal standards that you ignore the right of *audiatur et altera pars*, that my side must be heard as well?' I stood and covered the three metres between me and my judges. I planted myself in front of Quirinia, crossed my arms with more confidence than I felt inside and looked down at her. She kept her eyes down on her sheets of paper. I was angry that she wouldn't even look at me. 'What a miserable state you've come to,' I said.

'Don't you dare judge us,' Calavia said and leapt to her feet.

I glared at her. 'You've already found me guilty without due process. Even the lowest-ranking soldier knows that's illegal. You should be stripped of your commission for such wilful ignorance.' She was young and passionate, so in my head I gave her some slack. But their collective behaviour was inexcusable.

'Sit down, Calavia,' Volusenia said. She looked up at me. Her fingers were tapping the table. She glanced at Quirinia, who still avoided looking at me, but Quirinia nodded at Volusenia. 'Very well,' the latter said. 'Say what you want to.'

'We are all in a state of loss and hurt so our emotions are flying high,' I said. 'I would therefore ask you to hear me calmly,' I began.

Volusenia's expression tightened but she gestured me to continue.

'You, Colonel Volusenia, have known me for fifteen years since the time you guarded my child in the palace against Caius Tellus. We stood in that same palace four months ago, fighting Tellus when I ordered you to take Silvia Apulia to safety. Not, I think, the actions of a traitor.'

'You, Pia Calavia, guided *Consiliaria* Quirinia here and me to safety. When you and I returned to Roma Nova to look for Silvia Apulia and were captured by the nationalists, I thought we were both dead and the mission finished.' I waved towards the audience. 'There are so few personnel here qualified or competent to continue the search so it was vital that you and Atrius should somehow be freed to carry on. I bargained with Tellus for your lives and release.'

'You found a way back into your life in Roma Nova like a good

politician and took the easy way out by shacking up with Tellus.'
Calavia's voice was uncompromising.

'Oh, grow up,' I snapped. 'The only reason you're sitting here
sniping at me is because I went down on my knees and begged him
for your life.'

'Literally?'

'Yes. It was a moment I shall look back on with nothing but shame,
but it was the only way to save you and Atrius.'

She said nothing.

'The days that followed, I had to obey his every whim until I had
proof you were both across the border.'

'But you were intimate with him. I saw it myself.'

'No. He gave that impression and threatened that if I didn't play
along, he'd execute you both out of hand. Do you think it wasn't the
most repulsive thing, being so physically close to him?'

'He said you were his companion in every way.'

'Tell me his exact words.'

'He asked me to think about why you had come back. Was it really
for Silvia Apulia? You'd exerted authority as an imperial councillor
and senior senator for so long, you naturally gravitated to the centre of
power. Perhaps you were being a realist? You'd been defiant at first,
but were settling into a new role at his side. You were to be Livia to his
Augustus.' She glanced up at me. 'This would be confirmed by your
new appearance. Then when you came into the room in tunic and
sandals, you looked like something out of history.'

'For your information, that's all I was given to wear.'

'Then—' She paused. 'You didn't resist when he held you close to
him.' She looked at me with fire in her eyes. 'I hated you at that
moment. Good bloody riddance.'

'You believed the traitor who killed his way to power, who
executed your own grandmother, over me?' I stared at her, but she'd
bowed her head. 'Listen to me, Calavia. Ever since we were children,
Caius Tellus has tried to destroy me in front of others. He has the
knack of charming others to believe him. If that didn't work, he'd
destroy people's faith in somebody or something by dropping just the
right amount of doubt into their ear. He is a charming, manipulative
predator and you fell for it.'

She looked furious and embarrassed at the same time. She was so young despite her military competence; she took everything she saw so literally. The passionate fighter who'd led our escape out of Roma Nova with such expertise and unflagging optimism now looked like a crushed child.

I looked at Quirinia last. Her face was resolute, but two dark red patches burned in her cheeks.

'You, my childhood friend,' I said, 'I expected more of you. We've served together under Imperatrix Justina and her daughter Severina until Caius Tellus's coup. But even you were nearly taken in until that Families meeting after Constantia Tella's funeral. We froze together on that mountain escaping from him. Tell me, please, what has convinced you to judge me, even after you saw for yourself what he was like?'

'I—' She rubbed the fingertips of one hand with the fingers of her other.

'Yes?'

'I refused to believe what Calavia said when she came back. We couldn't get hold of the *Acta Diurna* for ages – they stopped printing it. But the first international version we got hold of, there you were named as his companion. I still couldn't believe it.' She looked up at me and searched my face.

'I escaped that night, Quirinia. His political troops pursued me, helped by the damned tracker he had me fitted with. They wounded me and eventually captured me.'

'Why did you delay escaping after Calavia and Atrius were released? Volusenia shot at me.

'I hardly call three days a significant delay, colonel.' She flicked her fingers at me as if dismissing it. 'Two things,' I continued. 'Firstly, he threatened my daughter through his friend in the EUS security services. Marina should have been safe in America with her husband, but Caius Tellus said it would take one transatlantic call to destroy her. I managed to send a covert warning to her husband and prayed he would take appropriate measures. Secondly, it's not easy to acquire walking clothes, boots and equipment for crossing an alpine range in winter when you only have access to indoor tunics and sandals. I'd managed to gather a few basic things together when I saw that damned notice in the *Acta Diurna*. Although I wasn't fully ready, I went that night.'

'But you had help?'

'Yes.'

'From whom?'

'I'd rather not say in open session, but will tell you privately.'

'We have no secrets here.' She swept her arm round to include the fifty-odd souls in the room.

'Nevertheless, it is poor operational security.'

She didn't reply, but the muscles on her face tightened. What on earth was wrong with them all? Volusenia jerked her head at Numerus who left the room. I dropped down onto my hard bench; my legs were trembling. We sat in silence for a few moments, but I turned at the noise of the door opening and watched Numerus and another tall figure escorting a slighter one between them. As they marched up to the front, everybody stared, watching their progress. The trio halted by the side of the trestle table where my three judges sat. Numerus resumed his place, but the other two stood. At first, I didn't believe who I was seeing. I stood up to get a better view.

'You remember Turturus, who wanted to join the rescue mission?' Quirinia said.

I would never forget him. A frightened adolescent, yes – the grim-faced guard was gripping his arm none too gently – but a conniving little bastard all the same. This was Caius's spy who'd been responsible for my arrest – along with that of Calavia and Atrius – and for Atrius's ill-treatment at the hands of Caius's punishment squad. What the hell was he doing back here?

'Oh, yes, I remember him well.' I gave him what I hoped was a look that would freeze him to the furthest cell in his body. 'I stood before Caius Tellus, manacled, and this little traitor was brought in. Tellus explained to me that Turturus followed us in a fit of pique and offered his services to the nationalists to spy on us. Apparently, he was fed up with being told what to do by a woman – me – and having his masculinity stamped on, so he'd come back to Roma Nova seeking a "better way". As far as I was concerned, he'd been far too young to take on an extremely dangerous rescue mission.' I glanced away for a few moments.

'Perhaps it was my misjudgement, but I never dreamt that any loyal Roma Novan would betray a unit seeking to rescue the imperial heir, certainly not this miserable child.' I jabbed my finger in the boy's direction. 'His actions not only brought our mission to an end, but he was directly responsible for a loyal guard who had befriended him being subjected to hours of pain and humiliation. And he put another, Calavia, under threat of summary execution.'

I heard Calavia gasp. When I glanced at her, her lips were parted, a surprised expression stamped on her face. So Turturus hadn't told them that little morsel.

The boy's eyes bulged, then he slumped in the guard's grip.

'He tells a different story,' Quirinia ventured.

'Really? And what is that?' I tried to keep the sarcasm out of my voice, but it was too late. Quirinia flinched.

'We have to hear all sides, Aurelia,' she snapped. 'You said that yourself. Please sit down.' Turturus shot a look at me, and quickly transferred his anxious gaze to Quirinia. She smiled in an encouraging way.

'Now Turturus, tell the court – I mean, hearing – what you told me when you arrived.'

'I didn't know *she* would be here.'

I sat arms crossed and stared at him. Even in this dim light, I saw his cheeks turn dark red.

'Does that change your story, young man?' Volusenia's tone was fierce.

'N—, No, ma'am, but she's staring at me.'

'Well, ignore her and speak up.'

'I wanted to find out what had happened to my friends at the cadets' training school. So I went to the nats. They took me to his number two, Representative Phobius, then the first consul himself. I was a bit scared when they asked me to follow her and Lieutenant Calavia. Anybody would be.' He looked at me, then Calavia, and sniffed loudly. 'The nats promised to reunite me with my friends if I did well. The first consul dismissed me after he'd called me in to see *her* when they'd caught her. I shut the doors behind me and asked Phobius to take me to where my classmates were. That was our deal. He just laughed, and threw me in a cell. Then they made me skivvy in the back kitchens. He was a right bastard, that cook.'

I agreed with him about the cook, but I couldn't remember seeing Turturus when I was there.

'Continue,' Volusenia ordered.

The boy gave me a malicious look, then drew himself up.

'Well, I didn't *see* her, but I heard all sorts of stuff. I heard her voice once, bawling out the cook. He smacked us all afterwards. She was definitely in charge of the staff – I saw the order pinned on the staff notice board. And she was upstairs in the guest suite, one of the girls said. Typical patricians keeping together.' He made a face, then gave a sly smile. 'And she wasn't sleeping alone, they said. One of them had to take the first consul a drink up in the guest room one morning and she was asleep in the bed.'

The night he raped me. All three stared at me, Volusenia with a deep frown. Oh, gods. Hadn't Numerus told them what I'd said to him when I lay in the hospital with three gunshot wounds?

'Show them the ring around your wrist, Turturus,' Quirinia said.

The boy half raised his arm for a second, but there was no doubt what it was. Gasps came from the audience. Calavia stared, but Volusenia looked grim.

'And tell everybody what it means, please,' Quirinia said.

'It's what they put on slaves' wrists there. An' they can flog you an' everything.' He waved it around as if it were an emblem, a mark of passage.

Cries of 'no', people pushing forward to see, crowding round the boy in sympathy and shock, forgetting what he had just said. Slavery had never been allowed in Roma Nova, not even in the first days. The guard was elbowed aside by the sheer numbers. A man put his arm round the boy's shoulder, women grasped his other hand and arm. Protesting voices, full of indignation and disbelief grew louder every second.

'Quiet,' Volusenia roared. 'Sit down. This is not a damned arena.' Murmuring and mumbling, people drifted back to their seats, several darting hostile looks in my direction. I caught the word 'traitor' and 'coward' a few times. One man spat at my feet as he made his way back. Ironic that the collaborator was getting more sympathy than me. I stayed where I was, sitting upright, determined not to show how their words and actions hurt me.

Quirinia's expression was grim. Her voice cut through the babble. 'On this evidence, we cannot conclude anything but the worst, Aurelia Mitela.'

6

I waited until the room fell completely silent.

'Is this the "evidence" against me?'

'First we had Calavia's testimony,' Quirinia replied. 'Turturus arrived a few days ago and provided us with valuable corroboration.'

Calavia went to speak, but Volusenia shook her head.

'Well, then,' I said, 'I have a few observations, if I have the court's – ah, no, the *hearing's* indulgence.' I raised an eyebrow and slowly panned round the faces.

Quirinia gave a brief nod.

I stood and walked to the end of the table near Turturus, but a few paces away from him.

'Firstly, as I reported to ex-Senior Centurion Numerus when he visited me over three months ago while I was in intensive care, Caius Tellus raped me.' I closed my eyes for a moment as the memory of the humiliating violation flooded back. 'To him, it was a demonstration of power. He was under some delusion that once he had possessed me as an object he could do what he liked with me.

'Secondly, he ordered me to run the household and assume duties as—' I swallowed hard '—his companion. I refused. But the domestic staff were terrified, apart from the cook who was a bully. I intervened on that one occasion that Turturus refers to.

'Thirdly, Caius Tellus has suspended much of the law. Citizens are liable to summary arrest. Tellus has ordered the dismissal of women from ministerial and government positions, uniformed services, magistrates, and teaching apart from pre-primary. When I left, all women business owners were being forced to sign over their assets to a male relative within thirty days. Do you *really* think that is *my* Roma Nova?'

I rolled up my sleeve. The flesh on my arm shivered in the unheated room. The steel ring that designated me as Caius's property glinted in the light.

'Contrary to what Turturus asserts, being a patrician is no protection from being enslaved.'

Gasps from the audience, but nobody came forward to comfort me as they had Turturus. I walked back to the bench without looking at any of them, sat down and folded my hands in my lap to stop them trembling. Perhaps Miklós was right; it was too soon and I didn't have either the mental or physical energy to cope with this.

Quirinia, Volusenia and Calavia huddled together arguing heatedly, but trying to keep it to a whisper. Suddenly Calavia slammed her hand on the table. She stood, jolting the edge of the table.

'I'm not taking any further part in this shambles,' she said. 'I withdraw my testimony.' She nodded curtly at Quirinia and strode over to the audience where she plumped herself down on a chair in the row behind me. I didn't react outwardly, but even though I was bone-tired, my heart leapt at her words. Thank Juno, somebody had believed me. But Calavia, of all people? Thoughts and questions ran round my head, all enveloped in anger, but with her retraction, I sensed we were near the endgame. I had to keep a grip, whatever my nerves wanted to do.

Volusenia turned her full-strength glare on Turturus. 'You need to explain exactly how you got back here.'

Turturus's skin paled and he trembled. 'The housekeeper gave me some boots and walking stuff. She told me to run through the side gate in the car park between patrols.'

Gods, Drusilla, the palace housekeeper. She was still alive, or had been when this boy had fled. I closed my eyes for a few seconds and sent a silent prayer up to Juno. I sincerely hoped this waste of space hadn't brought her under suspicion. I stood and turned to face him.

'Something else I'm sure the hearing would like to know, Turturus,' I said. Quirinia leant forward and opened her mouth, but

Volusenia raised her hand in Quirinia's direction, silencing her, then nodded at me to continue. 'How did you convince the housekeeper to help you escape?'

Turturus shifted his weight from one foot to the other and looked away.

'Well?' Volusenia said. Her strong features were tightened into a stare that would frighten the toughest soldier.

He tilted his head at me. 'I… I told the housekeeper I'd report her for helping *her* to escape if she didn't help *me*.'

The anger rocketed up through me. I went to hurl myself at Turturus but just in time remembered where I was and why I was here. I had to keep calm, at least outwardly. But this treacherous child had nearly put another loyal Roma Novan's life in danger. Was there no end to it?

The crack of a chair falling to the ground and heavy, slightly uneven footsteps marching across the wooden floor interrupted us. A tall figure, black-haired and with blazing blue eyes, marched up to Turturus and struck him full in the face. The boy dropped to the floor, his face covered in blood, and the man kicked him hard before the guard and Numerus grabbed him and pulled him away. Atrius, my comrade-in-arms, tortured by Caius Tellus's punishment squad, was struggling to break away from the two men who restrained him. His breath came in short heavy gulps as his eyes spat fury at the boy on the ground.

'Stand down, Atrius,' I shouted, almost by instinct. I was by his side in a second and grasped his forearm. 'Stop. It's done.'

He turned his head and I saw fury and agony mixed. He gulped and then took a deep breath. He stopped struggling against the grip the two men held him in. I nodded at Numerus, who released him, and I led Atrius back to my bench and pushed him gently down onto it. I remained standing, but laid one hand on Atrius's shoulder to reassure him.

'I think we can now conclude that Turturus's evidence is flawed,' I said in the driest voice I could muster in this room full of emotion. 'If we were in Roma Nova in normal times, I would arrest him and send him to trial for treason. However, we are not. If we are to survive and then fight back, we need to develop a process and structure to deal with these kinds of circumstances.'

'You take a lot on yourself, Aurelia, considering you are under proscription and outside this community,' Quirinia shot at me.

'I will, of course, await the hearing's conclusions, Maia Quirinia,' I said, exercising every ounce of constraint to keep the sarcasm out of my voice. 'However, I rather feel the first was dealt with earlier and reversal of the second is the subject of this hearing.'

I stared at her until she dropped her gaze and studied the table. Volusenia shook her head and gave a brief 'Ha!' in my direction. Quirinia shuffled paper and whispered to Volusenia, who nodded.

'Please step forward,' Quirinia said. Her whole demeanour and her voice were stiff with embarrassment.

As I covered the space between me and my judges, Calavia and Styrax, the ex-legionary who had sat behind me, moved to my left and right. Styrax nodded at me and drew a little nearer. Calavia didn't look at me, but stared straight ahead. I released my breath slowly, heartened by such support.

'Aurelia Mitela,' Quirinia started. 'The Roma Nova *Decuria* of Exiles recognises your right of citizenship and withdraws its proscription.' She swallowed. 'It invites you to join the community of exiles.' She stared at me for a second, a dull flush in her cheeks, then looked down at the table and brought her hand up to support her forehead. She looked utterly crushed. Before I could say anything to her, Numerus, my faithful supporter, had marched over and clasped my forearm in a military handshake and placed his other hand on my shoulder.

'Welcome back, major.'

I closed my eyes for a moment and opened them to find his grey ones looking steadily at me. Through the hubbub surrounding us, I heard his words distinctly.

'Thank Pluto you're back. Perhaps you can kick some sense into these sorry-for-themselves idiots.'

7

'Let me through!'

A young girl, red-brown hair flying loose round her face, was wriggling between people, gently pushing bodies apart where she needed to. Her drown eyes, normally steady, glistened.

'Aunt Aurelia?'

'Oh, gods, Silvia.' I folded her into my arms and moulded her to me, almost crushing her. Silvia Apulia might be an emancipated adult of sixteen but she clung to me like any lost child.

'I *knew* you hadn't gone bad,' she said into my shoulder. 'Whatever anybody else said.' She pulled back. 'They wouldn't let me answer your letters, although they let me read them.'

'Well, that's all finished now, darling. I'm here, where I belong, among my own people.' I smoothed her hair. She grasped my hand and looked at me with a solemn face.

'I cannot imagine how horrible it must have been to be so often in that man's company. And him forcing you like that.' She turned her head away.

'I will never forget that, Silvia, and when we take Roma Nova back, there will be a reckoning between Caius Tellus and me.'

'Do you think we can do it?'

'That's why I'm here.'

•　•　•

Calavia pulled the door open and almost snatched the tray of food and tea from the man who had knocked on the door. At least it broke the silence. Volusenia, Quirinia, Numerus and I perched on rickety fold-up chairs in what had once been a drawing room. The clean lines of the cornicing and the fireplace with running plasterwork decoration were filled with dusty neglect. I was sad to see how rough the parquet wooden floor looked as Calavia's boots tramped across it. Silvia sat on the one good chair, but hunched in on herself as if she were the uninvited guest. I'd insisted she should be present. If we were ever to form ourselves into a government in exile, we needed a constitutional head. And she *was* the imperial heir.

Eating delayed the inevitable for a few minutes. I set my plate down on the bare wood, then studied them one by one, but none of them looked back at me for more than an instant. Well, we'd be here all day if I didn't start. I began with Quirinia.

'In your letter, you invited me here to discuss the recent murder of a member of my household and the rumours of a connection with Roma Nova. The simple truth is that Caius Tellus sent an assassination squad to terminate me. Instead, they murdered my driver who was also a friend of my companion's. The *pugio* they stuck through the poor man's heart and the note they stuffed in his mouth leave absolutely no doubt.'

Quirinia stared back at me, eyes wide and lips parted. She looked horrified. 'The driver?' she said after a few moments. 'Why him?'

'To make an example the ancient Roman way,' I replied. 'And also Caius's way – remote terrorism.'

The afternoon sun shining through the windows did nothing to dispel the dismay that Caius could strike at will, and across a national frontier. Calavia shifted in her seat and looked down at the floor. She'd tasted Caius's brutality first-hand.

'However, I'm sure you wanted to discuss more than that,' I continued. 'I would have been naive to have thought otherwise. Now you have accepted that I'm not a traitor and collaborator, we must plan for the future. We cannot sit here and let Caius dictate the course of Roma Nova.' I paused. 'Nor of our own lives.' Quirinia glanced at me, then down again. Silvia stared at me like a fawn waiting to be dispatched; the two Praetorians sat back, stony-faced.

Numerus was right; they looked completely disheartened.

'Very well,' I continued. 'I would suggest we establish exactly who is here and what our assets are. It looks as if there are fewer than a hundred people here. I would have thought more would have arrived.'

'I have a list, major,' Numerus offered. 'But—'

'Yes?'

'Others have been here, but were not admitted.' His voice dwindled to a mumble.

'Roma Novans?'

'Yes.'

'And why were they not admitted?'

'They were a group from… from Castra Lucilla.'

Dear gods. My estate manager and my people.

'Led by a man called Gavinus?' I said.

'Yes,' he replied, and looked at Quirinia.

'And what has happened to them?'

'We don't know.'

I stood up, too angry to speak for a few seconds. I folded my arms and paced around. Those loyal people, barely recovered from the attack by Caius's thugs, escaping with their lives, leaving their homes and everything behind them they couldn't carry in one bag, had been denied refuge by their own people. They'd set off at the end of the first week in October. We were now at the end of January. Juno knew where they were now. When I reached Quirinia, I stopped and glared down at her.

'I suppose this was your doing? These people were desperate, but because of your prejudice against me, they're out there holed up somewhere, probably sleeping rough, completely cut off from everything. Well done!'

'You know the penalty for proscription applies to everything to do with the proscriptee!' she shot back, her face a deep crimson.

'Yes, but it wasn't their fault. Mars' balls! This is a crisis of extreme proportions and you refused them shelter on a technicality. You should be ashamed of yourself.' She flinched as if I'd struck her. I took a deep breath. 'My first priority is to go and search for them. Do what you like in the meantime.' I yanked the door open and was halfway out when Volusenia grabbed my arm.

'*Consiliaria!*' she said. 'You cannot abandon your duty as senior minister and head of the Twelve Families.'

'My duty, colonel, is to those poor sods your cosy little *decuria* threw out on the street in the middle of winter. They are my *familia*.' I removed her hand from my arm. 'Don't *you* presume to tell me my duty.'

'Your place is here to lead the exiles,' she replied. 'Under the authority of Silvia Apulia, of course,' she added as an afterthought. We both glanced down at the poor girl, looking totally bewildered.

I dropped down and knelt down by Silvia's dilapidated armchair. I took her hand. 'I'm sorry, darling, we're all being bad tempered, but you see I must go and look for them?'

She nodded, then glanced at each of us in turn as if she didn't know what to reply.

'I'll go,' Calavia's voice came from behind me. 'It's the least I can do. And your estate guard Sentia knows me.'

Miklós poured a slug of brandy into the large cup of tea I was warming my hands on. Our temporary home, the government apartment, was warm, almost stifling, but I was cold with exhaustion.

'You should rest for a day or two, *drágám*.'

'You know I can't. There is so much to do.'

He folded me into his arms as if wishing to hold me forever.

'When are you moving in there?'

'Tomorrow.' I wriggled round to face him. 'But you're coming with me, aren't you?'

'No, you need to reintegrate with them and heal rifts.' He stroked my face with the back of his finger. 'I don't think I'd be very welcome anyway.'

'But—'

The finger touched my lips. 'I will be close by. I'll stay at the house to tidy up after the police release it, then I have some business to attend to.' He reached into his shirt pocket. 'This came for you from the police.'

I handed him my empty cup and opened the envelope stamped *Landespolizeidirektion Wien*. I scanned the sparse ten lines. They were 'pursuing several leads', but we were released from the enquiry, subject to advising them of our forwarding address.

Styrax collected me from the government apartment building at seven the next morning. In the lobby, Miklós kissed the back of my hand, then lightly on the lips while the young policeman on guard tried not to watch.

'Go with your gods,' he said. He smiled that little lopsided, almost rueful smile that I always wanted to kiss.

'Miklós—'

'Go now, or you won't do it.'

I pulled him to me once more, savouring the warm masculine scent of his skin, the faint tang of pine. I looked up and his dark eyes shone. He kissed my forehead, then turned me round and gave me a light push out of the door.

Once in the dark street my breath plumed in the freezing air. I turned and looked back into the cheerful lights just before I stepped into the warm fug of the taxi. Miklós smiled through the glazed door, raised his hand, gave a little wave and then just stared at me. I swallowed hard. This wasn't goodbye, just a temporary separation, I told myself. I sniffed hard, dragging in the cold that filtered through my body. I wiped tears from the skin below my eye as the taxi pulled out into the early morning traffic. Oh, gods, how lonely it would be without him.

At the safe house, only fifteen minutes away, I looked up at the tall rectangular windows. A few were lit, glowing in the dark of the cold Viennese morning. The yellow street lamps scattered light onto the frozen cobbles without much effect. The door guard nodded, then promptly opened the door. Volusenia was waiting for me in the hallway.

'Morning, *consiliaria*,' she said in her gruff voice and held out her hand. I took it; there was bound to be some awkwardness, but we couldn't afford to be precious in our current circumstances. Still, there were some curious looks from the two clerks pretending to shuffle paper at the side table. 'Please come with me.'

Volusenia led me across the dusty tile floor of the front hall, up the ornate staircase onto a wide landing. She nodded to the guard outside the second door along and opened the door slowly. She held her finger to her lips. I dropped my bags in the corridor, careful not to make any noise, and we crept in. The room smelled of old dust and new mattress. Pinned up at the window, a rough-woven blanket didn't quite exclude the artificial light from outside. A rickety dining chair draped with clothes was the only furniture apart from a modern shiny kit bed and mattress complete with white quilt and pillow.

The figure in the bed stirred as we crossed the bare boards, but she didn't wake. The quilt was drawn up tight behind her neck and under her chin and from the curves of her shape under the quilt I could see her knees were drawn up. Her mouth was slightly open. She looked twelve, not sixteen. We crept back out and in the corridor Volusenia leant back against the wall and faced me.

'We need you, *consiliaria*. More, Imperatrix Silvia in there needs you. She's only a kid. Full of grit, though. By the time we'd crawled through the Geminae pass and down the other side, she was exhausted. She didn't bleat once. It was only when I noticed blood seeping through her woollen gloves that I realised her hands were badly cut from climbing the gravel banks and slopes.

'When we had definite confirmation that Imperatrix Severina and Julianus Apulius were dead, you can imagine how hard that news fell on her. Mother and brother gone. And her father – we've heard nothing of him either. Poor child. She curled up in the chair and shook for minutes before she started sobbing. That night the medic gave her a sedative and we put her to bed. She still cries out in her sleep now and again.'

I wiped my fingers across my forehead and shivered as I remembered the hard trek over the mountains I'd had to force Marina to make last year when we were escaping Caius's thugs. These poor girls; they should have been dancing at parties, staying up half the night in the student bar tipsily airing political ideas or gossiping with their friends after a shopping expedition, not fleeing scared out of their wits from murder and tyranny. Volusenia showed me to a room opposite where I dropped my bags. She led me back downstairs in silence. Just before the hallway, she stopped, pulled a hip flask out of her pocket, unscrewed the top and thrust it in my direction.

'A good gulp. No less.'

I complied and felt steadier.

'Numerus has convened a general meeting for 08.00,' Volusenia said. She fixed me with her stare. 'Will you be able to work again with *Consiliaria* Quirinia, given her attitude at your hearing?'

'You don't take prisoners, do you, Volusenia?' I gave her a brief smile, hoping I'd hidden my bitterness at Quirinia's betrayal. She'd been such a good friend since we were girls, then had turned from me so easily. I knew the escape from Roma Nova had deeply upset her. Spending hours enclosed in a rubber body bag with three tiny air holes, being jolted along in a funeral van and terrified of being discovered would have been traumatic for anybody. But for her to change so fundamentally was unnerving. 'Quirinia and I will need to consider our personal differences when we have time,' I said. 'For the moment, we can't afford such luxuries.'

Volusenia led me to the kitchen where about twenty people were eating at a bench table. The smell of bread and strong tea surrounded us. Nobody spoke much as we joined them in eating rolls spread with margarine and sugary jam.

An hour later we made our way to the cavernous but shabby ballroom. Our miserly group of barely fifty souls was lost in it. Volusenia and Silvia sat behind a trestle table facing the rest of us. I gave Quirinia a brief nod when she took her place in the front row with Calavia and me. Scanning the audience, I recognised and beckoned forward one of the younger Cornelius brothers and an Aquilia and Sella, both members of Volusenia's troops. Of the Twelve Families, it was a poor showing, but if we did nothing else, we were going to formally pledge our support for Silvia as imperatrix even though she wasn't in her powers.

Pale but composed, Silvia listened to Volusenia outlining the current position: our assets were the house and those funds the fleeing Roma Novans had managed to bring with them. One or two had an account abroad, but none here in Vienna.

'The PGSF guards pooled their emergency field reserves,' she began, 'but the four thousand gold *solidi* are nearly exhausted. Some of you have found local employment and contribute a generous proportion of earnings. Unfortunately, but I suppose understandably, some people who have secured jobs have left the community and set up separate households.' She paused. 'We are economising and attempting to be self-sufficient, but the financial burden of keeping us all fed and warm is difficult. *Consiliaria* Quirinia tried to access her accounts here, but they've been frozen. We have no fall-back resources nor any even to prepare a plan to retake Roma Nova.'

I stood up. 'How have the finances been administered so far?'

'We've kept a cash book like a regimental account.'

'I see,' I said. 'Well, I intend to put all the Mitela assets abroad that I can access at the disposal of Imperatrix Silvia. This may involve significant sums, some cash, some investments, some in financial instruments. May I suggest that to ensure the most efficient use of current resources and my contribution, we ask *Consiliaria* Quirinia, Imperatrix Severina's budget minister, to manage them?'

Quirinia's mouth opened and she stared at me.

'Families?' I turned and asked, using the traditional system for obtaining consent.

'*Aio!*' No dissenters.

'People?'

'No disrespect, *consiliaria*, but I have a question,' a voice piped up in the middle. 'Wasn't *Consiliaria* Quirinia part of the weak government that led to the collapse? As were you?'

'Please identify yourself,' I said.

A young man, late twenties, was pushed to his feet by his companions. He brushed their hands away, then squared his shoulders.

'Marcus Lentilius, *optio* PGSF from Aquae Caesaris. Well, until ten days ago.' His face sagged as he said the second part.

'Excellent question, *optio*,' I replied, to a few gasps. Volusenia gave him a stern look and opened her mouth, probably to tell him to hold his tongue. 'No, it is, and something that we must consider. While there are so few of us, we must be transparent and agree amongst ourselves. If we aren't united, we'll never succeed in regaining our homeland.'

I walked to the side and turned so I could see everybody.

'I'll be honest with you, even if it is hurtful to anybody present.' I took a deep breath praying that Silvia would forgive me. 'Severina Apulia was not especially blessed with an ability to see things realistically. Quirinia and I disagreed on many things with her and often had to argue her out of unwise decisions.'

After I said that, the silence was so complete you could almost hear people's hearts beating. 'It is chiefly due to Quirinia's stewardship that Roma Nova wasn't bankrupt. Other government departments were not so fortunate in their ministers, notably Interior. I lay a great deal of the blame at that department's door.'

I held up my hand at the murmurs of anger. 'However, there were many other reforms that should have been implemented years ago, such as abolishing decimation of the armed forces if they rebelled. Of course, no commander in her right mind would condemn her troops to that. But that law still being in the codex supporting the Twelve Tables meant that the military were paralysed on the night of the fires.'

'Well, then, it applied to us Praetorians as well, but we knew we still had to act, whatever the consequences,' replied Lentilius. 'Why couldn't the other forces?'

'Well, Lentilius, the PGSF are exceptional.' I grinned at him. 'One of their outstanding characteristics is pig-headedness, after all.'

He laughed, shrugged and sat down.

'Any other questions, or do we agree on Quirinia's appointment?'

'I have something to say.' A light, but firm young woman's voice. Silvia.

I bowed in her direction. *'Domina.'*

She looked startled as I addressed her so formally, but she took a breath and stood up. Her light frame was bundled in a thick roll-neck jumper and cord trousers, but she held her head high.

'Some of you know me, but for most of you I'm just a name. Like everybody else, I'm trying to make sense of what's happened. I've never been so scared, ever. Aurelia Mitela and Colonel Volusenia saved my life.' She paused for a second or two, blinked, then looked first at Volusenia, then me. She returned to the audience. 'Like you, I didn't want to leave my home or my family or Roma Nova. Leaving my mother on the night of the fires was the worst.'

People were still as statues as they listened to her young but steady voice, so unlike her mother's hesitant one. 'I've lost my mother and my brother, Julian. And probably my father.' She looked down for a second. 'But I've lost people I don't know and people whose only crime was to support my mother.' She looked straight at me. 'Aurelia Mitela said some harsh things about my mother—'

Juno save me.

'—but she's right. When we get back to Roma Nova, it will be different. I don't know how we'll do it, but it *will* be different.' She looked over at Lentilius, an even more solemn expression on her face, and waited. His face reddened, he pinched his lips together, but clambered to his feet. '*Optio* Lentilius, you were right to ask about *Consiliaria* Quirinia. Everything is so confused. But we do have to try to make some sort of decisions.' She glanced at me and I nodded. 'If you could agree in this case, it would be really helpful.' And then she aimed a full-beam smile at him.

He blushed even redder, bowed to her, apparently incapable of saying anything further. He kept his eyes on her, then thrust his arm in the air and shouted '*Ave, Imperatrix*'. The room echoed his shout. Silvia blushed, her eyes liquid. Her hand trembled, but she kept the smile on her face and her back straight. I was so proud of her; that slight teenager was showing signs of growing up fast.

8

A council of eight was formed including Lentilius, who looked a little dazed to be included. Silvia insisted, saying she wanted somebody unafraid to speak up. Volusenia and I exchanged glances. Silvia was too inexperienced to realise that what she'd done had been to make him her slave for life, but neither of us commented.

The most important things we needed were information, security and money, but money was key, so Quirinia and I set off for the Argentaria Prima Vienna office the next morning. As it was only twenty minutes away we walked, followed overtly by Styrax and covertly by Balia, her comrade-in-arms from the rescue mission to find Silvia.

'Aurelia…?' Quirinia began hesitantly.

'Yes?'

She shook her head, but didn't say anything more. We walked on along the icy pavement for a few moments in silence, then she stopped. 'Why did you nominate me to look after our funds?'

I turned round and, squinting in the white morning sun, I said, 'Because you were the obvious choice. Whatever personal issues lie between you and me, we as a group need to make use of the capabilities we have. You can manage a complex budget. And I believe that your actions, however misjudged, were made out of sincere loyalty to Roma Nova. The rest is irrelevant.'

'No, it's not.' She grabbed my forearm with such a strong grip I had to stop. 'You might want to leave it there and retreat behind your superior attitude, but I can't, no, I *won't* take it from you.' Her eyes were blazing now.

'Excuse me for being dense, Quirinia, but you're not in any position to snipe at me.' I prised her hand off. I didn't want her to touch me.

'Yes, you're always so right, aren't you, Aurelia? The tough warrior and perfect Roman. Well, we can't all live up to the superwoman standard. Some of us are mere human beings.' She sniffed, dragging in cold air that made her nose drip. 'I often wondered why you wanted to have me as your friend when you had all those close soldier comrades, and mixed with the palace people. Even at school you outshone me.'

'Finished?'

She looked up and down the street for a moment or two, then gave a tiny nod.

'Firstly, I have made some monumental foul-ups in my life, so where you get the idea of me being perfect, I haven't a clue. Secondly, was I supposed to pretend to be stupid at school? Oh, sorry!' I bit back what I really wanted to say, but she flinched at my sarcastic tone. 'Thirdly, I never analysed our friendship. We just *were* friends. That's the whole point. We celebrated and commiserated with each other, laughed at the same things, felt the same way about other people. And we were naturally there for each other. There is no element of tit for tat, seeking advantage or doing favours between friends. Friends are just friends through thick and thin.' I stamped my feet to warm them up. 'That's the theory and that's how I experienced it. Obviously, it doesn't work in practice when shit comes to bust.'

I looked back at Styrax and nodded.

'Come along, Quirinia. We'll be late,' and I strode off down the street, desperate for physical activity to dispel my hurt. How dare bloody Quirinia throw those things in my face?

I heard footsteps behind me and presumed Styrax was bringing her.

. . .

'I'm very sorry, Countess Mitela,' the Argentaria Prima manager explained. 'Your accounts have been frozen. Just as Maia Quirinia's were.' He gave a hesitant half-smile. 'We've had a specific instruction from the new finance minister.'

'No doubt, but it's illegal. And as you know, you should disregard illegal instructions.' I held out Silvia's letter. 'Here is the authority from Imperatrix Silvia confirming our status and requesting free access to our accounts. That should satisfy the auditors.'

'I... I apologise, but the situation is unclear. I must seek further instructions.'

He squirmed, glancing at Styrax, who stood by the door with crossed arms and a grim face. His gaze darted at his wall paintings, his bookcase, the carpet, anywhere but at us. After a long five minutes of silence, I got to my feet along with Quirinia.

'Very well. I will report back to the imperatrix. Be assured that once she is restored, she will take a personal interest in your future career prospects.'

I turned and stalked out through the grey and white banking hall, Quirinia and Styrax in my wake.

'Hades take him,' I said as we marched down the Schottengasse.

'Technically, he's right, Aurelia,' she ventured. 'He's just being very careful. And so will most people be.' She sighed.

'Perhaps they haven't forgiven me for exposing their wonder child as a rogue silver trader all those years ago,' I said. The Argentaria Prima manager in Vienna, and those in many other cities around the world where they had branches, acted as the Roma Nova government's representative for certain transactions, including silver trading. Valeria Festa, the manager in the late 1960s, had been caught not only making illegal trades personally, but also actively assisting Caius Tellus when he was attacking Roma Nova's economy and enriching himself by manipulating the silver market. I'd been the investigating and arresting officer, exercising my Praetorian warrant. That had been fifteen years ago, but perhaps it still rankled.

'Haven't you tried to withdraw money before now?' Quirinia said.

'No, I've been in hospital, then convalescing until recently.' Miklós had taken care of everything financial. Damn, I should have contacted the Argentaria earlier. 'Good thing we have Plan B.'

My great-grandfather Soane had been English, from London, and following tradition had joined his family firm, a private finance house. He'd been 'displeased' when his eldest son Henry, my grandfather, had emigrated to Roma Nova and, unusually, married my grandmother. She'd been a diplomat posted to London; they'd met at a weekend house party where she'd outshot him.

Peter John, my grandfather's younger brother, had continued to run the business from London, expanding it through Europe and the Americas as Britain became an industrial powerhouse. Their Vienna branch had been established for over a hundred years. Peter John had based his generation's success on steadily increasing a highly confidential list of clients, which included royalty, but one of whom had been my mother, his niece, and then me.

When I'd exported part of my assets after that terrible Families meeting last summer, it was to Soane's Bank in London that I'd sent half of them.

The Vienna branch, located in a bland, stone-faced nineteenth-century block just off the Ringstraße, resembled a lawyer's office from the outside, complete with a modest brass plate engraved with the single word 'Soane's'. I glanced up at the camera discreetly perched on the window recess above the glass-panelled front door. Inside were subtle, neutral colours, a thick carpet and a hushed atmosphere.

I gave my name to the receptionist, who looked as if she'd escaped from a fashion magazine, and asked politely to see David Soane. He'd visited me when I'd been convalescing and had sponsored my application for political asylum so I was certain we'd be talking to him within minutes. But the receptionist looked us up and down and suggested we make an appointment with one of their advisors next week and to please bring our passports and proof of residence. I produced my Hungarian passport which carried Miklós's name, with my own name on a different page, not obviously visible. Quirinia had nothing to show.

'I'm afraid I cannot help you without correct proof of identity. Good day.' And she bent her dark head down to her desk and ignored us.

'I think you misunderstand the situation,' I said. 'I am Peter John's great niece and my cousin David is the head of this branch. Now please announce us to him.'

'That is not possible.' Her voice was chillier than the air outside. 'If you don't leave the premises, I will be obliged to call security.'

'Good, please do. We'll wait here.' I jerked my head at Quirinia towards a dark leather sofa. The receptionist mumbled into a telephone handset, casting eyes in our direction several times during her call.

Five minutes later, a tall man in a suit and wearing an austere expression on his thin face appeared. The receptionist pointed in our direction.

'I am Anton Drexler, Mr Edward's assistant. I understand one of you ladies is claiming to be Countess Mitela of Roma Nova, but you are refusing to produce any identification to back this up.'

'Edward?' I said. 'Is David letting the children run his bank?' I was genuinely amazed. Edward couldn't be thirty at most.

Anton Drexler didn't say anything. He stared at me for a minute, went over to the receptionist's desk and used the handset. A few minutes later, a medium-height young man, light brown hair topping a serious face bespattered with freckles, walked out of the lift, his fingers giving a tweak to the knot in his tie as a schoolboy would.

'Great Mars, it *is* you, Edward.'

'Hello, Aunt Aurelia.' He smiled like the child I remembered him to be. 'I'm sorry for the mix-up. Dad's had to go back to the UK. Grandfather isn't very well. What can I do for you?'

Quirinia put the pen down an hour later after signing the last of the five forms. I countersigned the specimen signature cards as she passed them across to me and we were finished.

'We'll get a cheque book to you the day after tomorrow.' Edward gestured to the taciturn Drexler, who set an envelope down on the polished table in front of me. 'And we've prepared a letter of introduction which should guarantee you credit for anything you wish to order or buy in the meantime. Let me know the number once you have a telephone line installed.'

He handed me a second envelope, slightly bulging. 'This should tide you over until we've made a transfer from London. Don't hesitate to contact Anton if you have the least question.'

Anton stood there motionless, a blank expression on his face. I wasn't sure he would be at all happy to be contacted.

Quirinia and Volusenia went into overdrive spending my money on making our building habitable. Those troops not on security duty turned themselves into labourers, painters, decorators, furniture builders. Atrius, a farmer's son, persuaded some of his comrades to form a working party to dig up a sizeable area of the garden for a vegetable plot. It was cold work in February. He looked exhausted one afternoon three days later when I went outside for a breath of fresh air. He bent over, leaning his body on one of the shiny new spades.

'Don't overdo it, Atrius,' I said. 'You're still on the light duties list.' He looked down from his considerable height and caught his breath.

'I know, ma'am, but I feel happier doing something.' He stood up and shoved the spade into the turned earth. 'I'm sorry I lost faith in you. That bastard Tellus had me convinced. And as for that little prick Turturus, I'd be happy to dump his corpse in the Danube, if you want.'

'You know we can't do that. Where is he now?'

Atrius jerked his head at a small figure at the far end of the garden, jabbing a spade at the hard earth under the supervision of Styrax's comrade, Balia. 'We keep him busy.' He grunted as he reached down for his jacket. 'Then we lock him up in the cellar at night.' He gave me a long steady look.

'Keep him healthy, Atrius. I want him to stand his trial when we get back.'

He said nothing, but gave me a brief bow and walked back into the house.

Volusenia suggested I tutor Silvia; the council of eight appointed me her advisor. I agreed as long as Quirinia taught her finance and one of the PGSF guards gave her some grounding in self-defence and personal security. The thought of Caius mounting a snatch was in the front of our minds.

Silvia had received a first-class education in arts and languages, history and basic sciences by a clever English governess, but she knew nothing about politics or the art of practical governing. Apart from letting Silvia to sit in the imperial council meetings as an observer during the last six months of her reign, Severina had allowed her daughter to reach emancipation at sixteen with minimal instruction about her future duties as imperatrix.

Silvia applied herself conscientiously, but struggled with the archaic Latin of some of the early law tables. Luckily, the Vienna University library had been able to supply both original and translations into modern Latin for her. She was chewing her pencil one day writing some notes on constitutional functions and, distracted, glanced out of the window. I sat opposite her, coordinating information about contacts in Roma Nova who we thought would support a resistance movement.

'Aunt Aurelia, there's a crowd of strange-looking people outside, like beggars.'

'The guards will deal with them. How far are you with your notes?'

'But I think they're coming here.' She stood up and pulled the curtain back from the window.

I rose out of my chair and went to the hallway, just in time to see Calavia burst through the street door, a satisfied look on her face. Following her, a group of around twenty bedraggled figures shuffled in, four smaller ones among them. Their clothes were dirty; dull eyes looked out of grey faces muffled with scarves. They looked round, worried and fearful, but they looked somehow familiar. Then under a soft peaked cap, I recognised my estate manager from Castra Lucilla.

'Gods! Gavinus.' I gripped him by the shoulders. He closed his eyes, shook his head then looked up.

'They said you were here now. Are we truly safe now, *domina*?' he said in a low voice.

'Yes, yes. Come into the warm.' I looked round. 'Where are the rest of them?'

His eyes tightened and he looked down at the wooden floor. 'Dead.'

As the new arrivals devoured hot soup and bread in the kitchen, the safe house's original exiles stood around only half listening; some carried on with their own conversations.

I sat at the table bench with Gavinus. He told me how they had piled into the lorries at Castra Lucilla and headed for the border. As there were too many road checks and they had none of the authorisations issued by the new regime's authorities, they'd abandoned the vehicles as planned, piled on their warmest clothes and set out on foot. They had water and food, and the guards had weapons, so Fortuna was on their side. They'd made good time and were in the woods within five hundred metres of the New Austrian border when they were overwhelmed.

'There must have been fifty of them, *domina*. Not regular troops, nor nationalists, but a mob of wild people, men as well as women. They ripped everything off us, all our food, torches, gloves, boots, even emptying the children's backpacks, taking the few toys they had with them. Sentia, Albia and their troops tried to hold them off, but there were too many. They died there. Those animals beat us and left us in the snow to freeze.' He reached for a glass of water and gulped it down. 'But we knew we had to go on. Somehow we crossed the border – I didn't know for sure we had until we found an old barn on a farm with the name in Germanic. The children were past crying. I know it was wrong, but we broke into their food store and dairy and stole milk for the children.

'We slept well past dawn, and when the farmer found us mid-morning he held a gun on us and threatened to call the police. I pleaded with him and while he was thinking about it, two others jumped him. I apologised, but he swore at me. We tied him up and left him in the barn. We walked from there, hiding wherever we could. Sometimes we had to steal food and clothes.' He smacked his hand on the table. 'Damn Caius Tellus to the depths of Tartarus!' Gavinus bowed his head and brought his hands up to support it. He gave a deep sob, then his shoulders shook. The other refugees stopped eating and stared. The early exiles had gathered closer, now completely silent.

Numerus moved forward but stopped a couple of paces from Gavinus when the farm manager jerked his head up and glared at him with a ferocity I'd never seen the mild-tempered Gavinus display before.

'We thought we'd find refuge in Vienna, here.' His voice couldn't be more bitter. He looked round. 'They wouldn't let us in, *domina*.

They said you were proscribed. We slept in the park that night. Juno, that was cold.'

I covered his hand with mine.

'A charity canteen gave us a hot meal next day and let us sleep in their storeroom. We've been there ever since, helping out, cleaning and doing maintenance jobs for them.' He gave a short laugh. 'Somebody welcomed us at least.'

9

———————

'This will not happen again.' Silvia's cheeks were red with anger. 'No Roma Novan will be shut out, whatever the reason.' The council of eight was silent while she shouted herself out. When she stopped for breath, I took her hand and pulled her gently back onto her chair. For a second, she looked daggers at me.

'I think Gavinus and the others appreciated you talking to them yesterday, Silvia, and comforting the children. This is such a fraught time and many don't know how to act in the circumstances.'

Quirinia glanced at me, then blushed and looked away.

'Now we're growing in numbers, I suggest we draw up a set of guidelines,' I said. 'We need an operating procedure to cover most eventualities. It should be simple, clear and establish a chain of responsibilities. Some people will have to work the day-to-day aspects of our collective life, others will need to have decision-making power. Obviously, we'll change it as circumstances change.' I looked round at the other seven. 'Thoughts?'

'Do you think many more will join us, Aurelia?' Quirinia asked.

'If Caius carries on as he has so far, I think we should be prepared for a considerable number.'

Telephone engineers installed lines and even one of the new data hubs; essential according to Volusenia's acting signals officer, a former telex supervisor who'd been thrown out of her job. But she didn't have any deep technical knowledge, as I explained to William and Marina when calling them the same evening.

'I'll order you some individual personal computers. Your people will need to collect them from the New Austrian distributor's warehouse,' William said. 'A special delivery will arrive from Brown Industries in a few days, Aurelia,' he continued. 'I'll send two technicians along as well. It's the least we can do.' He paused. 'We'll talk further after their visit.'

William Brown's crate arrived a week later on the same flight as two technicians. They went into a huddle with Volusenia's signals officer and two *optiones* in the room where the New Austrian telephone engineers had fixed the incoming line. The five of them went out in two hire vans and came back with them jam-packed with cardboard boxes – the promised computer equipment. I looked in the following morning; data terminals lay on the floor in a horseshoe shape around the room. Gavinus, his skin now a healthier shade of pink, was working with my former estate carpenter making benches from the pile of timber that had been delivered that morning from the local sawmill. They emerged the following afternoon and one of the BI technicians handed me a shiny handset and a full-teeth American smile.

'For you, ma'am.'

'Hello?'

'Aurelia, it's William. Now I'm satisfied you have a totally secure line, I can talk openly. Anything, whether voice or data, carried on your line will now be encrypted. Hank has run through the protocols with your signals people, but I wanted to outline what you can do with this. Once they've fitted the antennae and parabolic dishes, the system will give you two main functions – communications and monitoring.'

'We're blind and deaf at the moment, William. We have no idea what's going on in Roma Nova apart from the public broadcasts and they're only four times a day.'

'I expect you'll want to monitor military and police traffic as well as propaganda broadcasts. The new equipment will enable you to intercept signals, so you can gather good quality intelligence. It's using the information that's the tricky part.'

I blinked. That was exactly what Plico, my now dead intelligence chief, used to say.

'If you like, Hank can stay over for a few weeks to take your people through the basics of traffic analysis with this new equipment.'

'Yes, that would be very helpful.' We needed every grain of help we were offered.

'Your military exiles will know what equipment the Roma Novan forces were using a few months ago, the probable frequency range and where the main transmission stations are. Obviously, the crypto settings will have changed, but Hank will show your technical people some techniques to get the most out of the decrypt equipment. It's not a hundred per cent, but you should get some useful material.'

'Won't the New Austrians spot our activity?' I said.

'I recommend remote monitoring as near the Roma Nova border as possible, then you can use a standard telephone cable to get the yield back to Vienna. If you can set them up, I recommend two outstations to the south, one east and one west to provide triangulation.'

They would have to be completely covert. Not a whisper of our capacity should reach Caius or he'd take immediate countermeasures. We'd have to start cultivating a despairing exile image for public consumption.

'William, why are you giving us so much?'

When he answered, I could tell from the tone of voice that he was smiling.

'Marina said you'd never give up. And aren't family members supposed to help each other?'

Four weeks after I'd arrived, I was running through other European government institutions with Silvia so she would have some comparisons with the Roma Novan ones when there was a knock at the door. I didn't have time to answer before Atrius entered the room.

'Apologies for interrupting you, *consiliaria*, but the colonel asks you come to the hall, stat. We have, er, visitors.'

He glanced at Silvia, then back at me, a world of warning in his eyes. I ordered him to stay with Silvia and hurried to the front hall.

Volusenia stood ramrod still with a thunderous look on her face. Two PGSF guards hovered between the street door and the visitors.

Two grey-uniformed members of the Austrian gendarmerie, one an officer with a red-edged peaked cap, stood a shade behind a neatly-dressed man with an assured air and who carried a brown leather briefcase. He was trying to hand Volusenia a large envelope, but she stood, arms crossed, refusing to take it. Attempting to defuse the tense atmosphere, I stepped forward but didn't hold my hand out.

'Grüß Gott,' I said. '*Wie kann ich Ihnen behilflich sein?*'

Volusenia stared at me. She was used to me speaking Germanic, but perhaps she didn't like my conciliatory tone. Well, always best to start diplomatically in the face of foreign officials.

'I speak Latin,' he replied, in a clipped, huffy tone as if I'd questioned his intelligence. 'My name is Riegler, from the federal foreign ministry. I have come to serve notice on you.'

'For what?'

'As you have no residential status you are required to depart within fourteen days. Failure to do so will result in forced eviction.'

I bit my first reply back.

'On what grounds?'

'As stateless persons you should have applied for asylum on your day of arrival.'

'I think you mistake the situation, *Herr* Riegler. We are all citizens of Roma Nova and have full freedom of movement and settlement under the European Economic Area conventions.' I'd signed off the most recent amendment at the European Council of Foreign Ministers last summit, so I was on firm ground.

'We have a formal notice from your government that you have all been stripped of your citizenship and are thus stateless.'

I couldn't say anything for the next moment as a cold wave washed through me. Then it flowed back in hot anger. Bloody Caius. But this smooth bureaucrat was enjoying himself too much.

'You will be aware that the current regime in Roma Nova is illegal,' I said in my coldest voice. 'It came to power as a result of a *coup d'état*. None of its instructions carries weight. As the legally appointed Roma Novan foreign minister, I reject your notice and request an immediate interview with my Austrian opposite number, who I would advise you is a personal friend of mine. He was one of my sponsors for my own political asylum application which was granted last autumn within two weeks. At the minimum, kindly arrange a meeting with his assistant *Herr* Goss who knows me. That is all.'

I nodded to Volusenia who signalled the guards to open the door. I brought my haughtiest look back to Riegler, daring him to say anything more. He looked away, muttered something to the gendarmerie officers and stalked out with them in his wake.

We stood like tailor's dummies for a few seconds.

'Get me Edward Soane on the line, stat,' I snapped.

'The position is awkward, *Frau Gräfin* Mitela, but not impossible,' the lawyer said in her soft voice. She might have been a partner in a firm with a prestigious practice on the Schubertring, but she looked about eighteen and sounded younger. However, she absorbed the details of our case very quickly and Edward said she was as sharp as Mercury. 'As a group you are economically self-sufficient, that is, not in need of social assistance, and sufficiently proficient in Germanic.' She looked up from her file. 'Have you heard anything back from *Herr* Goss at the federal foreign ministry? Or the minister?'

'Not yet, but it hasn't been forty-eight hours yet. To be honest, I don't want to insist, as it might be politically embarrassing for the minister and thus *Herr* Goss. If we can resolve this without resorting to personal favours, I'd prefer it.' I shrugged. 'If not, then I will.'

She twisted her pencil round her fingers, glanced at Edward Soane who looked puzzled.

'Your Praetorians and the other military…'

'Yes?'

'Technically, they're foreign combatants and should be interned. We will fight that, obviously, and invoke the European Defence Cooperation Treaty, but it will hinge on the nationality and political asylum question. They may have to surrender to the federal authorities until their status is clear.'

'Well, the female officers and guards won't be affected,' I replied. 'All their commissions were cancelled by Caius Tellus as soon as he came to power. In his regime's eyes, they're civilians. The men?' I looked at her steadily. 'Numerus is a pensioner and the others all resigned the instant they crossed the border.'

'I see.' She knew I was stretching the truth, but made no further comment. 'Have you not thought to contact your legation?'

'To be honest, we haven't attempted it. They must be aware of the exile group's presence but we've heard nothing from them. The staff will mostly take the *nuncia*'s lead.'

'The *nuncia*?'

'The ambassador. If they've accepted the regime change and represent Caius Tellus, they will be hostile. If they haven't, they will be treated as a stranded embassy by your government and have little power or influence to help us.' I gave her a steady look. 'I didn't contact them myself before Saturnalia and I'm certainly not willing to risk any of our people stepping inside the legation building, being taken into custody and bundled back to Roma Nova to face at least rough treatment and possibly worse.'

'I still think it would be worth exploring, even to establish that fact. If they support your compatriots, it could further strengthen their case.'

'Very well, then we need a neutral place to meet.'

'Perhaps I could approach them to arrange a preliminary meeting at my office?'

I nodded.

'And in the meantime, I'll file opposition against the current Roma Novan regime with penalty costs and compensation for unlawful harassment under the European Acts. We should be able to get your people temporary protected status. It's a European measure for the admission and residence of conflict refugees. After what I've heard today, I would say you all qualify.'

I hadn't seen Livilla Vara since I'd given her letters of appointment to the New Austrian president three years ago. She swept into the lawyer's office four days later, fur-collared long coat against the chill March wind flapping round her. With her was an entourage of three men. She hesitated, gave me the briefest of nods and sat down on the chair parallel to me. She avoided my eyes and fixed her gaze on the window behind the lawyer's head.

Pia Calavia, who had insisted on acting as my security guard that day along with Styrax, stood by the wall to my side and gave Vara a measured look. Vara ignored her. Calavia's grandmother hadn't thought much of Vara or her mother, if I remembered correctly, but Vara had been an effective civil servant so I said nothing. At least she had come to this meeting – a good sign. But she looked as if she was sitting on a bag of upturned nails. The lawyer glanced at me, then addressed Vara.

'Thank you for attending, Ambassador. This is an informal meeting for my client to make a first contact and to discuss some practical issues.'

'Well, I really don't know why they haven't approached the legation. A simple courtesy call by Aurelia Mitela would have saved everybody's time. We have had a change of government and there have been a few adjustments, but as far as we are concerned it's business as usual.'

Calavia took a step towards Vara, murder in her eyes. I held my hand up and mouthed 'No'.

'I rather think that Livilla Vara is simplifying a very complex matter, perhaps from ignorance,' I replied. 'She's been here, observing from the outside and cut off from the latest updates. As foreign minister and member of the imperial council, as well as the late Imperatrix Severina's appointed personal advisor, I have been at the centre of events.'

Now Vara was looking at me.

'Speaking plainly, there has been a *coup d'état*, murder of the reigning monarch, forcible dismissal of the executive council, subornation of several ministries, rioting, prejudicial pursuit of the imperial heir and her protectors, crushing of personal freedoms, let alone Juno knows how many deaths.' I took a deep breath. 'I do not call that a mere change of government.'

'You exaggerate, *consiliaria*,' Vara said. Her features drew together and red flushed through her face. 'I mean, Aurelia.'

'You were correct the first time, *nuncia*. I am still the minister and Imperatrix Silvia has confirmed my appointment.'

'Silvia? A child!'

'Be careful, Vara. She is your lawful sovereign. Never forget that.'

'No, those times are over. A child can't run a country in crisis. A stronger hand has taken over and will restore order and prosperity.'

I could hardly believe what I was hearing. But when I looked at her properly, I saw that her face had paled, the muscles in her neck were stiff with tension and she wouldn't look at me. She grasped one hand in the other to stop her fingers trembling.

'Vara, are you ill? Because if you aren't, that's treason, *laesa maiestas*. You could go to Truscium for that.' Unlikely, but I had to shake her out of this somehow. She said nothing but took a deep breath. After a few moments she unclasped her hands, then looked at me. She seemed calmer.

'You must recognise Silvia and disown Caius Tellus's seizure of power,' I continued. 'His regime won't be recognised internationally. Remember your basics – *ex injuria jus non oritur* – unjust acts cannot create law. They'll throw it out at the next council of foreign ministers in Geneva.'

'Which you will not be going to, Aurelia. You're no longer Roma Nova's foreign minister. Remember, *ex factis jus oritur* – the existence of facts creates law.'

'Oh, for Mercury's sake, stop twisting words with me. I cannot understand why you can't see the basic principles, let alone justice.'

I leaned across the gap between us and touched her forearm.

'Come on, Vara, think it through.' I saw a movement on the edge of my peripheral vision and glanced up. One of Vara's staffers pushed forward to intervene, but Calavia got there before him and blocked his approach. He was tall and well built, and moved with the confidence of a heavy rather than the diffidence of a civil servant. In fact, all three looked as if they came out of the same factory. But Calavia was quicker, more agile and coordinated. Styrax was eyeing the other two. This wasn't right. They weren't bureaucrats, nor diplomatic protection which was normally PGSF. And they looked at Calavia, assessing her as an opponent, not as colleagues each protecting their principal.

'Let's all calm down,' I said and stood up. 'Everybody back to the walls. You, too, Calavia.' Reluctantly, they all moved back, the three musclemen keeping their eyes on Vara. They must have thought I represented an overwhelming danger. She glanced round at the oldest one. It was a look of fear. Then it clicked; they weren't protecting her, they were guarding her. I had to speak to her on her own. I turned to the lawyer.

'*Frau Rechtsanwältin*, I think Livilla Vara and I will take a little walk round your hallway to clear our heads.' The lawyer frowned, trying to decipher what was going on, but nodded. I stood up, took Vara's arm and made for the door. One of her detail stepped in front of me.

'Stand aside,' I said.

He stayed where he was.

'Are you challenging me?'

'We're not allowed to let the woman out of our sight.'

'Woman? How dare you refer to the *nuncia* in such terms? Move out of my way. Now.'

He hesitated. I was not in prime condition, but I reckoned I could take him. Being sensible, though, I didn't want to cause an incident in the lawyer's ultra respectable office.

'The *nuncia* and I will talk in the lobby. I mean her no harm – we are old friends.' I applied a light pressure to Vara's arm, praying she wouldn't contradict me. 'You may stand by the front entrance and watch us from there.'

He jerked his head at the other two and, preceded by them, Vara and I walked back into the tall, glass-walled hallway. I waited until they'd reached the entrance, a good ten metres away.

Out of earshot, I stopped and released Vara. I fished a handkerchief out of my handbag and pretended to dab my eyes. I eased a small black-plastic covered device out of the handkerchief folds and pressed a button to switch it on. I slid the button to max and clipped it to lock it.

'This scrambles our voices so if they have a bug planted on you, they'll get distorted voices in their receiver. Now kindly tell me what's going on.'

'Really, Aurelia, I don't know what you mean. You're so dramatic with all your spy stuff, just like that dreadful little Plico.'

'That dreadful little Plico is now dead, having sacrificed himself to buy us time to save Silvia. If you say one more word against him, I will not be responsible for my subsequent actions,' I hissed at her.

She took a step back at my vehemence.

'I can't say any more,' she said.

'Can't or won't?'

She said nothing.

'Look, Livilla, I don't know what you know or not, or why you're under guard by three heavies and not the PGSF diplomatic detail. Tell me.'

'They really can't hear?'

'No, these are the most advanced scramblers in existence.'

'They've got my mother.' Her face crumpled. 'If I step out of line, they'll kill her. It's the same for most of the legations.'

'You've been using the confidential channel?' It was a system for heads of legation to talk frankly and confidentially to each other.

She nodded. Caius most likely knew about it and was relying on the *nunciae* talking amongst themselves to reinforce the fear his threats to each of them had caused.

'How many of these heavies are there at the legation?'

'About a dozen. They're all armed and their chief has the keys to the armoury and the signals office.'

'Gods, they did organise this well, didn't they?' I muttered, almost to myself.

'I don't know what you think you can do.' She sniffed. 'If you start leaping around playing heroines, people will get hurt.'

'And nobody's going to get hurt as a consequence of Caius's dictatorship? Wake up, Vara, this is just the beginning. I'm not discussing complex matters of *jus legationis* or swapping diplomatic niceties. Nor am I asking you to help us directly. Just don't impede us. And don't encourage the New Austrians to harass us. Remember this. We are not going to let Caius Tellus get away with this. We're going to liberate Roma Nova. And believe me, we intend to succeed.'

10

'Out of the question,' Volusenia rapped out. She stared at me as if I was insane. 'You want my people to risk their lives getting some cantankerous old woman out just to make Vara happy. Livilla Vara should get a grip and open the legation to us and work with us. She should do it for her country. If old Countess Vara is a casualty, then that's a pity, but one of those things. We're at war.'

'I agree with your sentiments, colonel, but we have to be practical. Vara feels a deep bond with her mother – it's natural.'

'Maybe, but we have to put our personal feelings aside. My older sister is stuck there, but she knows her duty. You know what she's like – stubborn as Pluto. She'll probably spit in Caius Tellus's face. Not likely I'll see her again. But we can't deal with this now – the death lists have come through.'

Silvia stood, several folds of perforated-edged green and white printouts in her hand. The shabby, vaulted ballroom was silent as a tomb. Fifty anxious pairs of eyes were fixed on her face. Her hands were shaking, but she held herself still.

'We've called this meeting because there are so many rumours flying round and we need to tell you what's really going on. Brown Industries' new equipment has let us listen in to the... the rebels' messages and read some of their documents. These casualty lists have been compiled by the rebels.' She paused at the murmurs from her audience and glanced down at me. I nodded in encouragement. I thought she was too young for such a grim job but she was determined to do it. I'd helped her with her speech, but as long as she spoke from her heart, nobody would mind if she stumbled over a few words. She cleared her throat and waited until the murmuring stopped.

'As we are such a small number we must work together. We must also face horrible news together. It doesn't make it any pleasanter, but we can help each other to deal with it.'

I handed her a glass of water. She gulped half of it down, placed the glass back on the table and started.

'Here are the names: Severina Apulia imperatrix, Julianus Apulius, Fabianus Apulius born Mitelus – missing suspected dead, Senator Gaia Calavia, Major Terentia Fabia PGSF, Senator Julia Cornelia, Sextus Aemelius born Aquilius...'

She continued for nearly fifteen minutes, her voice becoming more strained as she went through the sheets. Sobs and gasps punctuated the numbed silence, with some crying and soft swearing. When she'd finished, she sank onto her chair and put her head in her hands. Her shoulders shook. I pulled her towards me and held her. After a minute or two, I released her and stood up.

'I think we need some time for reflection, but the imperatrix has said she would like to see everybody, either one at a time or in families, later this afternoon or this evening. We have to decide what to do next.'

'Did you prompt her?' Volusenia asked as we walked in the garden. Volusenia cupped a cigarette in her hand, attempting to hide the smoke.

'No, not directly, but she insisted on doing it. She said it was her duty. I know she's an emancipated adult, but she shouldn't have to do this sort of thing. I give her full marks for carrying out a shitty job well. And that will go to people's hearts. They know she's lost every member of her immediate family. She's growing up brutally fast.'

'Well, I think you should brief her before she starts these interviews.'

'Don't worry, I'll sit in with her.'

'Good. We need to know who will fight, who wants to stay here, who will wait and see. It'll be a tough, gritty struggle just to get started.' She threw the half-burnt cigarette on the ground and squished it with her boot.

Our meeting with Livilla Vara had depressed me. Caius had terrorised our nearest legation, the one that could have helped us. I felt sorry for Vara personally; a terrible decision to have to make, choosing between one's country and one's beloved mother. On the positive side, Edward's lawyer had met *Herr* Goss at the New Austrian foreign ministry to pursue documentation for the exiles and Vara had promised to do her best not to hinder us in this.

My list of possible helpers still left in Roma Nova was skimpy; I talked to the exiles and it grew by one or two names after each interview. But it wasn't enough to start even the most basic network. I sat back in my chair and stretched my arms to release the tension in my shoulders. The yellow March sunlight was clear and strong. I glanced at my schedule; I had two free hours, so I asked one of our taxi drivers to take me out to the suburbs.

I stepped out of the back of the car, pushing the passenger door shut. The driver's companion, my bodyguard, was by my side as I approached the black railings on the edge of the property. The house with its grey slate roof looked a little smarter since the day Miklós and I had left it; no police striped incident tape, the windows gleamed and tubs with daffodils and just-budding tulips stood each side of the front door. I released the breath I hadn't realised I was holding. Although I'd been weak recovering from the gunshot wounds and we'd had to live with an armed bodyguard, I would always treasure the weeks here with Miklós. I'd had no responsibilities, he'd been determined to look after me and we'd had time to love each other, sometimes fiercely passionate, other times just folded into each other's arms in warm contentment.

Just as I was going to turn away, the door opened. My heart thudded. Miklós? But a stout man in his late fifties, blond hair turning grey and a frown on his face, stood in the doorway.

'*Ja, bitte?*' he challenged.

'I'm sorry to have disturbed you,' I said. 'I used to live here, with my... my husband.' What a strange word. 'I just wanted to see the house again. Sorry.' I fished out my Hungarian passport from my handbag, opened it and held it up against the railings. He came down the pathway to the gate and peered at it, then glanced at my face.

'Oh, I see.' He almost smiled. A woman, her face slightly anxious, appeared in the doorway, then walked up to join him. It was such a quiet neighbourhood, my visit was probably the event of the week. She leant over and whispered to him. He nodded and she disappeared. She returned and handed him a small packet.

'I was going to take this to the land agent next week,' he said as he passed it through to me. 'But it says "Urgent" so you might as well take it now.'

He passed it through the railings. The padded bag was about twenty by fifteen centimetres with a typed label addressed to 'Aurelia Mitela c/o Farkas'. I could feel a rigid box inside. The couple looked at it, then at me, but I wasn't going to satisfy their curiosity. I thanked them and we returned to the safe house where I stopped in the hallway and opened the packet. The pure white top of the cardboard box it contained disarmed me for what lay inside.

I shuddered as I awoke. A light at the side of me. Gods, there was a ton of bricks on me. No, it was bedding. I reached a hand out to throw some of the stifling weight off.

A figure rose from a chair by the window.

'Oh, thank Juno!' Quirinia grabbed my hand and burst into tears. 'I know the doctor said you'd sleep it off, but I was so frightened you'd die.'

'Quirinia?'

She released my hand and darted to the door, opened it and spoke to somebody outside. She came back to my bed and helped me to a glass of water.

'I know I've been stupid and selfish,' she said in a low voice. 'But I would have been devastated to have lost you. Will you forgive me?'

'Quirinia, you know I will. Welcome back, my friend.' I smiled at her and I felt an invisible weight lift off me.

The door burst open. Volusenia stood on the threshold stiff, frowning and radiating anger like the senior Fury.

'What in Hades were you playing at, sitting out in the garden for hours in this freezing weather? If *Consiliaria* Quirinia hadn't found you, we'd be building your pyre once we'd defrosted you. For the gods' sake, you can be sentimental on your own time, not Roma Nova's.'

Quirinia stared at her. I concentrated on the ceiling.

'Well?'

'I'm not answerable to you, colonel, so rein your temper in,' I retorted.

'No, you're answerable to a far higher authority than me, the people of Roma Nova.'

I struggled up onto my elbows. 'The box, the packet addressed to me with the white box. Did you find it?'

'This?' Quirinia opened the drawer on the bedside table. 'It was on the stone bench at your side when we found you.'

'Push the door to, colonel,' I said. She gave it a good shove. I sat up and glanced from one to the other. 'Come closer.' I opened the box, but not the sealed transparent plastic bag inside.

Quirinia went white. 'Oh, gods. Oh gods,' she shrieked and clamped her hand over her mouth.

Volusenia look grimmer than ever if that was possible, but her eyes flickered in reaction. She recovered first. 'Why have you been sent a severed finger and whose is it?' She laid her hand on my shoulder. 'Not your companion's?'

'No, thank Juno. The ring on it belongs to my cousin, Fabianus, Severina's husband. And the scar… You see the scar running down the length of it? That's the result of him pinching his older sister's *gladius* when we were children. He almost lost the finger.' Then it hit me. 'Oh gods, Caius was there, sneaking around when it happened. The bastard.'

'What a foul thing to do, desecrating a dead body,' Volusenia said.

'If Fabianus was dead at the time.'

Both women looked at me, shock on their faces. My fingers trembled as I closed the box on the miserable thing.

'I must get up,' I said, scrabbling for the sheets and blankets, but Quirinia pushed me back.

'No, at least a good night's sleep before then. I'll have them bring us some supper up here.'

'Oh, very well.' I gave in, not because of her stern tone of voice, but because my legs felt like wool and my head a block of wood. The three of us stared in silence at the box, fully absorbed by the physical manifestation of Caius's cruelty.

After a few moments, Volusenia coughed. 'If you wish to keep the ring, *consiliaria*, I will dispose of the remains myself.'

'But not one word to anybody, especially Silvia.'

'Mars, no,' Volusenia replied. 'We tell her nothing.'

'Tell me nothing about what?' came a young voice.

Hades! Silvia stood at the half open door.

11

'You have no right to keep secrets from me, I'm the imperatrix!'

At that moment she looked like nothing more than a spoiled teenager stamping her foot.

'Darling, we didn't want to upset you.' I put my most conciliatory voice on.

'Upset? My life is a complete upset. Death, no, murder of my entire family, fleeing in terror for my life, living hand to mouth in this horrible house with a guard watching my every move and you all expecting me to be on my best behaviour all the time. Of course I'm bloody upset!' She glared at us all in turn.

'I apologise, *domina*,' I said.

'Don't patronise me, Aunt Aurelia. Just tell me the truth. I must be able to trust you to do that.'

'You're right, of course, but—' I glanced at Volusenia and Quirinia who both nodded. I gave her the brief details of how I came to have the sad remains of her father's finger.

'Show me.' Her voice was as neutral as the expression on her face. She didn't flinch, but her lips almost disappeared as her mouth retreated into a tight line for a few moments.

'On the night of the fires, I kissed my mother and Julian farewell,' she said. 'I knew in my heart I might not see either of them again. Dad had gone to see that dreadful man without even a goodbye.' She gulped as a single tear ran down her face. 'I haven't got any bodies to burn but I will honour *him* with the rites of the dead. That's the least I can do.' She wiped her hand across her face, then straightened up, turned and left without giving us another look, closing the door quietly behind her. When I shuffled past her door later on my way to the lavatory I heard sobbing.

The whole exile group gathered in the garden the following evening around a tiny pyre; we pulled the stone bench into service as an altar. It was so sad, it was almost ridiculous. We were diminished even in our rituals. Silvia was stone-faced as she lit the makeshift torch and set it to the small pyre. With no priest in our group, I led the prayers as head of Fabianus's birth house. Desperate not to let Silvia down by hesitating, I drew on my past Senate speeches to make up what I couldn't remember. Silvia and I walked round the burning pyre the requisite three times and watched as it flickered and smoked.

Quiet crying and murmuring broke into the silence and people pushed forward to throw small tokens onto the fire as libations. The gods knew they had little to give, but they gave nevertheless. Calls of *'Vale Mitelus, vale Apulius'* grew into shouts. The flames roared, now fuelled by the libations. The babel of voices grew and rose to shrieks. The ground pounded with stamping feet. Then came the throbbing of a chant. *Ultio! Ultio! Ultio!* Revenge – they wanted revenge.

Gavinus, my former estate manager, the gentle engineer, snarled and shouted as well as any of them. Even Quirinia, the practical accountant, was caught in the emotion and waved her arms like a professional mourner. My throat was dry, not just from the smoke. I shouted, chanting with the rest of them. We could have been back in the primitive ancient times, even before kings reigned in Rome.

Silvia stood rigid in front of the pyre, tears streaming down her face, arms raised and, contorted with rage and grief, the ugliest look I'd ever seen on a young girl.

Then she screamed, *'Delendus! Delendus! Delendus!'* She was invoking total destruction on Caius Tellus.

Catharsis was how psychiatrists described it, but exhaustion followed. As I walked down the stairs and into the entrance hallway the next morning, I noticed that people were moving quietly, looking ahead, but not talking. Perhaps like me, they were trying to absorb what had happened last night. I followed others into the former ballroom where Silvia stood at one end watching people file in. A solemn, drawn expression on her face made her look twice her age. She waited until everybody had settled themselves on the chairs with merely a glance at me as I joined Volusenia and Quirinia on the front row.

'People of Roma Nova,' Silvia began. 'Thank you for joining me last night in honouring my father's memory. I think it helped us relieve some of our sadness and anger. Now we must use our energy to drive out the cruel disease in our beloved country.' She panned around the faces. 'I can't believe Roma Novans really want Caius Tellus's regime.'

Cries of 'No!'

Her face relaxed slightly, almost into a smile. 'My grandmother Justina was tough and uncompromising. But she never killed, she was never underhand or terrorised anyone. She cared for her people. I believe even Caius Tellus's own supporters will realise how wrong and unnatural his regime is. Aurelia Mitela and Colonel Volusenia say we must find out what is going on there and start preparing for our fight back.' She placed her right hand over her left breast. 'I vow to you now, with the gods' help, to put myself at the service of *all* my people. So that we can free them and given them their lives back, or we'll die in the attempt.'

Volusenia leaned over and whispered to me, 'I think at last we have an Apulian with some steel in her spine.' I nodded and rose to my feet with her and the rest of the exiles to applaud the imperatrix.

Edward's lawyer had managed to shortcut the procedure for obtaining residency status by going through *Herr* Goss and coaxing temporary protected status documents out of the New Austrian government within three weeks. This not only quashed any more moves to deport us, but let us travel outside New Austria and more importantly re-enter the country.

Now the exiles weren't going to be handed back to Caius's regime legally, Volusenia stepped up security on Silvia, convinced he'd try to snatch her. Silvia at his side, however unwilling, would legitimise his regime. It had caused ructions enough last year when he'd captured me and announced that, although no longer the head of the senior Family, I was now his 'companion'. People had started to think the Twelve Families supported him. If Caius forced Silvia to legally contract with him, it would double our task, if not kill it dead.

The council of eight tasked Volusenia to head a steering group to develop a plan to retake Roma Nova; she co-opted Quirinia, Calavia and a male logistics specialist who was married to one of the PGSF *optiones*. He'd been a transport manager; he knew every road and back way in every part of Roma Nova and had followed his wife out.

In the meantime, I spent a few days in London including a visit to the head office of Soane's Bank. We were going through *solidi* at a fierce rate and I needed to liquidate some of the assets I'd exported there before the night of the fires. Juno Moneta knew how many sale certificates I signed in those austere premises. The portraits of my great-grandfather and various great-uncles and cousins seemed to be frowning down at me as I liquidated long-held assets. David Soane, who had now taken over in London, gave no opinion.

On my return to the Vienna safe house, a soak in a hot bath and something to eat were my first objectives. But as soon as I'd greeted the guard inside the door, and picked up my case to go up to my room, Volusenia cornered me.

'I know you're busy doing everything else, *consiliaria*, but we need some political animals of some sort – a few senators or even a junior magistrate or two would do. If what we're working on succeeds, what in Hades do we do once we get back? That bastard Caius took the country over by gradual political manipulation and we need people as crafty as him on our side.'

'I'll put some senators on the shopping list when I next go to the Roma Nova shop, shall I?'

Volusenia stared at me.

I rubbed my hand across my forehead and down over my face.

'I'm sorry, that was unnecessary. I didn't mean to be rude. I'm a bit tired from the travel. Gods, I'm so unfit. I need to start training again or I'll never keep up.'

'Yes, you've let yourself get out of condition. No excuse for it.'

I stared at her with resentment, guilt and tiredness. When in Hades had I had the luxury to trot round the pavements?

'Gods, Volusenia, you must have been a holy terror for your troops.'

'I still am. Don't underestimate me. You've never officially resigned, *major*, so be careful I don't recall you and start loading you up with training weights and make you work for your living.'

I grinned at her, my headache receding, but she just harrumphed. I glanced up the ornate Biedermeier staircase, then sideways to check for eavesdroppers. 'Look, Marcella Volusenia, we're a tiny group, we don't have the critical mass to retake a border post.' She gave me a Vesuvius look. 'Well, a district *castra*, then. We'll never succeed without a strong resistance movement inside Roma Nova. Too many people still support Caius.' I looked away. 'We may have to wait months until we're ready.'

'No! We need to strike before his system is embedded. Otherwise, people will just accept it and get on with their lives, like all occupied peoples.'

'Yes and no. If the rumours are true about these hellhole work colonies and the executions we've heard about, people will stop supporting Caius fairly rapidly. What we need to do now is to develop an information network to counter his lies and propaganda.'

12

Before I wrote one word of any take-back plan, I had to rid myself of one last piece of pollution from Caius – the damned slave ring. I'd vowed to wear it until I went back to Roma Nova as a reminder of the brutality we were fighting, but in a way I had returned. *This* was the true Roma Nova; a tiny group of exiles compared with the one and a half million inhabitants in the country itself, but a group that represented its true values. I found Numerus in his office.

'Have you got five minutes, some strong cutters, a chisel and hammer?'

It took an hour and my wrist was bleeding and bruised despite the rags I stuffed round it as protection. We had to find the old blacksmith's anvil in the stables in the end. I gave myself another few minutes, some strong tea and a slug of brandy to recover.

I drafted in Lentilius, Silvia's protégé, to work with me on the counter-information campaign; he had good common sense and knew what would appeal to ordinary working people as well as those who had served in the military. They would be anxious, even afraid, and we needed to give them reassurance as well as ask for their support. Of course, not everybody, however patriotic, would want to risk themselves and their families. We'd be unrealistic to expect that. All we needed was enough.

The logistics specialist on the steering group said that, as we had no planes to drop leaflets, we'd have to do it the dangerous way – smuggle them in to distribution points inside Roma Nova with the risk of the couriers and local distributors getting caught. He didn't say another word after that. But we agreed to buy a small litho printing press and prepare leaflets ready for the time when it became practical, and safer, to distribute them.

At least we could listen to what was going on now in Roma Nova. William had set up new electronic systems for us, but we couldn't use our two monitoring points as broadcast stations, or it would give away their locations.

Volusenia disapproved of me leaving the relative safety of Vienna when I scheduled a trip in one of the second-hand vans we'd acquired. At her insistence I took a couple of guards with me. We drove south-west for a couple of hours, parked under trees, then trekked on foot through the snow for another kilometre to the monitoring post she'd set up east of Graz. Cleverly, it was disguised as a mountain rescue communications relay station.

A second listening post one was two hours west, on the site of Virunum where Julia Bacausa, the mother of the first Apulians, had been born in the fourth century. Perhaps that was sentimentality or perhaps it was because it was one of the highest hills around. It was masquerading as an archaeological dig and had just opened up again now it was April. Between the two of them we were able to listen in to vast chunks of the communications spectrum used in Roma Nova.

The hut east of Graz nestled high in the trees on the edge of a drift of conifers. It needed open access on the side facing Roma Nova. We waited a few minutes to make sure there were no planes or helicopters in the sky. I didn't think the New Austrians would take kindly to our covert presence here and we didn't want to give it away by too many people being seen wandering around the site. Crews changed over at night for that reason alone. And the regular snowfall helped.

I knocked on the door in a prearranged sequence, my guard detail flattened against the wall out of the line of sight of anybody opening it.

'*Consiliaria!*' The *optio* looked surprised.

'Everything all right, Diana?'

'Yes, ma'am, of course. We didn't know you were coming, that's all.' Her face had a worried expression. 'We're a bit untidy.'

'As long as you're not holding an orgy, I won't report it.' I smiled at her. 'But it would be nice to get out of this chilly wind.'

The three of them were clad in dark green jackets and shirts, brown trousers and leather boots like the official mountain rescue teams, but without any insignia. One man wore headphones and leaned back, his face a picture of concentration, as he played with a pen between two fingers, his ankles crossed on the edge of the bench. Diana prodded him and glanced in my direction. He scowled back at her and pointed at his ear. He made a half-circle in the air with his left index finger, sat up and started making notes on a pad. Diana leaned towards what looked like a standard transceiver and flicked a tiny switch at the side. Within a nanosecond, Caius's voice boomed out, a little distorted but unmistakable.

'... and so we had to take action to save our great country from these rotten elements that were promoting internal decay. As you know, the old families structure strangleholding progress was abolished and a new system based on neighbourhood groups with a local leader has been guiding your everyday life. Some of you found it strange at first, but you discovered that if you obeyed your local leaders, and observed the curfew, all was well. Regrettably, a few isolated antisocial elements have caused us to extend the temporary emergency regulations. If we are to strengthen our new society, people must learn to obey, but opportunities are there in plenty for right-thinking patriots to rise in our new society.'

Six of us were crowded together in this hut. Despite the fug, I shivered. Caius spoke in a friendly and reassuring tone, like a favourite uncle outlining treats available for good children. Then his voice tightened.

'Traitors who have fled abroad have been proscribed and exiled. Their property has been taken into state guardianship for the benefit of all. Traitors at home are being tried in the new people's courts and punished appropriately. To maintain order and stability, lawbreakers and subversives must be punished as an example.'

I shivered as I remembered the 'punishment' his henchman Phobius had wanted to carry out on me.

'Regrettably,' Caius continued, 'three females, supposedly *leading* some of our prominent families, showed their true colours and actively resisted, causing misery and death. The so-called Countesses Calavia, Aquilia and Volusenia have been tried and publicly executed. Calavia was implicated in the death of Severina Apulia, the last of the *imperatrices*.'

Sour fumes rose up my throat. I clamped my mouth shut. I could still see that doughty woman holding the unconscious Severina's hand in the wrecked council chamber, and shooing me away. I felt the tears run down my face.

'On the positive side, men have taken their natural places leading councils, businesses, professions, trade, retail and industry. Women have, for the most part, returned to their proper feminine roles. Some are permitted to work in service or auxiliary jobs until they marry and have children, or if they are widowed. You will see no more women bearing arms, or giving men instructions – a repugnant state of affairs – but carrying babies and holding their children's hands as Roman women should.'

I felt so angry at this rubbish which sounded so reasonable. I was the emotional one scarcely controlling my feelings; he was the rational, sensible one.

'Fathers have now taken back their authority at the head of households and our society is the path to coming back into natural balance. Some misguided people are attempting to block this. There is no place in the new Roma Nova for such people. We must unite to root them out. Citizens – you, your children and your household must be alert and watchful at all times. If you suspect anything or anyone, you must report it to a member of the Roman National Movement or the *vigiles*. This is now more important than ever if we are to complete our transformation. I will leave you now with three watchwords: *patria, sacrificatio, vis!*'

We stood like statues in a public park as the harsh martial music blared out. I couldn't trust myself to say anything. People exchanged glances, uncertainty in the eyes of frozen faces.

'Well, fuck him!' The operator wearing the headphones smacked his hand down on the bench making everything rattle. 'That manipulative bastard needs taking out. And I want the pleasure of doing it.'

'Not before me, soldier,' I said. 'I was in the queue before you were born.'

They all swivelled their heads in my direction.

'It's a long and sour story but, believe me, it's both deadly and very personal between us. And I won't rest until it's ended. Neither will he.'

One by one, I talked to Colonel Volusenia, Pia Calavia and the young Aquilia lieutenant in the privacy of the room I slept in. There was nowhere else. Volusenia came in first, taking one look at my face before I said anything. She stared into the old empty grate as I gave her the details of Caius's speech and of her sister's death.

'I feared it,' she rasped, 'but it's still hard. My sister was fifteen years older than me, more in the way of a mother, but I loved her better than anybody else in the world.'

She dropped down onto the wooden chair and stared unfocused at the floor. 'He's an idiot, that man. He thinks he'll terrify us into inaction but all he's doing is pissing us off. No, that's a stupid word.' Her fists clenched. 'At this precise moment, I want to rip his head off his shoulders.' She breathed in quickly and heavily as if preparing to spring up, but after a few moments, her own shoulders drooped. When she looked up, her eyes were moist, but she'd reassumed that angry vulture look I remembered from the night of Marina's rape.

'I'll prepare letters for my brothers. Will you let me send them to Quintus Tellus via the Swiss legation?'

I'd been keeping that line of communication to Caius's brother for emergency only, but how could I refuse her?

Pia Calavia was dignified, but white-faced, when I told her about her grandmother's fate.

'I did my weeping when you showed me Quintus Tellus's letter back in December. My grandmother knew exactly what she was doing when she stayed with Imperatrix Severina. She was dying, you know. A malignant cancer. She only had about six months left at best.'

'Pia,' I said, as gently as I could. 'He had the three of them executed publicly. I'm so sorry.'

She clamped her hand over her mouth and just made it to the

bathroom opposite my room. I held her hair back as she knelt over the lavatory pan, throwing up the contents of her stomach.

'How could he do that?' she whispered. 'He didn't even give her the dignity of *liberum mortis arbitrium*. The barbarian.'

None of the three had been allowed to commit suicide privately. Caius had treated them like the worst common criminals.

Pia got to her feet and washed her hands and face. 'I'll stay with you, if you like, while you tell Aquilia. She's only a kid, just out of training. Juno.' Pia's voice was a little shaky, but her eyes were hard.

Twenty minutes later, Pia led Paula Aquilia away, sobbing her heart out. Countess Aquilia had been her grandmother's sister, not close, but it was a huge shock for a young woman who had seen her world collapse and who hadn't had time yet to develop coping mechanisms for dealing with violent death.

At the evening meeting, all three women sat stoically as I gave everybody else a summary of Caius's broadcast. After the silence, like a collective caught breath, at least half the room were on their feet, fists shaking; all were shouting or wailing.

I let them go on for a few minutes then put my hand up. Nobody took any notice.

Volusenia leapt up, spun round and faced the rampant noise. 'SILENCE!' she barked. 'Enough! Sit down.'

A few murmured, but facing her ferocity, they settled down.

'Thank you, colonel,' I said. 'I know you're all deeply shocked, but I would ask that you please show some sympathy for the families who have lost relatives in such a barbaric way. They need quiet calm and, of course, our support. In the meantime, we must learn to channel our indignation and anger into more positive action. The council is developing an outline of the preparatory work for a take-back plan.'

This time, there were gasps. Now I had their complete attention.

'The next thing to do is to change the way we organise ourselves. We'll go back to the traditional families structure that's been our strength down the years. I suggest you start now.'

I smiled as a certain amount of chair scraping and people shuffling took place. In the end, many of us were single representatives of our families, but there were, surprisingly, some groups, one even of four.

'Please select one person as representative who will collect and exchange information, instructions and tasks for the family. We are a small group, so with guard and monitoring work it may seem a little muddled, and those jobs must take priority at this stage. After today, I believe more people may find their way to us and we must be ready to receive them.'

13

I was called to the signals office the next evening. The duty operator was busy at a keyboard, but an *optio* rose from a small desk overflowing with paper as soon as I walked into the small room.

'We have a call from Brown Industries for you, *consiliaria*.' She gave me the handset of the secure telephone unit.

'Aurelia, it's William. I've been monitoring the broadcasts from Roma Nova. Grim. I won't let Marina watch them. Especially at present.'

I bristled at the thought of a man preventing a woman from doing something as simple as watching the news, however tragic it was.

'Why? What do you mean?' I heard the sharpness in my voice.

'Relax, I'm not being the tyrannical husband. It's that I don't want to have her upset in any way just now. Let her explain.'

I heard him call her as if she were in another room. After a minute or two, she came to the phone.

'Mama, exciting news! I'm going to have a baby. I had a scan today. Everything's perfect. She'll be born in August.' She sounded breathy, like a fifteen-year-old going out on her first date.

'Darling, that's wonderful. Sit down and tell me everything.'

After formally congratulating me and the Mitela family the next morning, the council of eight turned back to its business. They decided I should resume my function as foreign minister publicly. I acquiesced with a smile on my face, not really taking it in after the previous evening's news from Marina. We had no territory, but I could see the sense of showing the world we were still in the game. Nevertheless, I felt faintly ridiculous, as if I was wearing borrowed clothes, when I boarded my first flight to a Roma Nova legation abroad.

Nuncia Cornelia in Paris simply handed over her keys saying everything was at our disposal. She had told Caius in diplomatic but certain terms what he could do with himself. Cornelia's young cousin, Claudia, had been my extremely efficient assistant at the foreign ministry, loyal to her bones and a prime example of the stiff-necked Cornelian pride. She was Marina's age, but a world away in experience and, being honest, grit.

'I'm so pleased you've contacted us, *consiliaria*, we've felt a little at sea,' the older Cornelia continued.

'I'm extremely grateful for your support, *nuncia*, but how will this impact on your family at home and those of your staff?'

I explained about my encounter with Livilla Vara.

'Vara does not fully appreciate the extremely serious situation, *consiliaria*. I think it would be wiser to seek your main support elsewhere. Yes, we all have families, but this monstrous power grab threatens not only our country and our way of life but our very existence. What do you want us to do?'

I nearly fell on her neck with gratitude. Over dinner, we discussed the options.

'I think the best thing would be to close the legation,' I said. 'Install security and bring your people to Vienna. We're a load of rough soldiers, a few patricians and waifs and strays, plus my estate farming staff. We need some diplomats, but also some solid clerical backup. You're fourteen, fifteen Roma Novans, plus guard detail?'

'Yes, twenty-five altogether.'

'If anybody wants to stay here because of family or personal commitments we'll have to support them, of course.'

'No, they'll all come, *consiliaria*. They know their duty as Romans. I'll send an advance party to Vienna tomorrow. The rest of us – apart from a few to close up – will follow shortly.'

I paused. 'Have you heard anything from Claudia?'

The *nuncia* looked down at her plate.

'No, don't tell me she's dead.'

'She's alive, recovering. They arrested her at the foreign ministry, dragging her off in the night. She had a bad time, but had the sense to bend her pride and play dumb. In the end, they sent her to one of their new work colonies. They herd them in there, make them dig foundations for huts, then work ten hours a day building them. That's all I've heard, but it must be Tartarus. My brother Octavius got her out. He's one of these Roman National Movement idiots, but he couldn't leave her there. He said she'd lost a quarter of her body weight. She's staying on his farm now, working there, keeping her head down. He's a miserable piece, but he'll make sure she's safe and fed.'

'Oh, gods.' Claudia had been my loyal assistant. Was she the first of many who'd been broken?

London proved the same. The *nuncio*, a tall, lanky man bearing the completely appropriate name of Gracilis and wearing a Savile Row suit replied in his very cultured tones that I could be reassured of his complete support.

'I suggest I remain in post, *consiliaria*, as we may need the longstanding extremely close relations we have with the British government.' He studied my face. 'I assume we will be recovering the situation in the near future?'

'While I have breath in my body, Gracilis, I will be striving night and day to bring this about.'

He smiled gravely. 'But not at the expense of a few hours' sleep, I trust?'

Two weeks later, Berlin. I decided to leave that legation open as well, given that it was the biggest in the region and located near the headquarters of the European Economic Area. My meeting with EEA officials was polite on my side and cautious on theirs, but I came away with the impression that they wouldn't hinder us. The EEA president even asked me to drop in before I left.

'A bad business, Aurelia,' he said, frowning. 'This is completely off the record but let me know if I can help with anything.' He poured out a cup of coffee for me from the tray his assistant had brought in. 'Tellus sent us an obnoxious young oaf called Felinus. Apparently his vast experience included holding a junior commerce portfolio in the previous government.'

'I remember him from the last full imperial council meeting,' I replied. 'He's one of Caius Tellus's personal stooges.'

'We listened to what he had to say, which was mostly bluster. I have the impression they consider they are conferring a significant honour upon the EEA by continuing to belong to it.' He gave me a little smile.

'Oh gods, you know that's not Roma Nova's true stance.'

'Of course.' He stretched out his hand with a small card. 'My home telephone number. Just in case.'

Our Berlin legation *nuncio*, who'd been appointed over five years ago, was formal and businesslike. He'd simply shut down the communications lines to Roma Nova and refused to take an open telephone call from the so-called first consul's office.

'We'll reduce to half running, *consiliaria* – we can manage with that. I'll send the rest of the staff to help you in Vienna. Pity about Vara.' And that was all he said about her.

I hadn't been to Washington yet, but I used a video link from the Berlin legation communications room to speak to our *nuncia* there. I was encouraged and heartened by our diplomats. They swam cleverly through the difficult waters of international diplomacy, often acting to the limits of flexibility but, Vara excepted, they had no trace of a doubt about where their loyalties lay. As we rode back from the Maria-Theresia-*Hauptbahnhof* to the safe house, I thought how I'd love to have seen Caius's face as he received each legation's reply to his approach.

We heard the noise first; shouting, cries, police whistles, dogs, van doors slamming. As our taxi driver turned the corner, a sea of people confronted us. There must have been between two and three hundred mobbing the front door of our building, pushing and shoving. The

New Austrian gendarmerie, arms stretched out were trying to contain them, but there were only a dozen officers. Then I saw children, lost and shivering on the edge of the crowd, one mite in a tunic and quilted jacket, sucking her thumb, clutching a bewildered older child's hand, and staring at the crowd. He looked blankly ahead, a walking stick in his hand – he was blind. What in Hades was going on?

I leapt out of the taxi onto the wet street, followed by Atrius and Zosia, my escorts, close to each side of me. I was about to push through when I heard a child's voice.

'Help us. Help us for the love of Juno.'

I froze for a couple of seconds. He'd spoken in street Latin. The blind boy.

I crouched down. 'Who are you?'

'Lucius, I'm Lucius.' Then he burst into tears.

I pulled him to me and put my other arm around the little girl. Neither could have been more than seven or eight.

'Where are your mother and father?'

'Gone – they left us.' He started sobbing again.

'Right, Atrius, get me through this lot.' I stood and grabbed a child's hand in each of mine and followed Atrius's large frame through the crowd. Then I realised the shouts were all in Latin. Who were they? Where had they come from? Angry, despairing faces crowded in on us. Zosia bent down and picked up the boy and I scooped the girl up. We'd lose them otherwise.

As we reached the door, a voice shouted, 'They're getting in. Now's our chance!' They surged forward, knocking over those nearest and pushing against one of the two New Austrian gendarmes guarding the door.

I saw faces at the window to the left of the door and waved my free hand madly. The door opened a few centimetres, then widened to let out a half-dozen PGSF guards with long staves. They raised them in front of their faces, criss-crossing them with their neighbours, and stepped forward as one to make a space for us. The crowd retreated a good metre. We slid in with the children. The PGSF guards stayed outside, standing braced and looking grim.

The noise cut immediately as somebody shut the door and slid the bolt. I let out a long breath.

'Will somebody tell me what the Hades is going on?'

'The first ones appeared this morning, about twenty of them, then it got to about fifty or so, and they started thumping on the door and the windows so we called the police.' A woman of about forty whom I vaguely recognised answered me. She stepped forward and took the little girl from me.

'Who are you?'

'My name's Grania, *consilaria*. I'm one of the Paris legation staff.'

Of course. I shook my head to clear it and waved at her to carry on.

'By the time the gendarmes arrived, there must have been over a hundred shouting and chanting continuously. And the rest have appeared in the past half hour.'

'Where's Volusenia?'

'The colonel's gone with *Consiliaria* Quirinia to the New Austrian finance ministry for a meeting.'

I heard a movement behind me. Pia Calavia came down the stairs, tucking her shirt into her trouser waistband. She shrugged on her jacket and yawned. Her eyes were red with tiredness. She glanced out of the window by the entrance door and looked stymied.

'We have to get to the bottom of this,' I said. 'Lieutenant, detail another half-dozen guards to the door inside, then go out there yourself and bring me a selection of those people – half a dozen, max. And check the status of the gendarmes. Bring them in if you think they're in danger.'

A shot rang out. A roar, followed by a police whistle. Calavia ran for the door with her group, threw the bolt back and barrelled through the entrance. Others pushed the door shut behind them. I ran to the window. Calavia had her knee in the chest of a man lying in the gutter, her fingers circled the man's wrist and she was smashing the back of his hand down on the cobbles. A heavy service revolver fell out of his bloody fingers and clattered on the stones. Another guard dropped to the ground, grabbed it and stowed it in his pocket. The two of them pulled the man up and thrust him through the door before he'd had time to grab his breath.

'Medic,' I shouted, as he stumbled in and looked wildly about. Another three figures followed, plus the two gendarmes. Calavia and her detail slid back in and the door was bolted once more. Breathing a little fast, Calavia nodded at her troops and they took up positions surrounding the newcomers.

I crossed my arms and looked at the bedraggled group. I saw now they were clad in thin, dull clothing, one with a jacket, the other a jersey, the older woman swathed in a shawl. The man Calavia had relieved of the revolver sat on a chair while his hand was being bandaged. His shoulders slumped but he looked up at me truculently, and angry as Jupiter. He looked like a countryman in his rough clothing, but his voice was straight out of the Septarium, the nearest thing Roma Nova city had to a slum.

'We came here for help, not to be beaten up by your heavies.'

Calavia took half a step forward, but I waved her back.

'And what exactly did you expect?'

'We was told you'd give us money and somewhere to live. We got nowhere to go. We been sleeping in the park until these grey scarabs threw us out.'

'And who told you this?'

He gave me a sly look. 'I'm not saying nuffink more until I get some money.'

Atrius swooped down on him, grabbed him by the collar of his shirt, lifted him off the ground and shook him. 'Answer the bloody question. You piss around anymore, sunshine, and you won't have a mouth left to whinge out of.'

'Relax, soldier,' I ordered. Atrius loosened his grip and pushed the man back down onto his chair. 'Now, let's start again. What's your name and where are you from?'

He sat sullen for a minute or so. 'Burrus,' he muttered. 'From the city.'

'And why are you here, Burrus?'

'Got chucked out.'

'Why was that?'

'Owed money to one of those nationalist bastards. He turned up one day, dragged me out of my bed and threw me on a lorry with some others. Then they drove us over the border, turfed us out and left us there with the address of this place. We tried to go back but they shot some of us, so we legged it. We slept in the park last night, then came here.'

'All of you?'

'Yeah. Some of them are in a bad way, some only little kids like those two.' He pointed to the wall where my two protégés were crouching on the floor.

'Where did you get the revolver?' I said.

'Lifted it off one of those grey scarabs.' He snorted and shrugged. 'Easy.'

'You're obviously a man of talents, Burrus, but not ones we can use.'

'You chucking me out?'

'Not if you behave. Can you do that, I wonder?' I searched his face for reaction but all I got back was an expression of hurt and surprise.

Before I could ask him anything else, there was heavy thump on the door so loud I thought it would cave in. Calavia glanced out of the window.

'Police. A lot.'

Damn.

'Better let them in before they break the door down,' I said.

She opened the door cautiously and four grey-clad and black-jacketed gendarmes strode in, two carrying our luggage from the taxi. As if that wasn't strange enough, it became almost surreal when I saw their commander. It was my cousin from Berlin, Joachim von und zu der Havel.

14

———————

I was so surprised I couldn't stop my arms falling to my sides. I gaped at him, unbelieving. I hoped I didn't look half as stupefied as he did. His curly hair under his cap was more grey than blond and shorter, but the blue eyes were the same, although surrounded by many more wrinkles. And he could still produce a grim expression. He wore the police grey, but with a half-colonel's pips on his shoulders. I took a step forward.

'Achim? Joachim?'

He continued to stare at me, but said nothing. His colleagues glanced around as if assessing danger only to be met by cool stares from Calavia and her troops who shifted slightly, but definitely, in an encircling motion. The gendarmes rested their hands on their leather pistol holsters, Calavia's detail clutched their staves and they all eyed each other up, waiting for the slightest movement from the other side. I gathered my wits together and drew myself up.

'Grania.' I waved my hand toward the two children, instinctively frightened by the tension. 'Take the little ones to the kitchen and give them something warm to eat and drink. Actually, take the adults, too. Atrius, you go with them, to address any, er, security concerns.' Atrius nodded and pulled Burrus off the chair and followed Grania and her charges.

'*Oberstleutnant,*' I addressed Joachim formally, 'if you and your colleagues would follow me?' I turned to Calavia. 'Lieutenant, rotate your troops outside. Get somebody on the roof and take some photos. I want to know about any change as it happens.'

One of the police spoke into his radio as we walked through to the ballroom. There were half a dozen of the former Paris legation staff at one end working at some tables, with a row of filing cabinets separating them from the main area. We had no other place for them to use as a general office. There was a low level hum of VDU terminals, drawers opening and shutting, subdued conversations in measured tones. In another corner, two clerks were tapping at the cork-lined walls, pinning up a large-scale map and lists of tasks for this evening's main meeting and shooting glances at us. I drew Joachim away to one end.

'What the hell are you doing in Vienna?' he began. No preliminaries.

'And how are you, too, after a fifteen-year gap?' I mustered as much sarcasm as I could.

'That's irrelevant.' He waved his hand. 'Are these scruffs outside your people?'

A wave of hot anger rolled through me.

'How dare you call them scruffs? These *refugees* have been hounded out by a cruel and monstrous regime which murdered our ruler and has started executing dozens without trial. These *citizens* were driven over the border and dumped. When they tried to go back, they were fired on.' I was tired. Tired of travelling, tired of being a petitioner, tired of scrabbling around in the confined world of this building. 'You bloody New Austrians, sitting here in your comfortable, sanitised sugarcake town. You've been minus nil help.' I heard my voice getting louder, but I couldn't stop. 'Don't you bring your self-righteous attitude in here.'

I paused for breath and became conscious of silence. Every person had stopped moving and was staring at us. I waved at them to get back to their work.

'Well, they have to go somewhere,' Joachim said. 'They can't stay on the street. I'm not having three hundred refugees sleeping rough in this weather. God knows what would happen.'

'Clutter up your tidy little town, would they?'

'No, actually, I'm more worried about what would happen *to* them. You've got quite a lot of old people and children.'

'Haven't you got any empty barracks or some kind of holding facility? If you could house them for a few days, we can try and sort this out.'

'No, nothing. I'll contact the Red Cross tomorrow, but something has to be done now. These people must be off the streets by nightfall.'

'But that's in three hours. How the hell do you propose we do that?'

He shrugged.

'We will take them in. They are our people.'

I spun round at the light voice. Silvia.

She raised an eyebrow. 'Aurelia Mitela?'

I bowed. '*Domina*, may I present *Oberstleutnant Freiherr* Joachim von und zu der Havel?' I looked at him. 'Oh, excuse me, are you known by your matronymic, Huber?'

He ignored me and inclined his head to Silvia. '*Oberstleutnant* Huber of the *Neuösterreichische Gendarmerie, gnädiges Fräulein.*'

'You address the Imperatrix Silvia,' I said, crossly.

'Excuse me, I understood she was—' He stopped, gave Silvia a warm smile and bowed. 'I apologise, *Majestät*. I have been misinformed.'

She didn't return his smile. 'Romans do not fail in their duty to their citizens.' She looked down her nose at me. 'These poor people must be admitted and fed. Arrange it with the housekeeping team. Now. And no more argument.' She turned her back on me and beckoned Joachim to walk with her. I could only watch with open mouth, stunned by being treated so peremptorily.

'Countess?' A man's light voice to my left. 'If I may be of assistance? I'm Vibianus, from the consulate section, Paris legation.' A tubby man with a smile on his round face. 'Would you like me to organise the admission and documentation? I can liaise with the housekeeping team so that we are not overwhelmed.'

'Yes, yes, that would be perfect. Thank you, Vibianus.'

He beckoned to two women assistants who placed a table, chairs, papers, card index by the ballroom entrance. One of them set off in direction of the front lobby and came back with a group of a dozen refugees who looked round warily. Then another group, mainly children, with two women. The other woman assistant sat by his side and started processing some of the people while the first one hurried off towards the kitchen. She brought back Burrus with Atrius in close escort and the three others. Within ten minutes, sandwiches, tea urns and water jugs appeared, carried in by the kitchen staff and set out on trestles.

I caught Joachim as he left. He was walking towards the entrance door. His men had left earlier.

'A minute, if you please, *Oberstleutnant*,' I called to his retreating back. He stopped, but didn't turn. I caught up with him.

'Are you going to spend the rest of your life being bad-tempered with me, Achim?'

'It's not a question of temper. I don't have anything to say to you.'

'And why is that?'

'After the Berlin fiasco I decided to make a clean break. And that included everybody I'd known, including you. Especially you.'

'Why?'

'Do I really have to explain it?' He sighed. 'Every time I think of you or Roma Nova, I see Hasi and how you, and it, destroyed my life.'

'Now, wait a minute, you can't blame me for your partner's criminal behaviour. Hasi was on the take from Caius Tellus. Please don't lump me together with that unspeakable creature. He was responsible for my daughter's rape and the attack and murder of people at my farm. I barely escaped with my life when he launched his coup. In no respect does he represent Roma Nova.'

I waved my hand in the direction of the queues of people registering at Vibianus's table or devouring food at the hastily set up trestles.

'Neither I nor these refugees have done anything to you.' I stared at him until he broke his gaze. 'Don't blame us for other people's criminal behaviour.'

I turned and stalked away, impatient with his petulance. I presumed he left as I didn't see him after that.

Within the three hours the ballroom was full and the street empty. I noticed Burrus had shrugged off his guards and was busying himself organising his fellow refugees who seemed to accept his authority. Or maybe they were too tired to do anything else. Perhaps it had been bravado in front of authority that had made him defiant when he'd arrived.

After Silvia's speech a few weeks ago, we'd began to amass

supplies, making provision for refugees, but I hadn't realised how efficiently it was being run. Blankets, inflatable mattresses and pillows were found and by ten that evening the refugees were bedded down; some in rooms and quiet corridors, some in the ballroom itself.

The scheduled evening meeting turned into just a council session. I didn't say much but let Quirinia and Volusenia hammer out ideas of how to manage the new influx. For some reason, despite the fact that I'd sincerely wished for it, I was finding it hard to adjust to Silvia's newly-developed self-assurance.

I joined Volusenia in the frosty garden as she smoked her last cigarette of the day after the council broke up.

'You didn't say much. Anything wrong?' she said.

'No, not really.'

'That bad, eh?' She threw a quick glance at me. 'Calavia told me Silvia had been brusque with you. She getting too big for her boots?'

'Probably me getting tetchy. I've hardly slept these past few days with all this to-ing and fro-ing.'

'Ha! I don't know how you came by a reputation as a good spook when you lie so badly. Silvia's doing well, better than I ever thought, but she's still a teenager. Don't take it too hard. You're a powerful woman, Aurelia, and you're not used to being snubbed by young tykes, however august their descent.'

We walked on for a few minutes in silence.

'Now I've got the legations on board and we've worked out a *modus operandi* with the EEA, I feel somewhat redundant.'

'Bollocks! We need you to liaise with these New Austrians. I really have no patience with their genteel little ways. And Silvia needs you more than ever as her first councillor.'

I smiled at her, but said nothing more.

The next morning, I dragged myself out of bed to join Calavia on an early run. It was hard after days of rich food, meetings and travel, but it cleared my head. Nearly twenty of us jogged our way along the pavements, then to the green paths up to Empress Elisabeth's stunning Hermesvilla, the hunting lodge her husband built out of love for her. It *was* beautiful, no doubt, but not quite as enticing as Roma Nova. I closed my eyes and thought of the view from the old castle of

Roma Nova, overlooking the Golden Palace, the sinuous river, the roofs of the old town, the forum and Senate building dominating it.

I wiped away the moisture in my eyes. The breeze was fresh this morning. In a week's time, the Lainzer Tiergarten would be open until winter and we'd be able to puff our way up to the top of the Weiner Blick from where you could see the whole city spread out below. Then I realised what I'd thought. I'd automatically assumed we'd still be here until winter.

After queuing behind three of the refugees, I eventually got to the shower. I shivered more in the lukewarm water than I had outside in the early morning chill. I nearly fell over two more women sitting on the floor in the corridor waiting for their turn. We had to do something about accommodation, and fast. The house was large – twenty bedrooms – but people were packed into every one as well as the corridor and lofts. The plumbing system alone couldn't cope with three hundred and fifty people. I would bury my temper and contact Achim after I'd had some coffee. To my surprise he appeared later that afternoon.

'No, we don't have anything like a handy empty ex-barracks.' He snorted. 'If you remember, they were all demolished after the Great War as part of the Allied powers' retribution. The old imperial ones were turned into housing. Can't you rent somewhere?'

'With what? We don't have finite resources. I've sold almost half my overseas assets, the others have liquidated what they can. Some have taken jobs to bring money in.' A good number of the PGSF were working as taxi drivers or security until the refugee influx. Now we needed them here to keep order. 'We'll try and get the refugees into employment, but a lot of them are old or disabled. It won't be quick.' I looked away. 'If there was a time we needed Fortuna with a large farm or a rambling estate to spare in her horn of plenty, this is it.'

'I'll talk to a few people, but don't expect any sudden results.' As he stood up to go, he fished in his inside jacket pocket and brought out a visiting card. 'Here,' he said, 'I almost forgot. My mother asked if you would drop by tomorrow afternoon for tea.'

His mother? Tante Sabine? I hadn't seen her for a while. I hadn't even thought about her in all my busyness. Although I called her

'Aunt' and she'd been very kind to me when I'd been a student in Berlin, she wasn't strictly a relative. One of my now dead cousins had married her late husband's father. All my generation called her Tante Sabine. She'd moved back to Vienna after Achim's father had died. I was really too busy to make time for private socialising. But then again, Tante Sabine had connections…

The shallow flight of steps and the wide old-fashioned porch belonged to the 1800s; the security cameras did not. Upstairs, Sabine welcomed me into a modern oasis of daylight, beige sofas and herringbone wood floors.

'Soulless, isn't it?' she said and chuckled. 'But the designer was so sweet I couldn't find it in my heart to say anything that would crush him.' She took my hand. 'Sit, sit down, Aurelia, and let me look at you.'

Her elegant hair was swept in a soft curve from front to back and moved like the gentle swaying of July wheat. Her smooth skin, perfect make-up and designer clothes along with that confidence of a high-cultured sophisticate made me feel dowdy and provincial. She looked my age, but I knew she'd married late and had to be in her mid-seventies by now. She waved a manicured hand at nobody I could see and a sober-suited man appeared with a silver tray covered in the type of china and exquisite cakes I hadn't seen in months.

'You look tired, darling,' she said. 'Probably overdoing it, like Felicia used to.' She shook her head. 'You Roman women!' Then she laughed. 'Don't look at me so seriously, Aurelia.'

'I'm sorry, Tante Sabine, it's just a difficult time at the moment.'

'So I understand from Joachim. And you're all crushed together in that scrubby little merchant's house.'

'It's not so bad,' I fired back. She lived a comfortable, safe life, free to go to concerts, travel, shop at the smartest stores, to see and be seen at Vienna's most exclusive parties. I wouldn't have called her flighty to her face, but she'd never lacked for anything, nor had she ever had to make any sacrifices.

'Why don't you move in here with me? You'd be so much more comfortable in the guest flat. I'll take you to all the parties and we'll have such fun!'

'Sabine, I can't. We're living on a knife-edge and we have to stay together. I'm deeply grateful for your offer, but I can't desert my people.'

'That's ridiculous – you have to have some sort of life.'

'Why don't you come and see us for yourself. We're not quite as uncivilised as you might think.' I smiled at her.

To my surprise, after we'd finished our tea and talked family trivialities, she called for her coat and car. She looked up at our merchant's house, sniffed and pulled her shoulders back. Inside, she was gracious and polite, but I felt her withdraw when there were too many people around her. She bobbed a curtsey to Silvia and murmured '*Majestät*', which surprised everybody.

Afterwards, as we stood in the chill dark of the late April evening only relieved by the weak street lighting, she laid her hand on my arm, stretched up and kissed my cheek.

'I may have something for you in the next few days. *Bis später.*'

15

———

I didn't think any more about Sabine that next week. Perhaps she meant she would have one of her charity fundraising events for us. But seeing her had been a temporary escape into a more pleasant world for an afternoon.

I made myself a mug of tea in the kitchen, ironically a quieter place than most of the house; people were always too busy in there now to stand around gossiping. And they were trying to make something special for the Floralia meal tonight. We had no circus to stage the usual competitive games or public spectacles but we could start the evening with a sacrifice to Flora and follow it with theatricals and indoor games.

After the playlets would come comic speeches and story-telling. The most original would be awarded a garland and a prize. Floralia was an occasion to dress up in gaudy clothes and let our hair down. Even in our exile bubble, we were determined to keep up traditions if we could; it reminded people what we were struggling for.

Several of the younger ones had been out looking for wild flowers and picking up cheap leftovers from florists and supermarkets. It was spring, after all, with all that implied. Flora might be the goddess of pretty things like flowers but she also represented fertility. We'd have several babies in nine months' time, no doubt.

Silvia would lead the public observances at the beginning and place flowers and grasses on a temporary altar. People had chosen

Burrus as master of ceremonies – not my first choice if I was honest. Floralia at home in Roma Nova was often raucous and wild and the wise didn't go into the street on the last night of the festivities. However, Lentilius, Silvia's pet follower, was by Burrus's side and would keep him in check.

I had to admit that Burrus had settled into the community, acting as a people's representative and settling minor squabbles. Even Vibianus who'd sniffed at Burrus's intervention at first conceded he was surprised at his effectiveness at managing the new exiles.

'An unrefined piece of silver ore, *consiliaria*, but he's been useful.'

On the surface, Burrus was meticulously polite and deferential but I'd caught a few glances from him when I thought he was unaware I was watching. Whether it was speculation or dislike for authority, I couldn't tell. When I attempted to pin him down about who exactly had told him we would give him money, he'd merely replied he couldn't remember. Well, Lentilius had befriended him, so I gave him the benefit of the doubt. Perhaps some of Lentilius's integrity would rub off on Burrus.

With scarcely forty Praetorians as a guard force, keeping order wouldn't be easy. Six manned the monitoring stations and we couldn't abandon them even for a single night. Although contained theoretically by their family groups, squabbles had inevitably broken out amongst the people struggling to manage when they were confined in a building designed for a tenth of their number. Atrius had stopped one knife fight before it got out of hand and Quirinia had noticed petty theft from supplies. The office area was cleared each night now and, despite the frequent open meetings, people still grumbled. With the prospect of everybody drinking themselves stupid tonight, I shuddered. The gods knew we all needed a break, but I was uneasy.

A light touch on my arm. Silvia. I stepped back and bowed.

'*Domina.*'

Dressed in a white tunic she had made herself, hair drawn back and held in a simple ribbon, she looked twelve years old. Her face wore a stricken expression and she looked as if she was going to burst into tears.

'Aunt Aurelia, please,' she whispered. 'I've been so stupid.'

I said nothing, but waited.

She twisted the fingers of one hand round a thin silver bracelet on her other arm. After staring at the wall for a second or two, she raised her eyes to my face.

'I was very rude to you when that policeman called. I apologise. He and his officers made me nervous. Sorry.' Her cheeks started to turn pink.

'It's all right, darling,' I said and clasped her shoulders. 'You're growing up very fast and doing so well, it's a bit of a surprise when you go back to being a normal girl.'

'I realised what I'd done, but I was too embarrassed to say so,' she said. 'When you were so quiet and correct at the council, I knew I'd stabbed myself in the foot and didn't know how to get out of it.' She heaved a huge sigh. 'It's so hard always being on my best behaviour.'

I chuckled. 'I know. I'll be honest with you, Silvia. I used to have to bite my tongue most of the time with your mother. I've had practice.'

'Yes, I expect you did. I loved her very much and I miss her, but she was silly sometimes. I want my sensible, clever cousin back as my friend.' She glanced again at my face.

I smiled at her. 'Friends?'

'Yes, oh, yes,' she said, and hugged me hard.

It began well; decorous but relaxed. By midnight, it was all going to hell. At home in Roma Nova, the most cautious citizens would lock and bar their doors after about ten and let the more rowdy elements get on with it. The *vigiles* would have a busy time and the next day would be a day of sore heads and magistrates' hearings. Unfortunately, the wise, the rowdy and the ordinary were all trapped in here together.

I sent Silvia upstairs with two guards to sleep in her room and we got most of the children into the far rooms with some of the more sensible parents. Some of the Praetorians were mixing in with the party to try and keep the atmosphere calm. But as people got steadily drunker, it was no use. There were just too many of them. Most of the flower garlands decorating the room had been torn down. Burrus, surrounded by a group of giggling young women, was shouting out more and more extreme forfeits to his little group. When they started pulling plainly terrified young girls into the centre where he and his cronies were sitting, I sent Calavia and her four in to grab him. She was swamped and failed to extract Burrus, but they brought the girls back. Pluto, they were only about fifteen or sixteen.

'Get them upstairs,' I shouted at her. We barred access to the upper floor and I sent some of the other Praetorians to extinguish as many of the open flame torches as possible without openly antagonising the partygoers. Apart from preventing the house being set on fire, perhaps it would give the hint the evening was coming to a close. Instead, things became louder, the torches were flickering solidly round Burrus and his group and the music was thumping through the air. Then Burrus started chanting and punching his fists in the air in rhythm. First his cronies joined in, then those closest. It rippled out until the whole room was alive with drunken shouting faces distorted with emotion.

Burrus looked straight at me through the howling and flames and smirked. My blood ran cold. Just like the Roman Nationalist Movement. Oh, gods, Burrus was a plant. Caius's agent.

Merda.

I cast about for a trusted face.

'Atrius.' I tapped him on the shoulder. 'Take somebody else you trust completely, join up with the other two in the imperatrix's room and stay with her. If this lot get past us and you hear them coming upstairs, get her out via the roof windows in the loft. Go straight to the *Gendarmie* HQ and ask for Colonel Huber.'

He stared at me for a few seconds, then nodded and disappeared. I shouted in the ear of young Aquilia. 'Lieutenant, get that bloody music turned off.' She nodded and made for the side wall.

'Where in Hades are they getting all this drink from?' Quirinia, breathing heavily, eyes darting everywhere. 'We didn't order a quarter of this.'

'Pilfering or something like it. Never mind that now,' I shouted at her. The noise was deafening and starting to make my head throb. 'Get upstairs with the others.'

'*Consiliaria*, look out,' Volusenia growled beside me. 'They're coming towards us.' She stepped forward to meet the chanting surge of people, just as she had done in the forum several months ago. We had no firearms, just staves and short wooden nightsticks.

She roared at them to back off and disperse and raked them with her eyes. A number of them stopped, cowed by her fierce look, but Burrus egged them on. I went to stand by her side, the other Praetorians fanning in a two-deep half-circle behind us. If nothing else, we had to delay him so that Silvia could escape. Burrus stopped three metres from us, his henchmen and women clustered around him. They swayed, but he stood stock still, feet planted apart. The music cut abruptly, thank the gods, and Aquilia.

We waited. Eventually, the noise subsided to murmuring, then silence. I stared straight into his eyes, daring him to advance. He stared back. I heard coughing, a glass break, somebody crying, but we stayed there, not moving.

Eventually, he broke, thrust his hand and a home-made cudgel in the air and shouted, 'Take them apart!'

The first wave of bodies was pushed towards us by others behind them. We crossed staves and fended them off, landing punches on a few noses, or striking their legs with the nightsticks. Cries went up as they fell and started to retreat. Poor souls, they were fuelled by drink and high on Burrus's agitprop.

Volusenia and I took a step back to let people clear their injured, but I went forward again.

'STOP!' I shouted as loud as I could. 'This will get us nowhere. Go back to the tables and sit. We can talk.'

A bottle flew through the air at me. I jumped back and it glanced off my shoulder. Only when it crashed on the floor and shattered did I see it was full of nails. A mass of bodies flung themselves on us again. Our Praetorian line curved inward, the back line stepping forward to relieve the front. We had two injured now. The problem was that while they only wanted to attack, we only wanted to defend. We tightened the three-quarter circle guarding access to the stairs.

When the crowd pulled back after their third rush, we re-formed, in two lines of twelve. There were five metres between Burrus's rabble and us.

'We need to snatch that bastard,' Volusenia said in my ear. She beckoned Calavia and three others to come forward. Calavia's face was scratched, with a cut leaking blood down her cheek and chin. She looked a little dazed.

'I'll do it,' I said. I nodded at the other three. 'Still use the triangle tactic?' They nodded. 'Let's do it.' And I charged straight for Burrus.

One guard was right behind me, the other two a little to each side. We barrelled through, arms flailing at anybody in our path. I grabbed Burrus's arm and yanked it. The guard immediately behind me swung forward, grabbed Burrus's other arm and we turned a hundred and eighty degrees to frogmarch him out. Then a human wall roared and collapsed on us.

I pushed and pushed at the weight of people piled on top of me, but I had no strength. Hot alcoholic breath and sweat made it five times worse. I coughed and gasped trying to catch some air. My pulse seemed to beat in my ears. I saw one of the other guards near me, eyes shut and unmoving. I still had my hand around Burrus's wrist, but I couldn't see his face in the tumble of arms, legs, stomachs and chins.

I felt movement within the heap of bodies above me and Volusenia's voice muffled. Reluctantly, I let go of Burrus so I could lever myself up. When I stood up, I saw Volusenia's back to me. She was in the front curve of an extended sparse circle. They'd advanced, holding the staves between them to make a flimsy barrier which was working for the moment as the opposition was equally dazed. One of the other guards and I grabbed the unconscious guard and pulled him away from the heap of bodies. Volusenia's curve concertinaed back as we moved towards the stairs.

There was no sign of Burrus.

'Jupiter's balls, here they come again.'

We were down to seventeen. Then the rhythmic thudding started. Gods, what was coming next? Somebody or something was pounding at the fabric of the building. Was it all going to collapse on us?

I raised my nightstick in front of my face to counter a woman, red-faced, eyes glittering, rushing at me with a broken bottle. She was almost hysterical with drunken rage. She fell, sobbing with frustration, but the next figure rushed at me and the next. Burrus had reappeared, his face bruised, hair sticking to his forehead glistening with sweat. The pounding became louder but we were preoccupied defending ourselves.

My arm was aching, my thigh was sore as Hades where somebody had kicked me when I'd fallen. Volusenia's face was set and tight, the other troops struggling against wave after wave of people.

Then an almighty crash from the front of the building. Everybody stopped, mesmerised by the noise. But only for a few seconds. I heard

Burrus screeching encouragement at his rabble. Another rush of bodies flinging itself on us. My chest heaved, grabbing breath. I prayed my end would be quick.

We were engulfed, but the newcomers filtered through our ranks and to the side and hurled themselves on the rabble. Within a few minutes the rioters were contained and a voice roared at them to lie face down on the floor or be silenced permanently.

We stood there like statues in the forum for a few seconds, trembling and too tired to move, but watching the newcomers. They were all in walking clothes but every one of them wore land forces standard issue boots. I let my breath out, wiped my forehead with my sleeve and glanced in Volusenia's direction. She was sitting on the stairs nursing her arm and looked deathly pale. Before I could say anything, a tall woman detached herself from the group, and strode over to Volusenia.

'Centurion Junia Sestina, reporting for duty, ma'am.'

Volusenia stared up at her. 'Well, your timing's perfect, centurion.'

'Yes, ma'am,' Sestina replied. Volusenia looked out into the ballroom full of bodies and wrecked furniture. But I saw the half-smile on the younger woman's lips. A sense of gallows humour, then.

Junia Sestina had brought nearly a hundred troops with her. 'The women were all dismissed the day after Caius Tellus announced he'd accepted the duties of first consul.' She snorted. 'We were all told to return to our father's, husband's or brother's household and sit at our looms. What a load of bullshit.' She glanced at me, but I waved her to continue.

'Most of the women officers were imprisoned. Some have been released, dismissed with a warning to stay at home, but I heard some of the senior ones were sent to the work colonies.' She stared down at the floor. 'Bloody grim, apparently.' She sipped from her mug. 'Anyway, the rest of us kept in touch, using the resistance cell structure. Then we heard the nats were hauling in former women military from *optio* upwards for 'questioning', whatever that meant. We weren't going to hang around to find out so two days ago, we all walked out of our homes and made for the emergency assembly points.

'The men who'd stayed in their units when Tellus took over joined us. They didn't like the way things were developing – they were being used for political jobs. Anyway, they pinched transports from their depots six hours after the women had started on foot from their homes. We met up and travelled on almost to the frontier. The worst bit was dodging the *vigiles* patrols. Women are forbidden to be out after curfew,' she explained.

'All the old rendezvous points worked. We came over the mountains. I told my brother I was sorry if he got into trouble on my account, but I had to do my duty. He nodded, clasped arms and wished me luck.'

She said that all so simply, but I knew what a hard journey that must have been. In every way.

I radioed Atrius that it was safe to bring Silvia back. From the moment she stepped through the hall, she moved slowly, stiffly, disbelief all over her face. At the site of the first dead body, she clasped her hand to her mouth, but held on to her dignity. Quirinia came down from the upper floor and reported that everybody was safe, but nervous. We posted guards on the stairs. Lentilius, his face scratched but otherwise intact, pushed his way through to Silvia. He grinned, possibly in reply to the smile that lit up her face when she spotted him, but mainly from relief, I thought. A pity he hadn't been able to contain Burrus considering he'd been on friendly terms with him.

Half the rest of our original troops had some kind of injury, but Volusenia was worst with a broken collarbone. Luckily, it hadn't broken through her skin. She sat uncharacteristically still, while a medic immobilised her bulging shoulder. While we waited for the ambulance to take her to the accident hospital, she rapped out orders in between gasps to Calavia who tried to absorb her new responsibilities.

'You're promoted captain, immediate effect. You'll have to rely on young Aquilia as best as you can. After this disaster, I strongly recommend we impose martial law for a week at least to deal with these idiots and until things clarify.' She glanced up at me. 'Agreed, *consiliaria*?'

'I think it would be a wise step in the circumstances, with the imperatrix's consent of course.' I frowned at Volusenia. Silvia might be young, but she was still our ruler. And the military would still be subordinate to her. But Silvia nodded without saying anything. 'We have to process the rioters in a fair and proper way,' I said. 'We also need order and instant, known structure. The council agrees on the understanding we revert to civilian authority as soon as practicable.' I glanced at Quirinia, then Lentilius who both nodded. With Volusenia, Silvia and me, we were just quorate. 'Agreed, colonel?'

'Yes!' She winced.

'Very well, authority is formally transferred to the military for fourteen days as an emergency measure.'

'And I formally accept as officer commanding, but Calavia can't handle all this alone, so as senior rank I'm recalling you, major.'

'But—' I protested.

'I'm going to be laid up for a week or two with this damned shoulder, even after I get out of the hospital you insist on sending me to. There's no other option. You've never formally resigned your commission and the troops will respect you.'

Hades, she had boxed me into a corner as cleverly as any politician.

She almost smiled. 'I'm sure the imperatrix agrees with me.'

Pale and grasping the back of a broken chair, Silvia almost smiled back.

16

So the next day I found myself dispensing summary justice at the head of a military field court martial on a collection of bruised, battered and hungover scraps of humanity. Seven bodies were wrapped in blankets for disposal, including Burrus. The doctor, one of Cornelia's Paris legation staff, pronounced him dead from a blow to the head. I'd really wanted Burrus alive. What had been his motivation? Was he a spy or *agent provocateur* for Caius?

Two of the others had died from heart attacks, one from suffocation and the other three from trauma of some kind; all tragic victims.

I sat at the table with Calavia at my right and the newly arrived Junia Sestina on my left recording everything. As a centurion, she had years of hard experience of dealing with stroppy squaddies. This would be an easy run for her. We had no copy of the *Lex Militum* but the Paris legation had brought its civil one, the *Codex Civilis*, all twelve volumes of it.

Most cases were clear. We had no sanction apart from extra work hours and fines; with only one secure room, detention was impossible for so many. Some instinct kept us from involving the New Austrian authorities unless absolutely necessary. Thank Juno, Atrius hadn't been forced to resort to taking Silvia to Joachim Huber. I shuddered to think of the publicity and the pleasure Caius would feel reading about our disunity.

Almost overwhelmingly, the guilty were ashamed. We required

them to attend civil and social education. Many had left school too early and as well as poor job skills had a low sense of community. Something else to look at when we were back in Roma Nova. But we could at least start now.

By late afternoon, we were finished. But the overcrowding had gone beyond critical. The room I'd shared with Quirinia now slept ten. Silvia volunteered to house the same number in her room, but I had Numerus assign Calavia and a couple more Praetorians in there and none of the recent refugees. We started a twenty-four-hour shift system with the additional troops which meant only a third of them were occupying beds at any one time. And they were supervising the punishment work details.

Next day, Numerus set off just after daybreak with a three-vehicle detail and half a dozen Praetorians and was absent most of the day. All I knew was that he drove to the south-west of Vienna with the bodies. They returned exhausted and smelling of smoke as the sun collapsed below the horizon.

Despite the cool evening, I dragged the council members and senior military outside into the garden. Silvia's eyes peeped out from between her scarf and woolly hat like a schoolchild, and she wrapped her arms around her slight body to keep warm. Quirinia and Lentilius looked like barrels of wool in their swathes of scarves and shawls although I noticed he had a smart leather jacket underneath. The military ignored the temperature, but we all wore the black fleeces and walking trousers that were becoming a sort of uniform for us.

'I apologise for bringing you out here but there's nowhere to meet inside in private,' I started. 'We desperately need to find some additional accommodation. We can only just about sleep everybody but we can't administer them, let alone work on the take-back plan. I'd be tempted to rent warehouses and convert them, but the New Austrians would bleat about it infringing their housing regulations. Quirinia, what reserves do we have?'

'We were breaking even financially when people had outside jobs, but now we're eating into our reserves.' She took a deep breath, then coughed at the chill of it. She recovered and cleared her throat. 'Even being very careful, the reserves will be drained to nothing within five months.'

'We have to get people back into work, then, bringing some money in,' said Lentilius.

'Yes, good suggestion, but it takes time. I've tasked Vibianus from the Paris legation staff and his team to work on this. They have all the information about people's skills from when they processed the refugees after they arrived. But we must find more space, and now.'

I woke at half four the next morning after a short night's sleep. We'd ground to a halt, stuffed with liabilities and few resources. I dressed quickly and made my way over sleeping, some snoring, bodies in the corridors to the kitchen. Four staff were already working making bread, grimly kneading and rolling dough like automata. The whole place was piled to the ceiling with dried goods and eight tall refrigerators hummed out of unison.

I made a cup of instant coffee and left them to it. Back in the office area which had been restored at one end of the ballroom after the disastrous Floralia party, I pulled out the telephone directory for Vienna and started making a list of commercial estate agents.

For the next week, I visited more estate agents than I knew existed in Vienna. The only relief was a call to Marina in the EUS. My daughter, after a polite enquiry about my health, prattled on about choosing prams, blankets and soft toys and recounting how many times a day the baby inside her kicked. If a voice could glow with love, hers did. Even as a little girl in the palace nursery, she'd acted the mother with baby Julian. Perhaps this was her strength, her calling, nurturing the next generation.

Fed up with the unexpected summer rain – it was June, for Mercury's sake – I traipsed back late one afternoon accompanied by Atrius and one of Quirinia's finance team. Nothing was big enough or within our budget. Beautifully mannered agents had been very understanding, but… And they were itching to get away for lunch or for the evening. Achim's promise to contact the Red Cross had produced a nil result. We had endured nearly six weeks' overcrowding and it was getting on people's nerves. We'd had outbreaks of stomach upsets due to some people's sloppy hygiene and several fights had broken out. Tonight we were doomed to yet another night stuffed together, worse than in Septarium tenements.

I dumped my umbrella in the stand by the door and was fantasising about sitting down to the luxury of a rich hot chocolate drink with my feet up in a bedroom to myself, when Grania, the French legation staffer who seemed to have turned into our head receptionist complete with desk in the front hall and her own clerk, greeted me.

'Consil—, I mean, major, there's a visitor for you. She's in the drawing room talking to the imperatrix.'

Damn.

They were sitting at the table in the middle of the room. Silvia was staring at the visitor's face and listening intently. I walked between the bedrolls towards the table, bowed to Silvia and bent down and kissed the visitor's face.

'Tante Sabine. A pleasure to see you. What brings you here?'

'Dear me, Aurelia, do I need a reason?'

I felt the warmth rise around my neck. 'I'm sorry, I didn't mean to be abrupt. It's been a hard day.'

'Well, I think I have good news for you. Do you remember my late father-in-law, the one that married your mother's cousin? He had a *Jagdschloss*, a hunting lodge, not far from here. It's gone downhill – it's been shut for twenty years – but there's been a caretaker whom I allow to keep his horses there.' She waved her hand towards the bedrolls occupying every centimetre of the floor. 'If it will help, you're welcome to it.'

I wasn't optimistic about what we'd find, probably a small manor with a large garden that we could use to house thirty or so people. Junia and I drove up the winding tree-lined drive; clumps of grass and moss invaded the stony, broken surface. It seemed to take forever. I glimpsed a square tower between the overgrown trees; no doubt a folly built by some eccentric ancestor centuries ago. The driveway end, almost obscured by tall evergreen shrubs, opened out into an area the size of a parade ground in front of the biggest hunting lodge I'd ever seen. A full-blown five-storey baroque palace stood in front of us.

'Jupiter, it's bloody enormous,' Junia said. She glanced at me. 'Sorry, ma'am, but I've never seen anything like it.'

'Agreed, the Golden Palace in Roma Nova would fit into a quarter of this.'

Square stone columns ran up the central part of the clinically symmetrical building that jutted out from the dull yellow facade. One lonely statue decorated the parapet running each side of a pediment soiled by bird droppings. Peeling and patchy it might have been, but the building must have contained over a hundred rooms, plus a ballroom and a suite of large reception rooms.

We climbed out of our hire van and walked under an imposing gallery across the front facade, through the archway with a door jammed open, and into the interior court as large as the area in front of the house. Before us rose a set of wide, shallow steps leading up to tall double doors festooned with iron and studwork with peels of faded green paint falling away from the wood. A lighter metal hasp and staple were fastened with a padlock that looked as if it weighed a kilogram. The ground floor windows were too dirty for us to see through even though we rubbed hard with our hands.

'Let's find a way round the back,' I said and was turning when I heard the double click of a weapon being cocked.

'*Stillstehen!*'

We froze.

'This is private property. What do you want?' The voice was deep with a lilt. I turned very slowly, nodding to Junia to do the same.

A tall, dark-skinned young man in his early twenties with black hair, in an open shirt, leather jacket, riding breeches and boots, was pointing a double-barrelled shotgun at us, and frowning.

'We have the owner's permission to inspect the property,' I said. 'In fact—'

He snorted. 'Unlikely. Now get on your way. Out.' And he jerked his head in the direction of the archway.

'No. I have a letter from the owner, the *Frau Gräfin* von und zu der Havel.' His eyes flickered, but he kept the barrel pointing at us. 'She said you didn't like being disturbed.'

He stared at me for a second and I had the strangest feeling I had seen him before.

'Show me.'

I unzipped my jacket, reached very slowly into the inside pocket and held the letter out to him.

'Put it on the step.'

I complied and, keeping us covered, he bent down in one graceful movement and swooped it up. He ripped it open; the cream lined envelope floated down to the ground. After he'd scanned the letter and reread it, he lowered his shotgun.

'I am to show you round and open up any parts of the building you wish to see.'

He stalked off in direction of the opposite arch. Junia and I exchanged glances and followed our ungracious host.

'There are bedrooms on three floors, enough so we only have to share in twos, a ballroom that can be converted to more if we put in a false floor and there are more than enough rooms for offices, dining hall and meeting rooms. There's even a library and a games room. The kitchens are old-fashioned but all the services work. We could move in tomorrow.' The nearly five hundred faces stared at me as they stood listening at the last plenary we would hold at the Biedermeier house.

'*Consiliaria* Quirinia will head the task force supervising the move with Vibianus and Grania as her deputies. They will designate an advance party under Senior Centurion Numerus which will move out at 08.00 tomorrow morning. They will ensure the building is safe and has the basic requirements in place. The rest of us will move in over the next week or two.'

The murmuring held a tone of excitement and the noise level rose as people speculated on what the move would mean for them personally.

Before they broke up I called for silence.

'One last thing. Everybody will need to work to put the building into a fully habitable state. Family heads will be assigned tasks for their families, but skilled artisans in anything connected with building, carpentry, horticulture and agriculture should report to Vibianus now. Although we will keep the name of *Jagdschloss* Havel, this will become the headquarters for Roma Novan exiles, but more than that, it will be the spearhead for our work to take back our country from the usurpers and their brutal regime.'

• • •

By the last week in July, we had a clean, plainly furnished, functioning building. Somehow during the frenzy of the long work schedule, Vibianus had started sending people out to job interviews, the taxi drivers were back at work in Vienna and my former estate manager Gavinus organised a task force to clear the garden and grounds for late planting. I thought he was optimistic, but I left him to it. School started for the refugee children which wasn't completely popular with them, but their parents were grateful. The military under Calavia opted to take over a ground-floor wing and the rooms above as a mini-barracks; she said they felt more comfortable in a separated unit.

Silvia hadn't celebrated her seventeenth birthday at the end of January; we'd been too intent on surviving. The shock of the disruption and flight from Roma Nova had made people turn in on themselves and hardly notice external things like birthdays. Now, after the Floralia disaster, the idea of another party made us all shudder. As a very late celebration and a gesture of thanks, Silvia invited Sabine over for a quiet supper.

'Any problems with the caretaker?' Sabine asked me as I walked her to her car afterwards through the first-floor gallery, now the main office, by day full of clerks tapping on keyboards and shuffling paper.

'No, none,' I said. 'We hardly see him. Gavinus, who heads the outdoor team, talks to him now and again about practicalities, but your man keeps to the stables, the keeper's cottage or goes off on his horses. I don't even know if he has any family. I haven't seen one.'

'Lúkas is a bit of an oddball, but seems very well travelled. He knows Berlin and Prague and Bratislava well, even Marienbad and Budapest. I think he has connections on the Russian border. Maybe he's a smuggler!' She laughed. 'I don't need to know, Aurelia. He's kept this place ticking over for the past five years, so I'm content. He turned up one day on an old motorcycle, a kid of sixteen, seventeen, confident as God. I'd just sacked the previous caretaker who'd been selling off doors and decorations to a second-hand architectural dealer. Lúkas goes off sometimes, but only ever for a few days.' She sighed. 'I can't sell this place, it's entailed under *fideicommis* to Joachim, then his children, and we both know that's not going to happen.'

'Perhaps he can adopt?'

'That's up to him. It'll go back to the state eventually if no heirs present themselves.'

In April, we'd applied to the New Austrian court for a formal declaration of ownership for the Biedermeier house. Not a squeak came from Livilla Vara's legation protesting it was Roma Novan government property when the notice was published in the New Austrian government gazette. I knew Cornelia from the Paris legation had invited Vara to lunch in the town on the morning of the Floralia riot, but I hadn't had time to examine her report in detail and read between the lines.

I questioned Cornelia about it when we were preparing the paperwork for the final court hearing which was due on the last day of July. She'd smiled at me and said, 'Once I had insisted her guard sit away from us, I merely reminded Vara of a few essential facts of political life.' She'd refused to explain further. To my surprise they granted ownership within ten minutes. We put the Biedermeier house up for sale immediately to create a financial reserve.

Now settled in our new accommodation – I refused to call it home – we pressed on with our take-back plans. Volusenia, fully recovered, started training the troops hard. I thought she was optimistic as we were still just over the hundred, but she was concentrating on turning them all into special forces mini squads capable of operating in full isolation.

Working with Cornelia, I coordinated our relationships with European and North American governments. I worked long hours throughout the summer, often influencing and persuading across time zones. Sometimes people were on holiday or at conferences and I had to chase them through different intermediaries.

We didn't have good or bad relations with the Eastern European countries and my contacts reported no particular concern from them. Our legation in Moscow, which I hadn't visited, was as neutral as the administration there. But North America was different. The French-speaking countries of Quebec and Louisiane sided with their European colleagues in 'la francophonie', France and the Helvetian Confederation, and gave us their support. Canada followed its British partner in the Transatlantic Federation, but the EUS was strangely aloof. When I spoke to her two months after Floralia, the Washington *nuncia* reported continued polite interest from the American administration, but no enthusiasm for supporting us.

'I'm sorry, *consiliaria*, but I'm still getting a blank wall here,' the *nuncia* said. 'The EUS External Affairs Department are being very reticent. One of the assistants to their deputy secretary, a smart kid just out of Harvard called Hartenwyck, even made an allusion to the possibility of treating us as a stranded embassy.'

I sucked in my breath. The EUS had a practical policy about the recognition of governments. When I'd written to their president's protocol chief a month ago, he'd replied that the question of recognition did not arise; 'We conduct relations with the government in place.'

I had to assume that was exactly what they were doing with Caius's illegal regime. And that tied in with Caius's presence at Langley before the coup.

'Not to worry, *consiliaria*,' the *nuncia*'s voice came through the encrypted telephone. 'I told Mr Wet-Behind-The-Ears Hartenwyck that as we'd bought the plot for the legation in 1792 from Governor General Franklin, over seventy years before the EUS became an independent state, we were perfectly entitled to stay here and grow cabbages in the garden if we wanted to.'

I laughed at her robust attitude, but she was right. She'd fight it through every national and international court if necessary. And the Americans knew it.

17

Just over five hours after talking to Washington, I struggled into wakefulness. I swallowed a yawn and rubbed my gritty eyes. I had to get more sleep; my working hours were so irregular. A face hovered over me. Quirinia. I pushed up onto my elbows.

'Here, drink this.' She offered a large mug and then sat down on the chair she must have pulled over from the other side of the room. She watched as I gulped down the warm tea.

'Some marvellous news.' She was smiling, no, grinning like one of Bacchus's naiads, very un-Quirinia-like.

'What? Caius has surrendered himself or fallen on his sword?'

'No, you silly. Don't you remember you have a daughter? And that she's been pregnant? Well, no more. Marina was delivered of a daughter two hours ago. No complications. Both are well, William Brown says, but Marina is resting.'

Oh, Juno. I gulped the last of the drink down and reached for my clothes.

'No, go and bathe,' she said. 'Marina will be fast asleep for at least another few hours.'

'How does it feel to be a grandmother, Aurelia?' I could hear William Brown chuckling down the phone line. I felt like an old woman of eighty this morning, so didn't comment.

'Is she well? Truly?'

'She's tired, but the doctors aren't worried. She just needs to rest and regain her strength. The baby was quite big, a healthy eight pounds.'

Gods, over three and a half kilograms. No wonder my poor child was exhausted, bearing a giant.

'I must congratulate her when she wakes,' I said. 'Please ask her to call me as soon as she feels up to it.'

My arms almost ached with a longing to cradle Marina in my arms. She was little more than a child herself despite her twenty-one years. But, of course, Marina was thousands of kilometres away, sleeping in a hi-tech American hospital bed, monitored to the last hair on her head with beeps and electronic displays. Her daughter would be wrapped in a cellular blanket and lying separated in an open transparent plastic box at her bedside, not snuggled up to her mother and not surrounded by her family.

Downstairs, Silvia rushed to kiss me and congratulate Family Mitela on the birth of the new heir. The *phut* of a champagne bottle being opened and congratulations flying through the air filled the room. Volusenia, *Nuncia* Cornelia, young Aquilia and Sella stepped forward with Quirinia. The noise quietened down.

'Aurelia Mitela,' Quirinia began in a formal tone. 'The Twelve Families ask if you accept your daughter's child into Family Mitela.'

'I accept her.' I only wished I could be there with Marina. I wanted to pick the child up, to claim her and receive her into my family so she could be raised a Roman.

'Then we welcome her into our number. We are only six Families here including your own, but I speak for all of us. We shall enter her name in the record book in eight days' time if she still lives.'

I bowed to each of them. A tiny tear ran down my cheek. In normal times, I would have been at my daughter's side, the whole Twelve would have been there. The entire Mitela tribe would have been present at Domus Mitelarum at the baby's naming day next week with the house overflowing with food, drink and celebration. My throat hurt as I gulped down my sadness. Nevertheless, I raised my glass to them all and thanked them formally.

• • •

Eight days later, Quirinia and the other Families representatives gathered round in a semi-circle behind me as I initiated the link to the Brown home in New Hampshire.

Marina herself answered. I could see the bookshelves of William Brown's study in New Hampshire behind her as the black and white image settled. My daughter was dressed formally, her hair bound up above a pale but perfectly composed and made-up face. I wanted to pull her to me and hug her, but I had to speak the traditional words.

'*Salve*, Marina Mitela. I trust you are well. Do you have any news for me?'

'*Salve, domina,*' she replied in a clear voice. 'I wish to present my daughter to you.' She reached to the side and brought a bundle towards the camera. Screwed up features and tiny bubbling lips in a pink face. My heart leapt.

'What is her name?' I said.

'She is named Carina and is fully healthy.'

'Then I accept her into the Mitela Family.' I swallowed hard. 'I regret I am not able to tie the *bulla* around her neck myself. Please do this as my proxy.' Marina laid the child down and brought out the gold *bulla* and chain I'd had made by a Viennese goldsmith and sent by courier. She held it up to show me, then fastened it around the baby's neck. I looked down for an instant, then glanced up at Marina to see her kissing the child's forehead. The baby's response was to gurgle. I got up from my seat to allow the other Families representatives to gather round to congratulate Marina. I caught Junia's eye; she smiled and gave me a nod as I wiped a few tears from my eyes, then sniffed. I should be there with her, not living such an important event through technology. After a few minutes, the cluster of well-wishers dispersed and I slid back into the seat and stared into the monitor.

'Are you really well, Marina?'

'Yes, Mama, honestly. They were wonderful in the hospital. I'm a little tired, but I expect that's normal when you are up in the night. William has arranged a nurse to help me for the next few weeks.' Her face became solemn again. 'Thank you for the formal welcome for Carina. I know how busy you are.'

'Darling, I couldn't miss this. And this is what we are fighting for. I *will* come and see you as soon as I can.'

'How is Miklós?'

'He… He's away at the moment.'

'Oh.'

I didn't have anything to add.

'And William?' I said.

She turned and beamed to her left. William's face came into view.

'Hello, Aurelia, how are things?' He was smiling in that half-jokey, half-solemn way that characterised him.

'Let's not talk about me,' I said. 'Let me offer my heartiest congratulations on the birth of your daughter. She looks beautiful.'

The beautiful one then bawled her head off and Marina excused herself and carted the baby off out of view. William slid into her place and I heard the door shut.

'That's a lovely name that Marina's chosen.'

'She called 'Carina' to her just after the baby slithered out, but as she'll live her life here, we'll call her Karen, Karen Brown.'

No, William Brown, I thought, she'll be recorded as Carina Mitela in the family records, whatever you may think.

'She'll retain her Roman name, though, and when she visits us, I'll tell her about her family history,' I retorted.

'Of course,' he said smoothly. But he didn't understand. He wasn't Roma Novan.

Reassured that my child and her child were both well, and that photographs were on their way to me, I settled down to the minutiae of planning. Our activity and confidence grew over the next few months. The leafleting and propaganda campaign were progressing well now that we had a small but dedicated print room. But the most dangerous part was travelling back into Roma Nova. The monitoring stations reported show trials, executions and increasing draconian laws. And we had a steady stream of refugees. Burrus had taught us to screen everybody much more carefully, but we were starting to gather professional middle-class people who would have left a great deal behind. It must be getting grim now for them to run. But they brought talents and skills which only strengthened our capabilities.

I started my international lobbying again and achieved some informal economic sanctions at the European level as well as at the

League of Nations. Governments would hopefully look twice before doing business with the new Roma Novan regime. Unfortunately, our documentary proof and photographs were circumstantial although our communications intercepts helped. But the EEA president sighed at our meeting and said he had no control over the business sector and could do nothing until there was proof Caius's regime had broken international law.

A British investigative journalist had sent back some grim photos and camera footage from Roma Nova before disappearing. Caius Tellus dismissed the images as staged exaggeration by criminal elements and tried to reassure the international community his government was investigating the reporter's disappearance but few believed him. I pitied the poor reporter's family; unlikely they'd see him again.

Vibianus's staff was compiling dossiers from the refugees' stories; it was providing the jigsaw pieces to gradually build up the whole picture, but it was slow work. The positive result was that questions were being asked in the European press at last and on the broadcast media. Opinion was wavering about Caius in Europe, but not in the EUS.

'From the snippets we've picked up on the intercepts, we're pretty sure the Americans are supplying Caius. Not overtly, of course, but nothing else explains why he's still solvent,' Volusenia said at the council meeting in August.

'Well, he has the silver, of course,' I chipped in.

'Does he, though?' Quirinia asked. 'We've been monitoring transactions as best we can and the volume seems to have decreased steadily. It looks as if it's dropped to nearly fifty per cent of the previous twelve months. I'm sorry I can't be more exact.'

'My friend Prisca Monticola was the head of the Silver Guild until just after the coup,' I said. 'She was thrown out, of course, but she's been sending occasional letters via the poste restante office in Vienna. She hasn't once mentioned production or trading, only family chit-chat, her aunt's cat and household stuff. Knowing her, she's still keeping an eye on anything to do with silver, even from the sidelines. I'd have thought she would have hinted if it was going downhill.' I paused. 'Actually, I haven't heard from her for over five weeks.'

Vibianus looked up from the notes he was taking. 'Excuse me for interrupting, *consiliaria*, but do you still have those letters?'

'Yes, of course, but they're personal. Nothing to do with anything silver or politics related.' I made a point of looking at my watch. 'Can we get back to the agenda?'

'I'm sorry, I don't want to be discourteous.' He smiled his diplomat's smile. 'She may very well be using the silver traders' code. It's a form of confidential communication. It's not only military and political organisations that use codes.'

'Explain.'

'As you can imagine, silver is vulnerable to theft. To prevent information getting out about caravans, or mint deliveries, the miners and traders in the fifth century developed a system of codes. It didn't rely on substitution or mathematical formulae, but everyday phrases with set meanings.' He glanced at me. 'It's not designed to circumvent the transaction and reporting regulations in force these days, just a way of enhancing security and passing on market news.'

'How do you know this?'

'My mother's family were traders and she taught me some of it when I was considering becoming an apprentice in my uncle's business. I, er, stuck it out for a year.'

'Oh, gods, have we been missing vital intelligence?' I said. The rest of the council stared at Vibianus.

'Well, don't just sit there waiting for flies to nest in your mouth, major, go and fetch Monticola's letters,' Volusenia barked at me.

We abandoned the rest of the meeting and Vibianus started working on Monticola's letters minutes after I set the envelopes down on the table. Like a good bureaucrat, he carefully started a new page on his notepad, sorted the envelopes by date and opened the first one.

Volusenia paced up and down the office, disappearing into the garden every so often. The rest of us sat in various positions of unease on the group of chairs in the meeting room and waited. I couldn't bear it after an hour and a half and joined Volusenia in the courtyard.

'Anything?' she said, glaring at me.

'Not yet. He's rough-drafted some and is collating the rest. I have months of them – a good dozen and a half.'

'Pluto in Hades! If only you'd recognised them for what they were.'

'Don't get at me – it didn't occur to me this code system could exist.' I scowled at her. 'And while we're on it, stop calling me major and ordering me around like one of your barrack pets. I've relinquished my military role definitively.'

'Ha! Touchy, aren't we? Well, as it's a national emergency you're still on the active list until released by the imperatrix. You're stuck.'

'You're enjoying this, aren't you?'

'When you're as short-handed as I am, you'll understand why. We're training up a new officer corps by promoting some of our own people and co-opting some of the new arrivals that have at least three years' service in their background, but there are few who have practical combat leadership experience on the ground and you're one of them. We won't need a foreign minister when we invade, but I'll need an effective ground commander to lead the troops.'

I said nothing, but kept walking by her side.

'I apologise if I've been inappropriate. I'm only a rough old soldier,' she said gruffly.

I laid my hand on her shoulder. 'No, I apologise for being sensitive. Anxious times for all of us.'

But she was right. That evening I decided to divide my time between the political work and training with Volusenia's troops.

I'd sent everybody to bed at midnight, but Vibianus worked on, hunched over the table. The only sign of fatigue he showed was when I brought him a cup of tea at six the next morning. He stretched his arms out then raised his right hand to his face, drew his thumb and fingers together across his eye sockets to meet in the middle. He took a deep breath.

'I've done them all and written a summary and report of the most salient points. Perhaps I could take the liberty of asking you to present them to the council. I feel I must go and lie down for a little while.'

He finished his drink, set the cup down and stumbled to his feet as if his legs had forgotten how to work. I put my hand out to steady him, but he shook his head, turned and left. I picked up the sheaf of paper. His rounded handwriting on the first pages had degenerated into a scrawl, but perfectly readable.

• • •

'The first two are chit-chat,' I said to the council later that morning. 'There's nothing hidden that Vibianus could spot and he was keen to find something – they're the first he tackled. But at the end of the third one, Monticola makes a throwaway reference to our time in Berlin, except what she says isn't quite true.'

'What do you mean?' Volusenia said.

'We left the reception at eight and went to eat at an Italian place in Savigny-Platz, not lunch at the Hotel Adler.'

'Perhaps she didn't remember properly?' Quirinia said.

'That's what I thought. But that was the night she almost had her head blown off by a gangster. Not something you'd forget. But I didn't think anything of it, we had so much going on here. Vibianus has noted she used the German word for eagle, Adler, not difficult to see the connection to "Aquila".'

'Hardly a secure code,' Volusenia said.

'No, but Vibianus says it's one of a number of opening words meaning a message follows.' I picked up the fourth letter. 'Here's the first message: "State confiscation. Black forecast. Avoid trading." Pretty straightforward, I'd say. The next one is, "Breaking network. Implementing production slowdown." Then "Production seventy-two, distribution fifty-nine, stockpile." Vibianus writes this means production is at seventy-two per cent on the previous quarter and only fifty-nine per cent is being distributed. They're finding some way of hiding the difference.'

I laid the sheet of Vibianus's notes on the table. Silvia, at my side, stifled a yawn, but she picked up the sheets and examined them.

'Juno, if she and the others get caught, Caius will have them slaving on the silver-face at Truscium itself,' Quirinia said. 'But a significant blow to his finances.' She almost purred.

'The next few are reports of output,' I continued. 'It's falling all the time. This one says, "Full hostile audit. Arrests", then three months ago, "Mercenary takeover". Until Vibianus wakes, I don't know what that signifies. The last letter from her five weeks ago contains these phrases, "Crisis. Grave personal danger". This is why I got you all up at this time. Given all this valuable information, we can't leave her dangling – we have to get her out.'

Nobody spoke for a few seconds.

'Obviously it's regrettable that's she's in such a situation,'

Volusenia said. But we can't organise a snatch squad to save one non-strategically important person, however prominent.' Her tone was measured, almost sympathetic.

I took a deep breath to soak up some of the fury rolling through me. Then another to grasp some balance before I spoke. I glared at Volusenia, nearly hating her.

'Prisca Monticola has risked everything to get these messages out. The gods know what danger she's put herself in to even acquire this information, let alone send it out. Even you, Colonel Volusenia, must have a distant memory of how bloody difficult it is to gather intelligence let alone communicate it. Or is it so long ago that you've forgotten?' I heard the biting sarcasm flow out of me.

Silvia gasped, Quirinia laid her hand on my forearm, but I ignored her, locking eyes with Volusenia. The others shrank back into their chairs.

'You will withdraw that remark, *consiliaria*,' she bit back.

'Or what?'

'Aurelia—' This time Quirinia shook my arm, but I ignored her.

Volusenia refused to break, her eyes boring into mine.

'Stop!' Silvia cried. She leapt to her feet. 'Please stop.' I wrenched my gaze away from Volusenia to Silvia, refocusing my eyes after the hard glare. Silvia's cheeks were flushed in a white face and she looked ready to burst into tears.

'How can we do anything about this if you just fight all the time? I thought you were supposed to be helping me.' She turned and ran off, with Lentilius scurrying behind her. Just as he reached the door he turned, stared at me, then narrowed his eyes as if thinking something through. What on earth was that about?

I pounded round the edges of the Jagdschloss former pleasure gardens now showing the wilting leaves of winter vegetables. This October was surprisingly warm and clear. As I turned along the east side, the horizontal white sunlight nearly blinded me. But that wasn't why my eyes were damp. Prisca and I had not only bonded because of the attack in Berlin, we had met regularly for theatre or a simple meal. Each time we'd met we'd instantly reconnected, often laughing our way through to the early hours. I'd sponsored her daughter on an exchange to a silver processing company in Birmingham in England. She wasn't only a sounding board, someone to commiserate with or congratulate, she was my friend. I stopped and dragged breath back into my lungs. I would not abandon her, whatever Volusenia said.

I apologised to Silvia for my rudeness, but not for my point of view. She gazed at me with wide eyes, but a firm mouth and a defiant chin.

'I understand, Aunt Aurelia, but you're the one who says we have to take the wider view and not to let our personal feelings interfere with our goals.'

Gods, she was brutal as only a seventeen-year-old could be.

She relaxed her face a few millimetres.

'I'm sorry, but there are so many in similar situations. The best thing for everybody is to take back Roma Nova as quickly as we can.'

I'd taught her too well.

18

After a training session drilling field tactical basics into people who'd forgotten anything they'd ever learnt in their two-year compulsory service, I made for the bar corner in the barracks section mess and downed a large brandy. It wasn't French, but the local stuff. It stung as it coursed down my throat. Nevertheless, I took a refill. As I raised the glass to my lips, another figure in olive green sat down on the stool beside me. Calavia.

'Major.'

'Hello, Pia.'

Bit early, isn't it?'

'Don't you start,' I shot at her. 'Sorry.' I looked down at the counter. 'I'm fed up, tired and cross. Ignore me.'

'I heard the colonel had given you a hard time. She's quite correct. We have so few resources, even with the recent influx.'

True, we were up to just over fifteen hundred now. Quirinia had split them into *vici*, or village communities with separate councils to make administering them more manageable. But they were hardly an invading army – a third of them were too old or young.

'I know. Subject closed,' I said and returned my attention to my glass. But I burned inside.

Pia Calavia looked round the room; the steward had disappeared. We were alone. She fixed her gaze on the bar counter.

'You know Colonel Volusenia's been sending groups over the border? Just as a test.'

I hoped my mouth didn't hang open. And Volusenia had had the nerve to castigate me in open council.

'And how long has this been going on?'

'A couple of months.' Calavia glanced up. 'Only small groups of professional troops like Junia Sestina and only for a few hours. The colonel went herself last week for the day. Now she's planning a four-day one next week.' She shrugged. 'I thought you ought to know, but she's so worried about losing you.'

'Hades take her, what right has she to baby me? Well, there's one extra going.'

I caught Volusenia in the garden, puffing on her post-supper cigarette.

'You'll die of those things if you manage to survive your little holidays in Roma Nova.'

She broke into a coughing fit.

'Who?' she rasped. 'Oh, bloody Calavia, I suppose. You two are as thick as thieves. I'll talk to her later. Wonder how she likes scrubbing floors with her toothbrush?'

'Don't take it out on her. What in Mars' name were you doing, gallivanting off like some cowboy without Council's permission? '

She threw the butt in the hedge. 'Security.' She touched her shoulder. 'This taught me to be cautious since Burrus. I was going to inform the council at the next meeting,' she grumped.

We walked on in silence. At the garden wall I stopped and looked out over the parkland. 'It's a positive step, no question, and a wonderful opportunity to get hard intelligence and make contacts with any resistance. I'm going with them next week.'

'Out of the question,' she snapped. 'And don't try and change my mind.'

'Look, Volusenia, I'm not arguing about it. The op's planned already – you can't refuse me. Besides, one thing we really need is proof for the international courts to get tighter sanctions imposed. I know who to contact and what to look for. I go.'

I turned and marched off, leaving her calling my name.

I got to Silvia before she could, but she wouldn't budge either.

'If Colonel Volusenia says no, then I must respect what she says.'

She sighed. 'Sometimes, you make this really difficult for me. I respect you and your guidance, and your love, but I can't give in to you all the time. We daren't risk you being caught or even injured.' Her eyes pleaded with me. 'Please, Aunt Aurelia, don't.'

She twisted her fingers together as if she was asking to go out with friends to a late-night party. If only she was – that was what she should be doing at seventeen.

'Darling, I'm so sorry. I didn't mean to upset you. It's the last thing I want to do.' I touched her cheek with my fingers and gave her a smile I didn't feel.

I stalked back to my room. I knew in my head they were both right and I would have said the same thing, but that made me more angry inside.

The next day, I was training with Junia and her group. Our task was to approach the keeper's cottage without being detected. Maybe it would provoke a reaction from him. I hadn't seen him to speak to for a couple of weeks although I'd seen a figure riding a horse along a bridleway a week ago.

The dozen trainees were fit enough but they hadn't yet developed the instinct for stealth. Out of seven attempts they set the proximity alarms off four times. Junia creased her eyes into slits and her lips almost disappeared. Her chest heaved with frustration.

'You're a bunch of imbeciles – dead imbeciles, so perhaps the world is safer now,' she hissed at them. 'We're staying here until midnight, if necessary. If it goes past that, I'll decimate you myself.'

We stood in the shelter of trees across the way from the keeper's cottage. She glanced at me. 'Major, would you mind showing them how it's done?'

I cursed Junia in my head, but nodded at her. I grabbed a stave with a shoulder strap, which acted as a substitute rifle, from the nearest recruit and edged forward to just behind the tree line. Junia was using random pattern proximity alarms that Brown Industries had supplied. Mars knew where the coverage was. I only prayed I didn't set one off.

I crouched down and skimmed the stretch of ground. The cover was poor – in the back garden a half-metre-high hedge, vegetable patch with the remains of squashes and tomato plants, two rows of parallel bamboo canes for runner beans, but now no growth. Leaves and late fruit covered the apple and pear trees – we were in October after all – but not one of the trunks was a person wide. And there were two unshuttered windows overlooking the garden. Several had attempted this red herring and failed.

The front courtyard was a nightmare – total exposure. The ground to the windowless side wall was open, but only ten metres and the wall would give shelter. Five seconds max to cross to it. I stood up, shouldered the fake rifle and launched myself.

Back to the wall, I slithered along to the corner. No alarm scream. Nothing. Crawling along the ground, I cleared the first window opening and approached the door. I stood, fake rifle ready, took a breath and grasped the door handle. I felt a slight resistance as the spring in the handle mechanism contracted, but it made no noise. I eased the door open a few centimetres to slide in and met a double-barrelled shotgun in my face.

Miklós, my beloved companion whom I'd left in the city, was sitting on a wooden carver, a small table with a half-full glass of beer at his side. The chair was placed facing the front door. He wore countryman's clothes and a smug smile. My heart thudded, not from the sprint to the cottage. I took a half-step forward, put my hand out, but he didn't move towards me. Instead he took another sip of his beer, but kept the barrels pointing in my direction. I let my hand drop. Disappointment welled up through me. He didn't want to touch me.

'I thought somebody would get through eventually,' he said. 'I've been watching you all afternoon. Pathetic.'

'Really?' I hadn't seen him for months and he wanted to play word games. But his eyes sparkled. He burst out laughing. He broke his shotgun, laid it on the table in that graceful way of moving I knew so well and stood up. In one movement he stretched out his arm, grabbed me by the waist, brought my free hand up to his lips and kissed the back of my fingers. The fake rifle fell from my fingers and clattered onto the tile floor.

'Miklós.'

'Yes, wife?' and he laughed that rich, sexy laugh again.

I waved my hand feebly, but my heart was thundering. He brought his lips down on mine, crushing them. I grasped the edge of his waistcoat. I no longer cared if I breathed. I would be happy to die of pleasure at this very moment.

Which is precisely when Junia Sestina clattered in with her heavy boots.

'I thought your soldier friend's eyes were going to burst out of their sockets,' he said and chuckled. 'Her face was as red as the sunset when she left.' He pulled me back down, his arm clamping me across the back of my waist. I thrilled to the touch of his warm skin, the faint down on his chest, even the scar of the bullet I had put through him near fifteen years ago.

He drew the coarse cotton sheet up over us. This wasn't the most comfortable bed I'd ever lain in, but that wasn't important. Neither were the plain furnishings or floral curtains in the caretaker's cottage.

I flicked my fingers on Miklós's cheek.

'How long have you been here, amusing yourself at our expense?'

I tried hard not to sound accusing.

He traced his fingertip down my bare spine as I lay on top of him in the bed. I shivered at the soft electrical sensation.

'Only since yesterday.' He smiled up at me. 'This time.'

'What do you mean, "this time"?'

'I come and stay with Lúkas now and again. It's convenient for my business.'

'Why? Who is he to you?'

Miklós sighed. 'Aurelia, stop being a Praetorian. You're not interrogating me. He's a young man close to me. Just accept it.'

I seized his wrists. 'Tell me! Oh gods, he's not your son, is he?'

'And what if he were?'

'But—'

'Use your brain, woman. He's twenty-four, I'm thirty-eight.' He laughed. 'He's a cousin. You met him when he was nine. He was the boy who gave you my rose at the airport.'

I released him and propped myself up on my elbows. I'd been flying back to Roma Nova to pursue Caius who was targeting my daughter, then a child of five. Miklós had disappeared, but had wished me good hunting on the note attached to the rose. I searched

Miklós's face which was solemn now, then I looked away. He gave a long sigh and ran his fingers down my spine.

'You're going hunting him again, aren't you?' he said in a low voice.

I nodded, then buried my face in the space at the base of his neck.

'Surely you don't want to go on this routine exercise now?'

Volusenia was trying to sound reasonable. It didn't suit her. We walked on towards the back garden wall. The sun was warm for October with not even a light breeze to dilute it. The parkland was green and lush again, having recovered from the hot summer. Its softness was a complete contrast with the brutal place we were planning to go.

'It makes no difference,' I said. 'If it's as routine as you say, then how can it be risky?'

'I'm so fed up of trying to explain to you that I'm almost ready to let you go and Mercury take the consequences!'

'Look, this is an important intelligence gathering mission with specific targets. You say you can get me into the palace. Well, who better to find the evidence we want on Caius? I've handled more government paperwork than you've been on exercises.' Volusenia went to speak, but I continued. 'Yes, I have. I'm uniquely placed to identify exactly what we need to show the international community and tighten the rather pathetic sanctions currently existing against Caius.'

She was silent for a few moments then glanced up at me. 'Your daughter's baby is only a few weeks old. Don't you want to go to the EUS and see her?'

'I've already spoken to Marina and her husband. They completely support my decision to remain here.' I tilted my chin up at Volusenia. My heart had been wrenched at that decision but, strangely, it was Marina who had been most insistent during our last telephone call.

'I am only one daughter, Mama. You must stay for all daughters of Roma Nova, including the imperatrix. Silvia needs you more than ever.' She'd gulped, then said, 'I have some friends here now and William is taking the best care of me. I want my child to be able to come back to a free Roma Nova, not be condemned to be an exile.'

I could hardly reply, my throat had tightened so much; then transatlantic static had ended our call.

Volusenia's voice pulled me back into the present.

'And what would your little friend say if you didn't come back?'

'He's not little.'

She smirked. 'Well, you know best in that department.'

I swatted her arm with the back of my hand and grinned. 'He's my companion of fifteen years and in this place my contracted spouse, so some respect, please.'

She grinned back. 'All the more reason to stay and enjoy his, er, company.'

I grasped the top of the low wall with both hands and leant forward.

'I know you mean well, but I cannot ignore the call of going back. Roma Nova is in my blood, my heart and my head. It's not simple duty. It's as if Mitelus himself is standing beside me, from the end of the fourth century. He's wearing his chain mail *lorica*, *gladius* in his right hand, gripping his *scutum* shield in his left. And behind him all the later Mitelae, armed, ready for their battles.'

'Have you been at the brandy again?'

'No, and you know it.' I stood up. 'Marcella Volusenia, this is my battle in my generation and I won't shirk it.'

'You look so happy, Aurelia, at the moment. I think you're wrong to go, but I'm not going to stop you. If I'm honest, the troops couldn't have a better commander.' She chewed her lip. 'But if you get caught or injured, I'll come after you so hard, you'll wish you were already dead.'

'I'm trembling with fright.' But my body was singing already with the adrenaline coursing through it.

EXPLORATION

19

———

I dozed on the train from Vienna to Graz, at least I tried to. Last night, Miklós had made love with me so tenderly, I had wept, but he kissed the tears away.

'You have to go. I know,' he said. 'I'm not going to try and persuade you otherwise, but be very careful, Aurelia. Roma Nova is a brooding, destroyed place now. Trust nobody – friends won't still be friends. If they are your true friends, they'll be in camps or prison.'

I was repelled at his cynicism; it couldn't be that bad.

I shivered as I left his bed, dressed and trotted back to the kitchen in the main building to eat a warm breakfast with the others. Junia Sestina nodded at me as I poured my coffee.

Typical for October, it was fresh at six in the morning as we waited, dotted along the main Vienna southbound platform dressed like all the other commuters. The women carried small suitcases and the men black leather briefcases like accountants.

Two and a half hours later, we left the Graz station in ones and twos as if setting off for another boring day at the office. Four hours after that, now in walking gear, Atrius and I were climbing down the foothills onto the Roma Novan high alp. How different it was from the last time I was here, only a few kilometres to the east, shot by Caius with my life's blood seeping out of me. I shivered, but it may have just been the cool mountain breeze.

We rested overnight in a remote barn that the earlier recce groups had found and provisioned. Swapping into the more traditional clothes worn these days in Roma Nova, plus farmers' boots and cloaks, we started off for the city at five the next morning carrying heavy baskets of vegetables on our backs.

'Are you sure we don't look like something out of a previous century or two?'

'You're going to be shocked how things have changed. And don't, for Mars' sake, backchat any men, especially men in uniform or wearing rebels' armbands.'

'I was at the briefing, *optio*,' I said in my coldest voice.

'Yes, I know, but first-timers are rarely ready for it.'

I was too annoyed to answer. He knew I wasn't an amateur, so why was he treating me like one? I had the answer at the first village we came to. The dangling body, hands tied behind it, was a black silhouette against the late morning sun. As we approached the village centre, I saw it had been a woman. Her trousers were daubed with red paint and so was her face. The remains of her shirt flapped in the breeze. She had been flogged.

'Keep it together,' Atrius growled as I gagged. 'Look down at the road and walk as if your feet hurt.'

I leaned on my walking stave, stumbling along the pavement which had several potholes. I glimpsed left and right, but there wasn't a single person around. The small general store was boarded up and the inn looked as if it hadn't had a customer for years. The garage had the notice 'No more petrol' dangling at an angle from the middle pump.

Something bumped into my legs. A young girl, six or seven, barefoot, in tunic and short jacket. Her eyes were huge, unlike her body. She said nothing, just held her hand out, hesitantly.

I crouched down.

'What do you want, darling?'

'Eat.'

I set my basket down. In a flash, her arm went in, she grabbed a carrot and ran off.

Atrius pulled me up. 'Let's get out of here before anybody sees us.'

We walked in silence until we reached open fields. I stopped by a tree, fell on my knees and was sick. The lid on my basket burst open and vegetables scattered all over the road. Atrius wiped my face and gave me some water from a third-hand plastic bottle. My stomach had stopped spasming and I was about to stand up when I heard a vehicle approaching.

'Stay down, pretend to still be sick.'

A dusty black van with 'RMN 7th District' hand-painted on the side pulled up, braking sharply.

'What are you two up to?' A male voice. I heard the car door slam, then saw a pair of boots and black trousers.

'My mother's sick, she's just chucked up her breakfast.'

'She's got food to waste, spewing it all over the public highway? You want to give her less to eat.' I heard laughter from inside the van.

My arm was wrenched up and I was hauled to my feet. A man, about forty, with an inbuilt sneer under a nose that dripped looked at me as if I was a piece of stock.

'She looks too well fed,' the first man said and poked my stomach. I was about to retaliate, almost by instinct, when Atrius grabbed me by the waist and shook me.

'She's a lot skinnier than before I sent her out into the vegetable fields, sir.' He laughed.

'Good man,' the man said and patted Atrius on the shoulder. 'Show me your papers, while we're here.'

I glanced up at Atrius. I had no papers. Nobody had given me any. *Merda.* How could the mission team have forgotten something that simple? My stomach spasmed again and I retched.

'That looks all in order. On your way, then, and keep the old bat in line.'

'Thank you, sir.' Atrius bobbed his head as the man climbed back in his seat and they drove off. I scurried around and gathered up the vegetables. We stared at them until the last dust swirl had swallowed the car up.

'Kindly explain to me what happened there.'

'We have to keep moving. Let's go.'

'We're not going anywhere until I get a few answers. First of all, you can drop that huffy, abrupt manner. We have to act in character, but do not carry it over when we're alone in the middle of nowhere.

May I remind you I was leading undercover operations while you were still shitting your nappies.'

'Sorry, ma'am,' he mumbled.

'Accepted.' We started walking again. After a few minutes, I asked, 'Why haven't I got any papers?' I glanced over at him. 'I mean, they didn't seem too worried.'

He gave a short, hard laugh. 'You're a woman – you don't count. You're a footnote on mine.'

The *mansio* we stopped at for the night was comfortable, but dirty. At the evening meal in the large dining room, we sat at the long benches eating our stew, which was mostly vegetables with the odd lump of chewy meat. Food at these roadside hotels had always been plain, but this was ridiculous. The clerk was sullen as he assigned us beds in the dormitories, but took Atrius's *solidi* without comment. Caius's grim features decorated some of the coins, but Severina's nervous portrait smiled from the five *solidi* note.

We reached the city mid-morning the next day and went straight to the market. I remembered to stay slightly behind Atrius and keep my head covered with a scarf. Instead of the noisy, sometimes boisterous, seething mass of a year ago – shoppers, traders, hucksters and tourists, all pushing past and exchanging insults and greetings – it was dead. Instead of over two hundred stalls, there couldn't have been more than thirty. One or two had a good selection of fruit and vegetables at outrageously inflated prices, several were selling second-hand irons, toasters, hairdryers and electrical toys for just a few *solidi* each. Others displayed curtains, sheets, towels and tablecloths; all neatly folded, but faded. Grey faces, desperate faces, worn clothes and even some people without shoes or boots. It looked like the third world.

The *macellum* doors were guarded by two tall figures in maroon carrying riot gear. Why? It was only a shopping centre.

'Atrius.' I tugged on his cloak. 'Why are the *vigiles* guarding the *macellum*?'

'Because of the food riots. Now only the privileged can enter.'

'Juno.'

'Come on, here's our contact.' And he headed for a stall on the opposite side of the plaza with nearly empty plastic trays of root vegetables being rearranged by a grumpy-looking man with thinning black hair and a lined face. We introduced ourselves as Prima and Secundus.

'You took your time getting here,' he said to Atrius, ignoring me. 'Well, show me what you've got.'

Atrius signalled me to take my basket off and give it to the man.

'Well, don't dawdle, woman, lift mine down.' I stared at him for a second or two. What did he think I was? He was perfectly capable of dropping his own carrying basket to the ground. He gave me a fiery look, and I suddenly realised what was expected. I reached up, strained my arms at the weight. I handed the basket to the stallholder and backed off, keeping my head down.

'Oh, Pluto,' mumbled Atrius.

I looked sideways. *Vigiles*, and carrying nightsticks in their hands.

They stopped very close to us. I shrank against Atrius.

'Papers.'

As one read them, the other, taller one prodded at the vegetables we had brought, then upended my basket, covering the vegetables in another layer of dust. I didn't move, not wanting to break our cover, but I seethed inside.

'Well, pick them up, then,' the tall one ordered.

I grabbed the basket and started running after the rolling vegetables. I bent over to pick some up and the next minute I was sprawled on the ground, eating dirt. The bastard had kicked me in the bottom. And the two of them were laughing. I counted to ten. Then again. I got to my knees and eased myself up. I scrabbled around for the rest of my vegetables, but kept the two *vigiles* in front of me. My first thoughts were only of how I wanted to beak every bone in their laughing, bullying bodies. Then I wept for my Roma Nova, the misery around me, the hanged woman, that starving child. When I stood up, the tears were flowing freely.

'Here, drink this.' A smile and a friendly voice at last. The woman held out a mug of black tea. 'Sorry, we've run out of milk, but at least we have some sugar.'

I looked down at the quarter-filled creased paper packet on the table, but shook my head. I couldn't rob people of such luxuries. Four of us were crowded in a top floor room of a nineteenth-century block of flats. Atrius and the other man perched on the edge of a single bed. The end of a second bed against the far wall was just visible behind the edge of an old chintz curtain hanging from a rail on the ceiling. In the corner was a small basin and cooking unit. The table and two chairs where the woman and I sat were solid, if scratched. Bright sunlight from the roof light cheered up the whole room, but it was still a poor place.

The vegetable seller had brought us here after winding through the streets and cutting through courtyards and one passage even I didn't know. Atrius and I had trudged up three flights of stairs in the old block whose floors became shabbier as we ascended.

'My brother,' the woman nodded at the younger man. 'He studies engineering at the Central University and I'm graciously allowed to stay with him as his servant. They chucked me out, of course.'

'Marcia was top of her law class in her last year,' piped up the young man. 'So unfair.' His face looked like that of a fighting dog.

'Sextus,' she said, 'leave it.'

He shrugged.

'Let's get on.' Marcia looked at me. 'Prima, you're on the palace cleaning detail tomorrow morning. Our contact is the housekeeper.' I stared at her. Did she mean my old friend Drusilla who had helped me escape from Caius last year? 'She's a tough bird, but clever and a firm friend,' Marcia continued. 'She'll get you into the first consul's office, but warns she'll have to deny you if you get caught. If that happens, she'll be in trouble, but might get away with a whipping.'

'A whipping?' I stared at her and gripped the base of my throat. 'You don't mean like flogging?'

'No, they only flog men. Whipping's for women until first blood, so only a few strokes usually.' She looked at me, puzzled. 'Didn't they brief you about that?'

Volusenia had mentioned that ancient punishments, including corporal and capital punishment, had been introduced as standard. Phobius, Caius's sidekick, had threatened to flog me last year, but I hadn't believed he really would have carried it out. The reality of a woman with her hands tied above her and attacked legally with a whip until her back bled revolted me. I shivered.

'You'll have to do better than that, Prima,' Marcia said sharply. 'If you're going to wobble at the sound of a mild punishment, you'll be useless going near any of the work colonies. And that's where they'll send you if you get caught.'

I nodded, but didn't reply. She turned to Atrius next.

'Secundus, you'll continue as a vegetable seller and deliver to the palace in the morning. You'll have to sign Prima in as she's on your ID card. Once in the kitchen, ask for a glass of water. The red-haired sous-chef, Paulus, will pass you through and kit you out as a steward. After that, you'll have to find Prima on your own. Be a little careful with Paulus – he's brittle. He's very talented as a chef, but he's working under duress to stop his wife being sent to a colony.'

Marcia took hold of my hands and inspected them. I'd spent part of the evening in the barn rubbing gravel all over them to redden them, and jamming dirt into my nails. She poured the rest of the tea out of the teapot into a bowl and thrust it at me.

'Soak your hands for at least half an hour in this, then rub it into your face.'

That afternoon, I fished out the three fat envelopes we'd hidden in the bases of our bags. Climbing on Atrius's shoulders, I stashed them in the loft space above the ceiling in the communal bathroom.

The next morning, we slipped out of the building just before six. In the market square, a long queue had already formed outside the main baker's shop and a slightly shorter one along the front of a butcher's. It was mild, more than was usual in October.

We picked up baskets from the grumpy market trader, Atrius's larger one half filled with vegetables, mine full of fruit, and made our way on foot up the hill to the Golden Palace. Only a couple of vans, a legionary personnel carrier and the odd car were about. A bus chugged up the hill overtaking us; it was full of grey faces at the grey windows.

At the service entrance, armed nationalist guards thumbed Atrius's ID, searched his face, took their time, presumably to make him anxious. I stayed in his shadow, content to be ignored. Eventually, they told Atrius to sign in a register on the side table and add me on the same line.

One guard thrust a card attached to a lanyard at me.

'Make sure you wear that at all times. You don't want a whipping, do you?' He leered at me. I retreated behind Atrius and looked suitably cowed.

We made our way down to the kitchen and domestic area. Gods, it was so familiar, but the corridors were dingy, dirty marks on the door frames, the stone flags on the floor stained and chipped. How could Drusilla let it get into this state, if she was indeed still the housekeeper?

'You, with the vegetable baskets. I haven't seen you before.' Atrius froze at the voice behind us. I shrank back against the wall, eyes down, but watched sideways.

'No, sir,' Atrius bobbed his head. 'Fulso is sick and asked me to do the delivery. I'm his nephew, Secundus.' He proffered his ID which the guard read.

'Let's see inside your baskets.'

We had to take every vegetable and piece of fruit out. The guard picked over my fruit and helped himself to two apples.

'Who's the woman?'

'My mother. She's a cleaner here.'

'I don't remember her, but they all look alike to me.' He barely glanced at me. 'Pack all this crap up and get on your way. I'll have the same tomorrow and maybe her as well.'

'He's a charmer, isn't he?' I whispered as soon as I was sure we were out of earshot. Atrius merely grunted.

We knocked at the kitchen door and on cue the sous-chef beckoned us in.

'You come with me,' he said to Atrius, then looked me up and down. 'The woman should report to the housekeeper, next door along.'

I knocked on the housekeeper's door, heard 'Come' in reply in a harsh tone. Pluto. That didn't sound like the Drusilla I knew, but Marcia had told us the housekeeper was on our side. I took a deep breath, turned the handle and stepped into the room. The woman at the desk looked up and I was shocked to see how dull her eyes were in a face that drooped. Dark brown shadows filled the dips under her eyes. It *was* Drusilla, the one who had looked after me and helped me escape last year, but a very diminished one. Her original brown head of hair was now half grey.

'Oh, the new cleaner?'

'Yes, ma'am,' I said in my normal voice.

She jerked her head up, searched my face, then sat back in her chair.

'It can't be—,' she whispered. 'You're dead.'

I touched both my ears and raised an eyebrow.

She shook her head.

'Thank the gods for that,' I said. 'We can talk properly.'

'But how can you be alive? They showed photos of your body.'

'Well, I'm harder to kill than Tellus thinks. But he knows I'm alive. He sent an assassination squad, but they killed my bodyguard instead.' I swallowed, remembering Miklós's anger and sadness at his friend's murder.

Her eyes darted all over my face.

'What happened to your eyes?' she asked.

'Nothing.' I smiled at her. 'I'm wearing these new coloured contact lenses to dim the colour. Mitela blue is too well known.'

'Gods, yes.' She stared at me for a few more moments, then stood up.

'*Domina*, sit, please.' She offered her chair.

'No, I mustn't. Suppose somebody came in? The lowly cleaner wouldn't be sitting at her ease.'

I put my hand out and grasped hers. At last I saw some light in her eyes.

'Drusilla, I'm so pleased you're alive, too. That little bastard Turturus told us how he pressured you.'

'We manage, but it's so bad now. Every day that we're still alive is a bonus. As well as shortages, we all have to go to political meetings.' She gave a half-cracked laugh. 'Of course, as a woman, I can't join the nationalist movement so I'm spared that. But I feel so sorry for the men. Most people are just keeping their heads down, but some are starting to adapt to the new system despite the hardships.' She pressed hard on my hand. 'Come back soon, please. You must stop them before it's too late. Before they all fall in line with it.'

'Believe me, Drusilla, that's my priority. Thank you for keeping the faith.'

'That man's people killed my daughter. There is no question of doing anything else but resisting.'

Armed with mop, bucket, brush and duster, and wearing a grey overall and headscarf tied at the back of my neck, I followed the supervisor into the atrium.

'The first consul will be here at seven sharp. You have just over half an hour. Personally, I'd make sure to get it done in twenty-five minutes and be clear. But for Juno's sake, make sure everything is free of dust and stains. He has a fit if he sees either.'

I dampened the dust mop and worked my way to and fro across the vast area of marble. I reached Caius's desk after about five minutes. Just as I was reaching into my pocket for the tiny camera, I heard the door open behind me. My heart thudded so hard I was sure the incomer could hear it. Bootsteps sounded across the floor I had cleaned. Oh, Juno save me. Please, not Caius. My hands started to tremble. Should I turn? Would he recognise me? I hunched over, praying for my life.

'Get out of my way, woman!'

Caius!

Merda.

I bobbed a curtsey, shuffled sideways, bent my head and stood still.

He searched for something on the desk, snatched up a paper and to my horror, turned and looked at me. I fixed my gaze on the floor; my shoulders bowed, stomach out, toes turned in. Squinting through my eyelashes, I saw his frown. I didn't breathe as I waited. He shrugged, then marched off, leaving dirty footprints across my clean floor. A tiny surge of anger on behalf of cleaners of the world was drowned by the flood of relief. My fingers ached from gripping the mop handle so tightly. I wiped the sweat off them on my overall and took a deep breath to try to stop trembling.

Mop in hand again, I edged towards the desk again. I probably had ten minutes at the most before he returned to start his day's work. After a glance at the side windows to be sure nobody could see me, I flipped through the papers. Nothing. Beige file covers bulged in the in tray. I rifled through them, then found treasure – the sent folder of carbon copies of all Caius's letters. I flipped the precious file cover open and took my photos. Fifteen years of being a bureaucrat equipped me to see immediately what was important and what not. I closed the file and carefully replaced it and thrust the camera in my brassiere under the softest part of my flesh. I glanced around, especially at the side windows, then carried on with my mop, erasing all traces of Caius's dirty marks.

20

I was given a bowl of soup from the kitchen by Atrius, who was disguised in an off-white tunic and grey trousers as a kitchen helper. We sat in the adjoining domestic staff hall, just two of us in a room for thirty.

'Gods, this smells disgusting,' I muttered and tore a lump off the loaf in the middle of the table.

'It'll keep you going.'

'That's what I'm afraid of.'

He snapped out a short laugh.

Drusilla's underling, the cleaning supervisor, bustled in and glared at me.

'Haven't you finished yet? You've got five rooms upstairs to do this afternoon,' she said. 'You can't hang around in here trying to get off with the kitchen staff.' Her eyes in a round face bulged slightly as she looked at Atrius. 'You better be about your work as well.'

He glanced at me once more, then swung his leg over the bench seat and, smirking at the supervisor, sauntered back towards the kitchen.

'He's a bit cocky,' the supervisor said, although she'd watched him until he disappeared through the door. 'You want to watch yourself with that one.'

'He's my son.'

'Well, never mind that. On your feet and get cracking.'

. . .

As we trudged back down the hill into the town, I was sweating, not with the weather. Atrius handed me a bottle of water.

'You got what you wanted?' he asked.

'Yes, and more.'

He eased me through the next alley, then back out onto the next street.

'Can we get the pictures developed here to check? If the film gets exposed on our way out, we're stuffed,' I replied.

'We'll ask Marcia when we get back. But she may not have the right chemicals.'

We walked on in silence, winding through the streets until we arrived at the corner of the street near Marcia's block. We were both tired and desperate for a drink and a wash. I shivered. It all looked as it had been this morning; a half-derelict car, some plastic sacks of rubbish, crumpled paper in the gutter. An empty drinks can rolled along the pavement. Where had that come from? There was no wind to push it, no people rushing home from work, no kids on the street to kick it. Atrius went to turn into the street. I grabbed his arm.

'Keep walking,' I hissed. 'Something's not right.'

We crossed to the other corner.

'Shoe,' I said forcibly, but under my breath.

He knelt and fiddled with his shoe, while I glanced around, hardly moving my head. Atrius stood up and we moved quickly to the next block and the next before pausing.

'What did you see?' he asked.

'Nothing, and that was wrong.'

'Agreed.' He rubbed his forehead with his fingers and leant back against the wall. 'Now what do we do?'

We didn't have any idea where the other group was, only the RV point; for operational security, Volusenia had kept our briefings fully separate.

'I have an address,' I murmured. 'But we must be especially careful.'

'Why?'

'She's an er, informal trader.'

'A criminal?'

155

'That's a little harsh. She hasn't been convicted of anything.'

'Is it far?'

'At the lower end of the Via Nova.'

'D'you think we could go via my sister's? Just to look.' He didn't say anything but his eyes pleaded.

Last year, Atrius, Pia Calavia and I had sheltered in Paula Atria's dry cleaning shop. But that damned informer kid, Turturus, had led Caius's political troops there and we'd fled for our lives across the roofs of the old town, then through the dark wet streets. Would the shop still be there? More importantly, had Atrius's sister survived?

But there it was, thank the gods, lights on. We watched from the newsagent's across the street. I chose a magazine and almost fainted at the cost; eight *solidi* for one that had cost two-fifty last year. And the paper was coarser and thinner. Atrius pretended to flick through a tabloid while watching.

A man pushed open the glass door into Paula's shop and went in. Paula appeared at the counter. She was still alive and free, thank the gods. The man waved his hands about. She shook her head. He slammed his hand on the counter and a middle-aged man appeared to stand beside Paula.

'Pluto, that's that prick Firminus,' Atrius muttered. 'He's our mother's cousin. What's he doing here? Paula can't stand him.'

The customer turned, wrenched the door open, and left, huffiness radiating from him as he stamped off down the street. But Atrius was watching the plate glass window, his face set. We both saw Firminus grab Paula's wrist, bring his other hand up and slap her hard across the face.

I grabbed Atrius just about in time to stop him catapulting across the street.

'No.'

He gave me a savage look and jerked his arm away, almost pulling mine out of its socket. I grabbed his trouser belt, thrust out my leg and heaved him back over it. Atrius fell on the vinyl floor in a heap of arms and legs, He leapt up, but I was ready for him and blocked the doorway.

'Stop.' I fixed him with the sternest look I could muster. If I couldn't calm him down, he would not only sabotage the mission but get us both arrested and probably terminated. The newsagent had swung the top of his counter up and was bearing down on us.

Keeping an eye on Atrius, I smiled at the newsagent.

'Oh, thank goodness,' I bleated. 'Please sir, could you help me with my brother? He's bipolar,' I said in a stage whisper. 'The pharmacy's run out of his pills. We're at our wits' end with him.'

'Get off me, woman,' Atrius snarled at me. I didn't know whether he was playing along at this stage or meant it.

'Come along, son, calm down now,' the newsagent said, and pulled Atrius back from the door. He pushed him down onto the chair in front of the counter and gave him a beaker of water. Atrius grabbed it and gulped it down. The newsagent stood there, arms crossed and looking sternly at Atrius.

'Do you want me to call an ambulance or something?' He snorted. 'Not that anybody will be here within the next five days.'

'No, thank you, we'll just go home,' I said. 'Come on, Secundus. Ma will be getting worried.'

Atrius still hadn't said anything ten minutes later as he plodded beside me down the narrow street parallel to the Via Nova. The daylight was fading fast and we had to get off the street by the curfew at 9 p.m. or we'd be picked up by the *vigiles* or worse, Caius's nats.

'Atrius, we're nearly there. Are you ready?'

He nodded and we stepped into what was normally one of the most vibrant, if tackiest, streets of Roma Nova. Bright plastic shop signs, homemade displays, dubious cooking smells, tiny tables with fold-up chairs and people laughing and loitering on the streets – that was how this end of the Via Nova should have been. But this gloomy evening it was silent, apart from the occasional car or military vehicle roaring past and the odd late evening shop light. Three men and a woman stood under the lamp post nearest us, smoking. One or two others hurried by, intent on getting home by the curfew.

We strode past the smoking group who watched us, not with interest, but wariness. Trying not to look obvious, I glanced at the building numbers. Ten metres further down on the left we reached a faded maroon door between two shops. I entered the numbers Miklós had given me on the entry pad and pushed the door.

Enough lamplight invaded from the street to show a time-release switch on the hallway wall which Atrius pushed as I closed the door behind us. Dull beige walls and ceiling with a light bulb dangling from a wire and plain doors with heavy-duty locks to the left and right. A flight of uncarpeted stairs rose in front of us. I glanced at Atrius, then we started climbing. On the landing I signalled him to wait while I went forward. There were two identical doors. Hades. Which one? Miklós hadn't said. I had a fifty per cent chance of being wrong and possibly dead, but we had no choice. I took a deep breath and knocked at the nearest one with the sequence Miklós had given me.

A door chain rattled and the door opened about ten centimetres revealing a man's face. Dark hair and eyes, his face wore a frown.

'Yes?'

'Niklaus sent us,' I said.

'Never heard of him.'

'Are you János?'

The closing door stopped.

'Who's asking?'

'Niklaus's wife.'

He searched my face, then looked over my shoulder at Atrius who had come up to stand behind me.

'Who's he?'

'He works for me.'

The door closed before I could say another word, but reopened enough to let us pass into the room. I took a huge gulp of air, letting it out slowly.

'Wait here.'

I glanced round at the dark old-fashioned chairs, crochet antimacassars, a dresser stacked with a display of Samian pottery and coloured china, a vase of silk flowers, a television in the corner with a newscast mumbling at low level. All incredibly normal.

We turned as a petite woman came through a door at the side; she had brown hair and large brown eyes in a classically beautiful face. She wore a nondescript frock, and a hard expression on her face. She studied us. I returned her stare, refusing to look away. She wasn't just looking at me, she was trying to get inside me.

Apparently satisfied after a full minute, she gestured us to chairs.

'He said you were strong-willed. I see he was right.'

'Can you help us?'

'Depends what you want.'

'A bed for tonight and some food.'

Miklós had told me she was called Anna and her man was a friend of Sándor, the driver bodyguard Caius's assassins had killed in Vienna. She unbent a little as we devoured a plate of pasta, then tinned fruit. János didn't join in the conversation. Neither did Atrius.

'Niklaus sends his greetings,' I started conventionally.

'You don't need to pretend with me, Farkas *asszony*, I've known Miklós for years.'

Miklós used the German form of his name, Niklaus, for his trading activities, but if these two knew his real name he must trust them.

'Very well. Are you Hungarian as well?'

She laughed. 'No, I'm as Roma Novan as you. Maybe not so well documented down the generations, though.' Her eyes half closed as she sipped her glass of water.

'I'll be straight with you. Our safe house looks blown. I can't confirm it, but let's say I'm eighty per cent sure.' I glanced up at her as pasta slid off my fork. 'It's a lot to ask, but would you be willing to have somebody walk by and see if they think the same?'

'You're asking us to walk in the direct path of the *vigiles* and those nats and wave our thumbs at them? You've got a bloody cheek. We're keeping our heads down. Nothing doing.'

'Very well. Then at least lend me some clothes to disguise myself so I can do it.'

'Mercury's balls, don't you understand? Every corner is watched, every other human being a potential informer or denouncer.'

'I understand that, but I need to know,' I said. 'Our contacts there risk their lives every hour of every day. We've also stashed some important resources which we must retrieve. Of course, we'll recompense you,' I added.

'You think money will buy our services?' Her voice couldn't have held more scorn.

'Well, that's how you conduct your business, isn't it?' I bit back.

'Oh, so you think you're the only ones who can make loyal gestures?'

'Criminals aren't usually so inclined.' The words were out of my mouth before I could stop them. 'I apologise,' I added quickly, but the damage had been done.

In the small bedroom, with only a roof light as a window to the world outside, I lay on the bed. Atrius was asleep on a mattress on the floor, or so I thought until he spoke in a low voice.

'I know she was annoying, but I think you may have stuffed our chances.'

'You can't kick me any harder than I am myself, Atrius.'

'She's quite a looker, isn't she?'

I couldn't reply. How well *did* Miklós know her? But she had her man, János.

'We'll leave tomorrow morning,' I said. 'If we can't get those packets back from the roof space then we'll have to abandon them and run.' I wriggled on the lumpy mattress. 'I'm very sorry about your sister. It must be hell for her.'

'And I'm sorry for losing it back in that shop, but when we come back, I'm going to hunt that little turd down and give him the thrashing of his life.'

I didn't answer him. We had to plan for reconciliation afterwards and couldn't sanction revenge acts. But I wasn't going to tell Atrius that now. His anger was only contained by a very thin crust.

A faint glow of light from the roof light relieved the Stygian dark of the room. The street lights either weren't working or were switched off. Unlike my mind.

'We need to get to the RV point with the other team the day after tomorrow, whatever happens,' I said. 'Let's get some sleep.'

21

We woke at six the next morning. As I slipped out of the small bathroom after a quick wash, I saw a light coming from the kitchen. I hurried back to the bedroom and dressed. In the kitchen, the faded green curtains were still drawn against the dark morning. Anna was at the stove staring down at the eggs she was stirring in an old pan as if mesmerised by them. The boiling kettle clicked and snapped her out of her reverie.

Her face coloured when she looked at me, but she said nothing.

'Could we make a drink?' I said. 'Then we'll be on our way.'

'I've made you breakfast.' She spooned the eggs onto two plates and added a slice of tinned ham to each. I called Atrius and we ate in silence. Anna set mugs of tea down on the table, but hovered by the sink.

'János went out last night,' she said. 'He couldn't see anything.'

I twisted round to face her. 'But what about the curfew?'

She gave a short laugh. 'We don't let things like that stop us. He said there was nobody there watching, but the front door had been forced.'

Gods.

'He's gone to check this morning. There's a newsagent nearby, so he'll pretend to be going to buy a paper. He isn't back yet.' Her face tightened, but she merely turned and started washing up. I exchanged looks with Atrius.

'We'll go now, Anna. We can't endanger you further.'

'Every day is dangerous. You'd better wait for János.'

'We'll wait downstairs. Thank you for the breakfast.'

'Didn't you trust her?'

Atrius leant back against the tenement side wall, his knee bent, one foot flat against the brickwork. Hidden from casual passers-by in this covered passageway diagonally across the road, we could see Anna's entrance door between the shuttered up shops. If János was alone, well and good, if accompanied or followed, we could escape through the passageway into the *insulae* blocks behind us. Thrown up during a property boom last century, they were full of narrow alleys and hiding places.

'I'm not sure. Miklós told me to trust no one. He's dealt with this Anna for years apparently, but how do we know what pressures people are under these days?'

'Heads up,' Atrius said and peeled himself off the wall and set off up the street on our side.

János was ambling down the opposite side of the street, folded newspaper in one hand, cigarette in the other. He took a long puff, then threw the butt down in the gutter, blew out hard, stuffed something in his pocket and turned to press the keypad by the door. By then, Atrius had crossed over further up, checked for any tail and come up behind János. I glanced both ways to check again, then trotted across the deserted street to the door directly in front of János.

'Morning,' I said. 'See anything or anybody interesting while you were out?'

'No, and tell your boy to back off.'

I nodded at Atrius. He took one step back and then kept himself busy looking up and down the street without seeming to.

'There were lights on the third and fourth storeys and I saw a woman's face as she pulled back the curtains on the top floor. But that's it.' He shrugged.

'Thank you. I appreciate you going to look last night.'

'Somebody had busted in. Looked like a door ram, so probably those bastard *vigiles*. I'd be careful if I was you. Come back if you need to. She's sorry she was a bit off last night. She won't say so, though.

Typical stubborn Roma Novan woman.' He grunted. He held his hand out. 'I hope you find those bastards who killed Sándor. He was a miserable old sod, but he was my friend.'

'It's against procedure,' Atrius grumbled. 'And it's madness to return there.'

'Are you questioning my order?' I stopped, looked him squarely in the face and raised an eyebrow.

'No, of course not, ma'am, just pointing out—'

'Consider it pointed out. Now let's get on with it.'

We were still dressed in the drab clothes we'd changed into when we'd entered Roma Nova and I for one would like to have found a washing machine. Paula Atria's shop was out of the question. We walked on at a steady pace, but only a few people were about, concentrating on getting to work rather than looking at a couple of nondescripts. Twenty minutes later, we reached Marcia's building. Atrius went first while I watched the street. A short low whistle. I turned and followed him in. A crack in the entrance door to the building and a hole where the lock had been confirmed János's story. Boot marks on the floor and black scuffs on the walls of the first two storeys' corridors were telltale signs of the raid. A door on the second floor was open, but barred with white and maroon striped plastic tape.

I waved my fingers in an upward direction at Atrius and we crept up the next flight of stairs. No scuffs or boot prints. I nodded and we tackled the last flight, maintaining silence all the way up. At the top, we flattened ourselves against the wall each side of the door. I signalled Atrius back so he was out of the line of sight, gave one last look down the stairwell, then knocked softly on the door.

An unknown male face appeared in the narrow gap between the open door and the jamb.

'Yes?'

'Oh, isn't Marcia in?' I said, with a cheerful smile on my face.

'Who?'

'Oh, don't tell me she's moved again. And I've brought a chicken for her from her aunt in Brancadorum.'

The door slammed shut. I glared at Atrius who was trying not to laugh.

'It was the next phrase on the list, so shut up,' I hissed at him. After a full minute, the door opened again. Marcia, her face pale.

'Thank Mercury. I thought you'd been taken.'

She opened the door just enough for us to slide in. And we came face to face with an armed *vigilis* officer.

No.

I took a deep breath then shifted the weight onto the balls of my feet, ready to pounce or run. Was his backup already creeping up the stairs, ready to grab us? Atrius pushed Marcia out of the way, seized the door handle and wrenched the door open. I whirled round and was halfway onto the landing, Atrius centimetres behind me when Marcia cried out.

'Stop!

She lowered her voice. 'It's not a trap. He's one of us.'

'We found a hole to hide in last night,' I said as we drank black tea in an attempt to calm down. My heart was still thudding as I emptied my mug. 'What happened here?' I said.

'A raid.' She stood and walked over to the sink and leant back against it. 'I thought we were toast. I was working on an ID and had my print kit out all over the table. I just had time to shove it all away in the cupboard.' She looked up. 'But they would have easily found it.' Her eyes were red and her fingers twitched. The *vigilis* went over to her and put his arm around her shoulders. She leaned into him, then let out a sigh. 'The couple on the second floor were dealing in black market goods and had been denounced by a disgruntled customer, so Gaius says.' She looked up at him.

I studied Gaius standing there in his maroon uniform, jacket open, white T-shirt showing. He wasn't young or old, neither tall nor short. His mousey hair and brown eyes made him look like any other Roma Novan.

'So Gaius here didn't know the raid was coming?'

'No.' He looked down his nose at me. 'The special squads don't think to post such things on an open noticeboard for us common scarabs to read.' His voice was coated with sarcasm.

'Don't get snotty with me, *vigilis*. Given your corps' poor record, you have nothing to be proud about. Now tell me what you're doing here.'

'I'm Marcia and Sextus's cousin. I came round one day to see if they were okay, you know, after she'd been chucked out of the university. Not my sort of thing, but my mother said Marcia had been doing so well and it was a shame.' He stood up straight, releasing Marcia. 'It's not a shame, it's a bloody disgrace. I've been a *vigilis* for nearly twenty years, getting on with my job catching criminals. I've worked with some of the best police colleagues ever, women and men. When the women were chucked out it was weird, unnatural, but we got on with it. Then those bloody nats were there, "sharing law enforcement duties" as they called it.' He snorted. 'Now everybody's changed. Even some of my old mates have become louts. One woman came to the station complaining of being assaulted and they laughed and told her she was lucky to be getting any.'

He threw himself down on one of the rickety dining chairs and smacked his hand on the table. He was either one of the best actors I'd seen or genuinely distressed.

'I was going to make my way out, north to Vienna, but Marcia said it was too dangerous.' He glanced over at her. Her face took on a red tinge. 'I knew it wasn't true – there are loads of ways through. She talked me into staying and helping her and her friends. I can't do much, but now and again I hear something that might be useful and I can smuggle out the odd useful thing.'

If they caught him he'd have a doubly difficult time. I relaxed a little.

'You tread a difficult path, Gaius. I commend you. When we come back, we'll remember what you are doing now for Roma Nova.'

'Are you coming back? Really?' He looked up, his eyes doubtful. 'How can you?'

'That's why we're here.' I looked at Marcia. 'Where's your brother?'

'In his lectures, I hope.'

'Can he start actively recruiting? We need people inside every organisation. Students are usually rebellious by nature.' I smiled at her.

'He's sounded a few people out already, but the trouble is the nats are making them all go to political education classes and some of his friends are taking it in.'

'Then he'll have to find other friends. Tell him to look out for the quiet ones who seem to be watching but not saying anything. They're not confident to speak up in the presence of those throwing their weight around, but it doesn't mean they don't resent things.'

'I've had more luck with my women friends. We've started up sewing groups.' She rolled her eyes. 'We'll all be weaving like Livia soon if we're not careful, but it means we can meet under the nats' radar.'

'Excellent,' I said. 'What we need most is information on numbers of nats, what they do, their unit strengths, here in the city and out in the country. We need to know what shops and businesses are flourishing, which ones close, what farmers are supplying, how transport is running, the postal services. And most of all what people are finding hardest and what their feelings and opinions are.'

'You don't want much, do you?' Marcia said.

'It's all small stuff that will help us build up a pattern, a jigsaw, if you like. Then we can make connections. It's also important to note if things change.' I laid my hand on her forearm. 'They're things you notice in the everyday. That's why we need a lot of people to observe. But I don't want anybody getting either noticed or into trouble.'

'How are we supposed to get all this information to you?'

'Using the same transceivers you've been using so far.'

She looked appalled.

'But we only use them when absolutely necessary. Sextus said even tiny message bursts could be heard by the nats' monitoring people. We couldn't possibly send daily reports.'

'They brought new monitoring equipment into my station,' Gaius said. 'American. Well, that's what the stores clerk said. He's a puffed up little jerk – likes to sound important. Said I mustn't tell anybody. I said of course not.' He grinned.

'That's a pain, but we've brought something with us to help with that. I'll brief Marcia and she can tell you later.' He said nothing but looked steadily at me. I didn't know him and I wanted to talk to Marcia first. 'You're going to have to train the others in your groups,' I said to her. 'I suggest you keep your groups to five or six maximum, make one of them the leader who then belongs to the next level up.

Get each member of your core group to recruit their own group. Nobody will know any others in the network apart from their own group. This way, if any of you get caught, the nats would only ever get four or five other names at worst.'

Gaius looked at his watch then stood up. 'I'm sorry, I have to go on shift.' He held his hand out to me. 'I don't know your name and I don't want to know, but I'm honoured to make your acquaintance. You've given me hope.'

'We're going to rely on loyal people like you, Gaius, so stay safe.' He nodded to Atrius and left. I counted to twenty and jerked my head to Atrius who slipped out to follow him.

'So Gaius is your cousin. Is he reliable?' I look straight at her.

'I know you have to ask, but you don't know him. He's as straight as they come. I've seen him get more and more depressed over the past few months. He'd do anything for it to go back to how it was. Now he's got his dippy sister to look after as well. Her man's left her and joined the nats. She's just had a baby she didn't want and Gaius says she hasn't a clue as a mother. How little Marcus will survive, Juno knows.'

She fetched a bottle of beer and two glasses. It was gassy and weak, but just about drinkable. She slouched in her chair, sipped at her glass, but said nothing.

'What's the family name?' I asked to break her mood.

'Flavia.'

Well, I hoped little Marcus Flavius would manage to grow up despite a father who deserted him and a negligent mother.

22

Atrius reported that Gaius had gone direct to the *Vigiles* District VII station and disappeared through the guarded gate. Unusual. There had never been any need to guard stations before. He shrugged, then went to the bathroom to retrieve the packets we'd hidden in the ceiling.

When Sextus came back, he was starving and grumbled at the vegetable stew Marcia had made.

'Go out and shoot something if you want meat so badly,' she retorted.

'Sorry, sis, we had an ID check before the political education class and one of my friends was dragged away by those nats apes. He shouted for help but none of us dared move. We all just stood there, not believing what was happening.' He threw his spoon down. 'I feel so bloody helpless.'

'Sextus, you and Marcia are doing good work. It might seem low-level, but I can't stress how important it is. When you've finished eating, Secundus and I will show you protocols to start the work to drive these bastards out.'

Atrius and I drilled the two of them in the one-time letter pad cypher method so they could encode their messages. We practised for the rest of the evening but gave up at midnight. We started again with both of them the next morning, but Sextus had to go to classes at eleven.

I ran Marcia through recruitment techniques; she'd have more opportunity as a servant and could meet other women shopping and running errands. She seemed pretty savvy to me; setting up the sewing groups had been a brilliant idea.

Atrius and I slept in the afternoon with the door barricaded. We could, at a push, escape through the small roof light. When Sextus returned, I drilled them both in radio contact and lost contact procedures, and made them memorise a fresh set of personal contact passwords. Just before midnight, I gave them sets of pads that had been in the hidden packets to distribute to trusted colleagues once they had been completely checked out.

'We're going first thing in the morning.' I fished a small black plastic-covered device out of the third packet. 'This is a scrambler – the latest technology there is.' Sextus leaned forward, reawakened interest in his tired eyes. He was an engineer after all. 'You press this button to switch it on,' I continued. 'I suggest you slide the button to max if you are talking near *vigiles* or nats or anywhere you're worried about.' I took a loop of wire out with two jack plugs. 'Plug one end in the scrambler and the other in your transceiver. It will scramble your radio bursts. It runs on batteries. I've brought you four rechargeables plus a mini recharger. It'll keep you going for a bit. If they're starting to drain and taking less recharge, you must tell us as soon as you can and we'll get more to you.'

Atrius and I waited in the shadows of the main bus station. I shivered in my thin jacket, slumped against the concrete wall and closed my eyes while he watched. Those poor kids; they'd be lucky if Caius's thugs didn't get them. They'd managed for over a year, but how long would their luck last? I yawned and rubbed my face. I could have slept for a week. Drowsiness was seeping over me when Atrius nudged me with his knee.

'Here's the bus,' he whispered.

I eased myself up and peered round the corner of the bus station building. The thump-thump of the diesel engine broke the silence of the dark morning. The sun wouldn't rise for another hour, but the official night curfew had ended and we could make our way to the rendezvous point with the other team. We waited until the engine started to rev up and ran for the bus door as if we were late.

'You've cut it fine,' the driver grumped as he took our *solidi* coins.

Atrius mumbled an apology and gave me a light push towards seats near the back of the bus. At two further stops we picked up half a dozen half-awake early morning workers. I released a long breath. We'd done everything we needed to do; I'd taken the photos, we'd delivered the code pads, and given basic training to Marcia and Sextus. Gaius the *vigilis* was a bonus. Atrius had even pinched a directory from a phone box in the city – a valuable source of contacts. As the bus rattled on through the suburbs and entered the dock area, I felt at last we were on our way out.

The bus jerked to a halt. We were thrown forward. I grabbed the rail in front of me. Glaring light from a vehicle outside nearly blinded us in the dark of the morning. Spotlight. Only police vehicles had such powerful lights. Atrius half rose to his feet, then sat down fast as a nationalist trooper stepped onto the bus. Boots, black uniform, tight belt, black peak cap and that damned red armband with the mailed fist and fasces. Gods. Was he looking for us? We could take him as long as the other passengers stayed in their seats and didn't panic. Voices outside. How many were there?

'Everybody off,' he barked. Frightened eyes met other ones. 'Now!'

As Atrius reached the front of the bus, the trooper shot his arm out to block him.

'You. Why don't you have a party badge?'

'Me, sir?' Atrius feigned a country burr to his voice. 'I ain't fit for that. I just does veg on my uncle's farm.' He let his mouth drop open then gave the nat a grin.

'All right, turnip head, get off.' Atrius touched his forelock like a good peasant and stepped down, almost missing the lower step. I shuffled after him, not making eye contact with the trooper. Outside, there were three more of them. Two were checking papers. My heart thudded faster. Our ID was good, so we should pass. The fourth nat stood there, seeming relaxed but searching faces. I kept my eyes down. I cursed myself I hadn't put my grey contacts back in; my eyes had been too sore from tiredness. If I had to look up, I'd be stuffed. Few had the bright blue of the Mitelae. Hades.

The nat snatched Atrius's papers from his hand, glanced at me, then back at the papers. He was taking too long. Atrius grabbed me round the waist.

'This is my Ma. I look after her, but she's a bit shy.' Then he giggled.

'Simple as you, is she?' The nat sneered as he thrust the papers back at Atrius. We turned to get back on the bus, but the fourth man stepped forward.

'Just a minute.'

Pluto in Tartarus.

'You, the woman. Show me your face.'

I narrowed my eyes and opened my mouth to look as slow as Atrius.

'Unusual colour.'

Merda.

'The rest of them can go. These two stay.'

In the second after the other passengers had shuffled back up the bus steps, Atrius leapt forward, floored the fourth man, then one of the others. I hitched up my skirt, swung my leg and gave a full kick to the groin of the third one. He staggered back against his colleague and both fell heavily on the road.

'Into the trees,' I shouted. We dived into the copse, weaving between the trees. After two minutes, my breath was heaving, but I ran on, trying to keep up with Atrius's long strides. About twenty metres further up, sheltered still by the dark of the morning, and the nats' light shining in the other direction, we ran back out and sprinted across the road and dived between two dock buildings. We stopped for a second to catch our breath and listen for pursuit. Hopefully, they were bumbling around in the trees, but it wouldn't keep them for long.

'Let's get through and up the hill,' Atrius panted.

'Agreed,' I replied. 'To the caves.'

Then a storm broke along with the dawn. We pounded through the old dock quarter in the freezing rain, listening all the time for pursuit. The domed cobblestones reflected the pools of dull street light. We only slowed to a walk when we saw the odd lorry and occasional docker.

Most ships loaded and unloaded in the new complex Justina had opened eight years ago. Gods, that seemed a lifetime ago. The formal ceremony, a band playing its heart out, children with flowers, the new docks manager bobbing in front of Justina and proudly introducing his new staff all lined up on the red carpet, the priest strutting back and forward with blessings, speeches and finally shouts of 'Ave Apulia' had been followed by an alcohol-fuelled celebration into the small hours.

Two figures came towards us, heads down against the hard rain. They carried nightsticks in their hand. Hades, *vigiles*. But they were hurrying. Their radio buzzed and they stopped to listen. I grabbed Atrius's arm and pulled him round the corner of the next warehouse. It was built tall and loomed over the street, its defunct loading arm not quite touching the one opposite. We waited and listened. Rain poured onto our faces and fell off our chins. One of the *vigiles* spoke back into his radio, confirming they'd seen nobody but they'd keep an eye out for a man and woman acting suspiciously. We shuffled along to the warehouse door and flattened ourselves against it. I silently thanked the gods and the old builders that it was recessed. After a minute, we crept back to the corner. The *vigiles* were disappearing into the wet gloom.

'We have to cross the open yard with the train tracks to get to the bottom of the castle hill.' I glanced left towards the bonded area gate. A kiosk lit by a yellow light was occupied by two figures. The spotlight shining from its roof didn't reach beyond ten metres. If we were quick, they wouldn't see us, especially in this rain.

'Let's just do it. Those damned nats can't be far behind us.'

I took a breath and launched myself. Atrius' footsteps sounded behind me. Once across the yard, we edged round the base of the hill. At last we found a small gap where the wire fence had parted from the ground. Scraping and grazing our skin, but not caring, we heaved on it to make a hole big enough to wriggle through. Atrius bent it back into place as best he could to make it look undisturbed, but our priority was to get up the damned hill. I unclipped the cumbersome skirt now sodden and heavy with the rain. Atrius raised an eyebrow, but smiled when he saw I had my walking trousers on underneath. I rolled the skirt up and stuffed it behind a bush.

Thirty minutes later, we rested spreadeagled on the steep slope just west of the old castle ruins. Neither of us said a word. It had been a hellish climb; the rock was slippery and the thin layer of earth and grass turned to mud, trickled through our fingers, up our sleeves and spattered in our faces. My limbs trembled with the effort. The good news was that the rain had stopped. I took a deep breath, nodded at Atrius and pressed my feet on the ground to push myself on. We emerged in trees to the side of the castle visitor car park. I leaned back against one tree trunk and took sips from my water flask. Atrius crawled forward to the edge of the tree line. By the time he came back, I'd recovered my breath.

Behind the castle, around fifty metres away, rose a sheer rock face dotted with cave entrances. Some had been built across, even with doors and the odd window. Sometimes used by homeless people and those who lived on the margin, they often housed runaways and petty criminals. The *vigiles* used to raid them from time to time when the newspapers complained about 'lawless elements'.

'There's plenty of scrub in front of the caves, but we'll probably have to climb up to find an empty one. Some of them look occupied.' He glanced at me. 'Jupiter knows what sort of welcome we'll get.'

'With the nats after us we don't have any other option.'

23

———

We reached the first level easily, apart from a few scratches, but I was more worried at being spotted in the early light than caring about grazed skin and broken nails. I would have given anything for a rope ladder, though. The small cave we reached first was damp, lichen grew on the walls and it stank of human liquids and stale smoke.

I felt round the back for any passageway to other caves; many of them were interconnected. No such luck.

'I know it's vile in this hole, but we must stay covert during the day and get some rest,' I said. I could hardly see Atrius's face, but his figure outlined against the sunlight was slumped. We settled as far away from the foetid back of the cave as we could without being visible from the outside and fell asleep almost instantly.

I woke, uncomfortable and longing to stretch, but I couldn't move. Something pressed hard against my throat. It pinched my skin along a narrow line. A knife. And from the weight on my back, somebody was kneeling on it.

'Slow, real slow,' a male voice rasped.

I lay stock still. It was light outside, but all I could see was the gravelly floor, blurred. The pressure on my back eased and the pinch of the knife edge on my throat skin receded.

'Now sit up careful and slow like a good girl.'

I rolled over. As I struggled up a hand gripped the back of my neck with the strength of a vice.

'Now, on your feet and hands on your head.'

The grip on my neck lessened marginally as I stood up. A man's grip. I smelt sweat and smoke. To my side stood a young woman looking frightened but trying not to, and by the entrance two more carrying thick staves.

I blinked hard to clear my eyes. In front of me was a sturdily built middle- aged woman, dressed in boots, khaki trousers, a short-sleeved shirt and cloth waistcoat. A revolver that should have been in a museum was parked in an equally old-fashioned holster. Her face was as workmanlike as her clothes and carried a stern expression.

'We don't take kindly to trespassers – what do you want?'

I glanced around. Atrius stood to the side, hands on his head and flanked by two men dressed like this woman. I looked back at her.

'We're refugees.'

'What from?'

Who was she? Some kind of local militia raiding these caves? She was obviously in charge of these people so probably not, as a woman, part of the nationalists' regime. A criminal gang? Or possibly a dissident or even a resistance group?

'Well?'

'Who are you?'

'That's for me to ask you. Now answer the question.'

The fingers tightened on my neck. I couldn't even cough.

'We're running from the nats,' I croaked.

'That doesn't take a lot of working out,' she said and snorted. 'You'll have to give me something better than that to stop us slitting your throats and dumping your bodies over the cliff.'

Her eyes hardened. She was fast losing patience. One of the men by Atrius unsheathed his knife, a long-bladed hunting knife which gleamed even in the faint light. Atrius tensed. We were two to their seven. And they were armed.

'Very well,' I said. 'We're part of a reconnaissance group operating from outside Roma Nova.'

'Oh? I haven't heard of anything like that.'

'Well, you're not exactly on the inside track for news, are you?' I said.

She took a step nearer until her face was within centimetres of mine.

'Don't get arsy with me.' Her voice was low, but steely.

'Then cut us a bit of slack. We don't know who you are. You could be an unofficial citizens' militia working for Caius Tellus to draw in resistants. Unlikely with a woman like you leading it, but he's a devious sod.'

'And what do you know of Tellus?'

'Probably more than you do,' I retorted. She opened her mouth to speak, but I held my hand up. 'My name is Aurelia Mitela and he's been my enemy since we were both children. There's very little he wouldn't do to get hold of me.'

She stared at me. Her eyes widened, full of surprise and shock. The hand grip on my neck vanished. I put my own up to rub it, then looked at the woman.

'Now I've delivered myself into your hands, don't you think it would be courteous to tell me who you are?'

Her name was Lucia Palia. She'd owned and run a small engineering company.

We'd followed our captors, clambering up to a much bigger and drier cave two levels up, thanks to a rope ladder, and were now sitting in a circle on metal storage boxes and sipping black tea.

'I suppose we should have been more prepared when that bastard took over.' Misery coated every word she spoke. 'I thought that if we kept our heads down we'd be okay,' she continued. 'I'd only visited the lawyer to sign over the firm two days before.' Her eyes were full of anger. 'It was only going to be on paper. My accountant knew that. A man I could trust, I thought. He was the one who denounced me to the nats.'

She looked towards the open end of the cave, then shrugged and focused on me again.

'A dozen of those black-uniformed thugs stomped in one day, right onto the factory floor. They made straight for me. Paulus, my foreman, stepped in front of me, but they knocked him down. Two grabbed me and shoved me out through the door. Then they marched me across the yard, through the factory gates and threw me onto the street. Literally.'

I touched her forearm in a gesture of sympathy just below a red scar reaching up to her elbow.

'My ex-accountant is now in the black pit of Tartarus where we threw him,' she continued in a flat voice. She gestured at the women and men around us. 'These are what's left of my loyal workforce. Some stayed on in the factory, fearful for their families. I don't blame them. We're in contact with some of them now and again, when we go to, er, forage for food and other supplies.'

'So are there any other groups like yours?' I said.

'There's another one, based three caves along, all women. We say *salve*, but that's about all. One thing they told us was that there's another, much larger group at the top level.'

'I suggest we arrange a meeting with them,' I said.

'Why? We can manage on our own perfectly well.'

'I'm sure you can at present, but for how long? The nats will eventually get round to clearing the caves. You can be sure of that. And you know yourself how ruthless they can be.'

She said nothing, but looked at me like a bull resisting sacrifice.

'Lucia, we must take Roma Nova back before these bloody people become embedded. Each week, each month they stay in control, the harder it will be for us to dig them out. Already the *vigiles* are becoming brutalised and absorbed into the nationalist ethos. People are despairing and giving in, thinking there's no hope. Time is against us. This is why we're here, to make contact with those who refuse to join the regime. We must form active, but coordinated resistance that will be vital to the take-back.'

'Yes, but meeting these other cave-dwellers... We're only fourteen, *domina*. I think the women's group is about the same, perhaps less. We know nothing about the other one. They may be in the hundreds.'

'Well, one step at a time. When would it be a good time to visit the first group?'

Two stern-faced young women with crossed arms and braced legs looked down as we clambered towards their cave the next morning. Neither lifted a finger to help us as we reached the entrance. We pushed the greenery aside and heaved ourselves over the edge of the opening. A double metallic click of a weapon being cocked.

'What do you want?'

'Some common courtesy would be a good start,' I said as I stood up. 'Who is in charge here?'

'Who wants to know?'

I blinked. I knew that voice. A very slim figure, her face gaunt, with hollow cheeks and large brown eyes sunk in the sockets, stepped forward. She pushed a strand of brown hair laced with white back behind her ear. Her hand stopped halfway down and she stared at me.

'No!' she cried and launched herself at me. I folded her into my arms. She clung to me and sobbed as if she were a tiny child come home to her mother after years apart in a hellhole. Eventually, she looked up. 'Why have you come here? It's far too dangerous.'

'I've come to ask for your help, Claudia Cornelia, to serve Roma Nova at my side, just like old times.'

Claudia, my young assistant at the foreign ministry aeons ago, in fact only thirteen months ago. Then she'd been a sleek twenty-one-year-old. Now she looked like a malnourished woman in her forties.

'They burst into the bunker under the foreign ministry and dragged us all to a warehouse for two days. They shouted at us, beating us when we didn't answer. We had little water and no food. They gave the men the option of continuing and quite a number did. They disappeared the next day. We all pretended to be low-level clerks and, Juno be praised, all the women and the remaining men played along. They shot the security chief Fulvia in front of us all. One of the young girls shrieked and threw up over one of the nats, so he shot her. We had to clear the bodies away and dig their graves in the grass by the car park.'

She turned away and was silent for a few moments.

'Eventually, they shoved us into a lorry and took us out to a field north of the city and made us build a work colony.' She looked down at her hands, scarred and gnarled like an old woman's.

'The guards were nats. You can imagine what happened to us as women imprisoned there.' Her voice was toneless.

I took one of her damaged hands and pressed it.

'One day, two months after we'd built our hut, a car turned up and out stepped my cousin Octavius dressed up in one of those nats' black uniforms. I was working on the driveway, raking gravel over the tar surface with another woman, so I kept my head down. I couldn't have borne it if he'd seen me. He was such a snot. I'd snubbed him at the last Family Day.' She trembled. 'Then the camp governor came over to me with Octavius in tow. He ordered me into the car. I just stared at him and the governor slapped my face and told me to jump to. I wanted to hit back, but I'd had one beating. Never again.'

'What happened next?' I asked.

'Octavius didn't say a word for three hours, but drove to his farm near Brancadorum. He took me into the kitchen, told the housekeeper to wash the stink off, clothe me and find me a bed. I was to help her in the kitchen and keep out of everybody's way.'

She turned to me. The light from the harsh afternoon sunlight emphasised the hollows in her face.

'He didn't show me a scrap of affection nor even acknowledge that I existed, but he saved me, *consiliaria*.'

'So why are you here, Claudia, and not safe on your cousin's farm?'

'You, of all people, ask me that?' She raised her eyebrow in the old way, the supercilious Cornelia way, and I smiled to myself.

24

———

The women's cave was smaller than Lucia's but better organised with a sitting area furnished with rough stools and a table cobbled together from an old door and packing cases. A cooking area just below a natural vent in the rock boasted a paraffin stove, heat spreader, two pans and a stack of tin plates and cutlery. And at the back, a passageway through a curtain led to another cave laid out as a sleeping area.

'We're nineteen, all women, but four are out foraging at the moment. Two are former *vigiles*, three military, the rest are office workers and artisans. They've all been damaged in some way. Some are still fragile. Two I doubt will ever recover. But they're safe here.' Her voice was almost defiant. But she must have known they were living on borrowed time.

'Will you let me speak to your group?'

'Of course, *consiliaria*.' But she gave me a glance that was a mix of wariness and curiosity.

The foraging group wasn't back until gone eleven that evening so it was morning when I stood at the side, Lucia behind me, our backs against the cave wall. Claudia introduced me, which caused some murmuring and exchange of glances from the women sitting in the main cave.

'I'm not going to do a show lap round the arena—'

'That'll make a change from a politico,' somebody muttered.

180

Claudia frowned, but I held my hand up. 'Those times have passed,' I said in the direction of the voice. A brown-haired woman flushed and looked down. 'The plain fact is that I need your help to reconquer Roma Nova. You will be remembered with great honour and never be in want or threatened again.' Now they stared at me. 'You're living here as fugitives. Reasonably comfortably and in supportive company. But you must be aware that it's only temporary. There is no doubt that one day Caius Tellus's political troops will come here in force with the objective of clearing the caves.' I heard a sob and more mumblings.

'We will make our stand and if necessary die like Romans!' A black-haired woman jumped up and directed a fierce expression at me.

'Yes, and that would be very honourable. But you'd be dead. Wouldn't you prefer to live?'

Claudia shifted on her feet, but I ploughed on.

'The Roma Nova government in exile is obtaining and collating information and preparing a strategic take-back plan. But we need groups inside Roma Nova to help us.' I swallowed. 'I'm recruiting resistance groups to carry out specific tasks at the time we launch our operation. I see you have plenty of fighting spirit, but we will need you for more than that.' I paused and a few women looked at me, interest birthing in their eyes, fuelled by curiosity. Volusenia would have wolf cubs if she heard me now; recruiting was nowhere in my remit, but this was too good an opportunity to miss.

A blonde woman stood up. 'Former *Optio* Caelia, medical services attached to the XX Victis.'

'A good legion. You have a question?' I said.

'Exactly what do you want us to do, ma'am?'

'I can't give you exact details of your task at the moment, *optio*, but it will be a vital one. You can be sure of that. In the meantime you must keep everybody safe.'

'That was clever, making *Optio* Caelia responsible for security,' Claudia whispered to me afterwards over a cup of black tea.

'Do you think she can do it?' I said.

'Yes. She's fidgety and twice I've had to stop her going out and doing something silly. She's full of anger, as they all are.'

'Well, she'll help you drill them into a unit and select teams. She'll also be able to run evacuation drills. You must be prepared for that, Claudia. Caius won't wait forever. I'll use my Praetorian authority and make you a temporary lieutenant.'

'I'm honoured.' She took a few more sips, glanced at her watch. 'But that's not everything, is it?'

'How well you know me, Claudia.' I gave a little chuckle. 'No, now we must make contact with the larger group in the upper caves. I need to have Atrius with me as well as you and Lucia.' Her quick intake of breath told me the problem. I laid my hand on hers and looked straight at her.

'You and the rest of your group will have to get used to men again, to learn to trust them and work with them again. Atrius and those in Lucia's group will be completely respectful, but you will have to meet them halfway.'

She hesitated, then nodded briefly, but didn't say anything.

Back in Lucia's cave for the night, I managed to talk to Atrius privately.

'Neither this group nor Claudia's knows anything about our other team. They should be here by now.'

'Unless they managed to get out through the Helvetian route,' he said.

'We were supposed to fall back here, then leave together. The deadline expires tomorrow midday. After that we assume them lost.'

He looked away. He'd fallen into the nationalists' hands and knew exactly what would happen to them.

I didn't sleep well that night, imagining we would be overwhelmed by a feral group of hundreds from the upper cave, some kind of primitive and savage horde that had in desperation reverted to tribal behaviour. My rational mind told me I was being ridiculous, but neither Lucia nor Claudia knew anything about them. They occasionally glimpsed one or two figures climbing up or down on ropes, mostly at night. I woke early and boiled water on the little stove, sloshing it into cups to make black tea. I crept over to Atrius who blinked then yawned when I nudged him awake. He drank in silence, staring out into the dawn light.

'You're sure you're still happy to go first?' I said.

'Yes. They can only shoot me or club me to death. Then you'll know.' He shot me a quick grin and I punched him lightly on the arm, returning his grin.

'All the same…'

'Be careful. I know.'

It was more of a walk along a narrow ledge up to the upper caves than a full-blown climb. While Atrius went ahead, I glimpsed down and wished I hadn't. A hundred metres at least to the ground. If we failed to connect with these people, Lucia, Claudia and I would follow Atrius on that last fall and end up as piles of broken bones and shattered flesh. I wrenched my head back to the cliff face and nearly lost my balance. Claudia shot out her arm to steady me. I mumbled an apology.

The minutes ticked by. The sun became warmer and its light and warmth reflected off the crystalline rock. Birds swooped around us, no doubt curious about the invaders of their territory. Braced against the cliff face with a few centimetres' grace, my muscles were starting to stiffen and cramp. I didn't doubt Lucia and Claudia were the same. We'd probably been waiting a max of ten minutes, but it felt like an eternity. But all we needed now was some damned helicopter patrol to fly by and we'd be ducks in a shooting gallery. Gods, what was Atrius doing, renegotiating the Treaty of Westphalia?

I leant my forehead against the rock. A crack, a thump. Something flying through the air.

Please not… Not Atrius.

It bounced against the rock face, millimetres from my face. A wooden step rope ladder.

'What took so long?' I hissed at him as he helped us onto the deep ledge.

He laughed. 'You'll see.'

'Now look, Atrius, don't piss me around. We've been stuck out there having heart attacks waiting for your corpse to be thrown out. What's going on?'

Two men and a woman, booted and dressed in combat trousers, scruffy shirts and waistcoats, stepped forward. I nearly fell backwards off the ledge in surprise when I saw the woman. I hadn't seen her for at least a couple of weeks. Now I knew why.

Pia Calavia, aristocrat and Praetorian officer, looked like a wild guerrilla fighter from the South American continent. Criss-crossed across her chest were two bandoliers, the pockets part-filled with single rounds, part with magazine clips. Her long hair had been cropped to tight curls and she wore a knotted scarf like an ancient legionary's *focale* in the neck of a faded brown shirt. She brandished a rifle that should have been in a museum.

'What in Pluto's name are *you* doing here?' I'd recovered enough not to use her real name. If she was leading this group, she might well be using a *nom de guerre.*

'Waiting for you, Prima. Your deadline expires in three hours.'

I glanced at the two men standing with her, neither of whom I recognised. Their eyes were full of curiosity, but their expressions remained stern.

'Well, you can at least invite us in and find us a cup of coffee,' I said.

Their caves were extensive; there must have been over a hundred people living there, women and men. Their local leader, Frontius, had organised them into foraging, defence and logistic groups. A sturdy man with dark eyes that darted everywhere like a car trader or land agent looking over your shoulder for the next deal. He said little when Calavia introduced us as Prima and Secundus.

Calavia and two others had arrived about ten days ago with supplies, including precious transceiver radios, and the task of setting up cells of resistants.

'Has the other pair who set out at the same time as Atrius and me arrived yet?' I crouched with Calavia in a corner at the back of a side cave where she slept.

'One arrived yesterday with a gunshot wound to her lower arm. Her oppo didn't survive.' Calavia's eyes clouded for a few moments. 'She was more upset at leaving him in a ditch than worrying about her arm. Silly tart.'

'Don't be so hard, Calavia. It's distressing when a tent-mate dies at your side. First time?'

'Yes.' She tilted her head. 'Sorry, I didn't mean to be callous, but we can't afford it. We've dug the bullet out of her arm and patched her up.'

'I'll go and speak to her. What's the situation here? How far do the caves go back, really?'

'Right into the cliff until it starts sloping downward on the surface.'

'And are there any escape tunnels?'

She shifted her feet and dropped her gaze.

'Frontius has hinted, but hasn't given me any details,' she replied in a soft voice. 'I had a quick look around, but haven't had time for a thorough search.'

'He must have some sort of evacuation plan.' I would be having a word with Frontius; he had to trust Calavia with this or it could be disastrous if they were attacked.

'He's pulled this lot together,' she added. 'But he admitted to me it's getting harder to stay covert just because of the sheer numbers of them.'

'Any sign of the enemy?'

'Frontius says the nats have patrolled past here on the tourist road that leads up to the old fortress, but they haven't attacked the caves.'

'Hmm. Call me paranoid, but don't you find that strange?'

'Difficult to mount a frontal attack – the losses would be significant,' Calavia said.

'Yes and no. Numbers would decide it. But suppose you wanted to finish off all your opponents in one hit?'

She studied the opposite wall, then brought her gaze back with a look of horror. 'Oh, gods!'

'Precisely,' I replied. 'Classic tactic. You let them cluster, or if necessary herd them, over a period of time in one place, then strike. We can't wait for any warnings – they're going to have to leave the caves now and disperse. According to people we've talked to in the city, Caius has mostly squashed open opposition there and it seems the same in the countryside. He's not stupid. He'll be up here to clear them out any day now.'

25

———

The next morning, I took a group picked by Frontius plus two from each of Claudia's and Lucia's groups through the communication techniques and issued them with my last sets of one-time letter pads for encrypting messages.

'Give yourself enough time to work through the message and check it. Don't forget the identifier group at the beginning of the message. You must keep the pads in a metal box with matches and turps nearby. They are precious, of course, but if there is any threat or possible compromise you must burn them. If any of Caius's nats or somebody you suspect as a ferret or traitor could possibly have had access to them, they are worse than useless. They'll endanger more lives and could compromise the entire take-back.'

While Calavia went off for her regular radio schedule back to Vienna, Atrius organised the newly trained into groups to instruct the others. At least they'd all be competent to send a message if push came to shove. I went up to the edge of the cave and stared out. Tree branches moved in the breeze, the sky was calm with a few clouds, no noise apart from a few birds singing. But I felt uneasy; the cave dwellers were vulnerable living in a self-confident bubble that was overdue for bursting.

When she came back, Calavia gave me such a look that I knew something had happened. She didn't fuss but she had a sense of suppressed concern.

'Urgent info. We need to get the leaders together.'

I took her with Lucia and Claudia into a huddle with Frontius in a side cave with strict orders to the two guards to let no one into our discussion. Frontius was surprised, but then shrugged, when Calavia and I revealed our true names.

'I suppose I should have expected the Twelve Families to be involved in this. But we all thought you'd abandoned us.'

'Never, Frontius.' I clasped his upper arm and stared him direct in the eyes. 'We had to lick our wounds. Caius Tellus caught us all off guard. Now we prepare to strike back. But to do this we must put a network in place that can carry out tasks such as destroying their communications and transport routes, and securing the broadcast stations.'

'And just how are you going to do that, *domina*?' he said in a sarcastic voice. 'We're only just managing to survive.'

'Each group will have its specific task and train for it. But the first thing is to get you all into the city in safe locations.'

'The city? You're raving,' he said. Calavia shot him an angry look. Claudia and Lucia said nothing but looked unhappy.

'Staying here isn't an option,' I continued. 'The nats could strike any day.'

'They may not do it for months, if ever,' Frontius shot back.

'If I may, major?' Calavia fidgeted and I waved for her to speak. 'In my sched a few minutes ago with Vienna, the group that Major Mitela set up in the city has just reported a troop concentration yesterday in the Victis barracks. Six light personnel carriers and four covered cargo trucks. They couldn't see what was in the trucks, but something heavy from the how low the vehicles sat.'

'Victis barracks lies this side of the city,' I explained to the others and told them of my suspicions I discussed with Calavia last night I looked round at them all 'This means we move out now.'

'The safest place is right under their eyes where they least expect you.' I tore the city map out of Atrius's telephone directory and marked up locations.

'These are properties owned by exiled Roma Novans. Some are individual houses, some are shops with flats above or even simple rooms with shared facilities. They've agreed they can be used by resistance forces. You may have to break in, but I trust you will be discreet. My own *domus* may have been confiscated along with Countess Quirinia's, but if nobody's living there, then you'll need the passwords to get through the security. Well, if it's still working. I'll write letters of authorisation. Quirinia's steward knows my writing. If he's still there, that is.' I glanced at Calavia and Claudia, who both nodded. 'You may also use *domus* of the Calavia and Cornelia families, if available.'

'You've thought this through, haven't you?' Frontius said. He taken some further convincing, but now admitted to the wisdom of moving out in light of the message from the resistance group in the city.

'We've spent enough time planning,' I said 'Now we're into the doing stage.'

'You think you can do it?' Frontius pursued his lips.

'No, I think *we* can do it.'

He nodded his head slowly.

'One thing. In the properties you occupy… I trust you will respect the contents.'

'We'll have to live off something,' Frontius replied. 'We might have to scavenge.'

'Yes, but you can be sensible about it. The locked storerooms in the basements of the bigger houses should have good supplies of smoked and preserved meats and vegetables, if they haven't been looted. You should consume those first. If a steward is in place she, or he, will allocate you resources. We'll be in contact soon to ask you to get a job in a strategic target.'

'What sort of thing?' He scratched the back of his neck.

'Something like a cleaner or clerical assistant – one that people don't notice.'

'How long will it be for?'

'I don't have an answer, but it's been nearly fourteen months since that bastard Caius Tellus seized power. The sooner we're ready, the sooner we can act.'

He stood, thinking we were finished.

'One more thing, Frontius.' I gestured the others to stand. Frontius flicked the thick brown hair out of his eyes and looked at me with a wary expression. 'I understand you have dug escape tunnels to the surface from your run of caves here. Claudia and Lucia are going to bring their people up here in the next hour to be evacuated. They and Calavia need to know exactly where these tunnels are if we are to get everybody out safely. I suggest you share that information now.' I crossed my arms, stared at him and waited.

'Juno, I thought he was going to choke,' Claudia said. She was busying herself rolling her sleeping bag into a nylon bag. All around her the other women were packing up their camp; some were already ferrying their backpacks up to Frontius's caves. Calavia would direct the dispersal from there.

'I can see his point,' I said. 'This is the worst of Caius's pernicious regime – he's stopped us trusting each other. You don't know if your neighbour, a friend you've known for years or even your family member is one of these damned nats.'

I glanced round. The cave was pretty nearly empty.

'I'm just going down to check how Lucia's crew are getting on before it starts getting dark. I'll see you back at the top.' I patted her on the shoulder as I stood. I was used to clambering between the caves now. Somebody had carved out extra hand- and footholds and fixed a rope which made it even easier, but I didn't want to risk falling off. Whatever I would have liked to think, the reality was that I wasn't as agile as I had been twenty years ago.

'*Salve*, Lucia,' I said as I swung into the entrance to her cave. She stood a step back from the edge and looked harassed, but her people clustered ready to move with their bags and sacks at their feet. I noticed a few of them had rifles slung across their backs. They were chattering, some even joshing each other.

'Ready to go?' I said.

'I suppose so.' She rubbed the back of her neck with her fingers. 'This wasn't home, but we found some peace here.'

'I know. And it's going to be extremely disruptive in the next few months, but if we make a big push now, you'll be back in your own home this time next year.'

She smiled at me. I heard a sharp crack. Lucia looked startled. Her mouth opened without any sound. Blood dribbled out and she crashed to the ground.

'Down!' I shouted. 'Get back from the edge. And douse those lights.'

My pulse leapt. Pluto, they were here already.

More shots. A *thunk* from near the entrance. Then another. More above us. Then further up, but louder. Answering fire. I crept on my stomach towards Lucia. Her still eyes said it. I laid my fingers on the pulse in her neck. Nothing.

'*Vale* Lucia,' I murmured, then signalled two of her people to drag her body away from the edge. I grabbed my radio.

'Calavia, Mitela. Start emergency evac now. Be ready for enemy at tunnel exits. Over.'

'Confirm. Enemy below estimated at four times six. Over.'

'Pick your targets and discourage. Require covering fire for evacuation of lower caves. Over.'

'Will do. Out.'

Crawling on my stomach, I edged up to the entrance. Behind me some whispered snatches but mostly stunned silence. Nobody moved.

I glanced down. Calavia could observe better from the top cave, but I saw well enough. Three small armoured personnel carriers with a driver and six troops in each. Regular legionaries. And a jeep with the red splodge on the side and black figures clustered round it. Nats. Damn. The nats were fair game, but firing on regulars with the intention of neutralising them went against every instinct.

Shots rang out from above. Two black-clothed figures by the nat vehicle fell. I crawled back half a metre from the edge and turned to face Lucia's crew. Terrified eyes, angry faces and numb shock greeted me.

'Anybody a good shot?'

Nobody moved.

'Look, we have to move, and quickly. Some of us might not make it, but if we don't, we'll *all* be dead in minutes.'

A woman with dishevelled hair edged up to me.

'I—' She sniffed. 'My name's Tulla. I used to shoot for my legion when I did my national service, but that was a good twenty years ago.'

I grasped her shoulder. 'You're in the same place as I am. Welcome! Take the right edge at the entrance.'

She gave a brief nod and crawled forward. Somebody touched me on my shoulder. Two young faces, sixteen, perhaps seventeen years old, both pale, but eyes full of fire.

'We're gamers. Him and me, we play as a team. We can both aim really good. But we only ever used guns as cadets at school.'

Gods! Children.

'Apprentices?'

Both nodded.

'Take the left and tell me what's going on.' I edged back then crouched in the back of the cave, beckoning the rest of the group to follow me. One by one, they crawled into a huddle round me. Four of them still had their rifles.

'Can you use that?' I pointed to the weapon on the back of a middle-aged man with spectacles. He hesitated, then said, 'Yes, but my eyes aren't that good these days in this light.'

'Then hand it over to the two apprentices. Take them through it for a couple of shots first.'

He unslung it slowly and gripped the beautifully polished stock as if it were the imperial crown.

'It was my mother's favourite, I—' he said.

I held my hand out. He looked undecided. Then a shot cracked against the cave edge. He thrust the rifle into my hand and dived for the floor.

'Boys!' I shouted to the apprentices. They scuttled back.

'The legionaries are spreading out and hiding in the scrub between the castle and the bottom of the cliff,' one blurted out.

'Yeah, and Tulla, you know, the forewoman you said to shoot, she bagged one of them!' The other grinned for an instant. Then realising we were frowning at him dropped his gaze to the floor. I handed the first boy the middle-aged man's rifle.

'Listen carefully to this man and take great care of this. I want it back in the same condition.' Not a whisper of a prayer to Mercury of that happening, but they calmed. 'Now get cracking. Pick them off one by one. No wasting ammunition. No messing about.'

They took the rifle back to the left edge. The man crouched behind them, first instructing them, then encouraging them. My radio buzzed.

'Mitela, Calavia. Fifty per cent are out, no opposition at tunnel entrance. Your situation? Over.'

'Pinned down but targeting individual enemy. Limited ammunition. Move imperative. Over.'

'Agreed. Diversion imminent, prepare to move. Out.'

What in Pluto's name was she going to do?

Terrified, but lined up ready to go with a single backpack each, we waited. Tulla and the boys were still firing sporadically and shots from all three caves had kept the opposition pinned down. But they would have radioed for backup. How much longer did we have?

Even counting the seconds logically, two minutes took a lifetime to pass. The sun was dipping on the horizon now. If ever we needed the dark it was now. Then a shower of small objects whizzed past the cave entrance, then another. A crash on the ground followed by several whoomphs.

'Fire!' one of the boys shouted. 'The scrub's on fire and they're running like fricking pigs towards their trucks.'

'Go!' I shrieked and pushed the first one of Lucia's people toward the cave exterior. She grasped the rope and scampered upwards. I pushed them all out as if they were a parachute line. Then more missiles from above. The climbers carried on, but I ducked back. Smoke plumed up, joining that from the burning scrub. I jerked my head at Tulla and the boys, the only ones left.

'Get going! Now!' I shouted.

'But—' she protested.

'Do as I damned well say,' I growled. She stared at me for a moment, then slung her rifle across her back and grabbed the guide rope that led upwards. The boys followed close behind. I glanced down as I grasped the rope to the path upwards. The scrub was burning less and the smoke from Calavia's smoke bombs was dispersing. Claudia's people had gone ahead. As I neared Claudia's now empty cave, I was almost blinded by the beam of a massive spotlight on me. Oh gods, I was a target in a shooting gallery. I froze for a nanosecond. Shots came from above. The crack of glass splintering. The beam went out. Eyes still dazzled, I grabbed the rock face, pulling myself the last metre and threw myself on the cave floor, ducking the bullets that flew around me.

I gulped for breath, air rasping my throat. I lay slumped on the cave floor for a minute or two. The smell of ash, dirt, my own sweat, hit me. Ow, my face was sore. I sat up, and flicked gravel off it. My radio buzzed.

'Mitela, Calavia. Report.'

Her message was terse, but I could hear the anxiety in her voice. I pressed the rocker button.

'Calavia, Mitela. All in one piece, but bruised. Over.'

'Thank the gods. Can you get up here?'

'Give me five. Over.'

'Not possible. Look outside.'

I crawled to the edge. Snaking up the road in the dark, full headlights shining, were at least a dozen vehicles.

Merda.

I pulled myself up. My legs trembled. I stumbled to the cave entrance. At least the night had come down. I pushed the radio button.

'On my way. Out.'

Shots came from above. My cue to go. I gripped the rope as I made my way upwards. The top cave was twenty metres up, six floors of an average building, and my legs were like wet tissue. Shouts came from below, shots from above. I was caught between two worlds.

Luckily, the first part was along a narrow ledge rising steeply, but enough room to place both feet side by side. I plodded on, the staccato rattle from above continuing. Finally, I had to scramble up the last few metres then my fingers found the blessing of the rope ladder. Hands reached down. Atrius. I was so pleased to see his face, I grinned like an idiot. He wouldn't have seen – I was in the shadow – but that didn't matter.

Before I could thank him as he pulled me in, the cliff face shuddered and the cave next to ours exploded with a deafening boom. The blast demolished the wall of ours and rock flew everywhere.

'Back!' I heard Calavia shriek. 'Get the fuck into the tunnel.'

Atrius half pushed, half dragged me into the blackness. A cool breeze smelling damp touched my face. We rushed on for several minutes. Somebody lit a torch with a red filter. The tunnel became narrower, wound round to the side, the floor rose, the ceiling came nearer.

'Nearly there,' Calavia shouted back to us. 'Mind your heads.'

A minute later, the four in front of Atrius and me stopped. I eased forward. The stars. I saw the stars above us, then the moon. Luna, welcome! We climbed up through a shallow shaft and emerged onto the surface in a thicket of brambles and gorse.

'Quick, into the trees,' Calavia said. The ground shuddered under us as another blast hit the cave below. Mortars. They were using heavy mortars. If we'd been there, we'd have been blown into shreds of flesh.

26

Calavia gave me a quick nod before she busied herself directing people off to their allocated placements. Then she herself vanished into the gloom. The gods watch over them.

Frontius gathered Atrius, the young guard with the gunshot wound and me from the trees on top of the cliff and accompanied us through the city outskirts into the empty countryside. We pinched a bicycle to transport the injured guard; she was falling over with exhaustion and running a temperature after the escape through the tunnels. Atrius marched along, his arm round her waist and his shoulder supporting her weight. I sent a prayer to Mercury, patron of thieves, to ask forgiveness from the bicycle owner.

We holed up overnight in a farm outbuilding three kilometres out of the city. It was dry and the farmer gave us blankets, painkillers for the injured guard and meat rolls and water for us all. He said little, just nodded at Frontius as he closed the door. I didn't want to, but we stayed another day so the injured guard could rest. My stomach was in knots most of the day, but I managed to doze when I wasn't keeping watch. By morning the young guard's temperature was more or less normal, thank Juno, so we moved.

The horse and cart Frontius borrowed from the taciturn farmer made steady progress. Atrius sat up at the front, occasionally exchanging a few words with Frontius, but mostly silent. The young guard – she could only be in her mid-twenties – was sleeping. I'd made a rudimentary sling from a scarf to stop her arm being jolted all over the place as we drove over the rough surfaces, and pulled a blanket and one of the empty sacks over her. Our biggest worry was being stopped by nats or *vigiles*, but the farmer assured us the country roads were seldom patrolled now.

We hadn't seen a single private car on the road. With a collapsing economy the price of fuel had rocketed. I saw several garages with petrol pumps closed as we made our way west. The dirty signs, some with the plastic coverings broken and the unlit lamp showing through, displayed horrendous prices. Anger rolled through me at the dilapidation and desolation of my country and the misery Caius had brought about in such a short time.

After an anxious and chilly night camping in woods west of Aquae Caesaris when Atrius and I took turns on watch, we approached the frontier area. This could be the most dangerous part of our journey, but Frontius seemed unconcerned. At least the slow journey on winding roads had given us time to take in the shattering events at the caves. I only prayed Calavia had got everybody out to the safe houses.

Unlike the first and second times I'd struggled to get out of Roma Nova, this border crossing was unbelievably easy. We clip-clopped down a minor side road which soon ran out of metalling and became a grassy track which muffled the noise of the horse's hooves. I couldn't see very far in the dusk as we descended to the underside of a bridge over a stream. Frontius reined in the horse and cart and we clambered down. I patted the horse, whose breath sent warm plumes into the chill air, and sent a silent prayer of thanks to the farmer. I woke the young guard who blinked, sat up and shivered. After a drink from my water flask, she assured me she was perfectly fit to go on. I doubted that, looking at her pale face, but we had no choice.

Frontius backed the horse and cart into the trees and tied the reins to a stout branch. He said he'd return them to the farmer on his way to the city.

'You don't seem at all worried we might run into patrols, Frontius.'

'We bribe the frontier guards with coffee, chocolate and cigarettes not to patrol this area,' he offered by way of explanation.

'Where do you get them from?' I said.

'We acquire them from around here.'

'Acquire?'

He shrugged, glanced at Atrius who frowned at him, then looked back at me.

'I will arrange supplies for you in the future,' I said. 'The last thing we want at this time is a row with our neighbours over pilfering.'

We crossed the stream, walked along a track, scrambled up a steep bank and over a fence. That was it. In front of us was the main road to the Free City of Trieste. We were in the Northern Italian Federation.

We hitched a lift into Udine, cleaned up in the station facilities and caught the overnight train to Vienna. It was eight hours of boredom, but we managed to sleep some of the time, Atrius and I alternately on watch. The young guard with the gunshot wound was running a temperature again. I checked her arm. Blood seeped from the site where the bullet had been crudely extracted. Atrius gave her the last of his painkillers and tightened the field dressing on her arm. Thank the gods she was dozing when the ticket inspector came round.

Once in Vienna, I phoned the *Jagdschloss* and Junia came to collect us. We stumbled into the entrance, bone weary, but then I smelt coffee, proper Viennese coffee.

'I think you've done well, very well,' Volusenia said. 'Of course, you had no remit to recruit people but all in all that's a bonus. Now they're out of those caves and once established back in the city, they'll be invaluable.'

'What about Calavia?' I asked. 'Are you leaving her in the city?'

'For the time being. Now we have reasonably secure communication with these groups we can firm up our plans.' She looked up at me. 'Of course, we'll have to expect some losses.' I gripped my mug. I hated the thought of Marcia or her brother being grabbed in some dawn raid and hauled off by the nats for interrogation, or her young *vigilis* cousin. Or, Mercury forbid, Claudia Cornelia. I'd urged her to leave with me, but even before she said it, I knew she wouldn't. I shivered.

'Go and get some rest,' Volusenia said. 'I'll get the photos you and that young guard took developed. And collate your notes.' She glanced at her watch. 'We'll reconvene in six hours.'

I barely had the energy to peel off my clothes. I dropped like a stone onto my bed. It was only when my eyelids were pressing down on my eyes like lead weights that I realised that I hadn't seen Miklós. But I couldn't fight the weight of my exhaustion and sank like a dead weight into the arms of Morpheus.

Junia shook me awake early the next morning at six. I'd slept twenty hours.

'Why in Hades didn't you wake me earlier?'

'Because the colonel said to leave you. You were falling asleep in the van from the station.'

'The young guard, how is she? Is her arm all right?'

'Slightly infected, but the doctor's given her a shot of antibiotics and will keep her in the sick room for a few days.'

Atrius would have recovered fast; typical fit young soldier. But there was another man on my mind at the moment.

'Junia, where's Miklós?'

'I'm afraid I don't know.'

'Oh. Has he been made unwelcome?'

'Not at all. When you went, I think he went to stay with his nephew, cousin, whatever he is – the caretaker. '

'Lúkas.' I scrambled off the bed and caught the smell coming from me of several days in the field. 'Ah. I'll see you later after I've decontaminated myself.'

I skipped breakfast and even coffee. Downstairs, I made for the back door. The morning light was pink and lemon flushing out the grey blue of the last of the night. Frost crunched under my feet as I hurried over to the keeper's cottage. The downstairs shutters were already open and yellow light shone out of the windows. I heard voices and looked through the window. The television. Lúkas sprawled in an old leather armchair, a mug on the table to the side, and he was laughing. The sullen face he wore on the day I'd met him when Junia and I had first visited the *Jagdschloss* had vanished. He looked like a teenager as he threw his head back, narrowed his eyes and his mouth burst with laughter. But there was nobody else with him. I rapped on the door. I waited for a couple of minutes, and then went in.

He turned almost nonchalantly, then sprang up.

'What do you want?' The sullen face was back.

'Good morning, Lúkas. Is Miklós here?'
'Does it look like it?'
'It was a civil question. Is he here?'
'No.'
'Do you know where he is?'
'No.'
'Please, Lúkas, it's important.'
'He left three days ago, on his horse.'
'Didn't he tell you anything?'
'We don't stick our noses in other people's business.'
I stared at him, willing him to say more, but that was his last word.

'Well, these prove the EUS is directly involved.' Volusenia threw the sheaf of black and white photos onto the table. I passed them round the table to the rest of the intelligence group gathered in her office that afternoon; Junia, newly promoted lieutenant, Atrius, Silvia and Quirinia.

Silvia glanced round at all of us as if waiting for answers. The carbon copies in the 'Sent' file on Caius's desk that I'd been able to photograph included a letter in English from Caius marked 'Confidential – By Bag' in which he thanked his CIA contact White for the recent batch of technical equipment. Caius's initials at the bottom right-hand corner proved he'd seen and signed it.

'Gaius, that young *vigilis* Atrius and I met, specifically mentioned new equipment in his station,' I said. 'I'm going to ask the *nuncia* in Washington for her thoughts.'

'As long as she doesn't let on we know,' Volusenia said.

I gave her a long stare.

'Washington is one of the most senior diplomatic posts and only conferred on the most able and experienced officer. You may rest assured, Marcella Volusenia, that the *nuncia* knows how to keep a secret.'

'Don't poker up at me, *consiliaria*.'

'The *nuncia* there is old school,' I added. 'Not only did she come up through the *cursus honorum* but completed each stage with distinction. She's one of the strongest willed and craftiest women I know.'

'Sounds bloody terrifying,' Volusenia retorted.

'Not in your league, though, colonel,' I said.

Quirinia smiled and Silvia giggled.

'My point is,' I continued, 'that she will have picked a good head of station and will give her or him very specific instructions. It will be helpful to have her contribution if we are going to take the EUS's involvement in Roma Nova's internal affairs to the International Court.'

'Well, you know the political stuff better than I do, so I leave that in your hands,' Volusenia said. She consulted a pile of typed sheets. 'Next, you all report how run-down things are – closed shops, food shortages, unrepaired buildings, street lamps broken, petrol supplies cut off and the increased *vigiles* and military patrols. The photographs confirm this. How in Hades things have diminished to this state in this short time, I don't know.'

'I do wonder if there's been passive disobedience in the population,' I said. 'Fifty per cent of it has been disenfranchised and rendered invisible by law. That's a powerful force for resentment. You may remember the messages we had a few months ago about the silver producers deliberately reducing output and diverting distribution. On top of that, I wonder how many men are now seeing that their new, supposedly privileged, position isn't all it's cracked up to be. Information should start coming in about that via the resistance groups we met in our first few days in Roma Nova.'

'I can't imagine how peculiar it must be there now,' Silvia said and shivered. I took her hand and pressed it.

Volusenia looked at each of us in turn, then cleared her throat. 'In light of economic weakness, the reported discontent, our signals intelligence, the resistance groups and international support, I think we must now start more formal activity.'

Nobody spoke while they took in her words. Quirinia put her hand to her neck. Junia and Atrius leaned forward, as I did.

'Meaning?' I said into the tense atmosphere.

'The specifics of taking back Roma Nova.'

I took a gulp of water from the moulded glass beaker in front of me. At last, we had finished reacting to Caius. We were going on the offensive. Volusenia's eyes glittered as she continued.

'Now, that young guard you brought back with the shot arm, *consiliaria*, not only took some useful photographs but also managed to get wind of some of these damned work camps. Cross-referencing it with the signals information from the two listening posts, we're pretty sure we've identified their locations. The inmates will be weak and probably physically in poor shape, so we will need emergency medical support, but some will be ready for revenge. Our problem will be restraining them.' She smacked the flat of her hand on the table. 'Whatever happens, we must *not* allow a wholesale personal rampage, no *vastatio*. it's one thing to deny supplies and communications to the enemy, but on no account will farms and crops be destroyed. And looters will be shot.' She paused, then looked away, something very rare for somebody so self-assured. 'We'll have to use whatever forces we can muster locally to enforce order and provide support when the camps are liberated,' she continued, her voice tighter. 'Female ex-*vigiles*, local reservists who can be vouched for, even the remaining male *vigiles* if we have to, stiffened up with a few Praetorians.' She drew breath at last and looked up.

'May I speak, colonel?' Atrius said. Volusenia nodded. 'With your permission, I will work out a strategy to organise this. I know what it's like to be in the hands of the nationalists.' He looked down at the floor, his hands clasped together. After a brief moment he sat up straight. 'Claudia Cornelia's account of her time in that camp was invaluable. Apart from their physical injuries, malnutrition and exhaustion, these prisoners will be full of anger and despair and be overwhelmed with a way to express it. Yes, they will want to fight with us.'

'Work out how many people you will need and possible resources,' Volusenia replied. '*Consiliaria* Quirinia's team will cost it out.' She glanced at Quirinia who was scribbling in her notebook. 'Bring it back to the next meeting in two days' time, please.'

Atrius had lost his naivety, but also his self-assurance after being tortured by Caius's goons. There couldn't be a better person to handle this. It would give him a personal as well as professional route to reconciliation with himself. But it was, being brutal, a side issue. First we had to secure Roma Nova. I raised my hand.

'Colonel, we have plans on the intelligence, diplomatic and

humanitarian front and the earlier theoretical work my and *Consiliaria* Quirinia's groups produced back in April, but we must now develop the practical military one. We are still short of enough active forces to launch a full-scale invasion.'

'Our total numbers here are now up to 2,993, Aurelia, including five live births in the last two months,' Quirinia piped up.

'How many of that figure are between ages sixteen and fifty-five?'

'Just under two-thirds,' she replied.

'So we have a potential fighting strength of around two thousand, with half of that capable of front-line combat.' I looked around. 'I know Junia Sestina's been stepping up training, widening it to include all that age group. I know we have the resistance groups, but we need numbers or some strategy to combat their lack.'

Silence.

'Where do you suggest we get these magic numbers from?' Volusenia looked directly at me.

'Well, I wondered about calling in favours from military colleagues in other countries. I could probably muster a hundred or so who would help, totally unofficially.'

But I knew they'd have the covert backing of their military command. Soldiers looked after fellow soldiers even across national boundaries.

'To get sufficient numbers we need to plan to advance steadily, gaining people as we go, such as those female military who were thrown out when Caius Tellus came to power. This is Caius's regime's blind spot. They think they have subdued the women of Roma Nova and rendered them invisible. They will be one of our best-hidden weapons. Of course, they won't be as sharp as Junia Sestina's trainees; they're over a year out of condition.

'The second is what remains of the Twelve Families inside Roma Nova.' I nodded at Silvia. 'We know the imperatrix's cousins to the third degree have been imprisoned.' Silvia stared at me wide-eyed, then nodded. That particular piece of news had been hard to tell her. 'What has happened to the rest of them, we don't know,' I added. 'But the Families structure is still there. Can you imagine what the Mitelae, the Calaviae, your own family, colonel, and the others must be feeling? Yes, they'll all be keeping their heads down, but probably boiling with fury underneath.'

'My sister was murdered by Caius Tellus,' Volusenia said. 'The rest of them will either be in prison or being careful, but yes, I'd say they'll be ready for retaliation.'

I didn't mention the name of the Tellus family for obvious reasons, but I was worried about Quintus, Caius's estranged brother. I hadn't heard from him for months. Was he even still alive? Caius might have just shot him on a whim. And what had happened to little Conradus?

I shuffled my papers together. 'We need to contact them one by one and get them to leave the city and rally any people remaining on their estates and the surrounding areas. This will give us pockets of reinforcements. We'll sweep them up as we advance. They'll also help contain and stabilise their local areas when we take them back.' I looked away. 'My own people are here, of course, but I'm sure they'll want to come with us.'

Juno knew I wanted to see what had become of Castra Lucilla. I wept inside at the memory of that night we had to abandon the farm, leaving grain to rot, loosing all the animals into the open. Even more, it had been heart-wrenching for the estate workers to leave the homes their families had lived in for generations. Volusenia looked up from the notepad she'd been scribbling in for the past few minutes.

'We have just under three hundred Praetorians here,' she said. 'Even with my poor arithmetical skills that means there's another two hundred inside Roma Nova lurking somewhere. None of the photographs and none of the reconnaissance reports show any Praetorian on duty anywhere. We've heard of eleven confirmed executions, all senior officers, and only a few others imprisoned. Some may be in the work camps or in Truscium, Mars help them.' She paused to catch her breath. 'But signals intelligence shows no increase in movements to and from there nor any increased radio traffic. This leads me to conclude there are at least a hundred and fifty keeping their heads down. We need to find them.'

'Another factor is the attitude of the current *magister militum*,' I said. 'Has Caius replaced the previous one? If we can be reasonably sure that the country's top soldier would bring his troops over to us, or at least not deploy them against us, that would be a huge advantage.'

'That's a big "if", Aurelia,' Quirinia said. 'I know at the last imperial council, the *magister* was anti-Caius and you said he was still in post when you were, er, at the palace with Caius.' She blushed, remembering her own prejudice, I thought. 'He's very loyal to his soldiers and would do anything to protect them. You reported there were regular troops helping the nats when you escaped from the caves. So they *are* working for Caius at present. If the *magister* is still in post, he won't move until he's sure Caius is losing.'

A touch on my arm. Silvia.

'I know this is all technical stuff above my head, but would it help if I spoke to him and asked?'

Five pairs of eyes turned on her slight figure. Her skin flushed red, but her gaze was steady.

'He was very kind and polite when he came to the palace to see Mama,' she said. 'And he always brought me a birthday present.'

Volusenia rolled her eyes. Luckily Silvia was still looking at me and didn't see. Quirinia sent me a pleading look.

'That's a very clever idea, darling,' I said, trying to sound sincere. 'And one we'll keep in reserve. I think at the moment, we'll have to plan for the worst case.'

She gave me a mulish look back. 'Well, it was only a suggestion,' she retorted. 'I don't know why I'm in this meeting. There's nothing I can do to help.'

'I know it's difficult and perhaps a little boring,' I replied. 'But it's important for you to know exactly what we're planning to do in your name.'

'Oh.'

'You being here reminds us all why we're doing it.' I took her hand and pressed it. Poor child. What a way to spend your teenage years.

She nodded, crossed her arms and leaned back in her chair. Quirinia gave her a quick smile and a nod. Volusenia said nothing.

'It's the logistics of it all that will be the bugger,' said Junia, breaking the silence.

'Exactly so, lieutenant,' replied Volusenia. She looked at Quirinia. 'That Vibianus from the Paris legation, he seems a likely sort. I'd like to second him to work on the logistics, if you think he's up to it.'

'Well, I'd be most unhappy to lose him...' Quirinia looked dismayed.

'I know he's performing administrative miracles for you,

consiliaria, and our little colony is running smoothly because of it but that's not the object of our existence here.'

'No, I'm perfectly aware of that, colonel,' Quirinia retorted at her most huffy. 'But without good administration, we wouldn't be as stable and prosperous as we are.' Her right hand clenched around her pen as she glared at Volusenia.

'If I may?' I had to stop this turf war. 'The colonel needs Vibianus's expertise. That's beyond question. Why not promote his number two, Grania, to help you, Quirinia? She seems pretty competent.'

Both stared at me, one miffed, one cynical, but after a moment, Quirinia nodded.

'Now, next steps,' I said to move them on. 'Tasking. I suggest we establish two teams. One will work under Junia Sestina to make lists from the telephone directory that Atrius brought back, and from personal knowledge of friends and relations of the exiles here. This team will actively sound out potential supporters inside Roma Nova. The contacts from those lists will also act as a disinformation conduit. The propaganda war is as important as live operations. I did some preliminary work on this in March.' I glanced at Junia. 'Ask Numerus for the file. Then you'll need to draw up a contact schedule in liaison with a signals officer.' I glanced round at them all. 'We'll have to be extremely careful and do it in tiny stages. The potential for leaks is significant, but with our low numbers we have to try everything. I'll develop the approach messages with Junia. But before one call is made, we'll all have to slog away at the lists, vetting them to weed out any doubtful names.

'The second team headed by you, colonel, assisted by Vibianus, will plan each individual step of the take-back – objectives, timing, forces needed, expected reinforcements, feeding, resupply, logistics required. Timing and coordination will be crucial. One of the first things to plan is a schedule of specific targeted insertions to seize the main towns of Aquae Caesaris, Brancadorum and Castra Lucilla. This is going to have to be an invasion on a shoestring.' I smiled at them, but I wasn't feeling humorous. 'Whatever happens and whatever casualties we incur, once we start we must push through until we take the entire country.'

. . .

'Nightcap?' Volusenia asked as the others left.

'Just a quick one.' It was past midnight and I was yearning for my bed. 'What's on your mind?' I asked as I took the glass.

She stashed the bottle in her lower filing cabinet drawer and came to roost on the corner of her desk.

'It's all very well drawing up plans and tactics, but there's one big problem. Two, actually. Weapons and transport.'

'Agreed. I suggest that people draw funds from Quirinia and start buying rifles individually as from now. They'll have to apply for a licence and join hunting or gun clubs. Just a few at a time. The regime's pretty permissive here and most farmers have at least a shotgun. Handguns are out, but knives can be bought over the counter.'

'This is ridiculous,' Volusenia snorted.

'Of course it is, but we have no option,' I said. 'I'll make a few other enquiries for heavier *matériel* with international colleagues but I'll have to be ultra discreet.'

'And where are we going to store these weapons? The New Austrians will smell a rat.'

I smiled at her.

'What?'

'You remember in the original refugee group there was a logistics specialist, I think he was called Rex, no, Regulus. He's married to one of the PGSF *optiones*. He'd been a transport manager and followed his wife out. We made him part of Quirinia's original steering group back in March.'

'And?'

'He masterminded the hire and deployment of the removal vans when we moved here from the original safe house. At present he's driving a taxi. Well, we're going into the logistics and storage business and he's going to run it.'

She laughed heartily, then wiped her eyes. 'Well, I'll give you credit for inventiveness, Aurelia.'

'I'll talk to him in the morning to get it set up. I'm sure Edward Soane's lawyer has a commercial colleague who can push the paperwork through for us. There's a third thing...'

'Oh?'

I set my glass down and looked straight at her. 'Caius is not stupid, as I feel I have to keep reminding everybody. He was more than often one, sometimes two steps in front of me when we were younger. And he's just as sharp now. His only weakness is the belief that women are less able and should keep to the domestic side of life. And that's where we can snare him.'

'How will that help us now?'

'He'll think we're up to something if we don't give him something else to think about, something that confirms his belief. And we need him to be distracted. I have an idea I'd like to run past you…'

28

I set off with a rather overawed Regulus, the transport manager, to see Edward Soane the next day. His superior assistant Anton Drexler ushered us in. Edward promised that 'Klettermann Spedition KG' would be duly registered with the Austrian authorities and gave me an introduction to a commercial bank for its financial transactions.

'Are you diversifying your investments, Aunt Aurelia?' Edward asked as I signed financial guarantee papers.

'We can't squat in Vienna forever. Some want to settle down here to normal life like Regulus here, so he needs an income. He'll also be able to employ a good number of fellow exiles.' I hated lying to Edward, but Volusenia and I had agreed to start spreading rumours that we'd accepted the current situation and were planning to disperse and seek new lives elsewhere now that Roma Nova was closed to us. And Anton Drexler was listening, but pretending not to. 'Helping our people set up businesses or resettle elsewhere is important,' I continued. 'We all need to have a stable future. Now that Marina is settled in the EUS, I've been thinking about joining her. Or perhaps I'll go to London for a while.'

He shot me a speculative look, but courteous and discreet as his kind were, he said nothing as he gathered the papers together.

'Aunt Aurelia, if your colleague would excuse us for a few moments, I need to take five minutes of your time on a personal matter.'

I nodded to Regulus and he was escorted back to reception by Anton Drexler.

'What is it, Edward? Am I running out of money?' I laughed, not meaning it.

'No, not at all,' he said. 'In fact, your accounts have stabilised and been showing healthy balances. No, it's something I can't quite put my finger on, but I know something's up. Somebody telephoned us yesterday saying she was your representative, gave your code words and asked for a largish sum to be transferred to an account in one of the retail banks. Everything was perfectly in order, but the chief clerk referred it to me because of the amount and our relationship. I refused the transfer. You've always instructed us personally and this is the reason I put in my day report.'

'What do you mean when you say "a largish sum"?'

'A hundred thousand.'

'Jupiter's balls!'

'Quite.'

'Does this happen often?'

'Very rarely. We know all our clients personally. This is a private bank, after all. But I've put a warning on your friends' accounts and your group's accounts that all transactions must be referred to me. I've sent encrypted telexes to London, Frankfurt and New York as well.' He glanced at me. 'If you don't mind, I'd like to discreetly warn some of my banking colleagues here in Vienna in case there's some kind of general fraud attack going on.'

But I knew in my heart, and I think he knew in his head, who was behind it.

'Thank you, Edward. You are a good friend as well as cousin. I suppose they were bound to try it.'

'Well, let's change your code words now, shall we? And those of the other Roma Novan accounts.'

Quirinia turned almost white when I told her. We were wrapped up against the November frost and walking in the privacy of the garden. I pulled her down onto the cold stone seat before she fell onto it.

'Aurelia, you know we're very careful about security,' she gabbled in a high-pitched voice. 'We write nothing down. Only a very few people can sign cheques or authorise credit – me, you, Vibianus and Numerus. Surely you don't suspect any of us?'

'No, of course not. I don't know Vibianus very well, but *Nuncia* Cornelia vouched for him without hesitation. He's worked for her for over twelve years. His record is excellent, and remember, he was the one who deciphered the silver trader's code messages from Monticola.' I fixed my gaze on the rigid frozen leaves of the shrub in front of us. 'No, I think it's somebody very clever from Caius's people or maybe some of his new technology. We should warn everybody and tell them to alter their banking access codes immediately.'

In the communications room at the *Jagdschloss* I made some long-distance calls on our secure phones, then another two on an open line that anybody, including the nats in Roma Nova, could intercept. We would be naive to think they weren't listening in and monitoring our conversations.

We initiated the creeping propaganda campaign to throw Caius off the scent about the proposed take-back. Firstly, Quirinia's intelligence sub-group, mainly Atrius, Junia, some of the PGSF guards and a rota of carefully vetted civilians, were making open calls to any relatives, friends and contacts they had here in New Austria dropping in hints they were thinking of moving away or settling outside the exiles' colony. We didn't give them a script, just the instruction to include that they'd accepted they couldn't go back to Roma Nova.

That afternoon, I took Junia off that to develop second part of the campaign – delicate approaches to people still in Roma Nova.

'Unbelievable that the telephone system is still working so well,' she said.

'If I remember correctly, it doesn't need much of an electrical supply as it's the batteries in the exchanges that keep the whole thing running. If the mains supply is cut off or sporadic they can keep going for a good twelve hours. By then the mains would normally have come back on again. Unless something breaks, the system is pretty much self-sufficient.' I exchanged glances with her. 'A great weapon for us.'

'Were you a signals officer, ma'am?' She looked at me with raised eyebrows.

'No,' I said, and grinned. 'Just a random piece of information I picked up from a foreign ministry communications techie.'

After this second phase was set up and a rota of operators briefed and given a list of topics to discuss with their friends and relatives inside Roma Nova, Junia and Atrius handed over to Grania to supervise the whole thing. Every call was monitored, not only to ensure our own subtle messages were getting through, but to glean even the least intelligence from the other end. It was unusual to get a big breakthrough as shown in films; most intelligence yield was from slog, compilation and analysis.

As Saturnalia approached, we pushed the message of being surprised that things were so scarce in Roma Nova now and how wonderful past Saturnalia feasts had been. It had to be done so carefully; Grania held fortnightly refresher sessions on techniques to ensure nobody slipped up.

Saturnalia was different for us this year. As imperatrix, Silvia led the traditional observances on 17 December, assisted by Vibianus, of all people. With a wry smile, she surrendered her authority as imperatrix for the day to the *princeps Saturnalicius*, to whom Volusenia gave a stern briefing. The Floralia riot was burned into people's memories.

The former ballroom blazed with light onto trestle tables set out in long rows. Everywhere was covered in ferns, spruce and pine, and smells of roast pork, lemons and spices invaded the whole ground floor. For a few hours, the severe and stately *Jagdschloss* was overrun with Roman horseplay, noise, silly games taken seriously, toasts, forfeits, songs, dramatic turns and a great deal of alcohol consumption. Even Volusenia unbent and Quirinia was seen to collapse into a fit of giggles at an extremely off-colour joke.

Over the next few days, celebrations were more sober family affairs. On the twenty-third, the Mitelae estate workers and a couple of Mitela cousins and I sat in a small room off the kitchen, ate a light lunch and exchanged small gifts. I invited Silvia to join us; she was my cousin through her father, Fabianus, and although any family would welcome the imperatrix at their table, the poor child had no other blood relatives to sit with.

Miklós would normally have sat by my side during the Saturnalia season, shouting out encouragement to the wilder exploits on

Saturnalia itself. Where in Hades was he? I sipped my wine, twirled the stem of my chain store glass and wondered if I'd ever see him again or even drink one of my own Castra Lucilla vintages again.

As the next step in our propaganda war, Grania's teams started talking to their Roma Novan friends and relatives about specific resettlement projects. The message was that now this last Saturnalia was over, much of the Vienna exile community was going to disperse. Some of the operators were uncomfortable with this, so Grania pulled them off.

I received more than a dozen complaints against her for this.

'Can't you let them do the odd call, Grania? I'm sure with the success so far they know how to be convincing.'

'We need good liars, *consiliaria*, not uncertain ones,' she replied, pushing the bridge of her spectacles up her nose and gave me a steady look.

We had to wait out the New Austrian Christmas and Sylvester celebrations – a pity they didn't coincide with ours. Accompanied by Styrax, I went shopping for two solid days in the first week of January. Vienna had been the centre of elegance for centuries; beautifully gowned women, svelte tailoring, richness of design and creative genius. My arms ached with the weight of designer bags as we staggered back to the taxi driven by one of the Roma Novan exiles.

'Juno, Styrax, I hope we can find a suitcase large enough to take this lot.'

She grinned.

'I think you'll find, *consiliaria*, that a trunk has been ordered as well as the standard suitcase.'

Next morning, I dressed in my new designer winter wool suit, wide shoulders, wide lapels and nipped-in waist. Underneath I wore a multi-coloured silk blouse. Flashy gold earrings, a faux-fur collared camel coat with matching hat and low-heeled but decorated leather boots completed my new outfit. Apparently, this combination was the latest look. My hair had been dressed expertly by one of the exiles who had run his own salon. I felt a fraud but it was part of my disguise. Quirinia gave me a long list and a sheaf of paper along with her best finance minister frown.

'Please do your best to look after these items, Aurelia. They have consumed a significant proportion of our revenue resources this month. If you can do nothing else, leave them with the *nuncio* at the legation.'

'I'll look after your precious things, Quirinia, but stop talking to me as if I were twelve.'

She relented and gave me a look that was more that of a friend. 'I'm sorry, Aurelia, I didn't mean to be horrible. I should be wishing you luck.' She handed me a small wallet. 'Your ticket vouchers and Hungarian passport are in here with an initial supply of currency.' She leant over and kissed me on the cheek. *'Bona fortuna!'*

As Styrax drove me in my new finery to the Wien-Maria-Theresia Airport, a tear rolled down my over made-up cheek. I flicked it away with my fingertip. Was it nerves? Or tiredness? Who was I fooling? Miklós. He hadn't been there to fold me into his arms when I'd returned from that last dangerous mission to Roma Nova. Nor was he here today to wave me off and give me his 'good hunting' wish – *Weidmannsheil* – as he had in Berlin that dreadful time I was pursuing Caius Tellus back to Roma Nova fifteen years ago. Where in Tartarus was he? A strange heart ripple told me he was still alive; I would know if he wasn't. I knew he had to be by himself at times, but he usually told me he was going. Not that it was any easier.

I went through check-in and passport control on automatic, found my seat and watched the grey tarmac with some kind of mindless fascination as we taxied out to the runway. While we were waiting at the side of the main runway for our slot, a large plane landed less than smoothly in front of us. Purple and gold tail wing with its distinctive gold eagle. Air Roma Nova. Then the unmistakable burst of fighter planes above. They dropped out of the sky and landed moments before the passenger plane came to a stuttering halt. New Austrian red and white roundels on the fuselages. Seconds after the first military jet cut its engine, a figure in a dark flight suit leapt out and hurtled over to the passenger plane. Another from the other jet. Airport security blue-light short wheelbases and armed police barrelled towards the plane. Hades, what was going on? I vaguely heard some announcement over our plane intercom regretting we would be delayed, etc. etc.

Emergency slides sprouted from the Air Roma Nova plane and people glided to the tarmac. Once on their feet they hugged, rushed from one to another. One did a little dance. Two children rubbed their eyes – crying, I suspected. They were all rounded up by the gendarmerie and escorted onto a bus. But the aircrew were taken away separately with one of the military and two gendarmes. Thirty minutes later, with the Air Roma Nova plane towed away, we took off.

The other passengers' chatter about the exciting event of the day passed over me as I wondered what a long-range plane was doing on a fifty-minute flight from Roma Nova. In normal times, small planes resembling buses on wings did the Vienna hop. I dismissed the idea that after all these months the plane had made a long-haul flight and didn't want to land in Roma Nova; there were very few long hauls now and they were closely supervised by the nats, from what we had gleaned from signals intelligence. The only likely explanation was that somehow an aircrew had stolen a plane at Portus Airport in Roma Nova, got it refuelled and escaped with several hundred passengers. Gods, what an achievement! She deserved a medal, that pilot. Then two of my brain cells connected.

29

Three hours later, I was breezing through the VIP lounge in the West London Airport, full of self-importance and looking round in an expectant, entitled way.

'Darling!' A devastatingly handsome man around early forties, rich brown hair, sparkling dark eyes and a wicked grin sauntered up to me. Flashguns burst into life like Saturnalia fireworks. He bent down, laid his hand on my hip and kissed me on both cheeks as a close, a very close, friend would. The Hon. Charles FitzGlyn, society bad boy, ensured my arrival was as public as possible.

He whispered in my ear, 'How am I doing?'

'Darling,' I gushed in a loud voice. 'You're absolutely wonderful.'

He laughed, pulled my arm through his and slowly we made our way out to a luxury saloon, complete with uniformed and poker-faced chauffeur who held the back door open for me. I turned, waved at the photographers, gave them an all-teeth smile and slid into the back seat to land beside Charles.

'Sir Henry told me you were good,' he said as we rolled along. 'You're not good, you're bloody terrific.' His drawl had disappeared. He held out his hand. 'Charlie FitzGlyn, ex-Royal Lancers, now one of Sir Henry Carter's monkeys.' He grinned.

'Well, you certainly got the crowd's attention. Thank you.'

'Sir Henry says you want to make a splash, a really loud one. For some reason, the press seems to follow me around in my time off, so

I'm at your service. I have to say, it's the easiest assignment I've ever undertaken.'

'So what's the agenda?'

He handed me a list.

'This takes care of the next three days. I'll drop you off at your hotel, then I have a table booked for dinner at The Holly at eight. After that perhaps a club.'

I studied the list: lunches, fashion house show, tea, drinks, theatre, opera, parties, a vernissage, a celebrity book launch and more parties.

'Juno, I'll need a rest cure after this.'

'Probably. Oh, and you have a meeting booked at 8 am tomorrow with Sir Henry.'

Bolstered by a traditional English breakfast and surprisingly good coffee, I arrived a few minutes early at a nondescript office block in the financial quarter, the City of London; concrete panels, large windows in metal frames, anonymous and characterless. I checked the address again on the sticky note that Charlie had handed me last night. Hardly a place to meet Her Majesty's foreign secretary. But then, this *was* a confidential meeting so I'd dressed in a black suit and clipped-back hair like any City worker.

At a recessed doorway halfway along I paid off the taxi and pushed through the revolving door. In the pale yellow foyer smelling of fresh paint, a burly young man approached me and asked me my business here. Another watched me from the wall. Security, no doubt about it. I gave details of my appointment with Sir Henry Carter and produced my Hungarian passport as ID. Thank goodness it showed my true name as well as my married name. I smiled at the quaint way other countries called it a 'maiden name'. What nonsense! What was wrong with calling it a 'first family name'?

By the time I'd signed in a register and been given a visitor pass to loop round my neck, an older woman wearing a tweed suit and tortoiseshell plastic-rimmed spectacles had stepped briskly from the lift at the back of the hall.

'Good morning, Countess Mitela. I am Mr Hill's secretary. Sir Henry is using his office today. Please come with me.'

On the third floor we stepped out of the lift into a corridor with an armed policeman and another anonymous young man. This one was suited and equipped with an earpiece and wire disappearing into his clothing.

Inside, Sir Henry rose from a leather armchair to greet me.

'My dear Aurelia, welcome. I do apologise for the rather plain surroundings, but discretion, you know. Let me introduce you to Gerald Hill, who heads up the overseas branch of our security services.'

A thin, tall man with a receding hairline, wrinkled forehead and urbane smile stretched out his hand. His handshake was dry and firm; I could feel his bones through his skin.

'*Salve*, Aurelia Mitela. Honoured to meet you,' he said in accented but classical Latin.

'Mine is the honour, Gerald Hill,' I replied in the same language.

'Yes, well, we'll carry on in English, if you don't mind,' Sir Henry said. 'Bit rusty myself.' He gestured towards the easy chairs and waited until Gerald Hill's secretary had poured coffee and left. 'Gerald and Charlie will be your main contacts while you're here in London, but you need to tell me exactly how we can help you. We'll assist as far as we can, as long as it doesn't get sticky politically.'

'Have you ever met Caius Tellus, Harry?' I asked.

'No, but our man in Washington has. Bit of a charmer, I gather, but Gerald might have more.'

'Well, Foreign Secretary, our estimation is that he is an extremely deceptive and strong-willed individual,' Gerald Hill started. 'I'm sure I don't need to tell our guest how ideologically motivated he is. His record over the past seventeen months has been, in the mildest terms, disastrous for Roma Nova and disturbing for the rest of the world. Unfortunately, our friends in the EUS seem to think there is some advantage in supporting him. A most regrettable stance. Our head of station in Washington reports that a CIA operative called White is Tellus's chief contact. It is well known that the UK and Roma Nova have, or had up to Imperatrix Severina's untimely death, very cordial relations – something our colonial cousins seem to have forgotten.'

I had never met Gerald Hill until a few minutes ago, but everything I could remember from his dossier, especially a note about his polite but acute observations, seemed true. Like his late Roma

Novan opposite number, Tertullius Plico, it appeared he gave no quarter.

Sir Henry placed his cup down. 'The head of our American desk reports only minimal contact between Tellus's representative and British officials in Washington. I gather the Roma Novan *nuncia*, who is still received as such in Washington circles, gave the EUS External Affairs representative a flea in his ear when he suggested she should open her legation to Tellus's representative.' He looked at me and raised an eyebrow.

I laughed. 'Her reply was a great deal more robust than that. I hesitate to tell you what she said direct to Caius's obnoxious little man who called at the legation to demand she hand over the keys.'

'Quite.'

I looked over at the window then back again. I leaned forward and touched the back of his hand. 'Caius Tellus has caused so much misery, Harry. I saw that for myself in Roma Nova a few weeks ago. It can't have improved since then. We are determined to take back our country from him, but we need your help. I'm very grateful for your agreeing to this little charade at the moment. We need to distract him, to show him that we're giving up. If it looks as if I, his bitterest enemy, am considering making a new life for myself in London, then he may lower his guard. By acting in a shallow and rather selfish way, I may make him think I really am uncaring and "just a woman" incapable of providing realistic opposition. It's a gamble, but wars are often won on deception.'

'Indeed. Well, Charlie's the man to help you with this, but what else are you looking for?'

I glanced at both of them. Should I ask direct or keep to a political, blurred approach? Would they be shocked, or perhaps embarrassed if they had to say no? Would asking change the equal relationship into an obligation? Mercury help me. My stomach fluttering, I pulled up my courage.

'We need weaponry – personal weapons, light machine guns, mortars, grenade launchers and ammunition for all.'

Neither man moved. If I hadn't been looking, I might not have seen that tiny razor-sharp look that flashed between them. Sir Henry shifted in his chair.

'That's very direct, Aurelia.'

'I don't have the time to fiddle around playing games, Harry. We're moving into a critical phase now. Our strategy is decided, our plans are nearly completed. I would ask you both to keep that confidential.'

'Of course, Countess,' Gerald Hill said, rather too smoothly.

Sir Henry looked away and rubbed the tip of his nose. I stopped there. What else could I say?

'You must understand that any sign of direct military aid traceable to the United Kingdom is unacceptable,' Gerald Hill said after a few moments and looked me direct in the face.

'So you will not help?'

'Nothing would give us greater pleasure than to see that bastard Tellus kicked out,' Sir Henry said. 'But you must understand our position. If a single British firearm was discovered being used by a Roma Novan invading force, there'd be hell to pay.'

I swallowed hard at my failure. A flame of anger surged in me; our closest ally refused to help us. They wanted Caius gone but wouldn't help us to do it. Curse them.

'However,' Gerald Hill's voice interrupted my thoughts. 'Let me see if we have any odd overseas-made bits and pieces in the storeroom.'

I asked Sir Henry if I could use one of his secure telephones to make an urgent call to Vienna.

'Volusenia? Did you see the newscast last night? Was the Air Roma Nova that landed at Maria-Theresia on it? I saw the whole thing from my plane. We were waiting to taxi out to the runway and it landed in front of us. The pilot was taken off, presumably by police or military. Find her if you can, and her crewmates. And those passengers, there were a couple of hundred of them at least.'

'What about the plane?'

'Well, that would be a nice bonus, but the pilot is going to be much more valuable to us at present.'

I met our London *nuncio*, Gracilis, in the shelter of a clump of trees in Hyde Park. It was just before 07.30 in the morning and I had a headache. Although technically warmer up here in the north compared to frozen New Austria, the morning was damp; I was glad of my fleece tracksuit. I wriggled my toes in my trainers as the ground was cold. It was the third day of my social butterfly act and I was sick and tired of it with the emphasis on tired. If I had to have one more vapid conversation I would scream. But I was due to talk to Quirinia via one of Gerald Hill's secure comms lines later that morning to find out if there had been any reaction to our efforts. If so, then it would have been worth it.

Gracilis, accompanied by a man and woman, all three in jogging suits, appeared right on time. He paused, stretched, glanced at the trees, said something to the other two then dived into the trees where I waited for him.

'*Salve, consiliaria.*' He nodded, then leaned back against a tree trunk. 'I'm getting too old for this morning jogging business.'

'Oh, come on, Gracilis, you're only a few years older than I am. Perhaps if you did it more often you wouldn't feel the effect so much.'

'I know it's very fashionable, *consiliaria*, but I think I'll stick to the indoor gym.'

I laughed, but let him catch his breath.

'Report, please,' I said after he'd stopped wheezing.

'First of all, I want to apologise for cutting you dead at the EUS ambassador's reception last night. I know that was part of the act, but it seemed so unnatural.'

'Don't worry, you were perfect. Did you get any reaction?'

'Interestingly, yes. The ambassador's aide asked me privately what I thought about you. I merely commented that patricians had the choice and means to leave and go where they wanted. Other Roma Novans didn't have the option.'

Ouch!

'The aide nodded and said we should "get together" soon. So it seems I'm to have a rapprochement with the EUS representatives.'

'Excellent! I'll start making estate agents' lives here a misery and view some of their larger properties along with Charlie FitzGlynn. The newspapers seem to follow him everywhere. The British government is helping with that part of our operation at least.'

'Oh? Aren't they helping in other ways?' Gracilis raised an eyebrow.

'How well do you know Gerald Hill?'

'We belong to the same club and occasionally have lunch together.'

'So you are in his circle,' I said. 'What do you think of him?'

'Clever beggar. One of those quiet, deadly types, but sound.'

'Does he keep his promises?'

Gracilis wrinkled his brows. 'I've never known him go back on his word since I've been here. However, I'm not privy to all his little secrets.'

'Aurelia! Thank the gods you've called. Is your line totally secure?'

Quirinia's anxious face in the monitor and her agitated voice in my headphones made my heart sink.

'Yes, of course. What's happened?'

'You have to get back here now. Volusenia is livid, Silvia's crying and Numerus looks like thunder.'

'Quirinia, calm yourself. What's happened?'

'Lentilius, you know, Silvia's pet, that PGSF *optio* from Aquae Caesaris that she insisted should be on the council.' She gulped a breath.

'What?'

'He's disappeared.'

'What do you mean?'

'Vanished. Nobody's seen him since yesterday evening.'

Gods! Lentilius was privy to all our plans and he'd worked with me on the first wave of our counter-information initiative in April. Moreover, he knew about Monticola's part in sabotaging the silver production. Pluto in Tartarus.

'What have you done to find him?'

'Lieutenant Junia Sestina's taken a search party out and Numerus has supplemented that by a sweep of all the local bars. We've searched his room and all the papers he was working on but can't find anything – no letter, nothing out of the ordinary.'

'Look in the shredder and bins.'

'Oh.' She looked uncertain what to do next.

'Let me speak to Colonel Volusenia,' I prompted.

'Yes, of course.'

Volusenia's stark features resembled a vulture more than usual.

'Report,' I ordered.

'Lentilius is posted missing. The last time he was seen was shortly after supper last night. *Consiliaria* Quirinia has advised you of our actions to find him. We're including the railway stations and airport. We're checking his personal relations, friends here, outside contacts, all the usual.'

'Thank the gods he wasn't part of the intelligence group,' I said. 'Do you think he might have been snatched?' Poor bastard if the nats had him.

'It was my first thought, but his rucksack and some clothing are missing along with his boots and notebook.'

'Then we must assume the worst case, that he's run. Report him to the gendarmerie as a missing person, possibly kidnapped, but tell them to check the hospitals and clinics. Lock down all the files he might have had access to and interrogate his fellow team members. I'll be on the next plane back.'

30

I went out to dinner with Charlie in my usual socialite persona, but halfway through I complained about feeling queasy and having a headache. Escorted to the entrance by a very concerned maître d', I almost fell into the taxi. Charlie flapped around, his manner all concern. Back in my suite at the hotel, I rushed into the bathroom and cleaned my face of every scrap of make-up.

'I'll give out that you're ill and have gone to my family's place in the country to recuperate for a few days,' he called out from the bedroom. 'I'll get your stuff packed up and sent there.'

I pulled on jeans and a casual jacket and bundled my hair up in a ponytail.

'Are you sure you don't want a taxi to the airport?' he added.

'No, thanks,' I said as I emerged from the bathroom. 'I'll go on public transport. I'll be well hidden in a crowd.'

'Fair enough. One of my people will shadow you until you get to the gate, though. We don't want the opposition snatching you.'

A knock at the door. I stared at it, then exchanged glances with Charlie.

'Should be Jim with your ticket,' he whispered. 'But let's be careful.' He gestured me back behind the door, reached into his jacket and pulled out a service pistol. He held it to the side and a few centimetres behind. He grabbed the handle with his free hand and yanked the door open. His hand with the pistol was obscured by the door.

'Yes? Can I help you?' Charlie said in a crisp voice.

Not Jim.

Merda.

Charlie stretched the pistol out towards me and I leaned forward and grabbed it.

'Room service.'

'Sorry, we didn't order anything. Wrong room.'

'I don't think so,' the voice said and pushed Charlie back into the room. A big man, dressed as a waiter but toting a light machine pistol pointing at Charlie's chest. Nobody else followed him so I kicked the door shut and rammed into him, felling both men. Charlie scrambled up and I dropped hard onto the big man and thumped him on the nose with the pistol butt. The crunch of bone. He shrieked and struggled to push up. Charlie stamped on one of the man's wrists and grabbed the other. He pulled out a cable tie from his pocket and tied the man's wrists together. The big man looked at me with venom in his eyes. I could almost hear him thinking about how to attack. I jammed the pistol barrel onto the top of his eye socket, but not right into his eye.

'If I dip the barrel and pull the trigger, the round will travel direct into your brain,' I said. 'You'll die instantly. Understand?'

Charlie chucked me a cushion.

'And this will muffle the shot nicely.'

The man slumped where he lay. My heart stopped pounding at frantic level.

'Right,' I said to Charlie and jerked my head towards the phone. 'Can you get a clean-up detail here, stat?'

With his brown hair stuffed under a woollen hat and wearing a denim jacket, Charlie drove me to the airport in a specially converted white builder's van, a departmental wolf in sheep's clothing. It had started to sleet which made the light from the orange street lamps disperse in a hundred droplets on the windscreen. We'd hurried down the plain concrete service stairs of the hotel into the garage after Charlie had briefed the clean-up detail. I'd abandoned most of my luggage but I could reassure Quirinia it was being packed up by an efficient looking woman in beige slacks and a sensible jumper.

Charlie's radio buzzed. His eyes glazed while he listened through the flesh-coloured earpiece, but he navigated the roundabout leading to the dual carriageway to the airport without losing a moment's concentration. After a couple of minutes he blinked but kept his gaze forward.

'That was the office. That fake waiter was a Balkanite – no note of entry to the UK. Apparently, our Prussian colleagues know him. Second-league hitman, mercenary. They can't confirm who hired him yet, but they will.' He glanced at me. 'But I don't think we need more than one guess, do we?'

I said nothing, just gave a deep sigh.

'I would have thought Tellus would be content that you were looking to settle away from Roma Nova, that you were giving him a clear run.'

'No, with Caius it's always personal. Still, we diverted his attention, so not a complete waste of time.'

At the airport, Charlie drove into the cargo area. He had a miracle pass that the security personnel seemed to respect; they even tipped their hat to him. He stopped on a double yellow line outside a plain door with a keypad to the side. A feeble bulkhead light shone above the doorframe. Charlie pulled the handbrake on, then fished in his jacket pocket and brought out a white envelope.

'The door code is one-zero-two-nine. On the other side, turn left, follow the corridor and you'll be in the security area. The office has phoned through and you're checked in on the BA Vienna flight which leaves in forty-five minutes. The security desk will give you a boarding card.' He held out a British passport. 'Use this going out and coming back. It's in the name of Amy Smith. Let me have it back when you return.'

My own Hungarian one was stuffed in an inner zipped pocket of my jacket near to my heart. I clasped Charlie's hand.

'Thank you so much. You've been marvellous. And please convey my thanks to Sir Henry. We're all very grateful for such staunch friends.'

He leant over and kissed my cheek and whispered *'Bon voyage'* in a husky voice.

Feeling a little warmer than I should in the sleet and the dark night, I clambered out, reached back for my rucksack and ran for the door. I turned to wave, but the van was already pulling away. Charlie's instructions were perfect and once I'd collected my boarding pass I was escorted to the gate by a woman who looked like another passenger, but most definitely was not. I was boarded first. The other passengers must have wondered who this nondescript woman in jeans and a parka coat was. Probably some undesirable being deported…

Wien-Maria-Theresia Airport at two in the morning was a dull place. Wan-faced passengers waiting at the only baggage carousel operating, a single queue for passports, bored officials, students sprawled on seating, cleaning carts gliding over the hard floor and a single hopeful looking driver holding a name card. Unlike the daytime with shops, background music, cafés enticing you with the smell of arabica, everywhere was shuttered, closed and silent.

A dour-faced Styrax in casuals waited for me at the rope in the arrivals lounge. She nodded, took my rucksack and we marched over to the exit. At the *Jagdschloss* I fell into my bed but was woken at seven by Quirinia who had a worried look and a few more white hairs amongst the black.

'He's not back,' she said.

A shower and change of clothes and I was a few steps back from catatonic. I sipped coffee and chewed on a roll while searching the glum faces of those clustered at one end of the long kitchen table.

'Despite what's happened I don't think Lentilius has run away,' Silvia said. She looked round, her head held up and eyes sparkling. 'It would be against everything I know about him.'

'He has a staunch champion in you, *domina*, but the facts point in a different direction.' Volusenia was unusually diplomatic.

'Has there been any update or progress since *Consiliaria* Quirinia spoke to me in London?' I said.

'None. Junia Sestina and her team have been out all night again searching,' Volusenia replied. 'I've told them to grab some sleep for a few hours. Numerus's lot went out to scour the early morning markets and newsagents. Not a whisper.'

'The gendarmerie?'

'They weren't interested at first.' Quirinia. 'They said we had to wait at least twenty-four hours. Then I remembered your cousin. I hope you don't mind, Aurelia, but at the sound of *Oberstleutnant* Huber's name they started taking me seriously. But we haven't heard anything from them.'

'Which is all rather strange,' I said. 'Lentilius can't have vanished into the ether. I see two possibilities: either he's run, and let's assume the worst that he's hopped over the border to Roma Nova, or he's been snatched. Oh, a third one – he went on a bender and is sleeping it off somewhere in somebody's arms.'

'No, I'm sure he can't be.' Silvia's voice was shrill with protest, but I exchanged a glance with Volusenia who shook her head.

'Well, he's a PGSF *optio* and has become a valued member of the council of exiles,' I said. 'Betrayal is very much against Roma Novan values and unthinkable by a Praetorian. Potentially, he has everything to gain if he stays here and plays his part in the take-back. If he goes back to Roma Nova now he faces execution or at best being sent to a work camp once they've bled him dry of information. He knows that from Atrius's story.'

'You think somebody's got him, don't you?' Quirinia said.

'Yes, I do. Being brutally honest, he's not important enough to eliminate or even ransom. He's much more valuable as a source of information.'

Silvia covered her face with her hands.

I gave them a brief rundown of what had happened in my London hotel.

'That was different – a straightforward assassination attempt. A demonstration that I would never be out of Caius's reach. Needless to say, the British are underwhelmed by a political hitman operating in their territory. However, we must consider a fourth possibility about Lentilius, one that may be very uncomfortable. He may walk in the front door with a perfectly good excuse for his absence—'

'That would be wonderful!' Silvia's voice was full of relief.

'Perhaps, but we have to consider that he may have been turned.'

Quirinia looked appalled, Volusenia shrugged, but Silvia's face took on an ugly sneer. 'You always have to see the worst in everybody, don't you, Aunt Aurelia?'

'I'm just being practical. It's so common, it's almost a cliché. Read your histories. Despite the virtue of many noble souls, ancient Romans in the world of power and events changed sides as often as the moon rises.'

I was tired and didn't have time in the middle of this crisis to explain to a querulous and ignorant teenager how the threat of extreme violence and pain to you and yours would persuade anybody to take the easier route.

Silvia glared at me, then jumped up. We all stood up. 'Well, I for one will welcome him back with all my heart,' she said and flounced out of the room.

31

———————

'How's the operational planning work going?'

Volusenia and I were strolling in the garden, stretching our legs, mostly to get over the tension of the meeting.

'Mars give me strength,' she retorted. 'It's only been a few weeks since we started.'

'That's not an answer.'

'You must have been a misery to work for in the foreign ministry,' she grumped.

'No, I just want an update. Is that so unreasonable?'

She stamped out her cigarette butt.

'I was going to make it a surprise in the next intelligence meeting but I might as well tell you now.'

Now what had happened? I was fed up with nasty surprises and she looked grim.

'Don't look so depressed, *consiliaria*, it's good news.' She grinned, which looked completely foreign on her stern face. 'The detailed plan is done.'

'Impossible!'

'No, true. Vibianus should be crowned with laurels and put on a pedestal in the forum when we get back. He's certainly wasted as a diplomat. He's liaised with his former colleague Grania and *Consiliaria* Quirinia for costings and supplies. Then he took it to Numerus thinking the old centurion would look at the operational practicalities.

Ha! Numerus had plenty to say, but we've hammered and tempered it between us and it's ready for execution.'

I dropped onto one of the garden seats, ignoring the ice that coated it.

'When I said to treat it as a priority, Volusenia, I never dreamed you would do it this side of Parentalia at best. Bloody well done.'

'And young Regulus, the transport manager, has "Klettermann Spedition KG" bringing in excellent profits. The six small vans he leased for courier work has expanded to twelve. He's now master of nine medium vans, four fuel tankers and four flatbeds. His overt speciality is "emergency and interim solutions".' She snorted. 'Well, that's the fancy name he gives it. While this short-term work suits us strategically, he's also able to charge a bomb for it.'

After a few moments I stood up and we walked on in silence. This was much more than I could have dreamed of. Could I dare to hope that we could be thinking of setting a timetable, even an actual date?

'Anything else?'

Her eyes sparkled.

'What?'

'I found the Air Roma Nova pilot. I'll introduce you to her and her navigator; they're both here, along with all the passengers. Most of them are of fighting age and have done their national service.'

'I don't suppose she's brought her plane with her?' I asked flippantly.

'Ah. No, it's been impounded. One of Junia Sestina's promising recruits who used to work at Portus Airport says that for the moment they will have put it into a spare hangar at the airport while they sort out legal niceties. Unlikely they'll do anything as they'll need to write to the company's head office in Roma Nova asking them to remove it or risk decommissioning. That'll take ages, he reckons. They have other priorities. Pity.'

She continued in a very matter-of-fact voice telling me that just over fifty of our people had obtained rifles and were accredited members of different shooting and hunting clubs.

'Numerus has been able to acquire a good quantity of ammunition for them as well.'

'Good grief! I don't know why I came back,' I said. 'You're obviously perfectly capable of running everything without me.'

'Yes, we can organise the practical things but we need clear leadership, somebody to take decisions, and the responsibility. Somebody who knows the politics of it all. And importantly, somebody who can get outside help and support.'

'I'm not sure of that. Yes, we have plenty of support in words and good wishes, and the British helped with the deception we ran, which is supposed to still be running, but nothing practical. Only Marina's husband has sent us material supplies.'

Later in the afternoon two gendarmes visited for all of ten minutes to report nothing except that their hospital check for Lentilius was negative.

'We have to accept him as lost and compromised,' I said to the council of exiles the next day. 'Our prayers are with him and we will sacrifice to his memory.'

Silvia looked bullish, but said nothing.

'Vibianus, what was Lentilius working on?'

'Principally on the information campaign, *consiliaria*.' He looked at me steadily. 'We've sent coded warnings via radio to those inside Roma Nova who distribute the leaflets. Most have replied.'

'Most?'

'One in the city and one out at Aquae Caesaris haven't acknowledged.'

'Lentilius will know about the two listening posts, of course.'

'We've stepped up physical security,' Volusenia chipped in. 'We're scrutinising the traffic for any changes in volume or frequency and to check for possible disinformation.'

I rubbed my forehead with my fingertips.

'Very well. It's imperative that we act quickly. Let's look at it from the other way. What is actually preventing us from executing our plan?' I looked round the tense faces. I tried to repress my own excitement, but coupled with it my own fear. I hadn't used the phrase 'invading Roma Nova', but they couldn't be in any doubt. Silvia looked at me with wide eyes. Quirinia pursed her lips while Volusenia and Junia, who had been drafted in to take Calavia's place on the council, sat completely still. Numerus looked at me steadily and gave his little smile. I drew a great deal of strength from that.

Volusenia glanced at Junia, who took a deep breath before she spoke.

'Our second biggest problem is lack of transport. Regulus is doing his best, but acquiring the right vehicles so quickly for the best prices is not easy. Despite *Consiliaria* Quirinia's efforts to accumulate budget, our funds are not infinite. We don't have sufficient vehicles to deploy our forces to the locations in the proposed timescale.'

'And the biggest problem?'

'Weapons.'

They'd done very well to get fifty people armed and licensed in the time, but it was far too slow and they were far too few. Pathetically few, if I was honest. Damn. I closed my eyes for an instant and slumped in my chair. However optimistic we were about picking up supporters, we'd never make headway against resistance with access to the official armouries. Caius would have locked those down with double physical security and ordered a global change of access codes.

Volusenia laid her hands palm down on the table. 'We tried to make contact with the black market but haven't had time to reach the right people. Unsurprisingly, they're a suspicious lot. I didn't want to push it as we don't want to start any rumours.'

'Very wise,' I replied, knowing how cagey Miklós's contacts were. He'd given me a funny look when I'd asked him once about whether he'd ever dealt in firearms. He'd retorted how could I think he would be that stupid. I never asked again.

'We know one of Caius's first edicts was to demand all weaponry,' I continued. 'Even farmers' shotguns had to be handed in. Most would have done it, especially in the towns and city, but I'd bet my best boots that many out in the country held on to something, but we can't count on it.'

'So we're stuck,' said Quirinia.

'Yes,' I replied. 'And the worst thing is that every day we don't find Lentilius heightens the risk of Caius learning of our timescale and operational targets.'

32

—————

I went for a run with Styrax and Junia in tow to work off my frustration. I stopped to catch my breath at the far end of the Prater. I coughed at the freezing air. I'd run here with Miklós trotting beside me on a hired horse when we'd lived like a normal married couple in our suburban house. Well, not quite normal. Most couples didn't find their bodyguard dead in a pool of blood when they returned after their run.

I shook my head. Where *was* Miklós? Such a lot had happened in the months since October when he'd kissed me goodbye as I prepared to go on my sortie to Roma Nova. He hadn't even come back to Vienna for Saturnalia. Did he know that I was still alive?

'Are you returning to London, ma'am?' Junia's voice broke in.

'I don't know what to do, Junia. Really I don't. Colonel Volusenia is rightly anxious that Lentilius's disappearance is a massive security breach. Each day the risk increases. But if I don't go back soon, then my diversion won't be any good.' I wiped the sweat off my forehead with a cloth.

'We'll go back over our search and see if there's any chance we've missed anything, but…' She shrugged.

'I'm sure your search was thorough, Lieutenant. But it won't do any harm to retrace it. Lentilius may have moved or be hiding somewhere new.' I wasn't optimistic. I made a mental note to get Edward Soane to ask his commercial banking colleagues about

Lentilius's bank account. They'd never talk direct to me, but he might be able to circumvent their confidentiality rules. 'Let's check if any of the groups inside Roma Nova have seen any signs of extraordinary troop or vehicle movements near our targets.'

As we trotted up the main driveway of the *Jagdschloss*, a sturdy figure hovered at the main door. Numerus. His eyes were creased to slits and he twisted his head round as if searching. He must have spotted us as he stopped looking, then hurried towards us, waving his hands and breaking into a trot.

'You'll never guess,' he gasped.

'Not unless you get your breath back,' I said and then grinned.

He flicked his fingers at me. Junia frowned at him for such informality, but I didn't mind from an old friend. He obviously had something momentous to say.

'We've had a delivery.'

'Yes?'

'It was labelled "CKD furniture" – you know, self-assembly stuff – on half a dozen crates and "Domestic appliances" on twenty-odd boxes. The van driver and his two mates looked a rum lot, but they had proper paperwork and consignment notes addressed to you here. They unpacked, then pushed off sharpish.' His eyes gleamed. 'Did you order some new toasters? If you did, they're not the usual sort.'

'What the hell are you talking about, Numerus?'

Volusenia scratched her head. I ran my eyes over each container as it was unpacked. Junia poked and prodded at the contents. All three of us were silent. I could hardly believe that Fortuna was spilling the contents of such a generous cornucopia in front of us.

Numerus and Vibianus had found clipboards and were counting each item to make inventories. Some of the boxes had mixed contents, some more carefully packed in sealed bags looked as if they'd just come out of the factory. But they were all wrapped in fabric or their original packaging with layers of foam in between. After twenty minutes Vibianus handed me a plain white envelope.

'I found this in the wadding at the top of the second box, *consiliaria*.'

I turned it over. Nothing. I tore it open and found a postcard-sized piece of paper. On it were two words in Latin: *'Ex colle'*. I smiled to myself, then chuckled, then burst out laughing.

Volusenia's head snapped up.

'What is it?' she said.

I passed the note to her.

'From the hill. What does that mean?'

'It means that Gerald Hill and the British have sent us enough weaponry to start an invasion.'

I called Sir Henry Carter in London to ask him to thank his friend for the 'flowers'.

'It was very sweet of him and I really appreciate it.'

'Well, I'm glad you got back safely. Look after yourself and I hope the birthday party goes well.'

'I'm only sorry you can't make it, Harry,' I teased.

He laughed. 'I'm sure you have it all organised perfectly, Aurelia.'

Volusenia tasked Junia with setting up controlled access to the cellar that now housed our newly acquired weapons. It took the rest of the day to move and catalogue nearly two thousand pieces – pistols, rifles, light machine guns and the larger more powerful general purpose machine guns and finally rocket launchers – plus the ammunition and cleaning kits. Practice would start the next morning. It would be better to call it familiarisation, as those from the regular military would have used weapons very similar to these. Hopefully, those who had done their national service sometime in the past five years would remember something. But Junia started cleaning drills that evening. She supervised the issue of weapons, her eyes darting everywhere as she watched her two clerks. Centurions and *optiones* were detailed to show the less experienced or those who had forgotten.

She handed me a pistol without a word. I was surprised how strange it felt as I began to strip it. But my fingers and some deep memory remembered how to pull the slider off the frame and release the barrel. The methodical cleaning and wiping was soothing, the smell of the cleaning lubricant sharp but not disturbing. Although surrounded by others carrying out the same task I felt a moment of isolation, of quiet. Nobody spoke; it seemed as if they were gathering in their personal strength. Once done, I carried out a function check and pushed the magazine in. A satisfying clunk. Yes, it was ready and so was I.

Somebody was in the room. I lay in bed motionless but suddenly fully awake. No light shone round the shutter edges; it was a moonless night.

A warm human presence hovered in the space at the side of my bed. It came nearer. My flesh tingled. It leaned toward me. The smell of leather, a tang of sweat and horse. Gods, surely not.

I shot my hand up. Grabbing the other's clothing I pulled myself up and prepared to strike with my other hand, but a hard grip stopped me.

'Shh.' A horseman's voice calming a nervous animal. 'Is this a way to greet your husband?'

Four hours later, my alarm clock rang pitilessly. I stretched over and switched on the bedside light. Miklós stirred beside me. His arm encircled my waist and pulled me towards him. I lay there for a few minutes, content to rest my head at the base of his neck. He moved and I raised my head to look at him. Perhaps it was the dim morning light creeping in, but he looked tired. Brown shadows lined his eye sockets and he hadn't shaved for a day or two.

'Stop staring at me like that.'

I started at his voice. It rasped as if worn out. He'd whispered last night, but now he spoke naturally.

'You look and sound exhausted. Where have you been?'

He smiled and opened his eyes properly.

'Finding you and your band of rebels some special transport.'

'What do you mean?'

'If you shift over and let me out to the bathroom, I'll show you after breakfast.'

He walked me over to Lúkas's cottage. I hadn't mentioned his young cousin's surly attitude to me, but I had a million other things to think about now. Lúkas wasn't there, so we went to the back service yard and what had been the enormous stable block built round a separate stable courtyard. Even Regulus's vans and tankers hadn't filled half of it, just the carriage houses. Although dressed blocks on the outside, the stable block was lined with utilitarian rough stone inside. The fresh morning light emphasised the irregular contours of each stone; it looked rural, authentic, more than just a rich man's status symbol.

In the far corner a group of mechanics was clustered round Regulus's deputy listening carefully to her orders for the day. Whatever our grand plans, the work of the hundreds of support workers carried on everyday almost unseen. The figures dispersed to their tasks and the deputy spotted me. She looked like thunder and strode over in my direction.

Miklós chuckled. What was there to laugh about? She looked as cross as Hades.

'*Domina*, I really must protest—'

'Wait!' Miklós interrupted, holding his hand up. His voice was commanding and stopped the deputy in her tracks. He took my hand and pulled me towards a large opening on the nearest side of the courtyard. Inside were rows and rows of individual horse stalls, massive wood pillars adorned with elaborate ironwork dipping down to gates in the centre of each stall. To my utter surprise a good dozen of them were filled with black, brown and dark grey horses. I stopped by one and put my hand out and stroked the animal's head. He looked sturdy with an arched, high-set neck, broad and muscular back, and strong legs. He must have been fifteen, sixteen hands high. No sign of wildness in his liquid eyes. Lúkas was by another stall at the end, his arms almost encircling a horse's head, his cheek laid against the animal's, his eyes almost shut. I swore he was crooning to the horse.

'Great Jupiter!' I said.

'Exactly, *domina*.' The deputy stood right behind me. 'What are we supposed to do with these… these pets? The gods know they'll need a fortune in feed and then there's mucking out. And what use are they?'

'You need to do nothing, woman,' said Miklós. 'Just ignore them. My cousin and I will look after them. You may go about your business.' He waved his hand at her in dismissal. I'd never heard him be so rude.

The deputy stood there, lips parted, but no words coming out. She shot an angry look at him, then took a deep breath.

I stepped between them.

'This is unexpected, of course, and I will talk to Regulus when he is available. Perhaps you would ask him to come and see me?' I used my most conciliatory tone.

She nodded abruptly, threw another angry look at Miklós and stamped off hitting every cobble on the courtyard with furious intent.

'Well, that was a good start to the morning.' I turned to him. 'Why were you so rude to her?'

'She couldn't have shown more contempt if she'd tried. They aren't pets. They're all tough, well-built horses, bred to endure.'

The old Romans had used mounted units for scouting, skirmishing, and outpost duties, crucial when conducting operations over long distances in hostile or unfamiliar territory. We were certainly going into hostile territory, but not unfamiliar. Later Roman commanders had used mounted units more and more; for speed, mobility and shock value, they were unrivalled. But today?

'Miklós, they are magnificent. They remind me of Bátor, your first beautiful horse when we met in Berlin, but how will they help us?'

He looked at me, eyes half closed. 'Do you really think you are going to be able to sneak around Roma Nova with a convoy of noisy old trucks and vans? You say you are going to use surprise as a weapon, but you know yourself how good the Roma Nova military are at stopping the least opposition. But nobody is prepared for horses.'

'But what impact will a dozen or so horses have?'

'There are twenty here and another thirty at a stables south of Graz. They can ride cross-country at fifty kilometres an hour if required, don't need special refuelling and don't show up on any radar.'

PART III

INVASION

33

———

At a meeting of the heads of families and communities representing our three thousand souls, I explained that we needed to step up security as Lentilius, one of the council members, had disappeared in unclear circumstances.

Unfortunately Edward Soane had been unable to coax his colleague in Lentilius's bank to disclose any details other than 'more than sufficient funds to meet any contingency'. Lentilius had been receiving only a small allowance as a council member, so it was disquieting when the bank used those words; it usually meant substantial funds. But unless we could see his statements, we could prove nothing.

'We're still searching for Lentilius but in the meantime we need to take precautions,' I continued. 'I must now ask you to register whenever you go out of this building and when you come back in.'

Groans.

'I know it's a nuisance but everybody will be subject to it. We'll post notices by the exits and Praetorians will staff these points. The council would appreciate you informing your communities and families about the new checking in and out and the reason for it. We cannot be too careful, which brings me on to another matter. What I am about to say must not go beyond this room, however tempted you might be to share it.'

The mumbling and grumbling stopped and I waited until I was sure I had everybody's attention.

'Our *colonia* here in Vienna is temporary as our aim is to go back to Roma Nova. I accept that some may wish to start a new life here and I wish them *bona fortuna*. If anybody in your community wishes to do this, please ask them to give their names to Vibianus who will assist them to leave and settle outside. But I think that almost all of us want to go home.'

'*Aio! Aio!*'

'Well,' I said and then smiled. 'That may be coming sooner rather than later.'

'When? When?' people shouted. Many of these sober leaders rose to their feet and punched fists in the air, others glanced at each other, a few cried in each others' arms.

After a while I called for silence.

'This must be kept secret for the moment. Of course, rumours will leak out as activity steps up while our preparations are finalised. I count on you to disown them or at least keep them to a minimum. You can disclose Lentilius's disappearance as the reason for the inevitable additional security. I know it's tempting to want to reveal a big secret to impress others. We are human as well as Romans.'

A few smiles at that.

'But we must restrain ourselves. In the meantime, please encourage people to keep their fitness up and to attend every training session the military runs. We'll be allocating tasks and forming specialist tactical teams during the next week.'

People started murmuring again. I held my hand up for silence.

'One last thing. While we may be excited about returning to Roma Nova, we must remember that our fight back is dangerous; the odds are against us. We can't just drive up to the main border crossing and start shooting every nat in sight.'

'Why not?' came a shout. 'Kill the bastards!'

'A strong temptation, I know, but the *only* way we'll win this take-back is by being clever. Our tactics must be clean, sharp and coordinated. But I warn you that however smart we are and however strong your resolution and courage, we will lose friends and family members. Or they may be badly injured. We may experience small failures, we will certainly be frightened and exhausted. But we will liberate our country, lift oppression from our people and regain our homeland.'

Volusenia, Junia and Atrius spent the evening drawing up the lists of units and tasking squads for each specific task. A clerk sat filling in a pile of form letters with individual orders and stuffing them in brown envelopes. I left them to it; they didn't need me. I drew the door shut behind me as I left Volusenia's office and paused in the corridor. However fired up the leaders had been earlier, they might sober up when they handed out individual posting letters to their people.

Upstairs, I knocked on Silvia's door. She opened it only a few centimetres.

'May I come in for a moment?' I said.

'Um, I'm just doing something. Can we leave it until the morning?' She glanced away. What was she up to?

'I'm afraid not, darling. I'm going up to the listening posts first thing.'

'Oh. Well, I suppose you'd better come in.'

Inside, clothes, mostly jeans and walking trousers, shirts and two fleeces were lying across the bed. The drawers in the small unit were hanging open and draped over the chair were her training clothes and boots that all Junia's troops wore. Silvia had insisted, and I'd backed her, that she had to do the same military drills as everybody else. She had to be able to defend herself as well as feel part of it. And she was admired for her willingness to buckle down to the discipline and hard training with everybody else. She looked at me and flushed.

'Are you having a sort-out?' I said.

'No. Well, yes, actually. I want to be ready to go.' She looked up at me, her expression half defiant, half pleading. I sighed.

'Darling, you know you can't go with the tactical groups or even the reserves. Nor can you step a foot inside Roma Nova until we have a secure route to the city.'

'My place is with my troops.'

'Your place is to inspire them, to represent what they are fighting for, not leading in the front line. That's the job of the *optiones* and centurions.'

'I'm as fit and trained as the others of my age. I'm going.'

'No, you are not going with the assault groups.'

'You can't stop me. I command you let me.' Damn, this was a bad time for Silvia to play the truculent teenager.

'Look, Silvia, I can't fault your fighting spirit nor your courage. It's no less than I expect of you, but after all the effort we've made to rescue and protect you, I will not have you killed by a stray bullet or your throat cut by some treacherous nat.'

'You'll be going, of course,' she retorted.

'Well, actually, I won't. Not until the towns of Aquae Caesaris and Castra Lucilla have been taken. You have no idea how much it pains me not to be there fighting on my own land for my own people, but Volusenia has tasked me first with handling communications and reserves from here.'

'I'd like to have been there when she told you *that*.'

'I was disappointed, but I accepted it. Volusenia's plan is tight and precise and we have to play the part according to our competences.'

'Huh.'

'Besides, she outranks me.'

'*What?*'

'This next phase is purely military and she controls it. Once we take back territory, then I will regain my imperial councillor authority. For now, we all have to submit and that includes you, Imperatrix.'

Both listening posts now had a permanent guard of a dozen troops, plus disguised perimeter guards on the approach roads. Caius must have worked out by now we were listening and the posts would have been juicy targets. But once armed with the weapons in the back of our van that Styrax was driving, they would be extremely difficult to take. If he tried, the physical and electronic noise of such a firefight or bombing from the air would alert the New Austrians and they'd be sure to intervene. A kilometre out we passed a couple of hikers who smiled and waved at us. But as I looked in the mirror I saw one appeared to be talking into her sleeve. One of ours then.

'*Salve*, major,' the *optio* greeted me with a bright smile after we'd parked in the lea of the trees.

'Diana. Everything in order?'

'Yes, mostly quite boring, except for yesterday.'

'Oh?'

'Well, radio traffic has been diminishing steadily over the past month, not by much, but definitely downward. Last Tuesday there was nothing between the city and Castra Lucilla, which was strange. I sent the colonel a report, but then there was a movement of a small detachment of vehicles yesterday towards Castra Lucilla, and some new radio traffic. We sent it all back to Vienna.'

I hadn't seen Volusenia this morning as I'd set off before seven. Well, she'd brief me when I got back.

'Apart from bringing you these new toys'—I gestured towards Styrax and her colleague unloading the arms and boxes of ammunition—'I've brought this.' I gave her a brown envelope marked 'Eyes Only'. She shot a glance at me and ripped the envelope open.

'At last!' she breathed.

At Virunum I greeted the professor in charge of the dig with due formality. I'd dragged him out of his cosy department on a cold January day as my excuse for visiting a site so open to satellite surveillance. He was determined to show me everything. I followed him round in the freezing wind as he showed me foundations, lead water pipes, and a large, mostly intact mosaic. He was very enthusiastic about the amphitheatre excavation he was working on and praised the team we had provided to help him.

After twenty minutes I extricated myself, thanking him profusely. He was reasonably content as I'd promised him a hefty contribution to the dig when it reopened in May. After he'd driven off down the winding road, his car's snow chains clanking, I strode over to the administration hut. The only sign it wasn't entirely that was the satellite dish twenty metres away, shielded from sight by the tree line.

I knocked and a figure with a stubble chin and wearing a fleece and jeans with a small trowel sticking out of his pocket opened the door.

'Sergius. Digging much up?' I said as I entered the fuggy, warm room.

He grinned, but when he'd read the contents of the envelope I handed him his features became solemn. He watched in silence as

Styrax and her comrade walked through to the storeroom and deposited the weapons we'd brought for them.

'You're on active operational status as from now.'

We hit the Vienna rush hour, stuffed with tin boxes driven by normal people rushing home to their supper, then reading to their children at bedtime and settling down to a drama on the television or a chat on the phone with friends. As we escaped the worst of it and drove along the country lane to the *Jagdschloss*, we seemed to be stuck behind a small convoy of at least a dozen small lorries crawling along. The gods knew what they were doing here. I was more than surprised when they turned into the *Jagdschloss* driveway and then swung round to the back and through the archway into the stable courtyard where we also parked our little van. Tired as I was from the long day, I wanted to know who and what they were. Regulus, the transport manager, leapt out of the first one and waved his arms around. The other drivers gathered round him, shouting and laughing, flicking fingers at each other, sharing some joke. I walked over and they calmed. Regulus looked a little hesitant.

'I apologise if I'm interrupting, but what's going on? Something good, I think?'

'We've just come back from an auction, *domina*, and scooped all these vehicles. I couldn't believe it. They were being sold off as a job lot.' He shook his head. 'I expect they'll need a lot of work on them, but we can afford to cannibalise a couple of them. The colonel only wanted six more.' He grinned.

'Well, I think the beers are on me,' I said. 'Or maybe I'll put them on Colonel Volusenia's tab.' That made them laugh.

As we walked towards the back door, I told Regulus about Miklós's horses.

'Well, it's a bit unusual, but I can see his point. I'm not the strategist, thank Mercury, but it seems to me that making that first border crossing a surprise isn't going to be easy.' He stopped and looked at me. 'Look, *domina*, I just get what's needed to the place it's needed. I'm prepared to use whatever's available. Do you want me to talk to him about saddles and reins and stuff?'

I nodded. I couldn't say anything; I was just so grateful to the gods that this capable young man had fallen on us like a box of treasure.

'I've got something else to tell the colonel when I get her alone,' he continued. 'I've been able to call in a favour. A transport company in Graz I did business with before... before the rebellion still has the same facilities manager. I went and saw him on the off-chance and he's agreed to be a POL point.'

I stared at him. Being able to refuel at Graz would considerably increase our range and lessen our need for so many tankers.

'Mars' balls, Regulus, do you know what a genius you are?'

He blushed.

'You have just solved the last problem. Come with me to see Colonel Volusenia. She'll probably open a bottle of champagne.'

34

———

Regulus's reward was indeed champagne, but only one glass as Volusenia ordered him to draft in every mechanic he could find and get the vehicles up to standard, starting work at six the next morning.

'I've ordered a general parade in the ballroom for 07.00 hours,' Volusenia said as we took a late walk in the courtyard. 'We daren't risk assembling two thousand people outside in case the bloody surveillance satellites are working. We have enough trouble hiding all those trucks.'

'If Caius's EUS friends are helping with technical equipment as we heard from the groups in the city, then we have to assume the satellites are working and that they're getting a daily feed,' I replied.

'Well, all the posting letters have gone now, so I need to see what kind of rabble we are stuck with to get this operation active.' She drew on her cigarette. 'I'm not optimistic.'

'You'll just have to view them as irregular forces. They'll do their best but they're not going to look as shiny as your Praetorians.'

'Ha!'

'I've watched them training,' I said. 'Junia Sestina's worked miracles but you can't inject years of training in a few months or weeks. Don't you have confidence in your own plan?'

'You know, I can see why you're a politician. You can flip any argument back at your opponent.'

'Are you my opponent?' I asked in a quiet voice.

'You know what I mean,' she grumped.

'So when can we go?'

'Second day after tomorrow suit you?'

'I'll check my diary.' Then I grinned at her, stretched my arm out to grasp hers in the traditional salute. Her fierce grip and gleaming eyes said it all.

Crushed into the former ballroom, the parade went well; Volusenia even had seventy volunteers for the horse squads.

'I have to confess that although I love riding I never thought of using them operationally,' she said. 'We'll look like something out of a comic opera.'

'I don't care,' I said. 'I'll ride a giraffe into the city if it'll get me there.'

The very worst part of being part of the senior command structure was waiting; waiting to start, waiting for news, waiting for casualties.

Two days later at midnight, twenty of the mounted squad set off on horseback for the stables south of Graz; the remainder of the riders travelled with Miklós in two trucks with saddles and equipment for the other horses. I worried about training the riders; although they'd all been through Junia's hands and had some military knowledge, most were leisure riders. Miklós had spent the previous day assessing them. He'd only rejected eight, assuring me that horsemanship was the main skill needed. Tomorrow, the first riders would cross into Roma Nova by back roads either side of the western border post and meet up with Frontius.

The signals office had reported regular contact with Frontius and arranged a rendezvous with a fall-back point. Once the horse troops had taken that post our infantry, brought in by trucks, would take over. That western border post should be an easy gain despite Regulus's worry, as Frontius kept the border guards there sweetened with a generous supply of contraband goods.

Through the next day I assessed signals from the monitoring posts, from groups inside Roma Nova, reports from Regulus in Graz, from the field units mustering by the western border post. But nothing from Miklós. He wasn't military, but I'd assigned a radio operator to him with firm instructions to report in regularly. By seven in the evening I was pacing back and forward in the signals office until the duty signals officer asked me very politely to sit down or come back later.

I was dozing in a chair when a triple beep came through indicating field traffic. My heart thudded as I leapt up. It could only come from one source. It was only just eleven. All the operators and telegraphists stopped and watched the cypher clerk feed the message into her machine. Nothing but a gentle hum from the unit. I hovered, hands clutched under each armpit. Then the printer started clattering in the deep silence. I didn't register Volusenia entering the room, but there she was beside me. The printer stopped and a telegraphist leapt up to the printer and tore the print out of the machine. She glanced at it and handed it to me without a word. I felt the gaze of every person in the room on me as I read out the message.

FLASH. Western border post under imperial control. Proceeding Aquae Caesaris. Second horse squad proceeding Castra Lucilla. Farkas

I clamped one hand over my mouth and handed the message to Volusenia with the other. She beckoned to the duty signals officer.

'Send Lieutenant Junia Sestina the following: execute Phase I Tacita.'

Portable jammers and the ones in our listening posts would disable VHF radios used by the Roma Nova military and the nats. Even if we were only partially successful it would diminish the enemy's ability to communicate. William had sent us Brown Industries HF transceivers which would work over long distances and were less vulnerable to jamming. One of the first tasks would be to break into the telephone exchanges and throw the output switches from the battery rooms. The telephone system in each locality would shut down very shortly after that and communication to the city would be cut.

Volusenia turned to me. 'It'll take the horses a couple of hours to get to Aquae Caesaris and Castra Lucilla. Anything from the Families who live in the west?'

I was visualising Miklós on his black horse, galloping across the fields towards Aquae Caesaris where Mars knew what was waiting for him. I knew he was tough and strong, but I couldn't bear it if he were injured or worse... I'd always been the one going on operation with him staying behind. I closed my eyes and took a deep breath.

'Mitela! Your report, if you please.' Volusenia's harsh voice cut through.

'Sorry, colonel. I was preoccupied.' I cleared my throat. 'Representatives of Aquilia and Sella who have properties west and south of Aquae Caesaris sent messages last week to family members here and confirmed support. We expect to pick up another thirty fighting strength from them. Cornelia, we've heard nothing from. We know from when I met Claudia in the caves that her cousin has assumed head of their family and is a member of the Roman National Movement, so that's a blank. Quirinia phoned her niece – unbelievable the phones were *still* working. It seems their place only has a small workforce, but—'

'They'll fight, don't worry, Aurelia.'

I spun round. Quirinia stood by the door, her cheeks a little pinker than usual. By her side, Silvia.

'I have no doubt of that,' I said. 'How many do you think your niece can muster?'

'She couldn't be specific – about eight or nine – but they have a cache of shotguns and rifles they hid in the sheepfold when all weapons were confiscated. Honestly, Caius is an idiot. How can you run a sheep farm without a firearm of some sort, I ask!'

I smiled. Here we were in the middle of a military invasion and she was concerned about scaring wolves away from her precious sheep. But she was right on every count.

'We've had indications from all the city-based Families, apart from Vara and obviously Tella. They'll be ready as soon as we broadcast our messages, as will the resistance groups.' I looked at Volusenia and said in my most neutral voice, 'I sent Quintus Tellus a message via the Swiss Legation to find and safeguard his young nephew, Conradus. The child was living, if you call it that, at Caius's villa in the suburbs. I don't have a clue whether or not my message reached him. If it does, Quintus is not stupid. He'll know we're on the way.'

Every single person in the room stopped what they were doing and stared at me. Volusenia looked like thunder, Quirinia gasped, Silvia covered her mouth with her hand. Only the hum of the signals equipment and the odd beep interrupted the silence.

To my surprise Silvia recovered first, came over to me and took my hand.

'You were right, Aunt Aurelia. Conradus is in a dreadful place at that hateful man's villa. Uncle Quintus *must* rescue him.'

'Do you realise, *major*, you have committed an act of treason in time of war as well as breaching the military code?' Volusenia thundered at me. 'Contacting any Tella is expressly forbidden by imperial order in council.'

'Yes and no. It was a political decision, colonel. I know that we are in the military phase and you are the commander, but these next few days and weeks are not going to be a neat splicing of authorities.'

'What's to stop Quintus Tellus giving his brother a warning, or being coerced?' she barked.

'You don't know Quintus, do you?' I sighed. 'I've tried, but I see I haven't been able to convince you of the complete, visceral and unremitting hatred between the two of them. Quintus keeps it civil, something that unnerves Caius, but believe me, Quintus would die before he'd give Caius the drip off his nose.'

'Humph. I know you are the political authority here under Imperatrix Silvia, but if you do anything like that again while I control the operation, I will throw you in the secure room myself.'

I nodded, but said nothing. Silvia pressed my hand in support. Luckily, more field traffic came in and Volusenia was diverted.

'Centurion Atrius says his column has arrived within striking distance of Aquae Caesaris and is harbouring in the woods to the south. The horse squad set off for the town twenty minutes ago and he's expecting their signal any minute now. As soon as they've neutralised their targets he'll go in and broadcast his message to the groups there and proceed to secure the town.'

And so it went on. Castra Lucilla fell to the second horse squad. The motorised column followed close behind, drove into the square and broadcast Silvia's prerecorded message. I could see in my mind's eye the expressions on people's faces as they woke; suspicion giving way to disbelief as they realised it wasn't a dawn raid by a nats squad, but a liberation force. And in my own town. Gods, I'd have given anything to be there.

35

Aquae Caesaris and Castra Lucilla were easy gains. Volusenia would now send a column in a wide circle north of Roma Nova city to race to secure Brancadorum in the east, then a second one south to join up with them.

Now we had to wait.

The signals crew changed shift and Volusenia turned to me.

'Go and grab some rest, major.' She jerked her head in the direction of the door. 'It'll be at least four hours before the strike forces reach their new harbour points on the edge of Roma Nova city. Atrius has first to combine his front-line troops with those from the Castra Lucilla force. And I need to know that Brancadorum is secure before we move to the next phase.'

It was good practice, I knew; a tired soldier is a useless soldier, but there wasn't a hope in Hades I'd sleep.

A hand on my shoulder, pressing down. I blinked awake.

'For you, ma'am.' A telegraphist was waving a printout in my face. I sat up and shook my head. I glanced at my watch; sunrise in barely an hour. When I'd checked just before I'd gone for rest, neither Sergius nor Diana at the monitoring stations had reported any increase in signal traffic. But by now the nats had to be reacting. I swallowed, sat up, dreading what was in the decrypted message.

'Brancadorum secured. En route for harbour point east of city. Report capture of air cavalry base west of Brancadorum. Military personnel detained and secured. Light casualties. Aquilia.'

I leapt up, laced my boots and rushed out of the door, half running down the stairs and through the hallway to the signals office.

Junia looked up from the desk and grinned.

'I thought you'd be pleased to read that.'

'Pleased! That's bloody wonderful! Have you told Volusenia?'

'She only went for rest a couple of hours ago, so I didn't want to disturb her.'

'Quite correct. Okay, send back to Aquilia to advise us as soon as any women former air force personnel arrive. At least the fighter jets won't launch now, thank Mars. That would have been disastrous. But we need those damned helos up in the air.' This part of Volusenia's plan was extremely risky. Securing Roma Nova's military air force base had been crucial. They would have made mincemeat out of our convoys. Making contact with the women former helicopter pilots had been difficult; asking them to take to the air after a gap of over a year in the face of Caius's brutal regulations was tantamount to a sacrifice. If we failed, they'd be executed out of hand. But if we succeeded we'd have some air cover and fast transport.

At the last report, Volusenia had eight affirmatives and two maybes, plus three air traffic controllers and ground and safety crew. I sent a silent prayer up to both Mars and Mercury. The only problem would be dodging artillery launched from the bases around Roma Nova city.

A young telegraphist was by my elbow.

'The cypher clerk's compliments, ma'am. She said you or the colonel should read this.'

I took the sheet, read it and glanced at Junia. Gods! I dropped down onto the nearest seat.

'What is it?' she said.

'Atrius reports over a hundred people have turned up at the harbour area west of the city, some with weapons, some with knives, some as they are. We anticipated an element of this but not this many people this quickly. His unit's cover is blown, obviously.' I took a depth breath. 'Check back with Aquilia,' I ordered. 'Has she had the same?'

Within a second, Junia was dictating a message to the telegraphist who typed, logged it and passed it to the cypher clerk. As I watched these young volunteers going about their tasks as quietly and effectively as any regular military unit, my heart warmed. It was their dedication and hard work that would win us this war. It was up to Volusenia and me to give them the leadership they deserved.

A triple beep sounded.

Brancadorum airbase operational. Civilian irregulars arrived, est. 200–250, includes female former Praetorians and vigiles. Integrated into ground forces as tasked units, principally security and patrol. Ground units proceeding northern border post and northern and eastern harbour areas. Await your further orders. Aquilia.

I covered my mouth with my hand. It had almost been too easy. Roma Nova was only a small country, but to have covered so much territory and achieved so much in twenty-four hours!

A mug of coffee was thrust into my hand.

'Having a good war while I've been asleep?' Volusenia's voice sounded as gruff as usual, but I could hear the pleasure in it.

'Bloody marvellous one!' I grinned at her.

'So people have risen, as we suspected they would. What field strength do we have?'

Junia handed me a sheet with the figures. 'We started with just under two thousand exiles. With the locals who've joined us, we are now at three thousand five hundred on closest estimate. That's not counting the resistance groups in the city and anybody they've recruited. Vibianus has dispatched civilian teams to Castra Lucilla and Aquae Caesaris to take over, or at least supervise, the local *curia* staff running the towns. They should arrive tomorrow morning. He's organising one for Brancadorum but is fretting about the safety of the journey there. I've reassured him and said I'd send a fully armed escort.'

'Will putting these teams in work?' Volusenia sounded sceptical.

'It depends how far the local government employees have gone over to Caius,' I replied. 'But we can't leave a power vacuum anywhere, at any level. Just look at history for *that* mistake.'

'Well, you're the politician, you know best, but they'll have guards, certainly at first.'

'Prudent, but tell them to keep in the background. People will be jittery.' They wouldn't be the only ones. As I sipped my coffee, I wondered where the hell Miklós was. I stepped forward to the bank of screens and radio equipment where the duty signals officer was talking in a low voice to one of the operators.

'Anything from the horse squads?' I said.

'No, sorry, ma'am. We don't have a regular sched for them but I'll send a message to all of them asking for their status and location.'

I nodded and gave her a tight smile.

Volusenia and I stood back for a few minutes, each with her own thoughts. I knew what was coming. I chewed my lip while I thought about it. Dear Juno, I was more anxious about this than anything I'd done in the past few days.

Volusenia pulled me to one side. 'We have the smaller towns and the airbase, and our troops are in the harbour points round the city. Now we're ready to execute the next phase. Time to make that call.'

When Silvia had suggested the idea, I'd politely shelved it. But now we were about to gamble the whole operation on a teenager's suggestion.

I nodded, grasped the handset and punched in the number. The long ringtone seemed to repeat incessantly. But I knew it was his direct line.

'Yes?'

'*Salve, magister militum,*' I said in the firmest voice I could muster, but it came out shriller than I expected. I cleared my throat.

'Who in Hades is that?'

'Come, come, *magister*, don't you recognise my voice?'

'Aurelia? Aurelia Mitela?' A pause. 'Pluto in Tartarus!'

'Not quite yet, *magister*,' I answered drily. 'Do you have a moment?'

'Not now. I have a crisis to deal with. Somebody's invading and I have to muster my troops.'

'Yes, I know. It's me. And no, you don't.'

'What the hell is that supposed to mean?'

'Three quarters of the territory is back in imperial hands, including the principal towns and the airbase at Brancadorum. Local troops have joined us, and hundreds of former women military and *vigiles* have remustered in units commanded by us. We are coming after the traitor and usurper Caius Tellus and all those associated with him. The legal government of Roma Nova is still the imperial one, now headed by the Imperatrix Silvia. As her senior minister, I am ordering you to stand down your troops.' I took a breath. Would he do it?

'I have to obey the government in place whatever its type or character. And the military forces have to obey me. The Twelve Tables and the constitution bind us.'

'They bound all of us, *magister.* Unfortunately, Caius Tellus did away with them. Any new provision he has made since to secure your obedience is illegal, like all of his declarations and ordinances.'

'Fine words, Aurelia, but being realistic, I'm stuck between you and Caius.'

'No, you will be standing next to him when he's executed.'

'Are you threatening me?'

'No, just telling you what will happen if you field troops against us. Listen, it would break my heart to fire at any Roma Novan legionary, but I will give the order if that legionary gets between us and our objective. And it will be your sole and entire fault if he dies.'

'I… I can't give you my answer now.'

'You have the options, *magister*. Now is the time to use your brain and examine your conscience.' And I replaced the handset.

36

Volusenia looked as grim as Pluto himself when she dictated her message to go out to all ground units. No hesitation, no quarter if they met uniformed resistance. Simple words, but a soul-wrenching thing to do when faced with a former comrade. The horror of confronting a friend or brother, parent or even cousin at the wrong business end of a gun barrel and having to pull the trigger. Hades. We'd had to do it at the caves and it had haunted me for days.

'Execute Phase II Rubicon,' Volusenia barked at the assembled senior military staff and civilian officers. A dozen or so, we stood for a few seconds in a semicircle in front of her, notebooks in hand, tasks in our heads, but in a kind of stasis.

'Go!' she ordered.

I nodded to Junia and we grabbed our personal weapons and made our way to the hall to collect our already packed field rucksacks from our rooms. As I put my booted foot on the first step of the stairs, there was a thump on the main entrance door. We glanced at each other. The main gate at the end of the driveway was closed and guarded now round the clock; entry was only by escort from that gate. Nobody should be knocking at the door of the building itself. The young clerk on the reception desk flinched. The security guard by the door hesitated then spoke into her radio.

Another thump. The guard's radio buzzed. 'Gendarmerie.'

Merda.

I spun round to Junia.

'Go covert!' I shrieked at her.

She sprinted off in the direction of the signals room. The security guard was already relaying the same message to all posts. I ripped off my jacket and stuffed it with my pistol and rifle into the hall cupboard. The security guard threw her pistol and holster in the floor vase containing tall dried flowers.

I glanced round and nodded to her. She took a breath, grasped the handle of one of the double doors and opened it.

In strode my cousin Achim, in his grey police uniform, in full Commissioner Huber *persona*, his face as fierce as Cerberus. Two gendarmes followed him in. He glared round the hall, his angry glances darting into every space he could see. Eventually, his eyes came back to me.

'Good evening, Achim. Always a pleasure to see you. What can I do for you? Or is this a social call?'

'No, it isn't. What are you up to, Aurelia?'

I wiped my hands on my moleskin trousers.

'Actually, I've been in my grounds, pruning some unwanted growth, so you'll excuse my rather casual appearance. But you're welcome to come and take a coffee with me.' I looked over at the booted and armed policemen just behind Achim. 'And your, er, friends, of course.'

'I don't have time for *Kaffeeklatsch*. I have information you have an arms stockpile here that could start a war. As a courtesy I've left my troops outside the gate. But if I don't get a good answer – the truth – I'm going to tear this place apart.'

'Such a shame when it's your mother's house,' I murmured and sent a silent prayer up to Mars. Apart from a couple of dozen personal weapons, everything had gone south via Graz. 'Well,' I continued. 'Some of our people have licences as members of shooting clubs, as the *Gendarmerie* records must show. Obviously, they're kept in a locked cupboard. The caretaker has a couple of shotguns for killing vermin.' I looked him in the face. 'I rather thought we had all the necessary permits, but I will ask the steward to check.'

The gods knew what he would have said if he'd seen the convoys heaving with arms and equipment setting off the day before yesterday. They'd been disguised mostly in Klettermann Spedition lorries, but some had been in their original state; we'd had no time to do anything else.

'Get your steward in here. I'll take a look around while I'm here.'

'Of course,' I said as smoothly as I could. 'I'm not sure where he is at the moment, but we'll find him.' I nodded at the clerk who lifted her desk telephone and gabbled into it, relaying my message asking Vibianus to bring the housebook and gun licences for inspection.

'Come and sit down while we wait for him.'

I took a few steps up the corridor and opened the first door on the right, turned and extended my arm in invitation. He scowled but, gesturing his men to stay put, followed me. The clerk stared at me anxiously but I calmly asked her to bring coffee. Just before I shut the door I saw her scuttle off in the direction of the kitchen.

Achim sat there staring round at nothing. The room was furnished with four chain store easy chairs and a low table. A vase of fresh flowers stood on a small table behind us. The only other furniture was a bookcase in an alcove to the left of the fireplace and some shelves with a built-in cupboard underneath to the right. We used the room for visitors we didn't want to let into the main rooms of the house. I forced myself to relax into the softness of the plastic seat.

'Why are you so angry, Achim?'

'Because you have no regard for the law. You seem to think you can waltz through life doing exactly as you want without caring about the consequences for anybody else.'

'That's unfair and you know it. I'm sorry you wouldn't speak to me after the trial in Berlin – what, nearly fifteen years ago? I *did* appreciate your deep loss at your former partner's betrayal, but it wasn't my fault. Yes, I was the one who exposed that he was on the take from Caius Tellus's contact in Berlin, but I wasn't the one deceiving you. You must have had my letter explaining all that.' He shrugged. I put my hand out to cover his. He tensed, but didn't pull away. 'Nothing would give me greater pleasure than to reconcile with you.' I smiled at him. 'I've missed my big Brandenburg cousin.'

He said nothing. He gave me not a smile, but a lightening of the tension in his face. 'It still doesn't excuse any illegal activities you're up to at the moment,' he growled.

'Give me a little slack, Achim. You know I wouldn't do anything to upset our hosts here in New Austria. We keep ourselves to ourselves and don't ask anything of you.'

'I suppose not.'

'And who on earth thought we had an arms stockpile?' I laughed, hopefully in a convincing way.

His face closed up. Damn. In truth, I thought we'd been extremely careful. The Brits had delivered the weapons discreetly, probably with false number plates on their vehicles. We'd only had everything here for a few days, just time to clean and issue it. Gods, we'd better warn the depot in Graz. I fidgeted, trying to think of a way of getting rid of Achim, when the door opened with Junia carrying a tray of coffee. Why was she acting as a servant? I followed her movements, watching for any signal as she filled two cups and handed one to Achim. She half turned so Achim couldn't see her face and extended her hand with a cup for me. She winked once, then turned and left. Thank the gods!

'I don't know where the steward has got to. When you've finished your coffee, I'll show you around.'

The kitchen was full of intense chopping of vegetables, stirring and clattering of pans, the former ballroom with people packing up their files for the day, standing in ones and twos or tidying desks. The signals office was transformed into a 'training room' with people sweating over keyboards, struggling with the new concept of computers. One cried out with joy as he retrieved his printed work from the noisy printer. A stern-faced Volusenia, posing as a tutor, told him to get on with the next exercise or he'd never master it. Others sat around reading magazines with their feet up.

Out in the stable block there were no vehicles except three vans and a couple of old lorries in their garages, the mixed smell of motor fuel and manure and two people leading a pair of rather sluggish mounts over the cobbles for an early evening ride.

We found Vibianus in his office, clucking over a file and muttering 'damned water bill'. He looked up, his face showing annoyance at the interruption.

'Vibianus. Didn't you get my message that the gendarmerie were here and wished to inspect the gun licences?'

'*Domina*, I apologise. I've just had a crisis about our water and sewage bills and thought I could sort it out in a minute or two.

Obviously not.' He flipped the file shut with a sharp flick. I barely prevented myself from laughing.

'Very well, steward. Please find the gun licences.'

He looked baffled. 'I didn't think we were due to send in a return yet.'

Gods, he was playing it for all he was worth.

'Nevertheless, Commissioner Huber has come especially to check, so please find the file.'

Vibianus rummaged in the filing cabinet and pulled out a file. He opened it with an exaggerated gesture and a sigh and plonked it on his desk. As Achim bent to read it, Vibianus shot a look at me and nodded. He unlocked the gun cabinet in the room leading from his and made Achim a little bow. The rifles were placed neatly with individual barrel rests and dividers, name tags below, in almost offensive innocence. When Achim left with a brief nod to me, I let my breath out very slowly.

'Mars' balls! Make that a double,' I ordered the barwoman.

'Counter that,' Volusenia barked from behind me. 'You're going into theatre. I don't want you falling over drunk.'

'A single then.' I nodded to the woman behind the counter.

'I've bollocked the gate guard for letting that scarab through,' Volusenia said as we flopped down on chairs.

'Probably didn't have much option with Achim standing there in stroppy policeman mode with a couple of wagons full of riot police.'

'True, true. Well, it won't hurt for them to toughen up. But our cover-up worked well and we didn't lose much time. However, you and Junia Sestina better get moving. The convoy by the western border post is ready to move as soon as you get there. Your call sign is Aquila Zero. The Air Roma Nova pilot is standing by to take you. She was a little unhappy at flying such a tiny plane, but I explained it was her duty and she should get on with it.'

Just under an hour later, Junia and I were at the private business airport south-west of Vienna and twenty minutes after that squeezed into a tiny plane behind the grumpy Air Roma Nova pilot.

'I missed my first slot because of your delay in getting here and it was touch and go getting clearance for so late a flight.'

'Well, we're here now,' I said, fastening my seat belt and making a face behind the pilot's back at Junia. She grinned back. 'So shall we get going?'

The pilot was correct; dusk was nearly on us. Even though it took only a little over forty minutes to reach the tiny airfield west of Graz tucked in a valley just outside the Roma Nova border, the light had gone by the time we landed. A short wheelbase met us and soon we were on the road. Along with the throbbing diesel engine, my heart pounded. In less than an hour, I would be walking on Roma Novan soil.

Just before 9 p.m. we arrived at the New Austrian frontier post where the border policeman took one look at us then shouted something into his office. A brown-haired woman and man in dark green clothes emerged into the gloom only lit by an overhead lamp. They spotted my and Junia's gold badges clipped to our jackets, snapped to attention and saluted us.

'Good evening, ma'am. We were expecting you both an hour ago but were advised by central command that you had been delayed. If you carry on about fifty metres down the road, you'll find your convoy. They're flying blue flag front, green flag back, and I've been left this for you.'

She handed our driver a convoy flag: top diagonal yellow gold, lower diagonal imperial purple. A Roma Nova field commander's flag. I cleared my throat then swallowed.

'Thank you, *optio*, good to be home again.'

37

Phase II had been given the operational name of Rubicon to reflect the momentous crossing in 29 BC by Julius Caesar with an army in defiance of the *imperium* – the right to command – held by the consuls at the time. His swift action had caused Pompey and the Senate to flee en masse. I was no Caesar but thought that would be an excellent outcome today. Except we had to capture Caius; that would be our challenge in this century.

We passed a few checkpoints in the dark and stopped to let down troops to set up more in between. We had to ensure the road was completely safe before we could allow people like Volusenia, Quirinia and, more importantly, Silvia, to enter the country.

When we stopped to refuel, one of the women who helped us was in a Roma Nova land forces uniform.

'I hid it away, ma'am.' She looked at me under the shielded field light as we clustered under the camouflage nets. 'I buried it in a bin bag in the garden, but I knew one day I'd need it again.' She secured the fuel tank lid then wiped her hands on a rag. 'There you are, ma'am. She's full. That should take you right into the centre of Roma Nova city.'

I could say nothing but clasped arms with her.

The rhythmic vibration of the diesel engine was soothing. I thought I'd feel more excitement, but I was strangely calm, isolated even. I didn't even want to speak to Junia, my closest colleague. She sat back against her seat and stared blankly into the darkness. I dozed off as we trundled on for kilometre after kilometre.

I jerked awake as the driver braked hard. Two heavily armed figures in full military battledress loomed in front of us. I could see a few red half-lights dotted over a wide area ahead. We'd reached the perimeter of the western harbour point. After our ID was checked, Junia and I grabbed our rucksacks and followed a young woman who escorted us to the command post. Atrius was bent over a trestle table with maps spread out and held at the corners by small rocks. Half a dozen women and men stood around, murmuring and pointing. They looked up as we pushed the double canvas flaps aside.

'Major!' Atrius said. He stood straight and saluted. He had brown rings of exhaustion in the sunken flesh round his eyes.

'At ease, centurion,' I said, went over to him and clasped forearms. 'Congratulations on a well-executed operation. Imperatrix Silvia sends her compliments.'

He looked away for an instant. I might have been mistaken in the dim light but I thought he blushed.

'Report.' I was back in full military mode.

'We had some light resistance. Some *vigiles* and a couple of nats. We've interrogated the *vigiles*. But they had nothing of any significance, just routine checks now and again from their central station, paperwork and the occasional intervention by the nats. They kept it very formal with us. Then we tackled the nats. Easy to do, they're such cowards. Much more interesting – they had new handheld radios and new communication codes. One of my signals people said their frequency cards were in English.'

'Send them back to Colonel Volusenia.'

'Already done.' He grinned, then slumped forward. He thrust his hand out onto the table to steady himself.

'When did you last rest, Atrius?'

'No time,' he mumbled.

I pulled him to one side. 'You introduce me to your staff here and then you go straight for rest. And I mean immediately.'

Atrius's number two was a former estate manager from near Aquae Caesaris. She'd been reduced to working in her own fields; the only other option she'd been given was to be dragged off to a work camp. Although her workers ostensibly obeyed the new supervisor they'd stayed loyal to her. She had that crisp, managing air and seemed to have the rest of the troops, regular and irregular, well controlled. I was confident she would manage the harbour area with polite but ruthless efficiency while Atrius rested.

Junia confirmed staffing, patrol and operating procedures with her then ran a briefing group with the junior commanders while I dictated messages back to Volusenia and confirmed the coordinates for our next steps.

I only had to wait twenty minutes for Volusenia to give me the Phase III Scipio order. We had to keep going or we'd lose our advantage, but I was still worried about meeting regular troops and having to engage them. We still hadn't heard anything from the *magister militum* either way. He knew Volusenia and would talk to her while I wasn't there. If he wanted to.

After a quick coffee and meat rolls we climbed back in our short wheelbase, and with scouts ahead of us and our new convoy of nearly two hundred souls behind us, we set out for Roma Nova city.

'Incoming!' shrieked the radio operator in the seat in front of us. We shoved the doors open and dived for the ditches at the side of the road. I threw myself down so fast I winded myself. Gods, the pain that gripped my middle. Had to stay calm. Relax. Must get hands over ears. Too late.

The light and long whistle came first, then the brain-splitting noise of the explosion and the thump, the shock wave rumbling through the ground. I sucked in air, coughing and spluttering, trying to capture my breath. The second short wheelbase crew was already tracking the path of the ordnance. It had hit trees to the north side of the road; they burned white then yellow and orange, their black branches contrasting with the consuming firelight. My ears were ringing bells. I raised my head and my shoulders to see better, but Junia pushed me down into the frozen mud.

'Wait,' she hissed at me. From my restricted view, I could just about see a man and woman belly-crawl towards us across the verge. He had a radio backpack.

'Convoy centurion's compliments, ma'am,' he whispered. 'She says you are to remain here for the next ten minutes while we try and contact the scouts.'

I eased up and nodded. He spoke quietly but precisely into his mouthpiece. After a few moments his radio earpiece buzzed with a voice crackle.

'Scouts intact,' he relayed. 'No sign of military units.' He frowned. 'Say again,' he whispered into the microphone. He listened, glanced at me, then whispered, 'Out.'

'Scout commander confirms her original message – no sign of military.'

'Then who in Hades is lobbing ordnance of that size at us?'

'Incoming!' A shout travelled down the convoy.

We flattened ourselves, hugging the ground. This time I slammed my hands over my ears in time. As the ground rumble faded I looked round. My impression was that it hadn't been so loud, or the blast so strong. A cloud of smoke was rising a good way south of our route, at least a kilometre away.

'That's bloody sloppy shooting,' Junia mumbled.

I gestured to the radio operator. 'Tell the convoy centurion to get that DF'd and send a security detachment out to investigate the source. I'll eat my boots if those rockets came from a regular artillery unit.'

A chuckle from my side. Junia.

'That's a bit rash. Do you know how tough your walking boots are?'

'Ha!' I replied. 'If that detail can't pinpoint the source by some basic direction finding, then they can go back to Vienna and drive taxis.'

I fretted about the delay but we stayed down. Two larger vehicles with machine guns mounted on the cab roofs set off across the fields on the south side of the road. I tracked them with my night-vision binoculars. About twenty metres away they stopped bumping up and down and ran more smoothly. They'd hit a made-up road. They slowed down, stopped and troops piled out and formed into four small groups in a crescent shape. Classic pincer.

They advanced carefully on some black shapes which looked like a hut with a vehicle parked outside, but I couldn't see much more.

Suddenly, bursts of fire rang out. Our troops used four-to-one tracer rounds so we could watch where they poured on their fire. After a minute they stopped. Through the binoculars I watched them advance, the centre group enter the hut and drag out two, possibly three, figures. Ten minutes later they were back to the convoy. We stood up as the first truck braked.

Three men with nationalists' armbands, hands secured behind them, were pulled none too gently from the back of the lorry. One had blood dribbling from his nose.

'These miserable little shits thought they were big boy soldiers,' the *optio* said and pushed one forward. He had smuts all over his face and limped. 'They were making a pig's breakfast out of using the new SMAWs the EUS military are introducing. We've brought them with us and all the rockets we could find.'

'Show me,' I ordered him.

Three sleek tubes, complete with padded shoulder bracket, sights and trigger handles and four crates, three closed, of slim rockets lay on the bed of the lorry. I clapped the *optio* on the shoulder and smiled at him.

'Excellent work.'

I tasked Junia to liaise with the convoy centurion about placement and to designate firing teams.

I went back and stood with braced legs and arms crossed in front of the nats.

'Let's keep this simple. It's over. You either cooperate with us or you'll have a very uncomfortable ride back to a holding area. We are at war. As you fired on imperial troops of the legal government of Roma Nova, we may under law execute you here and now.'

I let that sink in.

'Your choice.'

The one with the bleeding nose spat on the ground where it froze. The *optio* smacked him in the face which made the nat cough violently. I raised my hand in the *optio*'s direction.

'Enough. Some pigs prefer to remain in the trough, *optio*.' I glanced at Junia who gave the tiniest nod in reply. 'Lieutenant, take him away. You and the *optio* know what to do.'

The young soldier pulled the nat roughly and the three of them disappeared further up the convoy. We waited a minute. The gunshot cracked loud across the empty fields, followed by a grunt and the sound of a body falling.

The other two nats looked at each other, terror filling their faces.

'We didn't mean nuffink. It was him, Statius. He made us do it.'

'Do what?'

'Get them bazookas out.'

Not an accurate description, but I wasn't going to engage in military semantics.

'What are you, political activists, doing with specialist military hardware?'

'It's… secret. Top secret, we was told.'

'Well, you can tell me your little secrets. They'll be quite safe.'

They exchanged glances.

'If you're not going to share, then we'll deal with you summarily.' I made a performance of looking at my watch. 'Lieutenant,' I called.

Junia strode round from the hidden side of the truck, in the middle of replacing her service pistol in her holster.

'Another one, ma'am?' she said.

'Both of them. We don't have time for this.'

The older of the nats fell to his knees, sobbing.

'Don't shoot me. Please. I've got kids. And a wife. If we tell, they'll kill them. You're women, you understand.'

Poor sod, he was completely stuck. The younger one chewed his lip so hard, it burst the skin and blood welled out. Whatever it was, it was important. And I had the growing feeling it was worth pushing for.

'We're Praetorians first, at a time of war,' I said crisply. They both flinched. 'There is no soft option. You have ten seconds or you will join your comrade.'

'No comrade of ours,' the younger one said and looked up. 'He's a complete bastard. He's my brother-in-law and knocked my sister about. Now he's gone, I'll tell you what you want to know.'

'A wise decision. I'm listening.'

'We was sent orders. Some rebels was trying to make a fuss so they told us to blow them… you… off the road.'

'And why were *you* doing it?'

'Cos… cos the military ain't coming.'

38

We sent the two nats back under guard to the holding area under Atrius's command where he had established a secure area for prisoners. As they climbed up into the back of the truck they looked surprised when a trussed up figure was thrown in after them; Statius, the one who'd spat on the ground and that Junia and the *optio* had hauled off. Now he wore a large purple bruise on his face, but otherwise he was living and breathing. Did they really think we would have shot him?

Volusenia's voice crackled over the HF encrypted radio, but I could hear the pleasure in it when I reported what the nats had said.

'So the *magister* has found his balls. Good. I've just given the signal to the resistance units inside the city. Calavia has confirmed receipt. No need to tell you to proceed carefully, though. Execute Phase IV, Aurora.'

Despite a long drink of strong coffee somebody handed me, I yawned. I fished a couple of energy pills out of my pocket and gulped them down. But they wouldn't be the only things keeping me going today. Volusenia's plan was working well. As we brought the main force in from the west and sent two centuries of troops to the north of the city, units from Castra Lucilla in the south and Brancadorum in the east would advance; together we'd draw the loop round the city tighter and tighter until we'd caught all the rats in the bag.

Light glimmered on the eastern horizon as we approached the

outer edge of the city; our objective was an industrial park. A pair of bolt cutters on the chain slung between the gates and we were in a factory loading area. Calavia's resistance group had done their reconnaissance very well. It was perfect. The peeling paint on the walls and weeds growing round the edges witnessed it was months since anything had loaded goods for dispatch. As quietly as possible, we parked all vehicles and formed up in centuries under the loading bay canopies. We were nearly at old cohort strength, four hundred and eighty, plus officers.

With Junia and the centurions standing to the side of the short wheelbase that I was using as my staff car, I clambered onto the seat and stood looking round at our troops, our task force. Although they all wore purple armbands with gold eagles, some were kitted out in old uniforms, some plain green trousers and jackets, some in black, dark blue and brown all jumbled up. Praetorians were mixed into each group along with women ex-*vigiles* and military. Some of our fighters were young, fired by patriotism and adventure, others, older, were more cynical, but all were prepared to risk their lives. As they stood easy, their fingers around the tops of the barrels of rifles resting on the concrete, I could sense the contained tension. I must not fail them.

'Free Imperial Forces of Roma Nova,' I began. 'Today, we go to liberate our country. We are entering Roma Nova city to free our own people from a tyranny they have endured for nearly a year and a half. Our argument is not with our friends and families, our colleagues and neighbours who have lived under such extreme conditions that it may have marred their judgement.

'Our argument is with a usurper and his henchmen, his destructive and grasping council of terror. I expect you to shake their world into pieces. Be ferocious in fighting, wipe them out if that is what they choose, but allow them to surrender if they choose otherwise.

'Civil war is uncivil. Thus, it must be quick and sharp if we are to stitch our country back together. We have survived over fifteen hundred years. My aim today is to ensure we survive for the next fifteen hundred.'

I saw a few smiles at that, but only a few, as it started to dawn on them that we were now plunging ourselves voluntarily into an unremittingly harsh situation.

'My intention is for every single one of you to be alive at the end of today, but some standing here and those preparing themselves in other imperial units or in resistance groups in the city may not be. We will treat their bodies with dignity and send them back to their families.

'Caius Tellus and his so-called nationalists should be in no doubt that we are their personal Furies. We will pursue them to their destruction, if necessary. But a word of caution – I want Caius Tellus alive to stand before a court of the Roma Novan people and be judged.

'Most of you have served in the military, at least fulfilled your national service. For some of you that may be a dimmer memory than for others. Many of you have received training in Vienna. Remember it, and obey your commanders even in the most harrowing moments. They will bring you through.

'But above all remember this: it is a big step to take another human life. You may not have a moment to think about it if your opponent is aiming a weapon at your head, intent on killing you. Your training and instinct for survival will kick in. But if someone surrenders to you then be firm, but gracious. We are not barbarians. The ones who are determined to fight on, well, we will not disappoint them.'

I took a breath and looked around. Bright eyes and serious, some grim, faces looked back.

'Roma Novans are fierce fighters; this is our history,' I said. 'Today with Mars' blessing we will add to that history. *Bona fortuna* and may the gods be with you.'

They stood in silence for a few moments, some glancing at comrades, others keeping their gaze towards the front as if not thinking of anything in particular – a sort of detachment. All we could hear were birds chirruping as they went about their early morning routine, completely uncaring about us or any other human. The centurions and *optiones* recovered first and gathered up their units. They left quietly, marching off in silence towards the city; only my own small detail, and Junia's, were left.

She spent the next ten minutes checking coordinates with the drivers and establishing radio checks, and advised our people to rest or relax for the next fifty minutes. I was so lucky to have such a practical soldier as my executive officer.

We had to give the task force an hour to march in and secure the first targets, so after receiving radio confirmation that the units to the north, east and south sides of the city had set off for their objectives, I closed my eyes and dozed.

When my watch alarm went off I shook myself out of my torpor and signalled to my driver to get us underway. Our three-vehicle convoy, followed by an infantry unit, moved through the first suburbs. It was early and the chill in the air bit, but nobody was in the street. Not a sign of local *curia* vans cleaning the street or collecting rubbish. No early shift workers or delivery vans or even the odd light leak at the edges of shutters. Street lights were all out, several with broken lamps. We veered round potholes as we proceeded between houses and were passed through a checkpoint one of our task force had set up. As the morning light grew, single houses gave way to multiple-storey *insulae* lining the streets as we approached the western end of the Via Nova.

Then I heard the sharp rhythmic noise on the tarmac. It echoed through the silence. More joined it. I signalled the driver to stop and we bailed out. Our detail took up defensive positions, our second vehicle crew manning the machine gun. The two scouts crept forward of the woman on point. I snatched my pistol from its holster and took a deep breath. One half of my brain had identified the noise immediately but the other half dismissed it.

Then the tall figure appeared, rifle slung diagonally across his back. He swayed with his horse's movement which seemed slow, but gained on us fast. The horse's breath plumed in the cold air. I thrust my pistol back into its holster and my temper back down into my core.

'Stand down,' I called to the troops. I raised my hands, put the backs together and parted them in a jerk. The scouts and point woman flattened themselves against building walls on each side of the street. Half a dozen more mounted troops followed, but halted a little way back.

'Where in Pluto's name have you been?' I blasted at their leader.

He grinned, swung one leg over the horse's back and slid to the ground in one fluid movement. He strode towards me and before I could react, he grabbed me and kissed me thoroughly. I struggled but his hard grip round my waist didn't relax. I had to admit I didn't really want to be released. He stroked my cheek and made shushing noises. After a few moments I pulled myself out the world of Miklós and Aurelia and came back to the cold deserted street in the middle of a civil war. I glared at the smirks on my troops' faces. Junia called them all to order and they slipped back into neutral military mode. I pulled Miklós to one side.

'Why the hell haven't you done radio checks?'

'We've been too busy for that.'

'What have you been up to?'

'This and that.' He waved his hand at nothing and glanced away.

'Miklós…'

'Well, after we'd taken Aquae Caesaris and Castra Lucilla, what was there to do? I sent the Castra Lucilla group to Brancadorum and came here with mine. We thought we'd have a little fun.'

'Fun? Describe "fun".'

'We scared the *vigiles* back into their stations yesterday.' His dark eyes gleamed. 'They ran like squealing pigs. We slept at a farm outside the city last night. The horses are rested and we are all ready for today.' He grinned again. 'What would you like us to do?'

A deafening explosion stopped my answer. We threw ourselves on the ground. A heart-rending scream as one of the group of horses collapsed and the rider with it.

'Get the fuck out of here,' I screeched at him. 'And switch your bloody radio on.' He leapt up on his horse and waved his arm vigorously at the other riders. I heard rather than saw the other riders gallop off, thundering down the tarmac.

'Move, move now!' I shouted and clambered into the short wheelbase.

We raced on for fifty metres, then dived down a side street to regroup.

Another blast to the street where we'd been. Damn, their aim was far more accurate than the amateurs we'd met before.

'Get a fix on that and relay it to the nearest two groups of the task force,' I said to the centurion in the third short wheelbase. 'Order them to go and deal with it. Mars' balls, we have to keep damage to the city to a minimum.'

The radio crackled. 'Message for Aquila Zero from Inferna One.'

I stretched my hand out. 'Go ahead.'

'Welcome to the city, Aquila One.' Calavia. She was still alive. Thank Diana. 'Care to join me for a drink at my grandmother's?'

Gods, she really did have a gallows sense of humour.

'Any traffic on the way?' I asked equally casually.

'A few mosquitoes, but we've squashed a good number.'

'There in thirty. Out.'

'Junia, get me reports from the units, and send a scout vehicle out down the Via Apulia.'

We made our way gingerly down the Via Apulia, passing through roadblocks our task force had set up. The reports were encouraging. Some resistance from nats' district and street offices and the occasional *vigiles* station; three were still resisting, besieged by our troops, but it was a matter of time. I could still hear ordnance exploding and gunshots, but only intermittently. We stopped just short of the forum and cut the engines: the silence, the deserted streets, dust and filth everywhere. Then a scurrying movement. Two rifles trained and cocked on the source within instants. This was supposed to be a clear route according to Calavia. A child of about six or seven clambered out from under a tarpaulin in a half-demolished *insulae* block, her rounded eyes pleading. She stretched out a skinny hand.

'Eat.'

The area was deserted, but we looked around first and guards slipped into position round our vehicles so we had a three-sixty view. It wouldn't be the first time a begging child had been used as bait.

I leaned towards the girl. 'Where's your mama?'

'Gone.'

I signalled an *optio* forward. He fished out an energy bar. The girl grabbed it, tore the wrapper off and ate it in three bites. She held her hand out again.

'Eat.'

The *optio* gave her a drink of water in the steel cup that topped his flask. She gulped the water down, glanced at him, then the cup. Too late, he went to grab her, but she'd fled back into the *insulae* block, the *optio*'s cup in her hand.

'The little tart!' He went to go after her.

'Leave it. She probably needs the cup more than you do.'

Nothing else happened on our journey except somebody took a pot shot at us when we turned off the Via Apulia. Junia took a detail with her and rousted out a teenager with a shotgun.

'For Jupiter's sake,' I said to the sulky boy when they dragged him out of the apartment block. 'Don't you have anything more sensible to do? And where in Hades did you get that shotgun?' I thought Caius had confiscated all firearms.

The boy said nothing, and looked down at the ground. He couldn't have been older than thirteen, fourteen at most.

'Answer me,' I said.

'Gun was my dad's,' he mumbled.

'Go home and lock your door. Stay inside with your family and don't come out until you hear a public announcement. And no more heroics.'

He looked up and flinched. His eyes reflected pure fright. 'Ain't you going to kill me?' His voice was shrill.

'Of course not. We're not barbarians.'

'They said—'

'Yes?'

'If ever the women came back they'd kill all the boys under sixteen.'

Then he gulped and snot ran out of his nose along with tears down his cheeks.

Junia gasped and one of the two soldiers holding the boy looked so horrified, she covered her mouth with her hand. I stared at him as if I hadn't heard correctly. But I knew I had. Bloody Caius.

'What's your name, child?' I asked.

'J–Justus.' He sniffed and wiped his nose with the back of his hand.

'Well, Justus, that was a lie, like all of Caius Tellus's lies. He and his nationalists tell lies all the time. We've come to save Roma Novans like you. All and every one of you.' And I pulled him to me and let him sob his heart out.

39

'So where are we, captain?'

I sat on a slashed and half-burnt leather armchair opposite Pia Calavia in the wreckage of Domus Calaviarum's atrium. Broken statues, furniture and columns had been moved to the sides, part-torn hangings and curtains were supplemented with plain cloth or blankets to keep light and inquisitive gazes out. Books had been thrown all over the floor and were covered in a year's dust.

Trestle tables with women and men handling paper, talking into radios and telephone handsets created a steady background buzz.

Calavia ran her fingers through her hair and consulted a scruffy notebook.

'We have the TV and radio stations but are maintaining a permanent guard there. Those nat bastards were broadcasting propaganda right up to the moment we burst into the studios. We brought in the former director of Roma Nova TV as soon as it was safe and she's organising a programme of music and keep calm messages. They're showing films out of the archives on a loop. I'd like you to go up there as soon as you are able, ma'am, and do a broadcast. Any chance of the young imperatrix doing the same?'

'You tell me, Pia. Is it safe for her?'

'The troops from the four columns of the task force have occupied the city itself. All the objectives on the list you gave to the resistance groups have been acquired.'

'This is wonderful, Pia.'

'To be honest, I think we were pushing against a three-quarter open door. People had had enough. Food is short, jobs have evaporated, services are nearly non-existent. People are talking openly about the brutality. My groups have been recruiting exponentially. In fact, it's difficult keeping tabs on them all and stopping them going off early. And your leafleting and broadcasts have been cutting through the crap.'

'Are there any central services left? What about the hospital?'

'Very few, but the Central Valetudinarium is just about functioning. A couple of my people work there, one as a doctor, another former surgeon as a nurse. She says they're having to put people in the corridors.'

'What about casualties? Surely they're getting attention?'

'We've had some, and yes, we've sent them there with guards to ensure they're treated as a priority. Thank Mars and all the gods, the military didn't turn out, though. I've sent a driver and escort over to find the *magister militum* and bring him here.'

'Good move,' I said. 'Since he chose not to turn out his troops against us, we should bring him in to thank him and get him to help us maintain order, even if temporarily.'

'I'd rather use my own people if we can until we've vetted his troops.' Her voice was flat, but I caught a note of wariness. Perhaps she was remembering how the regulars had captured us when she and I were trying to escape from Roma Nova a year and a half ago.

'Your call. But I'll talk to him when he gets here.' I waved my hand to take in the atrium. 'Are you using this house as your HQ?'

'Until we get Tellus out of the Golden Palace.'

'He's still there?'

'His political troops are taking too many of our people out, so we've drawn back to a safe margin.' She looked across the atrium at the clerks and then to the door where two guards stood. She lowered her head and leaned towards me. 'I don't know if Caius Tellus knows about the tunnels or their exit points but I'm playing it safe. I've stationed some of my people at the premises where they come out from the palace. All I've told the troops is that they're rendezvous points for the nats' fall-back.'

'Well done. I'll get Junia Sestina to reinforce them with some of her troops.' I glanced at my watch. 'It's half one now. I'll go and do the broadcast shortly. You don't have any food here, do you?'

She laughed.

'One of my own group is a baker. I just gave her the keycode to my grandmother's storeroom, showed her the kitchen and left her to it. What would you like?'

While I was eating chunky soup made of Juno knew what, with bread that could win a competition, a signal came through; Silvia, Volusenia and a civilian administration convoy were on their way with a heavy escort.

I left Junia at Domus Calaviarum as local military commander while Pia Calavia and I plus two Praetorians set off for the TV station. The streets were full of pieces of brick and stone, shattered glass, stinking rubbish and, the gods save us, at least half a dozen human bodies.

'We need to mobilise the refuse collectors, to clear all this and the *vigiles* to take these poor sods away. We can't leave people sprawled on the street. Have you found their prefect yet?'

'He's in the XI Regio station, refusing to let us in or to come out.'

'Hm. Let's see if he's so brave saying that to Volusenia.'

At the TV station, I recorded a reassuring speech, outlining what had happened and asking people to stay inside their houses for the next twenty-four hours for their own safety. Further information would also be broadcast over the radio. I hoped I didn't stumble too much; I was so tired. When we returned to her house, Calavia pushed me upstairs to a large room with a welcoming bed, removed my boots and closed the curtains. I was asleep within seconds.

I jerked my eyes open. My head shook with the noise of the blast. I sat up in a cloud of dust and noise, thrust my feet into my boots and grabbed my pistol. Shouting from downstairs. I tore down the graceful, now battered, central stairwell into the former drawing room.

'What in Hades was that?'

Pia whirled round, her face covered in dust.

'Those bloody nats are firing ordnance indiscriminately. They know they're done and just want to take the whole place down with them.' She turned and called to the centurion now coordinating her staff table. 'Report. Now.'

'Right, Calavia,' I snapped. 'We're not taking the siege option. We have to go in. I'm calling in all task force members with recent infantry experience plus Praetorians to meet here in sixty minutes. Please relay that to all units, stat.'

We were over two hundred by the time we set off. Junia would lead the main assault group which would slog it up the hill to the Golden Palace. Two other groups would attack from the side. Three parties of twenty, one led by me, were going down the tunnels. Stuff the secrecy now.

Calavia clasped my forearm.

'You've chosen the most dangerous way, Aurelia Mitela. *Bona fortuna.*'

I nodded to the guards standing in front of the old armourer's house in the suburb beyond the city walls. Calavia and I had escaped this way when we were trying to find Silvia and Volusenia the year before last. They had disappeared on the night of the fires when Caius had made his power grab.

The old armourer was still there, though with more grey hair and less body weight. Her muscular arms were diminished; she was now using them to pour drinks for the guards and irregulars lounging about in her sitting room.

'You!' Her eyes flared in recognition. 'I mean, *domina.* They said you was dead, the first consul s'posed to have shot you himself.'

'As you see, Armourer, I'm very much alive. Now we need to use the er, facilities.' I counted the guards here, mostly Calavia's group and a couple of mine. 'Four of you stay here. Keep the radio ready to relay a message back to Captain Calavia. The rest of you, come with me.'

Twenty-five of us followed the armourer down to her basement. Squashed in between her household detritus it was difficult to see everybody.

'We're going to the palace by this subterranean tunnel which does not officially exist,' I said. 'The ancients built them for emergencies. This is one of those emergencies. Two other groups are attempting the same. Expect the worst when we arrive. But if we can get into the palace and take it, we can catch the usurper and stop the bombardment of our city. Questions?'

Heads turned, glances were exchanged and a few muttered comments, but nobody raised a voice. I detailed two guards to stay in the basement within shouting distance of the house upstairs. We fixed red filters on our torches. Dim, but safer than white light. I nodded to the armourer and she put the key in the lock with a trembling hand and turned it.

We barrelled through the door three abreast in classic ram formation. No response. Back in a column of two abreast we walked steadily for about thirty metres, then came to a wider area with old cupboards, table and fold-up chairs. The harbour area. I flicked my fingers towards the long alcoves at the sides shielded by curtains. They were designed for sleeping or perhaps, in these times, hiding an armed guard. Curtains pushed aside with a rifle barrel, while another one aimed inside the alcove. All were empty.

Perhaps Caius didn't know about the tunnels after all. Nevertheless, we doused even our filtered torches, paused to let our eyes adjust. I took a deep breath, sent a prayer up to Mercury and touched my neighbour to advance at my side.

Taking short but steady steps, we advanced about another ten metres. I heard a soft click. I thrust my arm out to stop the soldier to my left side.

'Down!' I whispered. A light blinded us. Shots rang out. We flattened ourselves against the walls. I blinked, my eyes watering with pain. Grunts and profanities from behind us. They'd taken hits. We crouched, then scrambled back to the harbour area, dragging and pushing our casualties with us. Wild shots followed us, ringing and echoing through the tunnel, deafening us.

'Wounded back to the gate now,' I shouted. 'Remainder, regroup against the walls.'

I counted three minutes.

Silence.

'Advance with extreme caution,' I whispered.

Then came the rattle of a machine gun.

Gods, we'd be sliced into pieces of meat.

'Retreat. Now! Max speed.' We fled as if the Furies were after us. Two took rounds in their arms, one in her leg. She fell but her comrades pulled her along and we got everybody back the other side of the tunnel gate.

'Lock that bloody door and jam everything and anything against it.' Pushing my way through the bodies gasping for their breath and ignoring my hammering heart, I tore up the basement steps.

'Flash message Inferna Zero from Aquila Zero. Cancel tunnel operation. Extreme risk of termination.'

After arranging for the wounded to be taken to the Central Valetudinarium with a guard, I detailed two sections, around thirty troops, to guard the tunnel gate round the clock. It was very possible nationalists would use this route to flee. I told the *optio* in charge that she was to call for immediate reinforcements the minute there was any attempt to break through the tunnel door, or before if she felt it appropriate. And no more lounging around drinking cups of tea in the armourer's front room.

I drove back with the remaining half dozen, swearing long and hard under my breath. Dodging another damned rocket and veering round new shell holes in the road, I'd rolled up a fine ball of temper by the time we arrived back at Domus Cavaliarum. The guards let us through the gate and no sooner had the short wheelbase scrunched to a halt on the gravel, I was out and strode through the vestibule. I heard shouting the other side of the double doors leading into the atrium. I grabbed the handle of one of the doors and heaved it open.

My words were ready to shoot out, but I was stopped on the threshold by the sight of a very young woman with her arms wrapped round a boy sobbing his soul out. She stroked his blond head, and murmured words in a low voice. Two vulnerable children standing in the middle of dust, debris and war. The young woman turned, her face showing surprise and fear. She clutched the boy more firmly to her and stared at me.

'Imperatrix,' I said and bowed to her. She didn't react. 'Are you well?' She didn't answer. Everybody else was still. I could feel the tension running through the room. Why was Silvia holding little Conradus Tellus so fiercely? Where had he come from? And where was Quintus? Silvia glanced right. I followed her look and stepped forward. Quintus was standing between two men who gripped his arms. His suit jacket hung open, creased and torn, the silk tie that usually boasted an impeccable knot over a white shirt was binding his wrists. A purple bruise was developing just below his cheekbone. I glared at the men either side of him. They were *vigiles*. Their maroon uniforms were dusty but unmistakable. Behind them and Quintus stood two of our guards, their rifles trained on the group of three. I looked left to see Volusenia and Calavia, and a tall blonde woman dressed as an irregular but with a purple and gold armband facing them with an angry expression on her face and a rifle pointing at Silvia.

'What in Pluto's name is going on here?' I said. 'Why is Quintus Tellus under guard?'

40

The blonde woman spun round.

'Are you in charge here?' she snapped at me.

'My name is Aurelia Mitela. I am the Imperatrix Silvia's chief minister, head of the Twelve Families and location military commander. And you are?' But a memory was stirring. A cave at the back of the castle. She was the fidget from Claudia Cornelia's group.

'Oh,' she said. 'I know you.' The blaze in her eyes subsided as she looked at me. 'Caelia, former *optio*, XX Victis legion. I was trying to explain, ma'am, but nobody was listening.'

Volusenia snorted. Calavia rolled her eyes and went to speak. I held my fingers up. Calavia shrugged, crossed her arms and made a big show of seeming to listen.

'I'll listen,' I said. 'But first you must give me your rifle.'

She hesitated.

'No harm will come to you, but you must hand it over. Roma Novans do not threaten children.'

After a few seconds she relaxed and, her eyes still fixed on Silvia and Conradus, stretched out her hand towards me with the weapon. I leaned forward, took it and handed it to a guard by the door.

'Continue,' I said, trying not to show my relief.

'I was bringing a message here from Claudia Cornelia, but I took a wrong turning and found these three and the kid by a car.' She jabbed her finger in the direction of Quintus and the two *vigiles*. 'The scarabs said they'd stopped the car – they'd got him bent back against it – and he was resisting arrest. One of them kept looking at the bags on the back seat. I thought they were looting. I unslung my rifle and told them to stop. The kid was crying and tugging on the man's jacket, so one of them slapped the poor little bugger, really hard. I cocked my rifle. Then they told me the man's name. I wanted to shoot him then and there, but they wouldn't let me.'

She whirled round towards Quintus.

'That bastard and his brother are responsible for shooting my dad and raping me and my sister,' she cried out. 'I'm going to rip his guts out.'

She lunged at Quintus. She raised her hand then swung her fist down in an arc to strike him, but I got there first. She pushed against my restraining grip with all her force. I just managed to hold her by clutching her wrist hard, my fingernails sinking into her skin. I pushed back with all my strength.

'Stand down, Caelia,' I said, our faces centimetres from each other's. I gasped as I caught my breath. 'If there are accusations to bring, they'll be in a proper court, not in some vigilante summary execution.'

Gods, she was strong.

An instant later, the pressure ceased. Calavia heaved Caelia back, despite the woman's angry strength.

I nodded to Calavia and she beckoned a couple of guards forward to take hold of Caelia. I took a deep breath, swallowed and turned to the two *vigiles*.

They exchanged a glance and looked uneasy.

'Right, you two,' I said in a cold voice. 'You can untie Deputy Praetor Tellus and let him sit down. Then you can tell me exactly what you were doing.'

'We was only trying to help. We stopped his car to tell him it was too dangerous to be out and about. He was rude and told us to piss off.'

I raised an eyebrow. The urbane Quintus would never use such language, even in the most stressful circumstances.

'Then?'

'Well, we felt it our duty to reprimand him and, er, encouraged him to get out of his car.' The *vigilis* looked down at the floor. 'We searched him and found his ID card. Naturally, in the circumstances, we confiscated his stuff and thought we'd better hand him over to somebody. Thought there might be a reward.'

'And why didn't you take him to the first consul up in the palace?' I kept my tone as honey-smooth as I could. 'Surely he would have been happy to reward you for recovering his brother?'

'What? When he's as good as had it? You must be joking. We thought there might be a reward from your lot,' he repeated. 'We managed to convince that girl pointing her gun at us that we should bring him here. Oh, and it wasn't us that gave him that shiner.'

'Captain Calavia,' I said, without taking my eyes off the two *vigiles*. 'Have these two miserable pieces taken away and locked up somewhere for assault, attempting to kidnap a citizen and a minor, and looting.'

As they were led away protesting, Volusenia stepped forward to greet me, clasping forearms. I was so pleased to see her.

'Thank Mars!' she said. 'I heard the report of the shooting in your tunnel as we arrived a few minutes ago. Calavia tells me the other two details were on the point of opening their tunnel gates when your message came through.' She searched my face. 'Catch your breath and we'll try and find some other way of prising that bastard out without destroying the palace.'

'Agreed, but give me a few minutes.' I turned to Silvia and touched her hand. 'Are you okay, darling?'

'They were lying. The *vigiles* were lying.' She looked up at me. 'How is that possible?'

Where should I begin?

'Unfortunately, not everybody can stand the stresses of pressure. They give in and accept it,' I said. 'Some want to save their skin, others take advantage of people's misfortune. I have a horrible feeling we may discover more of it. The adult world isn't always a pleasant place, darling.'

'I know that – I'm not stupid,' she snapped back. 'But if we can't trust the guardians of the law, who *can* we trust?'

'I had many concerns about the *vigiles* before Caius's rebellion. One of the things we must prioritise when this is over is a total reform of the police service, even a new name, perhaps. But that's for later.' Silvia remained shocked and stood frozen, her arms still protecting Conradus. I knelt down, wiped the boy's tears away with my handkerchief and gave him what I hoped was a reassuring smile. 'I have to speak to Uncle Quintus now. Would you like to go to the kitchen and find some milk and biscuits?' He looked doubtful and clutched Silvia's hand hard. I looked up at her. 'Would you mind going with him, darling? He trusts you.'

I waited until they had left before I went over to the isolated figure on the chair.

'Quintus. How are you?'

'Relieved.' He stood up, then closed his eyes. 'You have no idea how much.' He opened them again and gave a tiny smile. 'I see you haven't lost any of your guile. That was well done with Silvia. That poor boy is so damaged. I don't know if he'll recover from Caius's beatings and neglect. I found him out at the villa, locked in a cellar. The servants have all fled, even the steward. I hope it gets thoroughly looted,' he added in a bitter voice.

'It's safer here for both you and Conradus.'

'Am I under arrest?'

'Let's say you'll have to stay here with us until we have time to decide what to do with you. There are more pressing matters to deal with.'

'I can imagine. I haven't seen Caius for weeks. He didn't look well then but he was still cracking out his orders. That slimy little toad of his, Phobius, is still terrorising the palace. You will have discovered yourself that he's put artillery emplacements in the public parks and turned the palace into a fortress.' He sighed. 'You may just have to blow the place apart.'

'Calavia's people have been able to map the known artillery emplacements from the trajectories,' Volusenia said. 'We should be able to take out at least two or three of the nearest ones with raiding parties. She's briefing them now. But we'll have to start targeting the palace building itself after that.' She looked away, then back to me. 'I know, it shrivels your soul to destroy all those years of history, but we must act now.'

'Agreed. He's sitting on the hill like a brooding presence. You're the location military commander now. You must do what is necessary to achieve the objective.'

'Excuse me, ma'am, but there's a message for you.' A signals clerk gave me a torn-off piece of paper from the printer and a strange look.

MY DEAR AURELIA, HOW TIRESOME YOU AND YOUR WOMEN ARE. YOU HAVE HAD YOUR FUN, BUT NOW YOU MUST WITHDRAW. BEFORE YOU HAVE A TANTRUM AND THROW THIS NOTE ON THE FLOOR, I SUGGEST YOU COME TO THE SQUARE IN FRONT OF THE GOLDEN PALACE WHERE I WILL SHOW YOU EXACTLY WHY. CAIUS

I looked at the printout to read it again. I couldn't speak. Bloody Caius. I felt rather than saw Volusenia snatch the message from me. She snapped at the signals clerk to show her the message heading and was swearing like one of her best centurions.

How had Caius penetrated our radio security? And what in Hades did he mean? There was no reason in this world why we would withdraw.

'Obviously, you can't go,' Volusenia's voice pierced my thoughts. 'It's just some ruse to get you into the open and shoot you. Wonder what he means, though.'

I took some gulps of water from my flask.

'We're stuck at the moment, Volusenia. It's a stalemate. Even if we take out some of his artillery positions he has at least half a dozen more. With the tunnels blocked and guarded he can't escape. But neither can our imperial troops get in that way. He's got heavy defences on the road up to the hill which are giving us more casualties than metres advanced. Yes, it will be hard, and it's going to take days as we tear down the walls sheltering him. We will prevail, of course, but our losses will be enormous. If there's half a chance we can shortcut this, we have to take it.'

'I suppose I'll be wasting my breath and patience trying to argue you out of it, won't I?' she growled.

'Yes, old friend, you would.'

. . .

The diesel engine rumbled as I drove up the hill with a white flag flying from the windscreen frame of my short wheelbase. The nats watched from their emplacements, some catcalling; one even spat, many gave me the fig. But I relayed their position, firepower, strength back to Volusenia via my radio. They'd be less cocky if Volusenia started targeting them if my mission failed. I told her to wait three hours and start her attack anyway.

I'd left her grim faced, Silvia tearful and Quintus protesting. I had no illusions about what would happen. Caius would kill me. But if I could get him to surrender in exchange, it would be worth it. Perhaps I was being naive, but something, anything to bring an end to this destruction.

Deep, cold sadness crept through me when I realised I would never see Marina's baby, nor Silvia received as imperatrix, nor Roma Nova restored. But worst of all, I would never lie again in my beloved Miklós's arms. I pictured him now, probably settled at the farm outside the city where he'd slept with his horses and comrades. He wasn't as impatient as I was and would wait for my message to come back into the city. I longed to join him more than anything. How tempting it would be to leave it all to Volusenia, Calavia and Junia. They had much more recent military experience than me; all three were full of strength and vigour. I swallowed hard. I didn't want to die.

But in my heart I knew it wouldn't be over until either Caius or I had gone into the shades. So in the fading light, I drove on.

41

———————

The barred gates to the main square were open. Unless the palace was to make an announcement they were usually locked. People could see through the railings, of course. I shivered as I passed through. The last time I'd been through this entrance, but going the other way, I was huddled under a blanket in the back well of Quintus's car, fleeing for my life from Caius.

The black-uniformed nats, each armed with a small machine gun that could cut me down in seconds, stood aside and tracked me with their hard eyes and frozen expressions as I drove through. At the far end of the square were half a dozen lorries and two saloon cars, one I recognised as the murdered Imperatrix Severina's official car. I stopped my short wheelbase in the middle of the square, took a deep breath and swung the door open. I stood a metre away from the vehicle and waited.

Movement from the sides of the square. Armed nats filed in and took up position at the edges of the square, one every ten metres or so. I instinctively placed my hand on my pistol holster, then let it fall. I would only be able to get off one or two shots before I was cut down.

People arrived. Women and men. Although here and there I saw a red and black nationalist armband, they looked like ordinary people. Some came close, but none stood in front of me. Most wore coats or jackets against the weather and all looked worried, even frightened. One face, a hand outstretched from a woman. Our eyes met. Locked.

Gods, it was Drusilla, the palace housekeeper and my friend. About fifty or so people. Then it clicked. They were the palace staff – cooks, clerks, drivers, stewards, messengers, cleaners – herded in to be witnesses, no, an audience. What the hell was Caius up to?

A man strode towards me, a long tall pole with splayed legs at one end in his hand and a wire trailing behind him. I tensed as he came within arm's length. He stopped, plonked the pole – a stand – down in front of me and clipped a microphone into the top of it. Busy with adjusting the trailing cable, he didn't say a word or even look at me. He scurried off in the direction of the far side of the square and disappeared into the crowd. Oh gods, Caius was going to make a circus of it.

The temperature was dropping rapidly. I'd wrapped warmly but the cold was seeping into my fingers and my legs were stiffening. Even if I attempted to escape in my vehicle, I wouldn't have been able to drive safely through all these people. Caius knew far too well how to spring a trap on me.

Suddenly a spotlight blinded me. I jammed my eyes shut, then slowly reopened them to get used to the full force of the light. I was caught in a pool of white light, sharply isolated from the rest of the crowd which I could scarcely see in the gloom.

'Delighted you could join us, Aurelia.' Caius's disembodied voice boomed out through the chill evening. I screwed up my eyes and looked up at the balcony that ran across the central part of the palace. The orange floodlight showed up the face of the building and the figure standing on the balcony. He was dressed in black with the usual armband. One hand grasped the top of the balcony rail, the other was raised in a gesture of invitation. Silence greeted him, but everybody's gaze was focused on him.

Unless he had a sniper trained on me, I calculated he wouldn't shoot me here among all these people. But you never knew with Caius. Well, if he wanted to make a spectacle I would give him one. I stepped forward and switched on the microphone.

'Good evening, Caius. For those who don't know me, I am Aurelia Mitela, senior minister to Imperatrix Silvia and head of the Twelve Families. Imperial troops have liberated most of Roma Nova and have the palace surrounded. I have come to accept Caius Tellus's surrender—'

A hand seized the microphone. Another pulled me away from the stand.

'Tut, Aurelia, you were not invited here to speak lies to these poor people who are wondering why they are being attacked.'

I pulled away the hand gripping my arm and kicked its owner's knee hard. He fell, cursing. A jab to the bridge of the nose of the one who'd snatched the mike. He dropped it and clasped both hands to his face as he let out a shriek of pain. I seized the mike.

'No lies, Caius Tellus, the plain truth.' I caught my breath. 'Why else would you be showering heavy ordnance on the town destroying people's homes?'

He didn't reply, but half turned and beckoned to somebody behind him. One of his nat guards stepped forward, pulling another figure with his arms drawn back behind him; tall, black curly hair, unmistakable.

Miklós.

I couldn't move. My words died in my throat. I stared at him. I couldn't see any detail at this distance, just a blurred face. An iron claw gripped my heart.

'I think you might like to surrender to *me*, Aurelia,' Caius's voice boomed out. 'Why don't you come and talk to me about terms?'

If I went to him now, all these people would think I'd complied. But I couldn't leave Miklós at Caius's mercy. Gods, what was Miklós doing here? How had Caius snared him?

I grabbed the mike and pushed the rocker switch.

'No, you come down here!'

'Unfortunately, Aurelia that is impossible. I offer you one more chance. I think you know what the consequences would be if you were so selfish as to refuse.'

Curse him. Curse him to the infinite depths of Tartarus. My fingers round the mike stem were so tight they'd become numb. I wanted to throw it up at the balcony to hit him between the eyes and fell him. It was too far, of course, and it would fall on the ground – a useless gesture.

I had no choice. I pushed my shoulders back and, ignoring the stares from those around me, strode towards the front entrance of the palace. I went under the portico and pushed against one of the tall wooden doors. No guard was there. In the vestibule, two nats armed with light machine guns barred my passage and pushed me face first against the wall. They removed my pistol. I should have expected that. Then frisked me. One ran his hand over my breast and smirked, then felt between my legs. I wanted to kick him in the balls, but remembered what I was doing and why. When he released me I stared at him as coldly as I could and memorised every feature of his coarse face. After a few seconds, he stopped grinning.

'You, I will remember,' I said. 'Have no doubt.'

Had women been subjected to this kind of thing as a matter of course during Caius's time?

Full of hot anger I stalked across the marble floor of the deserted atrium. At the top of the stairs a palace steward greeted me, but showed not a shred of emotion. He gestured me to enter the balcony room which ran the length of the central part of the palace facade.

Inside, the light of a crystal chandelier emphasised the harsh features of Caius's face. In his right hand he grasped a pistol and was holding it to Miklós's temple. The hard steel of the pistol barrel penetrated the black curls I'd so often run between my fingers. A piece of builder's reinforced tape sealed Miklós's mouth. He took a step forward and shook his head, ignoring the threat of Caius's weapon. His eyes were full of agony. Caius grabbed Miklós's arm and pulled him back.

'Dear me, how affecting.' Caius's tone couldn't have been more mocking, but his expression tightened. He was angry. No, it was something beyond that. He let his arm drop and holstered his pistol. He tilted his chin and two nats standing just inside the door marched over and took up position behind and a little to the side of Miklós. 'Those are two of my personal bodyguards,' Caius said. 'The moment you do anything I dislike, they will shoot your gypsy. Do I make myself clear?'

I nodded but I couldn't drag my eyes away from Miklós's face. It was both hard and easy to convey how strong and deep my love was for him. He searched my face as if committing it to memory. I'd been enthralled since I'd first seen him on his horse Bátor in the Grunewald forest. Our bond had strengthened and deepened over the following fifteen years. He was simply the other half of my being. His eyes were shining intensely, deep brown pools. I don't know how long we stood there; it could have been instants or hours.

Miklós struggled to say something despite his taped mouth. I desperately tried to understand. He shot an angry glance sideways at Caius, widened his eyes at me, then shook his head.

I groaned in frustration.

Caius laughed.

'You sound just as you did when you groaned in my bed.'

I spun round. 'How dare you! I was never "in your bed". You raped me.'

'Oh, really?'

'I never gave the least shred of consent.'

'You wriggled enough. How interesting to know how your gypsy compares.'

'He's Hungarian, not a gypsy!' I took a deep breath to steady my shouting nerves. 'You're confusing animal response with love.'

But when I looked back at Miklós his eyes were livid. Gods, Caius's words had worked their pollution. Miklós shook his head at me, then jerked it in Caius's direction. I'd told Miklós about that horrendous night once I'd escaped to Vienna. He'd replied that I'd had to do what I'd had to do.

'Well, at least you were tastier than your near virginal daughter.'

A heavy thrumming grew through my head. I couldn't move.

'So that *was* you behind the attack on her during the riot two years ago?'

'Did you doubt it? It was to teach you a lesson not to interfere in my plans.'

'Plans? First you rape my daughter, then my country. That was your plan?'

'Be very careful, Aurelia. Your emotional outbursts aren't helping, you know.'

My eyes welled, not with sadness, but hot tears of anger. My poor child violated by this monster and his thugs and terrified beyond her life for hours. But she was safe now, halfway across the world with a devoted husband and child of her own.

'Let Miklós go, Caius. You're only holding him to get at me. Now you have me here.'

'Yes, indeed. But now I wonder if I'll shoot him anyway. I think that would punish you a little. And you deserve it.'

'What in Hades do you mean by that?'

'All this effort of being forced to repel your little invasion. It really has taken up too much of my time.'

'Then surrender to me.'

'Ha!' He grabbed my wrist. 'That's what I've tried to ask you many times, Aurelia.'

I shook his hand off. 'Don't be ridiculous.'

He raised an eyebrow and glanced at Miklós, then brought his gaze back to me. Juno, was my rejection of him going to cause Miklós's death?

'You brought me up here, Caius. I've done as you asked. Now release Miklós.'

Caius sat down in one of Severina's delicate French dining chairs and crossed one leg over the other. He was completely still, apart from tapping the tips of his middle fingers against each other. After a few moments, he took a good swallow of whisky from the glass on the elegant occasional table beside him.

'Very well, I will release him. But first you will give me your word that you will order your forces to withdraw. And I want to hear you do it.'

Miklós shook his head vigorously. Caius nodded and one guard drove his fist into Miklós's middle. His legs buckled and he bent over, obviously in pain. I leapt towards him, but the second guard thrust his rifle barrel in my face.

'Leave him alone. Your argument is with me,' I said to Caius.

'Do I have your word?' He was insistent.

'You can't ask that of me,' I said.

'Surprisingly, I can.'

I stared at him, then at Miklós, then back to Caius. What choice did I have?

42

———

I hated him and I hated myself as I promised to give Volusenia the order to stand down. Caius would take me to his signals room himself to listen as I did it. He pressed a bell push on the wall. I heard the door behind me open and twisted round to look.

A man dressed in a business suit entered the room, followed by two other men in black suits. Curly wires from their ears disappeared between their shirt and jacket collars. They both carried machine pistols. I recognised the suited man, but couldn't place him. But I knew instinctively that he was a strong threat. I took a step towards Miklós, but Caius waggled his finger at me. The nats' weapons cocked. I froze.

'What a short memory you have, Aurelia. Be very careful or you'll see your beloved's brains scattered across the room. It would make such a mess.'

'You—'

'Yes?' Caius placed his elbows on the chair arms, his fingertips of each hand touching, and looked at me with a faux innocent expression.

I swallowed my words, lumpy and fiery as they were. I was walking on the knife-edge of Miklós's life.

Caius smiled at the suited man.

'You remember Mr White from the Berlin and Vienna diplomatic circles?'

298

'I remember him trying to pump me for information.' I turned to the American. 'Head of station now, I presume? Or are you merely supporting an illegal coup and a brutal regime?' I couldn't even be bothered to throw him a contemptuous look. He provided Caius's technical equipment – I'd found the documents proving it during our undercover mission – and probably funding, too. My old spymaster associate Plico had always thought the EUS had expansionist pretensions, even if only into the Indigenous Territories or French-speaking Louisiane on their own continent. Something about wishing to be an imperial power like Ancient Rome. But what were they doing here?

'Really, Aurelia, that was uncalled for. You will apologise to Mr White. Now.'

Caius's voice was as hard as steel. I blinked and glanced at his face. His eyes were like agates and as unforgiving. Apart from my self-respect, I had nothing to lose with a few words. And this was no time to be precious.

'I deeply apologise, Mr White, for wounding your feelings,' I said in English. 'I would not for the world have you believe that I harbour anything but the warmest feelings for you and your sterling work.' I made an exaggerated bow in his direction to ensure he knew exactly what I meant.

'So sincere,' Caius said and smirked. Even White had the grace to glance away. 'Well, I'm a man of my word,' he said and stood up. 'Your gypsy, ah, Hungarian friend, is released from my custody.'

I closed my eyes for a nanosecond and released my breath slowly. Thank Juno, Mercury and every other god on Olympus.

'However, Mr White and his friends would like to speak seriously to him about the destruction of some valuable property belonging to the EUS government, so naturally I am cooperating with our closest ally. He has a helicopter waiting for him. I do hope your women don't shoot it down.'

He couldn't do that. My hands shook. I clamped them to my sides.

'You promised.' I could only whisper, my mouth was so dry. 'You promised to let him go.'

'No, I promised to release him from my custody. You need to pay more attention to what I say, Aurelia. So incompetent.' He smirked at me. 'You will obviously wish to say a few words of farewell. I will permit this, but regrettably, not in private.'

He stood, strode over to Miklós and ripped the thick grey tape off his face. Miklós flinched at the shock and sucked in his lips, then coughed.

'I'm so sorry, *drágám*,' he said. 'They ambushed us. One of his informants—'

'No, don't.' I touched his lip with my fingertip. 'I can't tell you the agony of seeing you used here by this bastard to get at me,' I said softly. 'I will find you, wherever they hide you, whatever they do. You know I have always loved you and always will.'

'And I you.' His eyes were liquid and his smile sad but beautiful. 'Just remember Vienna.'

At Caius's nod, White's two stooges came over. I stood between them and Miklós. It was unbearable. I might never see him again. I folded myself into him and enveloped him in my arms. He gave a deep sigh as his neck touched mine. Tears flowed down my face. I was pulled off by Caius's guards and held while White's men marched off with the other life of me.

I wanted to retreat, to fall into a heap, to withdraw from this plane of existence, but I had a monster to deal with. One who had destroyed my world.

'Now, Aurelia, you have to send a little message,' he said. 'And if you make even the smallest mistake or attempt to send a covert meaning, I will rescind my generous gesture to Mr White and shoot your lover in front of you.'

I nodded. I looked at the floor; the rest of the world wasn't worth looking at.

'Now, I have to ensure you won't get up to any of your tricks on our way to the radio room. You have the choice – the indignity of being shackled or you can give me your word of honour.'

Merda. I would be as trapped by my word as by cold steel around my wrists. And he knew that, the bastard. But what did anything matter now?

'Well?'

'I give you my word of honour,' I muttered.

'At last, you have learnt to submit. Far too late, of course.'

My heart was breaking and he was still trying to score points.

'You see, you *are* just a woman like all the others, full of sentimental nonsense, unable to make a decision except through your emotions.'

'At least I've known the strongest emotion humans can experience. Nobody has ever loved you, Caius.'

He flinched. Then I saw the anger in his eyes. He raised his hand and I prepared myself for the blow. But it never came. Slowly, he let his hand drop. Perhaps he realised he needed me whole and alive, at least until I'd spoken to Volusenia.

He shoved me through the door and we traipsed along the corridor to the palace communications room, full of screens, banks of radios and printers. But it was deserted apart from two uniformed nats. They turned as we entered.

'Send a message to the women's rabble that their commander wishes to speak to them. Set up a voice channel so they know it's her.'

While the operator fiddled with frequencies and sending an initial message by telegraphy, I looked round the room. There were at least a dozen workplaces, all with folded card notices with station names. Pencils, logs, dirty coffee cups were strewn around. Headphones thrown aside. Manuals in English. Columns and figures chalked up on a situation board on the wall ended with a last acronym FUBAR – Fucked Up Beyond All Relief. They'd all gone. The Americans had gone, and so had most of Caius's own people.

I sat down at the set Caius's operator indicated and flicked the switch to receive.

'Mitela? Aurelia Mitela?' Volusenia's strained voice crackled out in the empty room.

'Please observe correct protocol, colonel,' I replied in the coldest voice I could muster. 'You will address me, as always, as *domina*.' I prayed that would put her on her guard. 'I have new orders for you.'

A pause.

'Of course, *domina*.' Her voice sounded subdued.

'And you do not need to run them past that child, Silvia. Her opinion is of no consequence.'

'None,' she replied. She sounded deferential now.

Had Volusenia caught on?

'I have taken advice from the first consul and we have agreed that all six columns are to withdraw at least to the outer city limits. I will issue further orders in four hours' time.'

'I understand, *domina*. I shall inform all the subordinate commanders.'

'With immediate effect, if you please. Out.'

I pushed the switch down to cut contact and bowed my head.

43

His goons threw me in a cell in the guardroom. It smelt of urine and terror. A light hung from the ceiling on its twisted flex. Ten minutes later a tin mug of water and a chunk of bread were pushed through the slot at the bottom of the metal door. I was almost too tired to eat or drink but my empty stomach won. After I'd devoured them, I flopped onto the wood bench.

Was Miklós still alive? What would Caius do with me now? Would Volusenia understand my hidden message? Had I betrayed my country yet again? Despite these questions whirling round in my head, I couldn't stay awake to think about anything. I closed my eyes, heavy with nervous exhaustion, and fell into oblivion.

The bench shook and I was thrown onto the concrete floor. The noise, gods, my head rang. Was it the end of the world? Another thunderous blast. The wall shuddered and concrete dust showered down on me. I coughed as I dragged myself up in the gloom. It must be five or six in the morning. I staggered over to the far wall but it was impossible to reach the tiny window slit at the top. Firing. Automatic gunfire. Shouts, a scream. Feet pounding across cobbles. I pounded on the metal door.

'Let me out of here!'

If another mortar hit the wall, it could fall and crush me. I wouldn't even be able to climb out.

Nobody came.

More shelling. After another long ten minutes, I heard footsteps in the corridor outside my cell. I stood back. Caius's goons barrelled in, grabbed me and pulled me along. I shook one off, but the other one smacked me on the head. I was stunned for a few seconds but they kept pulling me along up the stairs and eventually into the atrium.

Shards of glass and plaster lumps lay scattered on the floor. Shouting and gunfire all round us. Two armed figures raced past through the atrium garden heading for the side entrance. Purple and yellow armbands. Our people, imperial troops. But they didn't see me through the clouds of dust filling the air. Caius stood, legs braced, watching it all, but with an unfocused gaze. He brought his hand up to cover his eyes. And I caught a mumbled 'No!'

I heard footsteps behind me, slow at first, but then retreating fast. His last two faithful bodyguards were deserting him. Even they had seen the game was played out. Caius and I were alone in the destruction.

'You!' He waved his arms at me. 'You caused all this. The end of my dream.'

'A dream that was everybody else's nightmare.'

'Gods, you are still so bloody sententious. Don't you ever give it a rest, Aurelia?'

He strode over to me, hands like grappling hooks, his face twisted with rage. I dodged him. He was so strong that if he got his hands round my throat again, he'd choke me to death. I crouched, ready to attack. I'd go low for his crippled foot. I launched myself, my elbow jabbed his stomach. I sprang back, throwing my weight on my back foot, and brought my front one up to smash down on his.

'Stop!' A pistol barrel aimed right at my head.

Merda.

'Hands on your head.'

I hesitated. He struck my face so hard I almost fell. I pretended to stumble a few steps more than I needed to, then took a deep breath and launched myself at him, bodyslamming him to the ground. He was winded and couldn't move for an instant. Catching my breath, I looked round desperately for something to tie him up. He started to get up, so I rammed my foot down on his back, my heel hard into his kidneys. He grunted and flopped back to the floor. I didn't know what else to do so I thumped him on the head and he passed out.

'It was hard work, but here we are.'

Volusenia was calm now and gulped down tea in the palace kitchen, the only part still undamaged. I was holding a wet pad to my face where Caius had hit me. It hurt like Hades and I'd have a purple face tomorrow. But that was the smallest blow he'd dealt me. I hadn't had time to tell Volusenia the whole story. I would have to keep my heart's loss inside for a while.

When Volusenia had burst through the hole left by the destroyed atrium windows, the fire in her eyes had been intense, pumped by adrenalin. The rest of her detail were the same. Soldiers fighting their war.

I'd been struggling to tie Caius's hands behind him with a flex from a table lamp but it was slipping. Now he was in the most secure cell in the guardroom, shackled to the wall from his ankle and under twenty-four-hour watch.

'Thank Mars you understood my message,' I said.

'Well, you can be snotty sometimes but not that bad.' She grinned. 'When you mentioned six columns instead of four, I knew I had to take everything you said as bollocks.'

'Excuse me, colonel.' A young orderly hesitated. She couldn't have been more than seventeen. 'The imperatrix presents her compliments and asks that you attend on her in the state drawing room. And the *consiliaria*.' She glanced at me, then blushed.

'Thank you, young lady.' Volusenia nodded at her. 'Well, we'd better cut along then, *consiliaria*,' she said.

Silvia Apulia stood in front of her mother's carved chair. I glanced around. Calavia, Quirinia, Aquilia and some of the junior commanders, and a little to one side, Quintus Tellus with his arm around Conradus's shoulders. The boy stood straighter than I'd seen him for a while and he looked around in curiosity rather than fear. But I was surprised not to see Junia. People drifted in, until we were about fifty or so. White sunlight shone through the broken windows. And dust still floated in the air. Silvia waited until everybody present was quiet and still. She was dressed like a wild mountain guerrilla, complete with long boots, rough jacket and scarf hanging across her chest. Smuts and concrete dust were her make-up. But she stood erect and moved her head in a composed, almost regal way.

'Thank you for coming. I know there's so much to do. I will only be a few minutes. This last year and a half has been horrible for us all. The next few will be nothing but hard work. My heart goes out to those who have lost people.' Her eyes swivelled round and rested on me for an instant. 'But also to those who have been lied to. Now we must look after them all as well as reinstate order. Colonel Volusenia and the Praetorians will head up a security force until we can organise a new law and order service to replace the *vigiles*.' She paused for a moment.

Quirinia bent over and whispered something to her. Silvia nodded and continued. '*Consiliaria* Quirinia will organise food supplies and the reconnection of water and electricity. She and Regulus will get the buses and trains running again – the tasks of a new Agrippa.' And she smiled broadly at Quirinia, who blushed. Then Silvia looked direct at me. 'We need to reassure our legations abroad and our friends in overseas governments, but first we need a new government here in Roma Nova. So I need Aurelia Mitela to form a new imperial council and reinstate the Twelve Families.'

Gods, she didn't want much. But we'd all do it, of course. After all, we were home.

44

―――――

Twenty-four hours later I collected my miraculously intact staff car from the square in front of the Golden Palace. The engine sputtered and struggled as I got nearer Domus Mitelarum. The fuel gauge told me it was running on vapour. I abandoned it up the street and hurried to the tall gates guarding my home. Nobody was more surprised than I was when the entry code beeped and the service door opened at my push. I stepped through and was met by a ferocious woman pointing a rifle in my face. I sighed. It would be a good time when that stopped happening.

'At ease,' I said.

'Identify yourself.'

'Aurelia Mitela, the owner of this *domus*. Now let me pass.'

'I don't know you. Wait here.'

Ironic, kept out of my own house, but she was doing her duty. It didn't look too damaged; debris swept into corners in the courtyard, the garages still with doors, but only one battered van in the covered area. The honey stone facade was intact, but several windows were boarded or taped up.

A petite brown-haired figure hurtled down the steps. Claudia Cornelia. She threw herself into my arms.

'Oh gods, oh gods,' she cried and burst into tears.

'Steady, Claudia. It's over.'

'I know, but I thought you were dead.' She drew back. 'I apologise, *consiliaria*, but I am so pleased to see you.'

'Yes, I got that impression.'

She sniffed, then grinned at me.

Inside, the atrium looked like a field barracks. Rows of mattresses, camp beds and sleeping bags stretched across one side. In the formal drawing room my mother's blue velvet covered dining chairs were looking the worse for wear behind trestle tables with radio equipment, files and boxes. People looked up as we entered, but went back to their work after a second or two.

'We had to use what was to hand, so—'

I laid my hand on her forearm.

'Claudia, a few chairs and carpets are nothing in the account. But I bet the steward grumbled all the same.' I smiled at her in sympathy. Milo would have given grumpy an entirely new meaning when the resistance group took over his domain. I'd pulled him out of retirement two years ago to cover the crisis and give the household strong leadership. 'Where is he?'

She looked away.

'What happened?'

'A group of nats tried to storm the gates yesterday. Stupid really. Short of blasting them, those gates are impregnable. I told Milo to ignore them – they were probably looking for easy loot. But he insisted, took a rifle and two pistols, opened the service door and went out and shot them. Unfortunately, they wounded him. Badly.' She looked away. 'He refused to be taken to the hospital. He said he wanted to die in his home.'

In his room in the domestic hall, I held the hand of the grizzled old ex-centurion. His skin was near white and tinged with a translucent blue at the edges.

'Well, that was a stupid thing to do, Milo.'

'You aren't the only action hero, *domina*,' he whispered, then winced. 'I'm sorry I couldn't do more.'

'You've saved my house and my people, Milo.'

'I had to join their crummy movement or they'd have turned me out.'

'We've all had to make compromises these past eighteen months. You are not alone, old friend.' I pressed his hand gently. 'You've fulfilled your duty well, centurion.'

The shadow of a smile flitted across his lips and he released a deep final breath.

Five days later, Pia Calavia appeared at my door. I'd just returned from the first imperial council meeting followed by a session with the former Senate president. I'd asked the latter to re-form it and call a meeting so that Silvia could address them and hopefully be given formal consent as their new ruler.

Calavia looked as tired as I felt. She wore standard Praetorian uniform now with the captain's discs with stylised wreath on her rank badges, but she also wore a protective vest and laid a helmet to one side as she greeted me.

'Problems?' I asked.

'Looters, really, in the Septarium – the poor robbing the even poorer. We've just had a sweep through. I'll be thankful when *Consiliaria* Quirinia gets this new *custodes* police service up and running.'

'If it's any consolation, the new imperial council session was a long afternoon of self-justification and accusation. In the end I had to screech at them to shut up. Silvia looked appalled. I told them to behave like adults as the country depended on them. I'd take the Septarium any day!'

'I'm immensely relieved my aunt is representing our family on the council. Thank Mars I'm needed more as a soldier.'

'Your turn will come, Countess Calavia. You can't shirk it forever.'

She made a face at me and I grinned back. Then her expression became more formal. 'I have some news for you and a request. First, we found Lentilius's body in a cell. It... It wasn't in the best condition. Apart from being covered with burn marks and deep bruises from intensive beating, some of his fingertips were missing.'

'Oh gods!'

'He'd smeared a message in blood on the wall, "*Me paenitet*".' She looked down at the chipped marble floor for a second. 'But what did he mean? What exactly was he sorry for?' she continued. 'Did he come back to Roma Nova voluntarily and then regret it?'

'It could also mean he'd tried to resist but couldn't hold out.'

She didn't look convinced.

'Well, we'll never know,' I said. 'We couldn't get hold of his bank account details – damned Viennese confidentiality – but he seemed to have had a large amount of money in it. A suspicious person could use the word "bribery".'

'Do you suppose that bastard Burrus got to him?'

'I do wonder. They were quite friendly. If Burrus was Caius's agent – and I think there's no doubt he was – suborning somebody so close to the imperatrix would have been a gold strike.'

'Gods, what a tragedy.'

'All round. Well, we can't send him back to his family like that,' I said. 'Burn him in the public ground and send his family a message afterwards with the urn. What else is there?'

'We still haven't been able to get that Air Roma Nova plane away from the Vienna Airport authority, but the colonel has let the pilot and her crew go back to Vienna and lobby for it. The pilot's tough and grumpy, as you know. I expect to see it land at Portus Airport any day now. Next, Lieutenant Junia Sestina. She's in the Central Valetudinarium under the care of some prima donna called Doctor Faenia. Apparently, Faenia's some kind of neurosurgeon superstar. Even the nats let her stay on at the hospital. Junia was badly wounded in the assault on the palace and they thought she'd never walk again, but this Faenia has fixed her up. She needs a billet, though, where she'll be looked after properly and given something to do. Would you—'

'You don't even need to ask, Pia. Tell Faenia to discharge her here. As soon as it's medically possible.'

She fiddled with her uniform sleeve cuff.

'What is it?'

'We're not a hundred per cent sure but we think we've found Miklós Farkas.'

My hand flew up to my chest. Gods, that was quick!

'The colonel said you'd be torn between wanting to be off looking for him and reconstructing the government here. She said you'd do your duty but you'd fret. And that wouldn't be any use to anybody. So we've been watching out for any mention of him.'

'Where is he? Is he well? How can we get him out?'

'*Lente!*' She held her hand up. 'We think he's in a holding facility south of Washington, in the EUS. It's where people who are arrested but not charged are detained. One of the monitoring telegraphists found his name by pure fluke on a list for presentation at their first level court. Incredible. As White's role was covert, I'd have thought the EUS would hold a secret trial and we wouldn't get a sniff of it.' She glanced at my face, then hurried on. 'He's listed as Nicholas Farkas and accused of sabotaging valuable EUS property; his hearing is postponed for a month. I've sent a message to the Praetorian commander in the Washington legation to see if she can use her contacts to find out his state of health. I thought you might like to speak to the *nuncia* yourself to dig out a lawyer. As he's a Hungarian national she can't demand to see him herself, but I'm sure she can have a word with her Hungarian opposite number.'

That evening I waited for the call from the international operator. Calavia assured me the battery rooms in the central city telephone exchanges were all back to full strength but for the moment international calls had to be put through by hand. Gods, it was like being back in the 1950s. I had the encoding unit that Calavia had raided from the foreign ministry on the table ready to plug in. I was dozing off when the phone eventually rang at half eleven.

'Your call to Washington DC. Please go ahead.'

'*Salve, nuncia,*' I began.

'*Consiliaria.* Delighted to hear you again. Congratulations on a successful operation. We've all been talking on the confidential channel.' The heads of Roma Nova's legations across the world would have had plenty to say to each other. 'I understand from Pia Calavia that you wish to speak to me on a personal matter?'

She called me again the next evening to say she'd engaged a top New York criminal lawyer on my behalf and had been to see the Hungarian ambassador.

'The lawyer we've engaged, Thaddeus Smith, won't commit himself absolutely, but he thinks the charges are overstated, especially as the equipment Miklós Farkas destroyed was in Roma Nova illegally. He went on about export documentation and other technical infringements of EUS commercial law. Anyway, he's served the EUS government with a counter-claim for kidnapping, illegal detainment and cross-border rendition. He's asking for a million dollars in damages.'

'We don't want the money, *nuncia*. I just want him out of there and back with me.'

'Never underestimate the threat of money with the Americans, *consiliaria*. I'm sure the imperial treasury will take it off your hands if you don't want it. I mentioned to Thaddeus Smith that the imperial government had full documentary evidence of the EUS intelligence agency interfering in Roma Novan affairs and supporting Caius Tellus's coup.'

Yes, I thought as I listened to the crackle on the line. I'd provided that evidence with my clandestine photographs.

'I expect there'll be some posturing and negotiating,' she continued. 'However, we're reasonably confident that Miklós Farkas will be released fairly soon and be free to return to Roma Nova.'

I thanked her, leant back in my chair and closed my eyes. Thank the gods. Oh, thank the gods. The tears came at last, trickling down my face. After a few minutes I roused myself and poured a good measure of cognac and swallowed it down. Only one bottle had survived the rebellion and the resistance group's presence by being hidden behind books in my study.

The day we'd arrived in the city everything was broken, people desperate and fearful. There was little food, the hospitals were empty, the power stations were offline, no fuel, looters were rampant. The old police service, the *vigiles*, was enforcing its own kind of law. But thank the gods, we had the loyal Praetorians to reimpose order.

Now, a week later, we'd cleared the roads, brought in food, although limited, but enough grain to provide to the bakeries to make bread, and dried legumes for soups. Tinned meat and fish was doled out against ID cards. Gavinus, my loyal estate manager, was at the agricultural ministry with the logistics manager, Regulus, organising more supplies and getting the food chain up and running.

Atrius had found Prisca Monticola, my silver mining and processing friend, in the work camp north of the city. She looked terrible. Always slim, she was like a matchstick doll. Her eyes were huge in a face with cheekbones pushing her skin from inside. And her hair was white now.

'They hardly fed us,' she croaked. 'I was sent there on a charge of economic sabotage. I presume I was meant to die. I ate grass, dirt, sucked my tunic. We boiled up wood and nails from the huts to make a sort of soup. Some of the other prisoners hoarded stuff, but most used their brains and shared.'

After a very diluted tinned broth I hugged her slight frame to me then put her to bed in the room next to mine.

Quintus Tellus, who had done nothing wrong in my opinion, was treated harshly. He'd even supplied us with information from time to time when we were in exile. But he was tainted by association. He was tried, as were many in the weeks after the take-back, and stripped of all property and status. All Tella property was confiscated to the state. After I'd pleaded before the tribunal, he was permitted to keep the old Tella farm in the east. It was a ramshackle place, but quiet, somewhere that might help Conradus to recover. Quirinia managed to fix Quintus a part-time petty magistrate's job that would give them some income.

'Thank you, Aurelia,' Quintus said gravely on the morning they drove into their internal exile. 'We will manage.' The former urbane state servant looked out of place in farmer's sturdy clothes and boots. Conradus by his side looked at me, his face composed, but solemn. Another child that would have to grow up too quickly. I waved them off on that frosty morning, and vowed to help them whatever the tribunal had said.

Caius's trial was, of course, a sensation, albeit a short one. Silvia had insisted on seeing him the day before. She was composed in a black suit, hair bound up and her grandmother Justina's favourite silver and diamond brooch on her lapel which Caius couldn't fail to recognise. We'd found it in his personal safe still in its velvet-lined box; perhaps even he felt he couldn't touch such a strong symbol.

'I have to face him, Aunt Aurelia,' Silvia said as we waited. 'I was a frightened child when I saw him last. Now I'm the imperatrix of Roma Nova.'

I took my place to Silvia's right, Quirinia to her left.

Caius was marched in, manacled, between two guards with Silvia's Praetorian bodyguard closing up behind him.

He stood there arrogant and indifferent.

'Caius Tellus,' Silvia began. He raised an eyebrow as if he'd only just noticed she was there. Damned impudence. 'You will face your trial tomorrow before the people of Roma Nova. I wanted to see you first. I am curious about why you thought you could murder and brutalise the people of your own country and bleed it dry purely to satisfy your own ego.'

'Big words for a spotty teenager.'

Silvia blinked but didn't make any other movement.

We waited. After a few minutes, he shrugged.

'I have done nothing different from Romans in ancient times when you women knew your place.'

'Do you have no remorse?' Silvia asked.

'Change is sometimes hard. Remorse is a sentimental luxury along with all the other emotional nonsense you women wallow in.'

'You killed my mother.'

'A casualty of change.'

'And my father?'

'Fabianus Mitelus died well, stubborn to the end like all the Mitelae.' He glanced at me with his hard as stone eyes.

Silvia's shoulders rose as she took a deep breath.

'And my brother, Julian, whom your nationalists shot.'

Caius shrugged again. 'He was a soldier. They die.'

Silvia's throat spasmed, but she kept her composure. She jerked her hand to the guards and they marched him towards the door. He turned and looked at me.

'Oh, Aurelia. One thing. Your idiot mother shouldn't have parked in that street. You never know when traffic accidents might happen.'

I clenched my fists. I wanted to smash the bastard's face, to beat him to death. He'd killed my mother, raped me and my daughter and tortured my cousin, Silvia's father, to death. Only Silvia's outstretched arm stopped me. I could have batted it aside in an instant, but I couldn't undermine her authority in front of a piece of shit like Caius.

Even at his trial, he managed to convince one of the judges he'd been misunderstood; he had been acting in the best interests of Roma Nova, he claimed. But the other two judges convicted him without hesitation.

A week later on the evening after his execution, I gave Silvia a hug, then a small brandy.

'It's over now, darling, completely over.'

'He was a traitor, Aunt Aurelia, but more than that, he killed my mother. He deserved to die.'

Two days later I drove Silvia in my now refuelled staff car to the reconstituted Senate. Her Praetorians followed in one of our battered vans from Vienna. On the steps of the patched up Senate House we were greeted by the president, Publia Cornelia. Her grandmother had been executed in the forum by Caius after his power grab; Publia spent the following eighteen months in hiding, working on farms and as a servant. I wondered how the stiff Cornelia pride had suffered under those circumstances.

She led us through to the main chamber where we were greeted in silence. The circular benches were occupied by women and men, some in correct formal dress, most in everyday clothes. Silvia and I had neither *palla* nor *stola* to wear; everything, including most of our clothes, had been reused or looted during the past eighteen months.

I looked round. No hostile faces, some friendly, most neutral. The Senate president nodded at me.

'Senators,' I began the formal words. 'As head of the Twelve Families of Roma Nova, I present to you Silvia Apulia. She is the sixty-fifth descendant of Julia Bacausa and Lucius Apulius, founder of Roma Nova. Is it your wish that she now take on the duties as imperatrix?'

Nobody said anything. I held my breath. Juno help us, they couldn't refuse, could they? I caught Publia Cornelia's eye. She nodded her head.

An older man in full toga order stepped forward. Brancus. 'Old-fashioned' was too modern a description for him. And he had a strong following in the Senate. Despite my thorough briefing for Silvia, I knew we were in trouble.

'Silvia Apulia, you are young, perhaps too young.' He paused, looked down, then removed his spectacles. 'We suffered from your mother's weak rule. She allowed Caius Tellus in to wreck the country. What can you offer us? How can we trust you?'

'Senator Brancus, I salute you.' She bowed her head, then looked him in the eye. 'You knew my grandmother, Justina, well. And her mother before her. Is your memory of Apulians not a good one overall? I may only be just eighteen, but I have been fired in the forge of death. My mother was murdered, my brother died performing his duty in defending us, my father was tortured to death. I was hunted like an animal, I lived in exile cut off from my home, something no Roman should suffer. With my loyal servants, I have liberated my country and rid it of its tyrant.' Her voice was high but strong. She swept the assembly with a fiery gaze. 'And still you ask me what I can offer?' Then she gave Brancus a look that was so like Justina's I nearly gasped out loud. She'd wandered from the speech we'd prepared, but she delivered her words with passion.

'If you want an easy road from here, if you wish everything done for you, if you want me to fall in with your every wish, then you will be disappointed. If you do not want me to lead our people then I will have to accept it. We have so much work to do to put our country back on its feet and reinstil purpose, confidence and prosperity. This will be my personal task for the rest of my life, whatever your decision.'

She clasped her hands together and stood still as a statue.

Brancus looked puzzled, shrugged, then sat down in his place on the front bench. A woman raised her hand, then stood. She wore an old jacket and crumpled skirt, but looked determined. Was that young Sergia? Gods, she looked twice her age.

'I wish to propose accepting Silvia Apulia as imperatrix and granting her full powers as under her grandmother Justina Apulia. I for one am thankful for her determination and courage in consigning Caius Tellus and all his people to the darkest depths of Tartarus.'

Cries of 'Well said' and *'Ave Apulia'* echoed round the chamber. The vote was taken and, barring three against and five abstentions, it was unanimous. I let out a long breath in relief. Silvia grabbed my hand and gave me a quick smile. I saw tears in her eyes but they didn't escape. After the tumult died down, the Senate president addressed Silvia with the formal words.

'The Senate wishes you well, Silvia Apulia, and asks that you assume the duties of imperatrix. Are you content?'

'I am. From this moment we go forward.' Then she added the old Roman greeting. 'If you and your children are in health, it is well. I and the legions are in good health.'

45

———

Three weeks after Silvia had gained *imperium* from the Senate, I slipped away for a weekend to Castra Lucilla. Gavinus was still managing the food supply chain for the agricultural ministry, but he was confident his colleague Priscilla was perfectly capable of taking back the post of farm manager for my estate.

I stamped my feet on the cold ground as she showed me round. The returned estate workers were doing their best to repair the shattered and neglected farm buildings. All the farm vehicles had disappeared and the tool stores badly pilfered. I was surprised that the *pars dominica* – the house and family gardens – had been spared apart from the cellars and food stores.

'We've even managed to find some of the stock, out in the woods. A bit thin and only half the number – this is the second winter they've survived – but there are even one or two calves. But the rest – the pigs, the poultry, even the ducks – all dead and left to rot.' She was on the verge of tears as we toured the rear farmyard and watched the pyre of burning animal bodies.

I gave her the envelope containing a letter of credit to buy what she needed to restock and repair, if she could find anything suitable at present. Gods! It was going to take years.

That evening, I sat bundled up in a rug with a small fire of scavenged branches the only respite. Maybe it was the creeping cold of an old stone house unoccupied for so long, the freezing March temperature or pure tiredness, but I was overwhelmed by sadness.

More than the damage to the farm I was concerned by the trauma my people had suffered. Only half had survived when they'd fled months ago. Now back in their homes, they would see the missing dead everywhere. We had to organise a *commemoratio* for them as soon as possible and settle their spirits definitively during the Lemuria in May.

The shrill bell of the telephone pierced my gloomy thoughts. I stared at it. The exchange was functioning at Castra Lucilla, but I thought all the wires had been cut to the farm. Priscilla must have somehow got an engineer to reconnect them. It rang again. I stretched out and lifted the handset.

Six and a half hours after I left the central interrail station in Roma Nova city, I arrived at Maria-Theresia-*Hauptbahnof*. How easy it had been before the rebellion to hop on a short-range flight and be in Vienna in fifty minutes. Now, every plane in Roma Nova, whether single-seater or international passenger jet, had been commandeered into state service.

I looked round the station concourse expecting it to look different, but of course it didn't. We might have lived a surreal life here in exile, but the rest of Vienna had gone on as usual. I picked up my hire car at the station kiosk and paid with my Soane's account card. The Roma Novan banking system was operating on a very restricted basis and I couldn't risk not having a car. I was tempted to call in at the Argentaria Prima branch here and give the manager a piece of my mind for his refusal to release my and Quirinia's accounts eighteen months ago, but that could wait.

When the tower of the *Jagdschloss* came into view I slowed down, crawling up the rest of the drive like an apprentice. I parked in the forecourt and looked around. Windows shut, lights off, doors padlocked. It was tidy, but lifeless. Had I done the right thing coming here? I bit my lip. Suppose… No, I couldn't afford to suppose. I grabbed the car door handle and pushed the door open. The slam echoed round. Pulling myself up straight, I strode through the back towards the keeper's cottage. No lights there either. Was there anybody here at all?

In the stable yard it was silent except for snuffling noises from one of the old stable blocks. Then I heard a neigh. I peered towards it and saw a weak light. Probably Lúkas, the caretaker. I didn't want to meet *that* grumpy young man. Disappointed to my core, and my eyes filling, I turned away. The sun was sinking and my boots clattering on the cobblestones made the only sound in the cold gloom.

'Aurelia!'

I stopped. My heart clenched. Could it be?

'Aurelia, where are you going?'

I turned slowly, dreading that the owner of the voice wasn't him.

The luxuriant black curls had disappeared. A one-centimetre fuzz covered his head. His face was lined, tired, brown shadows round the eyes. But his tall slim figure was unbowed and the light in his dark eyes undimmed.

'Miklós,' I said in a breath.

The warmth of his arms thawed my heart as well as my body. Since the take-back five weeks ago I'd worked like an automaton; the tough, efficient minister, cajoling the new imperial council, herding the Twelve Families, remotivating my own staff, reconstructing my businesses. I hadn't even had time to book a flight from Vienna to the EUS to see my granddaughter. But all the time, my heart was empty. Only as I'd fallen asleep at night had I cried for Miklós. What would White's bastards be doing to him?

When the *nuncia* had phoned me at the farm giving me the news that he would be freed the following week, I'd hardly registered what she was saying about negotiations, damages and confidential agreements. As there were no international commercial flights yet to Roma Nova, he would be escorted onto a plane to Vienna. She gave me the flight number and trusted that was satisfactory.

He stirred under me. I felt his fingers run up and down the skin of my spine. I gave myself up to the sheer pleasure of the soft electric tingle. When I opened my eyes he was staring up at the ceiling.

I pulled myself up onto my elbows.

'What is it?'

'I don't know. When White's heavies took me away I thought they'd force me to my knees and put a bullet in the back of my head. Tellus had made you break your honour. I knew how much that would hurt you.' I lay down on him, nestling my head in the hollow below his neck. 'Yes, they roughed me up and manacled me like an animal in the back of their plane. When we reached the prison, they shaved my head and put me in a cell by myself for two weeks. *Two weeks*. And all for a smashed up relay station which shouldn't have been there anyway.' He stroked my back.

'Oh, Miklós.' He'd been uncomfortable enough at the two hours in the interview room at the *Landeskriminalamt* after Sándor's death. Two weeks' solitary would have been hell.

'I did it for you, of course,' he said. 'I knew how important it was to stop them coordinating any resistance.'

'You made the whole operation work, you and your horse troops. You'll receive a hero's reception when you come back to Roma Nova.'

He didn't reply, but kissed me on the top of my head and made love to me as tenderly as I'd ever known.

The bed was empty when I woke early next morning. I smelt leather polish. The cottage was warm now from the rekindled stove. I pulled on his shirt and found a pair of old sandals by the bed. Miklós was sitting at the kitchen table, a bridle and a rag in his hands, a pot of polish nearby.

'You're up early,' I said.

He smiled, but it didn't show in his eyes. He said nothing but moved to the stove and set on water for coffee. As he fiddled with cups and spoons, his back to me, I saw his whole figure move almost jerkily, not with the usual slow grace.

'Miklós, what is it?'

'I can't,' he said, not turning round. 'I can't come back with you.'

I shook my head. I must have misheard him. 'What did you say?'

'Not now. Not ever.' His voice was hardly above a whisper.

Despite the warmth in the cottage, I shivered. I strode over to the worktop and took his arm to ease him round.

Oh, gods.

A spasm went through my stomach. His face was drawn, his skin dull, almost grey, like a corpse's. He said nothing.

'I know you'll have some things to tidy up here—' I said, filling the silence.

'It's not that. I've always found living in a city stifling. I can just about bear it when we're on the outskirts like this. After that cell in the EUS…' He shuddered.

'Miklós, please don't leave me. I need you more than I ever did before.'

He took me in his arms and clasped his hands behind my waist. 'You know I will love you until I'm dead. That will never change. But I can't live with you in Roma Nova.'

'No! Your place is with me and mine with you.' My voice became shriller. I couldn't help it. I gripped his shoulders hard, not caring if it hurt him.

He put his finger on my lips. 'Your first love has always been Roma Nova and it still is. You'll die with its name on your lips. You have so much to do there now and so many people depend on you. Your duty and life are there.'

'You're saying that *our* life together is over and we'll live separately?' I stared at his eyes, trying to see if he'd tired of me but all I saw was sadness and, I thought, love. I blinked hard and tried to catch my breath and calm my heart. My head said he was right about my love for Roma Nova, but my heart was breaking for both of us.

He ran the back of his fingers down my cheek. 'I'll be travelling much of the time but I'll keep a base here and we'll meet from time to time.' He looked straight into my eyes. 'If you want to.'

I wriggled in his embrace and he released me. I turned, crossed my arms across my chest and stared at him.

He said nothing, just looked out of the window. I felt numb. I couldn't move. I was enveloped in disbelief. After the struggle of the past two years, the snatched time together, his unswerving support and love, it was ending like this.

Well, to hell with him! I ran back to the bedroom. I stamped around getting dressed, heaving my clothes on and thrusting my feet in my boots. I snatched up my coat and bag and stopped in the hallway just by the kitchen door frame. Outside, the orange ball of the rising sun sent fiery light into the kitchen, onto the table, the stacked plates, the polished bridle and onto Miklós's face. He looked ten, no, twenty years older. He looked up. Sadness? Tension? No, it was fear.

What in Hades was I doing?

Leaning back against the worktop, he'd crossed his arms and was now looking down at the tile floor. A strong man, now he looked wounded, crushed. This was the man I loved, my soulmate. My heart flooded with love and a strong desire to protect him, even from me.

I stepped into the kitchen, dropped my things onto a chair and folded him into my arms.

'I'm sorry, so sorry,' I murmured.

'As am I.' He locked me into his arms.

'I couldn't go and leave you with my bad temper.'

He pushed a lock of my hair back from my forehead and kissed it. 'You wouldn't be the passionate and determined woman you are without it,' he said, then smiled.

I'd lived without him before and I could do it again. Oh gods, could I do it? 'I don't understand your decision, but I accept what you say,' I lied.

He gave a little chuckle and I blushed.

'Perhaps you will one day,' he said. 'You must go and do your duty now, Aurelia. They need you. But come back to me whenever you can. Call me and I'll be here, waiting for you.'

You can follow the adventures of Aurelia's granddaughter, Carina, and discover how she came from the EUS to fight her own battles in Roma Nova and pursue her own love story. Here's the first:
INCEPTIO

WOULD YOU LEAVE A REVIEW?

I hope you enjoyed RETALIO, the danger, adventures and passions.

If you did, I'd really appreciate it if you would write a few words of review on the site where you purchased this book.

Reviews will really help RETALIO to feature more prominently on retailer sites and let more people into the world of Roma Nova.

Very many thanks!

HISTORICAL NOTE

What if Julius Caesar had taken notice of the warning that assassins wanted to murder him on the ides of March? Suppose Elizabeth I had married and had children? Or if or Napoleon had won at Waterloo?

Alternative history stories allow us to explore the 'what if' of history. They should show the point of divergence when the alternate timeline split from our timeline; how things changed after the split; and how that world looks and works.

RETALIO goes back to the mid 1980s in an alternative Europe where the small but tough country of Roma Nova has survived for fifteen centuries. But these are the dark days of the Great Rebellion when Roma Nova has been taken over by a charismatic tyrant.

I have dropped background 'history' of Roma Nova into the novel only where it impacts on the story. Nobody likes a history lesson in the middle of a thriller! But if you are interested in discovering more about the mysterious Roma Nova, read on...

What happened in our timeline

Of course, our timeline may turn out to be somebody else's alternative one as shown in Philip K. Dick's *The Grasshopper Lies Heavy*, the story within the story in *The Man in the High Castle*. Nothing is fixed. But for the sake of convenience I will take ours as the default.

The Western Roman Empire didn't 'fall' in a cataclysmic event as often portrayed in film and television; it localised and eventually dissolved like chain mail fragmenting into separate links, giving way to rump provinces, local city states and petty kingdoms. The Eastern Roman Empire survived until the Fall of Constantinople in 1453 to the Muslim Ottoman Empire.

Some scholars think that Christianity fatally weakened the traditional Roman way of life. Emperor Constantine's personal conversion to Christianity in AD 313 was a turning point for the new religion. By late AD 394, his several times successor, Theodosius, banned all traditional Roman religious practice, closed and destroyed temples and dismissed all priests.

The sacred flame that had burned for over a thousand years in the College of Vestals was extinguished and the Vestal Virgins expelled. The Altar of Victory, said to guard the fortune of Rome, was hauled away from the Senate building and disappeared from history.

The Roman senatorial families pleaded for religious tolerance, but Theodosius made any pagan practice, even dropping a pinch of incense on a family altar in a private home, into a capital offence. And his 'religious police', driven by the austere and ambitious bishop Ambrosius of Milan, became increasingly active in pursuing pagans.

The alternate Roma Nova timeline

In AD 395, three months after Theodosius's final decree banning all pagan religious activity, four hundred Romans loyal to the old gods, and so in danger of execution, trekked north out of Italy to a semi-mountainous area similar to modern Slovenia. Led by Senator Apulius at the head of twelve prominent families, they established a colony based initially on land owned by Apulius's Celtic father-in-law. By purchase, alliance and conquest, this grew into Roma Nova.

Norman Davies in *Vanished Kingdoms: The History of Half-Forgotten Europe* reminds us that:

> *…in order to survive, newborn states need to possess a set of viable internal organs, including a functioning executive, a defence force, a revenue system and a diplomatic force. If they possess none of these things, they lack the means to sustain an autonomous existence and they perish before they can breathe and flourish.*

I would add history, willpower and adaptability as essential factors. Roma Nova survived by changing its social structure; as men constantly fought to defend the new colony, women took over the social, political and economic roles, weaving new power and influence networks based on family structures.

Given the unstable, dangerous times in Roma Nova's first few hundred years, daughters as well as sons had to put on armour and heft swords to defend their homeland and their way of life. Fighting danger side by side with brothers and fathers reinforced women's roles and status.

The Roma Novans never allowed the incursion of monotheistic, paternalistic religions; they'd learnt that lesson from old Rome. Service to the state was valued higher than personal advantage, echoing Roman Republican virtues, and the women heading the families guarded and enhanced these values to provide a core philosophy throughout the centuries. Inheritance passed from these powerful women to their daughters and granddaughters.

Roma Nova's continued existence has been favoured by three factors: the discovery and exploitation of high-grade silver in their mountains, their efficient technology, and their robust response to any threat.

Remembering the Fall of Constantinople, Roma Novan troops assisted the western nations at the Battle of Vienna in 1683 to halt the Ottoman advance into Europe. Nearly two hundred years later, they used their diplomatic skills to forge an alliance to push Napoleon IV back across the Rhine as he attempted to expand his grandfather's empire.

And in more modern times?

Prioritising survival, Roma Nova remained neutral in the Great War of the twentieth century which lasted from 1925 to 1935. The Greater German Empire was broken up afterwards into its former small kingdoms, duchies and counties; some became republics.

Despite the legal reforms in the mid 1700s, there was little fundamental change in Roma Nova's governance. Until the late 1970s, tough female rulers drawing on centuries of experience and backed by the Twelve Families had provided active, solid if traditional leadership.

But in the early 1980s a weak imperatrix had opened up the opportunity for a power-hungry charismatic demagogue and his brutal nationalist movement who seized power (*INSURRECTIO*).

Now the Roma Nova refugees and exiles must lick their wounds and decide on their future. But Aurelia Mitela, former foreign minister and imperial councillor, left to die by her nemesis, Caius Tellus, has been rejected by the exiles and has little hope of escaping from her nemesis or of seeing her beloved Roma Nova again.

THE ROMA NOVA THRILLER SERIES

The Carina Mitela adventures

INCEPTIO

Early 21st century. Terrified after a kidnap attempt, New Yorker Karen Brown, has a harsh choice – being terminated by government enforcer Renschman or fleeing to Roma Nova, her dead mother's homeland in Europe. Founded sixteen hundred years ago by Roman exiles and ruled by women, it gives Karen safety – at a price. But Renschman follows and sets a trap she has no option but to enter.

CARINA – A novella

Carina Mitela is a new officer in the Praetorian Guard Special Forces. Disgraced for a disciplinary offence, she is sent out of everybody's way to bring back a traitor from the Republic of Quebec. But the conspiracy reaches into the highest levels of Roma Nova…

PERFIDITAS

Falsely accused of conspiracy, 21st century Praetorian Carina Mitela flees into the criminal underworld. Hunted by both security services and traitors she struggles to save her beloved Roma Nova as well as her own life. Who is her ally and who her enemy? But the ultimate betrayal is waiting for her.

SUCCESSIO

21st century Praetorian Carina Mitela's attempt to resolve a past family indiscretion is spiralling into a nightmare of blackmail and terror. Convinced her beloved husband has deserted her and her children, and with her enemy holding a gun to the imperial heir's head, Carina has to make the hardest decision of her life.

The Aurelia Mitela adventures

AURELIA

Late 1960s. Sent to Berlin to investigate silver smuggling, former Praetorian Aurelia Mitela barely escapes a near-lethal trap. Her old enemy is at the heart of all her troubles and she pursues him back home to Roma Nova but he strikes at her most vulnerable point – her young daughter.

NEXUS – A novella

Mid 1970s. Aurelia Mitela is serving as ambassador in London. Helping a British colleague to find his missing son, Aurelia is sure he'll turn up.

But a spate of high-level killings pulls Aurelia away into a pan-European investigation and the killers threaten to terminate her life companion.

But Aurelia is a Roma Novan – they never give up…

INSURRECTIO

Early 1980s. Caius Tellus, the charismatic leader of a rising nationalist movement, threatens to destroy Roma Nova.

Aurelia Mitela, ex-Praetorian and imperial councillor, attempts to counter the growing fear and instability. But it may be too late to save Roma Nova from meltdown and herself from destruction by her lifelong enemy….

RETALIO

1980s Vienna. Aurelia Mitela chafes at enforced exile. She barely escaped from her nemesis, Caius Tellus, who grabbed power in Roma Nova.

Aurelia is determined to liberate her homeland. But Caius's manipulations have ensured that she is ostracised by her fellow exiles.

Powerless and vulnerable, she fears she will never see Roma Nova again.

———

ROMA NOVA EXTRA

A collection of short stories

Four historical and four present day and a little beyond

A young tribune is sent to a backwater in 370 AD for practising the wrong religion – his lonely sixty-fifth descendant labours in the 1980s to reconstruct her country. A Roma Novan imperial councillor attempting to stop the Norman invasion of England in 1066 – her 21st century Praetorian descendant flounders as she searches for her own happiness.

Some are love stories, some lessons learned, some resolve tensions or unrealistic visions, some are adventures. Above all, they tell of people with dilemmas and in conflict, and of their courage and effort to resolve them.

www.ingramcontent.com/pod-product-compliance
Lightning Source LLC
Chambersburg PA
CBHW021143160726
47994CB00001B/56